DEAD MAN'S NUMBER

THE ROADHOUSE CHRONICLES BOOK 3

MATTHEW S. COX

DIVISION ZERO PRESS

Dead Man's Number
The Roadhouse Chronicles Book 3
© 2016 Matthew S. Cox
All rights reserved

ISBN (eBook): 978-1-949174-76-2

ISBN (Print): 978-1-949174-77-9

CONTENTS

THE MESSAGE

Unease kept the dust hopper stew bubbling in Kevin's gut. He put a hand over his belly and leaned back in his seat. Tris, seated opposite him across their new kitchen table, faded to a near-silhouette in the early evening sun beaming in the sliding glass patio doors behind her. Every few seconds, a flash of orange reflected from Abby's spoon. The girl sat with her back to the wall along the left side of the table, hunched over the bowl, stirring at her dinner, most of her face hidden behind a long curtain of straight, light-brown hair.

She wore a dress one of the locals made for her from a mixture of goat wool and hide. Abby especially loved her fur-lined moccasins, though didn't bother wearing them inside the house unless it got cold. Kevin glanced from her to Tris and tried to distract himself from his worry by knowing she had nothing on under her T-shirt with the dark navy sleeves and white middle. Whatever logo had been over the breasts had faded long ago, probably before she'd been born.

Abby raised her head enough to give him a hint of a smile and a pleading look before going back to stirring.

"I spoke to Crystal," said Tris. "She's okay with me being away for a couple of days. Seemed eager to have Bee up and around again. Cassie too… she can't wait to see a working android."

Kevin chuckled. "You have to request time off? Sounds like a prewar job."

Abby glanced toward Tris, who stared guilt into her food.

"We're not going to be gone that long," muttered Tris. "We've been there before, and it's not too dangerous."

"Almost a straight shot." Kevin glanced at the ceiling while envisioning the map. "Route 76 to 80, and pretty much 80 all the way to Eppley."

"If it's safe, take me with you." Abby raised her head and pulled her hair off her face. "Please?"

The last thing I need is for something to happen to her. Kevin sighed. "I dunno. Leaving the safety of Ned with a little kid seems like a foolish gamble."

Abby furrowed her brows, but the rest of her face remained plaintive. "She just said it wasn't dangerous… and I'm not little. I'm eleven."

"Nederland is safe, but it's not impervious." Tris let go of her spoon to rub her eyes. "I… I'd almost feel better bringing her along too, so I wouldn't keep worrying about her."

Abby shot Tris a quick smile before giving Kevin her most wide-eyed, imploring stare.

"It's not that I want to be away from you. I don't want you to get hurt." Kevin picked up his empty water glass and tried to drink from it for the third time. He held it out and frowned. "How's your friend Isla adjusting to Ned?"

"She likes it here." Abby gazed down. "But she's still scared at night."

Kevin leaned forward and gave Abby's shoulder a squeeze. "I think we all are."

Abby shot him a hard look; for a second, he almost regretted trying to 'play dad,' but her expression softened and she grasped his hand where it rested on her. He smiled until she let her arms drop in her lap and bowed her head. When the silence became pregnant, he stood. Two steps after he started to the patio doors, he swerved to the sink and held his glass under the faucet.

Still not used to working plumbing. Nederland had managed to get reasonably close to a prewar state. Perhaps due to its small size and relative lack of damage. No one saw fit to drop a warhead on a tiny little mountain town. Small wells and isolated septic systems didn't fall victim to the large-scale infrastructure collapse that devastated most of the country. Here, he could fantasize that the war had never happened. Almost.

Bill found his story of all the solar panels sitting around at Amarillo fascinating, and the town elders had spent days discussing an expedition, one they would likely ask Tris to lead. Despite the possibility of a couple hundred Infected in the area, it almost tempted him. Of course, he wouldn't bring Abby back there... too many bad memories. Nor did he much feel like leaving her here with her knowing where they went.

The town elders hadn't made up their mind yet either way. More panels would make expansion smoother, but they still had Boulder and Denver to scavenge from. Decent odds at least three-quarters of the homes in Boulder had solar panels that still worked. Most proper cities still had much to salvage... for anyone with big enough balls to risk concentrated groups of Infected.

Tris sidled up next to him and put an arm around his lower back while he refilled his water. She opened her mouth to speak, but paused, glancing through the window over the sink at Emma walking by outside. A thirteen-year-old in a tank top, camo shorts, barefoot, and carrying an AK-47 around did wonders to break the illusion the world hadn't been fucked.

Kevin tried not to think about little Zoe diving into a firefight against a raiding party. All of nine years old and she seemed to *enjoy* defending the town from bandit raids or Infected like some manner of game. Kids her age should be hiding whenever shit like that happened. He glanced back at Abby still picking at her food.

At least she's got no interest in guns.

"Hey," said Tris, a touch over a whisper.

He shut off the faucet. "Hey."

She waited for him to finish taking a long drink. "Abby's lost her father, and she's terrified about losing us."

He leaned on the counter, head down. "I know... I know. I'm just... after everything she's been through, I want her to be safe. We've got no idea what things are like out there with Amarillo out of the picture."

Tris put a hand on his arm and squeezed. "Nowhere's safe with Nathan after me. I... I'd rather keep her close."

He took another long sip and set the glass on the counter, but didn't let go of it. "Well..." He smiled. "Guess that's two votes for. I suppose we bring her."

"I promise I won't get in the way," said Abby.

"You're going to tell me she should carry a weapon next." Kevin gave Tris the side-eye.

"Do I have to?" asked Abby. "I don't wanna get shot. They won't shoot me if I'm not a threat."

"Some people will," said Tris. "And the kind of people who'd attack us and not be inclined to shoot you too will umm…" She bit her lip. "You'd rather be shot."

"Most raiders don't have time to bother with kids." Kevin folded his arms. "They left me alone."

Tris poked him in the stomach. "You were only four… and a boy. It's not the same."

He grasped her shoulders, held eye contact for a few seconds, and pulled her into a hug. "When did you get so cynical? I thought you saw the best in people until they showed otherwise."

"Easier to be an optimist when you don't have a child depending on you to keep them safe." She stared into his eyes, the worry another drone would find Nederland plain on her face.

"Okay. We shouldn't hit anything too dangerous… Route 80's travelled enough to be reasonably safe." He let off a sigh of resignation. "I suppose she should carry a Sig or something just in case."

"Do I have to?" asked Abby. "I don't want it to, like, go off on accident or anything."

Kevin's thoughts leapt back to the family with the semi-truck; the twins weren't much older than Abby. He liked to think they lacked killer instinct at their age; at least they didn't open fire on Bull with the rest of their family. Abby hadn't recovered from the events of Amarillo, perhaps she never would. Giving her a loaded handgun felt like a bad idea in more ways than one. He thought about his nightmare, running over grassy fields away from Infected, and scowled at the sink.

"We won't force you to," said Tris. "But it wouldn't hurt to learn how to handle a weapon. Even in a place like Nederland, you can wind up needing to protect yourself."

"Okay." Abby lifted a spoonful of stew to eat, but hesitated. "Isn't that what the militia is for?" She stuck the spoon in her mouth and took her time chewing, sitting in silence for a while after.

"You're a little young yet, but a town like this… everyone protects everyone." Kevin grumbled off to the side for a few seconds before looking at her again. "We're not saying you need to pull a Zoe. She's going to get herself hurt or killed."

"If I had a gun, would my father still be alive?" asked Abby, not looking up.

Tris shook her head in disgust. "I should've put a bullet in that bastard's head as soon as I saw him pointing a gun at you."

"Honestly?" Kevin walked around the table and took Abby's hand. "Probably not. If you had a gun on you, Warren might've been afraid you'd shoot him as soon as he started accusing you of being infected."

Abby sniffled. "An' Dad woulda gotten killed like they shot Tris for killin' Warren."

"It's a risk. Depends on if it's riskier not to have one." Kevin stared at his hand engulfing hers, hoping she didn't bristle at him for attempting to replace her father.

"I..." She shivered. "Guns scare me..."

"They scare me too, kiddo." Kevin smiled.

She managed a small smile in return.

"I'll show her the basics." Tris swiped at her empty hip, and froze.

"What?" asked Abby.

"Just got so used to always carrying that Beretta around. Feels strange not having it on me." She started for the living room. "Guess I feel safe here."

Kevin released Abby's hand and patted her on the shoulder. "I'm going to go check on the car, make sure it's up for a ride."

"I'll clean up." Abby stood and gathered the bowls.

Kevin headed out the front door and down the porch, which had only a few feet of clearance to the gravel road passing by—not that getting hit by a car presented much of a concern. *Hell, this place probably didn't have much traffic even before the war.* The Challenger sat in the grass a few feet east of the house. One downside of Ned came in not having a charging plug at the house. He stopped, hooked his thumbs in the pocket of his jeans, and sighed, missing the little garage he'd had in Rawlins. Of course, he could always build one here too. For the time being, he'd have to move the car to the downtown area for a charge, and either wait with it or walk home.

After keying in the security code with the rubberized buttons under the door handle, he hopped in and slid his thumb across the six rocker switches over the console. Everything lit up as it should. Of course, nothing going wrong with the car only fanned the fires of his superstition. Fate wanted him to head off on this trip so it could screw him harder when it would hurt more. The battery showed a seventy-seven percent charge, not quite enough to leave him comfortable about starting a long drive.

Abby emerged from the front door, having put her moccasins on. Tris followed a moment later. He tapped a square button on the left side of the central display screen, paging through the car's internal diagnostics. He found himself hoping something with the car failed, as if a problem now somehow guaranteed nothing major would go wrong once they'd gone a hundred miles into the wasteland. He chuckled, thinking about many nights drinking at Roadhouse tables with other travelers. *I'm being dumb. Why are drivers so superstitious?*

"Hey," said Tris, appearing by his still-open door. "Taking Abby to the range for a little while, see if I can at least get her able to hold a gun without her hands shaking."

Abby stared at the ground.

"Okay. Be careful. I'll probably wind up leaving this thing downtown for the night."

"Damn, sorry." Tris smacked herself in the forehead. "I forgot to ask Crystal about a car plug. I'm not sure they have an extra."

Kevin chuckled. "Another reason to go shopping in Amarillo I guess." He shut off the diagnostic with a grumble. "Not worth the bother. Ain't like I've got a need to do a lot of driving lately."

⸻ ⸕ ⸎ ⸕ ⸎ ⸕ ⸎ ⸕ ⸻

TRIS TOOK ABBY'S HAND AND LED HER PAST THE CHALLENGER, ACROSS THE road that came within four feet of the back of their house, and up the hill to the east. The local militia had a firing range set up at the northwest part of town where a nice-sized bit of mountain served as a backstop. They only had an hour, if even that, of daylight left.

Grinding gravel announced the car pulling away, Kevin no doubt heading downtown to plug in. *He's taking the death of his gods well.* It may or may not be worth a trip back there to salvage solar panels. Fair bet half the remaining proprietors had contemplated it, but maybe with the Code defunct and having to worry about defending themselves, the idea of running headlong into a city with hundreds of Infected would be too intimidating.

Not that she had a tremendous amount of faith in what the Enclave had taught her, but history class made it sound like solar power had wound up competing with nuclear as the dominant source of electricity in the years leading up to the war. A fair amount of areas where fear kept the nuke plants away already had the basic infrastructure for solar. Of course, even Amarillo's stash couldn't repair the entire country... hell, probably not even one whole city. She smirked to herself at the irony of cities filled with people terrified of living near nuclear power plants being bathed in radiation by warheads instead.

Abby swung her free hand at her side, walking with her gaze on the dirt. "It's nice here."

"Yeah."

"Do you like it?" The girl looked up.

Tris nodded. "Yes. I guess I do miss Rawlins a little bit, more than I thought I would, but you are much safer here than you would've been on the side of the road in the middle of nowhere."

"Is Kevin upset that I made you leave?"

"You didn't *make* us leave." Tris ran a hand over Abby's head. "Besides, he wanted to take me here before you showed up."

Abby blinked in disbelief. "He was afraid of *you* getting hurt?"

"I'm fast, but I'm not perfect. I don't know how long the nanites will keep working. And... he's a guy." She held her arms out. "I look fragile, so he's got this deep-seated need to protect me."

Abby grinned. "It's kinda cute."

Tris laughed. "It annoyed me at first... but, it's nice to have someone who worries about me."

"Yeah." Abby bowed her head and punted a small rock off into the grass.

Tris scowled at the sky. *Nathan, I hope you die painfully for what you did.* "I'm sorry I didn't shoot Warren sooner."

Abby kept quiet for a few strides before looking up. "Is that why you let me stay with you? 'Cause you think it's your fault my dad got killed?"

"Well, I guess that *is* a little bit of it, but the look in your eyes when you asked. It wasn't even a question for me." She managed a smile while pushing the range gate open.

The old wooden fence creaked.

"It's not your fault." Abby looked her in the eye. "If you killed Warren right away, it woulda been murder... even if he was an asshole. Everyone was so freaked out, they probably would've gone crazy."

Someone had already set up a couple of cans and paper plates on sticks at about twenty yards, decent enough targets. Tris guided Abby up to a brown folding table upon which sat two more cans, a few scraps of paper, and a gun cleaning brush.

"We don't have much light left, so I'm not going to waste too much time." Tris pulled the Sig out of her belt, removed the magazine, and racked the slide to eject the bullet. "Whenever you're around a gun you should always—"

"Treat it like it's ready to fire." Abby shifted her weight onto her left leg and tapped her right moccasin toe into the dirt. "Dad always said that. I had a little gun back in Amarillo, but I forgot it when we had to run out in the middle of the night." Her lip quivered. "He, uhh, gave it to me when I turned ten."

Tris set the gun on the table and pulled her into a hug. "I'm so sorry. The town's thinking of going back there to salvage some solar panels... if I go, I'll look for it."

Abby sniffled a moment or so later. "I'm not crying over a gun... I miss my dad." She wiped her eyes and picked up the Sig. "This is a lot bigger than mine. Is it gonna hurt my hand?"

"It's a 9mm, shouldn't be too bad. That's why we're here." Tris gestured for her to try aiming it empty. "I don't think you'll need to use it, but if you're afraid of what it's going to do when you pull the trigger...?"

"I'll get hurt, yeah." She sighted over it a few times, holding it in a two handed grip. "It's a bit different. Where's the safety?"

Maybe her dad did show her a few things. Tris pointed it out after Abby found the slide release and magazine eject without help. The girl grabbed the magazine and loaded it, but struggled to pull the slide back. After a moment of grunting and straining, she racked it, chambering a round.

Abby let out a sad laugh. "Guess I need to lift stuff or something." She aimed. "If someone tries to hurt me, I'll probably forget I even have a gun and just cry at them."

"The first time I had to defend myself, it happened before I could think it through." Tris cringed, expecting a gunshot any second. She hovered behind Abby, ready to catch if either gun or child went flying.

Blam.

The girl's arms bounced up a few inches and a puff of dust rose up from the dirt.

Abby adjusted her grip. "Wasn't trying to hit anything... Okay, it doesn't kick too hard."

Two methodical shots later, she nipped a can. Seconds before firing a third shot, a man and woman in green, followed by Emma, ran over with rifles. It took her a second to remember the dark-skinned woman; she pictured the building in Chicago, and a name came back to her.

"You okay?" asked Patricia.

Thirteen-year-old Emma eyed the clouds while squeezing and

relaxing her grip on an AK47.

Tris exchanged a knowing look with the kid before smiling at Patricia. "Abby's acclimating to a new weapon."

The woman nodded.

"If you don't mind," said the man Tris wanted to call Peter, "next time, give us a heads up. Unexpected gunfire gets people nervous... especially when it's almost dark."

"Sorry." Abby clicked on the safety and put the Sig on the table before backing away like the gun might spontaneously hurt someone. "I'll stop. I got a feel for it already." She eyed Emma before following the older girl's gaze to the clouds. "What's up there?"

"Nothing you need to worry about." Tris picked up the gun and smiled at the militia. "Sorry for stirring up a false alarm."

Another man in green camo emerged from the tree line, jogging up the dirt path to the range.

Patricia waved to him and yelled, "Clear."

Abby wrapped herself around Tris' left arm. "Can we go inside before it's all the way dark?"

Tris offered an apologetic smile to the militia. "That sounds like a good idea."

All three of the militia gave Abby comforting looks as she passed them.

A few minutes into the walk home, Abby broke the silence, but didn't look up. "Emma's from a settlement that used to be in Boulder. Her parents and brother got taken by Infected when she was like six."

Tris cringed. *I never had the cure to begin with... I didn't fail.* "I..."

Abby kicked at an egg-sized rock, sending it tumbling. "She's not afraid of them. She wants to kill them all. I hope she doesn't do something stupid and get hurt."

"Yeah." Tris sighed. *Why do I feel so guilty that I failed to bring the cure to the Resistance? Kevin keeps telling me it's not my fault, but...*

"Why are you crying?"

"I..." Tris dabbed at her cheek. "Don't know. I told you about the cure thing... It doesn't make any sense, but I feel like I screwed up."

Abby stopped and stared for a few seconds of earnest silence. "Please don't do something stupid because my dad got killed. I'd rather stay safe with you here."

"Stupid is subjective." She gave Abby a firm hug before resuming the trip home. "I promise I won't do anything foolish."

2

SPEED

Kevin hurried a few thin-sliced pieces of dust hopper meat around the pan with the tip of a wooden spatula. He dropped in six eggs one after the next and whipped the entire mess into a scramble. Tris walked in, yawned at the still-dark window, and squinted at him.

"What?" He smiled. "The sun will be up in ten minutes or so."

She collapsed in a chair and put her head down. "We're driving to Omaha, not going fishing... why are we up this early?"

"Huh?"

Tris shrugged. "People who fish always wake up before the sun for some reason."

"Historical documentary?"

"Yeah," she muttered into the hollow between her face and the table. "At least that smells good."

"Where's Abby?"

"Couldn't wake her up." Tris yawned.

Kevin shoveled the meat-and-eggs mixture into a large serving bowl and turned off the electric stove. "I can't get over how... creepy this feels."

"What's creepy?"

"This"—he gestured around at everything—"kitchen. This house. It reminds me of movies I've seen of before the war." He carried the bowl to the table and set it down. "Be right back."

"Mmm."

Kevin jogged upstairs and headed to the second bedroom which had become Abby's. He knocked twice and pushed the door in. The girl lay on her side with her arms and legs wrapped around the pillow, using a man's large sweatshirt for a nightgown. He walked over and gave her shoulder a gentle nudge. After a minute of no reaction, he did it again.

Her left eye popped open. "Mmm?"

"Breakfast."

She emitted a disinterested murmur and snuggled into the pillow.

"You can sleep, but we're heading to Omaha soon. I'd prefer you stay here where it's safe anyway. I'll ask Bill and Ann to check on you."

"Wait." She straightened her legs and stretched. "That's not fair."

"Trouble sleeping?" He sat on the edge of the bed.

Abby, eyes still shut, yawned. "Yeah. Why do we have to go so early?"

"More daylight for driving. I want to be sure we can find a decent place to spend the night, probably around Kearney. The Hastings 'house is not a happy place right now… might have to go past it, and I don't fancy spending the night in Omaha."

"Why?" Abby opened her eyes. "What's in Omaha?"

"A strange man who lives in an airplane. He's got information from Tris' head that she wants. Omaha was a big city, and I don't want to be near it any longer than I have to be."

Abby frowned at the pillow.

"We've been there before. It's not a bad trip. If you want to stay here with Bill and Ann, you don't have to go."

She pushed herself up to sit. "I'd rather stay with Tris and you. I'll come downstairs after I get dressed."

Kevin ruffled her hair and jogged back to the kitchen as Tris poured coffee into two cups. He winced at the idea of drinking fifty-year-old coffee, but it's not as if he hadn't done that before—or worse. He accepted the cup and slurped it, wincing when the taste hit him. *Erk. Instant.* Kevin suppressed the shudder. A minute or so later, Abby entered, wearing her new dress and carrying moccasins. She fell hard into her seat and stared at the portion of eggs and bread Tris put in front of her as if searching for the deepest secrets of the universe.

"You want coffee?" asked Kevin.

Abby stared at the fork; her expression suggested she couldn't quite comprehend its function. "Can I sleep in the car?"

"Sure."

"I'll skip the coffee." She fumbled the fork around into a proper grip and got to shoveling food.

After eating, Kevin collected the dishes and cleaned them with a few quick swipes of a sponge. Tris ran upstairs, returning in about five minutes, having changed from her T-shirt-and-nothing-under-it outfit to her favorite black T-shirt with the grey ankh design, jeans, and her Enclave shoes.

"Car's down by the militia building. I'll go get it so Abby doesn't have to drag herself across town." Kevin tried to give Tris a peck on the cheek, but she held on for a longer, deeper kiss. When she finally relaxed, he leaned back and smiled at her. "Be right back."

He headed outside and hooked a left, following the gravel. The air had a touch of chill at the hour, and a symphony of insects and birds filled the streets. An almost-mile walk brought him into the center of Ned, past the lot full of old digging machines rusting along the left side of the road. Bill Vasquez, dressed as always in his olive-drab fatigues, emerged from the tan building at the corner that the militia used as a headquarters, and offered a 'good morning' wave. A brick-sized light over the door brightened the area a bit more than the pre-sunrise sky could.

"Still going on with this trip?"

"Yep." Kevin unhooked the charging plug.

"Well, hope it's what you're expecting. You can send Abby over whenever." Bill set his hands on his hips.

Kevin walked with the wire as it retracted into the panel. "She's uhh, coming with us."

"What?" Bill blinked. "You're sure about that?"

"Nope. Not at all, but..."

"Outvoted?" asked Bill, chuckling. "Ann and Zoe gang up on me too."

"Something like that." Kevin shook his head, unable to resist a grin. "At least we did this trip once before and it wasn't bad. Abby's got herself convinced we won't come back and that whole situation with her father..."

Bill scratched at his close-cropped hair. "Well, figure you know the run. Always willin' ta watch her if ya need. Though, rather ya stick around."

Kevin smiled. "Yeah... that makes two of us, but Tris' *gotta* know what that strange little man found. We'll be back. This place is home now."

"I can't say I'd feel different in her position." Bill leaned forward, chuckling at the ground for a second. "She seemed pretty worried that a particular kind of problem would come out of the sky."

"Yeah." His jaw tightened. "I wouldn't put it past them to drop that shit here… I'm amazed they haven't done it already. Probably since Ned is so damn small. You guys see anything in the air that ain't flapping its wings, shoot it."

"Don't worry. We will."

Kevin walked around to the driver's side door and stuck one leg in the car. "Hopefully, this is a quick trip and we'll be back in a day or two. If that scrawny little bastard got her hopes up for nothing, I'm gonna bounce his head off his computer thingee a few times."

Bill laughed. "See ya soon."

Kevin slid down into place behind the wheel. As comfortable and familiar as the car felt, he found himself unenthused about leaving Ned. A couple days of 'safe normal' hadn't even gotten boring yet. He chuckled before muttering, "This is either going to send us off on some other ridiculous trip, or she's going to be crushed at another one of that prick's jabs." He'd only gotten a brief glimpse of Nathan the two times he appeared on screens, and he still wanted to twist the man's head off.

He drove back to the house, where Tris and Abby waited on the front porch. She picked the barely-awake girl up and carried her to the car. Kevin leaned over to push the passenger door open and pull the seat forward. After easing Abby into the back, Tris got in.

"Hope you don't mind if I let myself drift too." Tris reclined and closed her eyes.

"Go right ahead." He pulled a U-turn in front of the house and drove east toward the city gates, a pair of dump trucks flipped on their sides.

Socrates, the old man in the ancient brown trench coat, waved from atop the dump truck gate a few minutes later as Kevin pulled up. It took the elder a little while to navigate a ladder down and amble over. "What's yer plan?"

"Runnin' out to Omaha. Apparently, Tris got mail." He flared his eyebrows. "Should be back in three days."

"Safe trip then." Socrates waved to a younger man, likely only months past eighteen, who opened one dump truck bed before jogging across the road to move the other.

"Where's Emma?" asked Kevin.

Socrates smiled. "Gate duty rotates. Bill don't want her up here anyway. First place trouble shows up usually. That kid's got balls of steel, an' she's gonna get herself shot one of these days."

Kevin thought of Athena and her immortality complex, wondering where the fine line sat between feeling untouchable and plain old not caring about survival. He squinted at the sliver of sunlight peeking over the horizon. "See you in a couple days."

"Come back alive." Socrates tipped his hat. Long strands of cobweb-like white hair trailed around the shoulders of his duster coat.

"That's the plan."

With a final wave, Kevin nosed the Challenger past the gate. He took 119 east before hooking left into Boulder and proceeding northeast to Route 52. That afforded him a straight shot east without having to go into Denver. If his last experience there offered any clue, the place had to have thousands of Infected.

Route 52 had seen better days. Most people liked skirting around Denver, and many drivers had picked fights with potholes their cars couldn't handle. A few succumbed to traps of barbed wire and old telephone poles, the sort of thing marauders without wheels set up to catch cars for roadside ambushes. He kept his head on a swivel while driving around and among rusting hulks.

By the time he approached the ramp to Route 76, the road clogged with a river of bumper-to-bumper rust. The carnage in the eastbound lanes had to have been there when the bombs fell—the only way that many cars would've ever been in one place. He spent a few minutes in the lane once used for oncoming traffic, driving past hundreds of wrecks that hadn't moved since 2021, some fifty-two years ago.

The sight darkened Tris' mood. He squeezed her hand. Scenes like that always got her emotional, sending her mind whirling around what it must have been like for the people trapped in such a nightmare. Once they cleared the traffic jam, he left the oncoming lane and sped up, going as fast as the paving allowed. Tris settled down in her seat and closed her eyes again.

Kevin drove for hours while Tris and Abby remained asleep. A bridge spanning 76 proved intact, and soon after crossing it, he hooked a left past a barricade made of two smashed school buses crowned with concertina wire. He braced for a fight, but thankfully, whoever had tried to block off the southeastern end of the bridge hadn't remained around to harass them. Once on Route 76, he leaned on the accelerator and got up to 140 mph without a complaint from the car.

The vibrating hum of rubber on paving hammered at his willpower, threatening to drag him back into the sleep he too readily spurned earlier. He rolled down the window to let some air in. Although the early summer offered a warmish breeze, it wound up being cooler than the car's interior.

Tris stirred and sat up with a yawn. "Hey. Where are we?"

Kevin surveyed the land outside. "Probably getting close to Nebraska by now."

The rattle of a magazine ejecting and snapping back into a pistol came from the back seat.

"Good morning, kiddo," said Kevin.

Abby leaned her head into the front, one arm draped over each seatback. "Hey."

Tris fished some sandwiches out of a bag between her feet, and handed them around.

"We're moving fast." Abby munched while peering out her window. "I've never gone this fast before."

Kevin tapped the wheel, imagining a bit of old music that used to play at Wayne's. "This thing's got a bit more pickup than that van."

"That van is carrying a couple hundred pounds of machinegun." Tris winked. "And it has motors optimized for torque, not speed."

"Huh?" asked Abby.

Kevin sniffed at the sandwich reflexively before biting it. "She means it's meant for hauling heavy crap, not going fast."

"Oh." Abby leaned back and nibbled on her lunch.

He pulled over for a rest stop about two hours later. Abby insisted on holding Tris' hand the entire time. As the girls went one way, Kevin crossed to the other side of the road and watered the grass. Worry of Enclave snipers kept him glancing back out of the corner of his eye at her white hair until she returned to the car with Abby.

Kevin glanced down and coughed at a whiff of shitty coffee in the air. "Damn. That can't be a good sign… smells the same coming out."

Abby hovered close to Tris' side by the car during a few minutes of 'leg stretching,' while Kevin performed a neurotic check of the car. After they got back in, he twisted around to look at her.

"You okay?"

She smoothed her dress over her legs and nodded. "Yeah. It's creepy being alone out here. Like… there's no one left in the whole world."

He patted her on the knee. "It's okay to be scared. I never really knew how scared I was until I didn't have to be anymore."

"What's that supposed to mean?" Abby scrunched up her nose.

"Got a taste of it at the 'house." He faced forward and eased the car underway again. "First time in a lot of years I wasn't out here, not knowing if someone was looking at me over a gunsight, wanting ta take what I have. Wondering if I'll wake up if I try to sleep... 'Course, that rug got pulled out from under me."

"Sorry," muttered Tris.

"Not your doing." Kevin squinted. "That Nathan prick." He shot a quick glance back at Abby. "So, anyway... it never hit me how worried I always was, because I always was. With livin' in Ned for a bit now, it's different."

"Oh. Is it dangerous to drive?" Abby leaned forward. "Can I have water?"

Tris handed her a canteen.

"Depends on where you are. Route 80 is relatively safe since it gets used so much."

Abby squinted at him. "Wouldn't that make more people want to steal there?"

"Yes and no. Drivers who take this road are on long trips for the most part, which means they have cars they think can handle some nasty sh—crap." Kevin picked a crumb from the corner of his mouth. "There aren't a whole lot of cars left, and the kind of jackasses who'd attack a driver for the chance they're carryin' somethin' worth taking wanna find easier pickins."

"Oh." Abby drank a few gulps before returning the canteen. "What's it like being a driver? And you don't have to stop swearing 'cause I'm here. I've heard worse."

Kevin grinned. "Most of the time, it's just like this. Long times of watching road go by. The problem is those twenty second 'aww shit' moments when someone wants what you have and believes their guns are bigger than yours."

Tris ran her fingers through her hair. "Think that Komodo guy was right? More people can set up rest stops without worrying about bounties on them..."

"No clue." Kevin shrugged. "They still gotta find panels from somewhere, and with no Code, nothing's stopping someone from deciding they want a roadhouse and killing the guy running it."

Tris glanced at him, nose raised. "Didn't you say most people are decent?"

"Decent people aren't the type to spend their life out on the road." He glared at the decaying stripe of paint flowing under the hood.

"Oh, I don't know." Tris put a hand on his thigh. "You turned out okay."

"What's that?" whisper-shouted Abby. "There's something coming at us."

Kevin raised an eyebrow at the rear view screen, where a buggy made out of aluminum tubing with two huge rear wheels and tiny front tires appeared to be gaining on them. "Wow... that guy's desperate."

"Is he a bad guy?" asked Abby.

"Yeah, more than likely. That little thing is working too hard to keep up. He ain't drivin', he's tryin' to catch us." He smiled. "One way to find out."

He pushed on the accelerator. Red LED numbers in the center of the console ticked up past 140, 160, 175. Abby grabbed the back of Tris' seat and whimpered. Tris stared at the road ahead.

Eleven seconds after he hit 184 mph, a great plume of white smoke billowed out behind the driver of the buggy, engulfing the entire vehicle in a cloud, which rapidly fell away to the distance behind them.

"Yeah, he was trying to come after us." Kevin laughed. "Rickety ethanol rig couldn't keep up. Pretty sure he blew his head gasket."

"Can we slow down now?" whispered Abby.

He eased off the accelerator and let the car settle down to 120. "Yeah. Better for power."

The girl released her death grip on the seats and slid back to the center of the rear seat. "What did he want?"

"Probably the car." Kevin frowned. "Or what he thought we were carrying."

"Oh," said Abby. "Please don't let them catch us."

Kevin grinned, squeezing and releasing the wheel. "I won't. I've had a little bit of practice at this driving thing."

3

THE OPPOSITE OF ALONE

With the sun weakening in the sky, Kevin kept his eyes focused on the north side of the highway. By his estimation, they'd be somewhere between Lexington and Kearney by now, and he knew there should be a 'house in the area. Sure enough, the glowing red neon of a Roadhouse sign emerged from behind a small clump of trees about fifteen minutes after he started looking for it.

"Goin' to spend the night here," said Kevin.

Tris nodded.

He overshot it on purpose, pulled a U-turn, and headed off the highway onto a concrete lot with a bunch of dead semi-trucks left to rot. Beyond a row of rusting trailers, a sturdy brown-walled building bore a smaller version of the Roadhouse red sign, in paint. Some of the truck trailers closest to the building appeared to have been converted into homes. Two large German Shepherd dogs relaxed on the dirt by a stairway made of cinder blocks leading into one such home. He had the feeling another nuke could go off and neither would bother moving.

Old toys, a small pink bike with white tires, one of those red plastic pedal cars (faded to pink), and more rubber balls of various shapes and sizes than he felt inclined to count littered the area. Tris stared at the evidence of children and got that look on her face again, likely wondering if someone had scavenged all that crap up for a present-day kid, or if the former owner of all those toys had survived the war.

Kevin steered around in a wide right turn that lined up on the roadhouse proper, aiming for one of the defined parking spots out front with a charging plug. The sight of a roof laden with solar panels stirred the faintest hint of regret at walking away from his dream. Fitch would no doubt let him take over again if he went back there, but he couldn't risk some random lunatic shooting the place up and catching Tris... or Abby in the crossfire. Roadhouses were for men like Wayne, who had nothing worth losing but the house itself and no other warm soul who'd give a crap if they bit a bullet. More than his life, though, he couldn't bear to watch something happen to Tris. If anything ever did, he'd probably turn straight into Wayne—and go back to running a Roadhouse, not caring at all if he lived to see tomorrow.

By the time he brought the car to a stop, he had to blink water out of his eyes.

"What's wrong?" asked Tris.

"Dust." He smiled, and pulled her in for a kiss. "Just some dust."

She gave him a pouty look. "You miss it."

"No. Actually I don't." He caressed her cheek with his thumb, smiling. "I was thinking about the reason I don't."

A hint of blush shaded her face.

Abby fiddled around with the rope she'd been using for a belt, untying it to add a leather holster Tris had borrowed from the militia. Once she had the Sig on her side, she scooted out of the back seat. She spent another half a minute fussing with how it sat against her hip. No matter how she fidgeted at it, she couldn't get comfortable. Kevin locked the doors while Tris plugged in the charge cable, and they walked up four steps to a porch and into the Roadhouse.

The scarecrow behind the counter looked like he hadn't seen a decent meal in months: emaciated, bald on top with scraggly strands of brown hair draped past his shoulders. A pair of six-shooters hung in oversized holsters from his belt. The man regarded Kevin and Tris with a brief wary glance before his expression warmed to a smile as soon as Abby slipped in behind them. Apparently, having a kid along somehow proved they didn't intend to cause trouble. Multiple female voices murmured from a hallway beyond. All the tables were empty.

Kevin approached the counter, raising a hand in greeting. *He's twitchy.* "Evenin'. Charge on port six. What you got that's good eatin'?"

The man flashed a nervous smile. "Two coins fer' chargin'. Uhh, chicken's fried. Pretty decent. Best we got but tek awhile. Got some 'tato thingees too, but ain't quite's good as the one by Rawlins."

Kevin grinned. "Yeah, Sang's got a way with spices."

"You know the place?" asked the proprietor.

"Yeah. It's technically my 'house, but I'm havin' friends run it for me." He indicated Tris with a nod. "That's the runaway sheep."

"Oh, damn." The man's tension evaporated. He rendered an enthusiastic handshake as though they'd been brothers for years. "Name's Ben. True 'bout 'Rillo?"

"It is," whispered Abby. She wrapped herself around Tris' left arm.

Tris raised an eyebrow at him. "I don't remember ever hearing you on the radio."

"Ehh..." Ben grimaced. "I listen. Don't like talkin' in public much."

"Yeah." Kevin shook his head. "Whole thing was a pile of bullshit." He looked at Tris and Abby. "You two okay with chicken?"

They nodded.

"Three orders of the chicken then, some of those taters as well. And a room for the night."

"Seventeen fair? Usually charge five fer that chicken, but I'll do four for yas." Ben tucked a strand of greasy hair behind his ear.

"Sure." Kevin set out nineteen coins to cover the charge as well. "And turn on port six."

"'Ave a seat." Ben scooped the coins into his hand, gave them a quick count, and dropped them into a box under the counter. "Drinks?"

"Oh... right. Water's fine." He dropped three more coins on the counter.

Ben whirled around to a machine made of copper pipes and plastic tubing. A wire mesh rack held about a dozen paper coffee filters in a vertical stack, with a feed line mounted to the topmost basket. He held a glass to a spigot at the bottom and opened a valve up top, allowing water to run down through the series of papers.

Tris headed for a booth-style table near the back hallway, which left most of the room in front of them. Kevin chuckled to himself. *Old habits die hard.* Ben set three glasses of water up, and Kevin carried them over to the table. He settled in at the end of the bench seat facing the room with Abby at his left, sandwiched between him and Tris.

Ben ducked into the back for a little while before returning with the news their food would take about twenty minutes.

Abby leaned against Tris; the way she held her hands together at her chest made her seem younger, or more frightened. Kevin tried to make eye contact, still wondering if bringing her along had been a good idea.

Tris put an arm around her while smiling at Kevin. He allowed himself to relax a little, and let his mind wander along a fantasy of a prewar family going out to eat for the night like they did in some of the old movies he'd watched.

They sat waiting for their food for a few minutes before a rumble outside announced the arrival of another vehicle. Tris' smile faded to a look of caution. Seconds after the clatter of the roadhouse door opening, her expression of caution bloomed into the same rageful glower she had right before shooting Neon through both eyeballs.

Kevin twisted around to peer toward the door.

A man walked in with an assault rifle in his right hand, his left arm around the chest of a scrawny girl a year or two younger than Abby, with frizzy red hair down to her shins. She hung over his forearm like an annoyed housecat resigned to being carried. The child wore nothing but a dense layer of grime from head to toe and handcuffs on her wrists as well as ankles. She locked stares with Kevin for a few seconds, a mixture of curiosity, fear, and pleading on her face.

The man had the look of a raider—baggy brown pants and armor made from old tires wrapped around his dirt-smeared bare chest, with six-inch nail spikes on both shoulder pads. He approached a table near the door and set the girl down on her feet right next to a metal-framed chair with a battered red vinyl cushion. She hopped and shuffled a few inches before plopping down to sit.

"I'm gonna kill him," muttered Tris. "Cover me."

Abby gasped and shrank down in the bench seat.

Another man entered behind them, a bit older, dressed in army green complete with a Kevlar vest and helmet, also with an assault rifle. He had a muscular build and skin of deep, dark brown. As the first man walked away from the captured child toward the counter, the one in army green gave Kevin a 'hey man, what's up' sort of nod.

Ben's face blanched as pale as Tris. The look he gave the new arrivals said he shared the same expectations about the men's intentions toward their captive, but had frozen in fear.

"Do they think she's infected?" whispered Abby.

"No, sweetie." Tris grabbed her Beretta. "They're not going to be thinking much of anything in a second."

Kevin reached across their adopted daughter to hold Tris' weapon down. "Hang on. Don't go starting a gunfight while you're sitting right next to Abby."

Tris narrowed her eyes at him, muttering, "I wasn't planning to *start* a gunfight; I'm planning to kill a pair of goddamned slavers preying on a child." Her face reddened in anger. "*Look* at her. How could anyone do that to another human being, much less a little girl?"

"Wait." Kevin squeezed her hand. "There's two kids in here and I don't want either one of them catching a stray bullet. Got a feeling Twitchy McTwitcherson behind the counter is going to go crazy if something happens. That guy looks like he'd start throwing bullets everywhere."

The red haired girl raised her legs, set her heels on the edge of the chair, and fussed at the steel around her ankles with a demeanor more annoyed than desperate to escape. For a short while, the metallic rattle of her restraints held the room in rapt silence. Ben stared vacantly at the man in tire armor, oblivious to what he'd said. A woman in her early forties started out of the hallway, stopped short staring at the bound child, shifted her gaze to the man in tire armor, and backed away, eyes wide with fear.

"Yo, you alive?" asked the raider.

"Y-yes," Ben stammered, leaning away as if expecting to be hit.

"Enough." Tris started to stand, but Kevin held her down by a hand on the shoulder. She shot a glare at him. "What?"

Kevin watched the girl. Too thin, too dirty, far too casual about her situation. She barely gave either man any notice, continuing to fuss with the cuffs. "Gimme a minute..."

The dark-skinned man in army green sat in the chair next to the feral girl, showing little concern at her halfhearted attempt to free herself. Either he didn't care if she got loose, or knew she couldn't. Kevin squinted at her. *She's more irritated than frightened.* The kid sensed him watching and raised her head to make eye contact. He mouthed 'are you okay?' at her. She blinked, stared at him a little longer, and raised her hands before tugging the cuffs apart as if to ask if he could get them off her.

"This is exactly what I was talking about," whispered Tris. "That guy behind the counter is just going to stand there and let them make a slave out of a little girl. Look at him. He's scared shitless. What if this was our Roadhouse? What would you do if this walked into our place?"

"Hang on." Kevin patted the table. "Something's not right."

"No shit." Tris glared at him. She pulled at the Beretta, but he held her hand down again. "Slavery's horrible enough, but that's a child. Disgusting. A bullet in the face is too fast for anyone who would do that."

Abby slipped off the seat and curled up in a ball on the floor below the table.

"I don't think this is as bad as it looks like. Their body language is all wrong." He eased himself to his feet. "The kid is too calm. I'm gonna do the same thing I'd have done if this walked into our place—talk to 'em."

"What's to talk about?" Tris continued to glare while squeezing the handle of her Beretta. "They haven't put anything on her but handcuffs."

"Look at how long her hair is and how filthy she is. The kid's probably feral. Maybe she bit them or they're trying to take her to civilization and she kept running away. They found a feral back home when I was like fifteen; a boy, a bit younger than that kid looks. Took them six months to get him not to rip any clothing they put on him off in seconds, and they had to lock him in his room for a month to keep him from running back into the Wildlands alone. She doesn't seem afraid of them. She ain't even seriously trying to get free. That kid's more annoyed than scared. Got a feeling she's been stuck in them things a good while. Maybe these two found her like that. Give me a minute before you shoot two guys who might not deserve it." He paused. "'Course, if you turn out to be right, I'll tackle the one in green."

Tris nodded.

The man in the tire armor carried three plates of dust hopper burgers over to the table. He set one in front of the girl, who ceased chafing at the handcuffs on her legs and stared at the food as though it glowed with divine light. She managed to get a grip on it with both hands despite the metal on her wrists and jammed it into her face, snarling and chomping on it like a stray dog. The man in green leaned back in an overacted show of fear that he'd get caught up in her feeding frenzy.

"I don't wanna be a slave," whispered Abby from the floor. She looked back and forth from the other girl to Tris. "Are they gonna take me too?"

Tris started to raise the Beretta again. "No. They're not."

"Just... give me a minute." Kevin pushed the weapon down. "I don't think they did that to her. She's not trying to get away or screaming for help." Kevin flashed a wry grin. "Or offering anyone money."

Tris glared at him. "That's not funny."

"Stay with Abby a sec. Watch my back." Kevin hurried over to their table.

The red-haired girl gave him a wary look as he approached, hovering over her meal defensively.

Kevin raised his hands. "Easy, kiddo. I'm not gonna take your food."

The men looked up from their burgers.

"Somethin' I can do for you?" asked Green.

"Howdy. Interesting group you've got." Kevin smiled his most disarming smile. "I, uhh, couldn't help but notice the girl and… well, my lady friend back there's a bit touchy about the whole slavery thing. Mind if I ask what the story is before she does something violent?"

Ben got even paler and swayed on his feet. His fingers twitched over the gun on his hip.

Finished with her food, the girl let her hands drop in her lap and stared up at him, swishing her feet back and forth. Small scratches and smears covered her skin everywhere, suggesting she hadn't worn clothing in a rather long time. Unnatural red-orange spots in the grime on her chest and thighs made him raise an eyebrow. The discoloration didn't look like blood, or anything he could remember. *Some kind of chemical? What the hell?*

"Aw, shit." The man with the armor made out of tires chuckled. "Yeah, I figger this don' look so good. We found the little thing like that. She don' talk much 'cept to ask us to get them things offa her. We was south a ways from here, scavvin', an' find this strip mall looks in good shape, so we start with the left side, figurin' we work our way across." He made a chopping motion with his hand in the air as if to indicate several discrete spaces. "First spot's this 'lectronics place, but there ain't nothin' useful there. When we walk out, this one comes hopping up to us from a grocery mart two spots over. After we checked the place out ta make sure she's alone, we put 'er in the truck and started headin' home right away. Oughta get there like two 'er three t'morrah."

"Name's Ray." The man in olive drab offered a hand to shake. "That's Larry… we ain't get no name outta the little one yet. Think the only words she knows are 'take bad metal off.'"

The girl tugged at the cuffs on her wrists. "Bad metal. Want off."

Ray let out a resigned sigh. "Best I figure, she'd been livin' on her own for quite a while. Had to be hundreds of empty cans in that market. She had a little nest built up inside the shelves made outta sleeping bags an' stuffed animals. Probably two or three years livin' there based on the number o' cans."

"Hey." Kevin waved at the girl. "Are these two telling the truth?"

The girl stopped fidgeting and stared at him. Dark green eyes radiated worry and frustration in equal measure. She stared at him for what felt like two solid minutes of silence, before the anxiety in her expression faded to hope. "I 'lone. Live by self. Angry mans catch me when I outside 'sploring." She raised her arms and rattled the handcuffs. "They chase. Hold down. Put bad metal. Hate bad metal. Angry mans take me away home. Put me in box an' go to bad place. Sickers get 'em. They not come back. Angry mans sickers now. I kick box. Break box. Go home." She snarled at the cuffs on her legs. "Hate bad metal. No run. Slow walk. Hard eat." The girl twisted and pulled at both pairs of handcuffs until she got angry to the point of crying. "So hate. No want bad metal. Can't break. Try lots." She stared at him for long pleading moment before continuing in a quieter voice. "Scared people. Hide many lots. I…"

"Poor kid," said Ray.

She leaned into the man in green. "Not scared Ray. He laughing smiles. He not bad. He take 'way bad metal. Promised."

"Wow," said Larry. "That's more words come outta her in that minute than since we found her like five hours ago."

The girl hooked the cuffs on her wrists over one knee and pulled at her arms until her hands turned red, then slouched and gave up with an annoyed sigh. "Hate angry mans for do this me. Good they sickers."

Kevin rubbed his chin. "How long have you been alone?" He glanced at Ray. "She probably hasn't talked much in a while."

The girl looked confused, opened her mouth, and furrowed her brow. "I 'lone lots days. Mom Dad went 'way 'an I little. 'Lone…" She tried a few non-words on for size before scowling. "Years."

"She just sat in the back seat curled up like a cat the whole ride." Larry stifled a laugh. "Kid doesn't understand blankets. Thought we were trying to hurt her.'"

"Itches!" yelled the girl, shivering.

Ray chuckled. "Pulled a spare shirt over her head, but she didn't like having her arms pinned either. Took that shit right off."

The girl pouted at her lap. "Ray said help. Hate bad metal. I happy sickers got angry mens." She snarled. "They 'zerve be sickers."

"We ain't got the tools ta cut them things with us. Takin' her back up ta Douglas Grove. Nice ol' settlement there. Get her loose once we get home. Paulie's got a set of bolt cutters oughta work." Ray gave her an apologetic look. "A night here and a couple more hours on the road, an' we'll get rid of them things."

She grasped her knees and stared down, seething with obvious discontent. "'Kay."

Kevin looked at Tris and waved for her to come over. "I think we might be able to help now if you want us to try."

The redhead growled, pulling at her arms and kicking her legs, rattling. "Hate bad metal! Make gone now!"

Ray gestured at the girl in a 'be my guest' manner.

Tris jogged over.

"They found her like this." Kevin put a hand on Tris' back. "Sounds like this kid's been avoiding people for a couple years. Someone grabbed her while she was out exploring, but she got away. She's been stuck for a while. Still got your lockpicks?"

"I hide." The girl leaned into Ray. "Scared. Not want 'lone, but people bad. See home and come wanna steal, but I hide next a food in wall hole. No steal. *My* food." She frowned at the floor, looking ashamed. "Maybe people help, but I scared. Hide. Now hate bad metal more 'an scared bad people. Can't run 'way bad people, so hide all people. Hear Ray laugh. Not scared Ray. Ray nice. Ask help."

"Oh, you poor thing." Tris took a knee and opened the compartment in the sole of her left shoe. "Hi sweetie. What's your name?"

The girl stared at her as if deep in thought.

"You have a name don't you?" Tris looked back and forth from the girl to Kevin, before glancing at the men. "What did people call you? She's got enough language to have had contact with people at some point. She couldn't have been on her own *too* long."

"Mom Dad went 'way 'an I six." The girl's lip quivered. "Sickers took 'em."

Tris scowled at the floor. "I'm sorry…"

The child grimaced while trying to wriggle a hand out of the cuff. "Not talk… longs time. Uhh." She stared with rapt attention at a thin sliver of metal in Tris' hand. "Name Kay-bee."

"Kimmie, Kadie, Kimberly?" asked Tris.

She shook her head.

"Kaylee? Katie?" asked Kevin.

The girl's expression lit up. She nodded. "Kay-tee. Mom Dad call Katie."

"Katie it is." Tris grasped the girl's hand and turned her arm over. "She's been stuck in these long enough to grow. They're way too tight. Hold still, okay? I'm going to get these things off you."

"Pease!" Katie trembled with anticipation; she cried, but the tears seemed borne of frustration. "Want off. Make angry. Hurt. Hard eat. No run. Fall lot."

Tris raised the girl's arm to study the cuff, poking at it with the shim.

"Maybe whoever caught her was just a cruel son of a bitch and tightened them too much?" asked Kevin.

"I'm gonna see if that guy has anything that'll fit her." Larry unbuckled his tire armor and left it on the table. "Before he passes out thinkin' we're gonna shoot his place up."

Ray chuckled. "Tellin' you man, ditch that steel belted crap. Makes you look like a bandit."

"You do kinda look like a raider," said Kevin past a grin.

"I need armor." Larry stood.

"That's not armor." Kevin winked. "Any real gun'd go right through it."

Larry held his arms to the sides, smiling. "Yeah, but most people use swords and shit." He walked backward a few steps smiling, turned, and strode up to Ben.

"There's all kinds of dirt packed inside. This is going to be pain in the ass." Tris scraped the shim about, using it to clear crud from the mechanism. "How long have you had the bad metal?"

Katie sat so still she seemed to have stopped breathing, watching Tris work. "I got catched 'an it hot. Got cold, an' now hot 'gain. I try everything break, but bad metal no go 'way. Swim not fun. Try all break bad metal. Rock hit. Not work. Then put"—she gestured as if smearing something around her wrists—"white slippy. Not good. Not break."

"Summer to summer? A year?" asked Kevin, eyebrows up. "You've been alone for a year?"

The girl shook her head. "I 'lone from six. Much long than have bad metal." She tugged her legs apart to make the chain rattle. "Had bad metal year."

"How old are you now? Nine?" Tris emitted a triumphant squeak as the cuff popped open.

"Yay!" Katie bounced in her seat. "I dunno old. I not six."

"She looks about nine or ten." Kevin jumped at a sudden touch from the side.

Abby clung to him, her gaze locked on Katie. She seemed terrified at the sight of the handcuffs, as if they'd somehow leap off the redhead and fix her to a bed while Infected swarmed in. Kevin put an arm around Abby.

"Don't figure she's got much of a concept of time passing," said Ray.

"She had to be living there a couple years, but could'a been early fall to now. Couple months… who knows. Seems kinda unlikely for a kid to survive so long on her own, but she had a perfect setup in that store. Like some kinda squirrel, she'd put all the canned food in the vents where no one could get to it but a kid."

Tris shimmed the cuff off the girl's other wrist after a moment of scraping black crud out of it, and tossed them on the table. Abby leaned away as if they emitted lethal radiation. Katie stretched her arms out to the sides, beaming. She leaned over to Ray and grabbed at him, clinging to his arm. He pulled her into his lap and turned her to put her feet up on her former chair to make it easier on Tris. The cuffs around her ankles had more damage than the others, like she'd worked them over with rocks and hammers. Mud, paint, oil, and a few traces of cooking lard lurked inside the mechanism.

Larry returned with a brown army-style T-shirt. He tried to pull it over her head, but she whined and pushed at it. He shrugged and set on the table. "He ain't got nothin' kid-sized. That's the best I could find."

"Damn. She beat the shit out of these." Tris bit her lip and tried to force the shim into place. "Can't say I blame her."

"Openin' locks… That's a handy skill to have," said Ray.

"Yeah well." Tris grasped Katie's foot to hold her still. "I got a whole lot of skills I didn't think I'd need. This is much easier when they're on someone else."

Kevin raised an eyebrow.

Ray went to pull the shirt over Katie's head again, but she flailed and whined, so he gave up.

Katie hissed and tried to tug back on her leg. "Ow."

"Sorry." Tris paused. "I… can't imagine spending a year locked up like this. I'd have gone crazy. VR was bad enough, and that was only an hour."

"Kinda strange. Who'd they think would grab you that you'd need to learn how to escape those things?" Kevin scratched his head. "Why would Nathan load you up with that sort of skill set?"

Tris looked at him. "How should I know why that bastard does anything? Why'd he give me hand to hand training?"

"So you could survive to get to the resistance probably." Kevin chuckled. "If he believes those historical documentaries too, he's gotta think the world out here's a lot worse than it is."

"Pease!" yelled Katie. She grabbed the chain between her ankles in two hands and pulled at it. "No stop."

"Please." Tris got back to work.

"Please?" asked Katie, slower.

"Right." Tris grumbled. "This is going to pinch a little, okay?"

Katie nodded.

The girl emitted a muffled whine as Tris forced the shim in. After a bit of wiggling it back and forth, the cuff popped open. It took another thirty seconds or so to get the other one off. The second it released her, Katie hurled herself on Tris while emitting a loud screeching cry that caused Ben to dive for cover. Kevin grabbed the girl from behind, fearing she'd gone full feral, but the redhead broke into joyous cries for a few seconds before she leapt away and sprinted across the room.

Katie climbed up onto the counter and ran down the length, her reckless dash punting a few bowls of peanuts to the floor. At the end, she jumped from the counter to a nearby table, knocking it over, and darted, squealing with glee down the rear corridor, her calf-length hair trailing after her like a phantom.

"Well that's… different." Kevin blinked.

Happy screaming outside grew louder, drawing toward the front door —and right on by. A moment later, her cheering passed around the building a second time.

"If I'd been stuck like her for a year, I think I'd go a little crazy too at being able to move again. I doubt she'd been trapped like that for all that long though, or she'd be limping." Tris scowled at the rusty metal. "Change of plans. I want to take a detour to find those bastards."

"They're already dead." Kevin gave Abby a reassuring squeeze. "At least the kid seems to think Infected got them. I'm guessin' she calls them 'sickers.' You said a bullet would be too good for anyone who'd do that to a kid. Sounds like you got your wish."

"Bad scene on the way inta that town," said Ray. "Looked like an old city hall building. We cut down twenty or so on our way ta this little orange and white U-Haul trailer. They'd rigged it with a pull bar into some kinda wagon. Makes sense now. We found a smashed crate in the back. Couldn't figure out what kind of beastie they had in it since it looked busted open from the inside. I think she kicked her way out. Sumbitches nailed the lid on too. Good thing the wood was old and brittle."

Kevin nodded. "If that wagon was still there, couldn't have been *that* long ago."

"A few weeks in cuffs would've felt like years to her." Tris shivered.

"Oy." Larry nodded. "Figger they nabbed her, an' saw 'dat buildin' on the way out, 'cided ta stop in and check it. Lucky fer her."

"Found her at this strip mall about two, three miles north of the downtown. Little creek goin' behind it in a culvert. I can't imagine how anyone could tolerate livin' alone for so long, much less a girl her age." Ray shook his head. "Kid's tough."

Katie raced in and jumped on Tris again, hugged Ray, pounced on Abby, hugged Larry, and zipped off to run two more laps around the room before skidding to a halt on all fours and scarfing up the peanuts that she'd spilled earlier, eating them shell and all.

Abby made an annoyed face at her dress where the other girl had smeared dirt on her, brushed at it, and sighed. The same woman emerged from the back to talk to Ben. Katie jumped up, wrapped her arms around her, and grinned.

"Hiiiii," chirped Katie.

"At least she's happy," said Larry.

"I kind of expected her to be a little more wary of people." Ray shrugged.

Tris put her hands on her hips, watching Katie continue to run around. "You showed her some people are nice. She probably thought everyone would try to grab her again. She's gone the other way—she wants the opposite of alone."

Abby looked from Katie to Kevin. "Isn't she gonna put the shirt on? She's not going swimming."

"That's all she's known." Kevin patted Abby's shoulder. "She's wild."

Katie, a little winded after another few minutes of racing around, bounded up to the table and halted standing at Larry's side. She helped herself to what remained of his fried potatoes, cramming handful after handful in her mouth while breathing hard through her nose.

Ben walked over with two mason jars full of homemade beer and one with water. He gave the men a 'please control her' look before going back to the counter by way of picking up the table she'd knocked over.

Katie rubbed her bruised wrists and beamed at Tris before hugging Ray again. She reached for one of the beers, but Ray switched it for water. Trails streamed down her front as she tried to drink too fast. Ray pulled down on the end of the jar, slowing her.

Once she finished, she grinned at everyone. "Thank for kill bad metal. I go home."

She started for the door.

Ray grabbed her arm. "Hey… You can't go off alone."

"Why?" Katie twisted around to face him, tilting her head. "I got home. Food. Warm."

"Well, one thing, it's a three hour ride by car. You ain't walking that. Two, I ain't lettin' no little kid run off on her own, bare-ass, no weapons, no way to protect herself." He picked up the T-shirt and pulled it down over her head despite her squirming. "You're too young to be alone. You need someone ta look after you. There a bunch o' families back in Douglas Grove would take you in, give ya a proper life."

Katie picked at the T-shirt, making faces as if trying to decide if she liked the way it felt. Tris gathered the child's hair and pulled it out of the shirt before letting it cascade free, which made her less fidgety.

"You're right," whispered Tris while glancing at Kevin. "She looks like she has no idea what a shirt even is."

"I no have." Katie pulled at the fabric.

"What did you do when it got cold?" asked Tris.

Katie shrugged. "I stay all day bed. Warm. Run fast outside pee or get can food." She poked at an orange mark on her leg. "Pillows like best. Yellow bits blech, but eat 'cause food. Two cans day make last."

"Kid's got life figured out. Too cold out? Spend all day in bed." Larry reclined and sipped beer. "That's the life."

"You ate pillows?" asked Tris.

Now I get it. Kevin chuckled. "Canned ravioli… the orange spots all over her are sauce stains. Ugh. That kid was eating fifty-year-old food. No wonder she's so damn skinny."

"Not that it's an option, but do you really wanna be alone all the time?" Ray ran his hand over her head. "Don't you wanna be with people?"

"I 'lone 'cause scared." Katie looked around at everyone before grabbing Ray's hand and pressing it to her cheek. "Y-you want me stay? Real? I can?" Her eyes widened, her lower lip quivered ever so slightly. The genuine disbelief in her expression weighed on Kevin's heart. "You want me?"

Tris gave Kevin the 'if he doesn't, I will' look.

"Now look at that face and tell me you're gonna give her to some other family." Larry raised one of the beers to his lips. "Guess you'll be surprisin' Tabitha with a daughter."

Ray shook his head, smiling. "Guess so." He nodded at Katie. "Yeah. You welcome ta stay with me an' my wife if you want."

She climbed up to sit in his lap, looking surprised, mouth open, speechless. After a few seconds of staring, she clamped on, cheek pressed to his chest. As if all the fear she'd harbored for however long she'd been alone hit her at once, she trembled.

"Guess that's a yes," said Larry.

Katie nodded. "I like. So 'lone. Want more talk. Home quiet. Scareds."

Abby sniffled and wiped a tear before clinging to Tris.

A thin teenaged boy with a strong resemblance to Ben carried three bowl-shaped hubcaps full of fried chicken out into the room and paused with a look of confusion.

Kevin pointed at their table.

The boy nodded and set the food down.

"Thanks for the assist." Ray reached up to Tris.

With a little bit of guilt on her face, she shook his hand. "You're welcome."

Katie grinned. "I not 'lone."

Tris' smile lasted only until she turned away from the girl. Morose, she trudged back to their booth, holding Abby's hand. Kevin followed. After they slid into the bench seat, he took his spot at the end. The fragrance of fried chicken got him in seconds, and he dug in. Abby nibbled for a bit, but once she got a good taste of it, she proceeded to do an impression of Katie's 'I haven't had real food in years' mauling.

Kevin glanced over at Tris after his second drumstick. She still hadn't touched her food. "What's wrong? You want to keep her too?" He grinned.

Tris smirked. "No. She looks happy with Ray." She sighed. "I almost just killed two decent men. As soon as I saw her, I assumed the worst and wanted to shoot them."

"Most people would've reacted the same way to seeing a pair of rough-looking dudes with a chained kid…" He picked up a breast, fighting the urge to jam it in his mouth. "Though you did kinda skip over the pointing the gun at them and demanding they let her go part."

"I'm so wound up." She leaned her elbows on the table and held her face in both hands. "All I can think about is how I'm supposed to do something about the Enclave, and this cryptic shit from Terminal9 isn't helping."

Kevin took a few bites to think over his response. She probably didn't want to hear him repeat that she had no way to stop the Virus, and failing wasn't her fault. He'd been around and around with her, questioning how the two of them could manage any kind of threat to the Enclave… hovercraft, high-tech weapons and all.

"I almost killed them right in front of her and… shit." Tris leaned back and raked her fingers up through her hair. "How long did it take her to trust people enough to ask for help, and I would've sent her crawling right back into some dark hiding place."

"Please stop feeling guilty about something you didn't even do." Kevin took another bite. "Nwfm eam yrr fmm." He swallowed. "Eat your chicken before it gets cold. This is really good."

Hamster-cheeked Abby nodded with an enthusiastic, "Mmm!"

Tris picked up a drumstick. "What's wrong with me?"

"Nothing." He reached over Abby's head to pat Tris on the back. "If people had to answer for everything they *thought* about doing but didn't do, we'd be in a lot of trouble."

Tris forced a weak smile. A nibble became a larger nibble, progressing to a chomp.

Chicken wins. Kevin gnawed on the small winglet, debating a little gluttony and a second basket.

"You're right," mumbled Tris. She stared across the room at Katie curled up in Ray's lap.

"Yeah, this chicken is damn good. I might get more." Kevin patted his stomach.

Abby offered him her thigh piece. "I'm full."

"Save it for the morning. I can't take food out of your mouth." He winked.

"No, not about the chicken." Tris indicated the men with a faint nod. "Not everyone out here is a piece of shit."

He raised both eyebrows. "Still nice to see proof every now and then."

Tris shook her head. "That kid's spent most of her life on high alert. Look at her, passed out in his lap. How long has it been for her since she'd been able to *really* sleep? Feeling safe?"

Abby cuddled up to Tris. "Thank you for taking me in. I know you didn't have to. You believed me the whole time. You wouldn't let them hurt me."

"That's it." Tris sighed. "Warren. That's why I was so ready to end those two. If I hadn't hesitated on him, then your father—"

Abby squeezed Tris' arm. "You're not like him. You can't kill someone without a good reason. It's okay. I understand."

Tris wrapped her arms around Abby and sniffled into her hair.

Kevin patted the table twice and stood. "Gonna get a room key… and more chicken."

4

SCARS

R andom vistas of sunsets played out across Kevin's dream, rich orange and blue swirling over the tip of an endless road. The flash of white paint down the center stuttered; individual dashed lines floated away from the paving and swarmed around the car like curious herons, diving and circling.

He reached up to rub his eyes. When he pulled his fingers away, he found the bizarre vision gone, though the cactuses outside had gone bright pink. Mountains approached; the road swerved to the right before plunging into a tunnel. The instant darkness surrounded him, he went from driving 140 mph to standing on his feet without a car around him.

"Hello?"

His dream voice echoed back to him with a metallic quality, as if he stood inside a giant, empty boiler. Hands raised, he crept forward until he found a wall, and felt around. Soon, he located a door and slid his hand down to the knob. It opened into a hallway with dingy white and green-checkered linoleum. To his right, a pair of doors led to bathrooms, each bearing a basic stick-figure label, one plain and one with a triangle skirt.

He crept down the hall, fragments of glass crunching under his boots, and entered a roadhouse-esque space with tables, chairs, and a counter—only the colors had gone crazy. Red and green on the floor, purple chair cushions, orange counter and tabletops. Wayne, in a duster coat and three bleeding bullet holes in his face, waved from behind the counter.

That's not right. They shot him in the chest.

A man in jeans and cowboy boots with a blurry mass for an upper body raised a mason jar in greeting, his face lost to an unformed memory.

Dad?

"What'cha havin'?" asked not-Wayne. "Usual?"

He pinched the bridge of his nose and tried to rub sense into his head. "Ugh. What the hell was in that chicken?"

When he opened his eyes again, Not-Wayne and the blurry apparition had vanished. The room retained its strange coloration, but he couldn't place it as any roadhouse he'd ever been to.

"Help... me," whispered a female voice.

Kevin whirled around.

A young, pretty, Hispanic girl in a slinky black dress stared at him. *Her...* She could've been anywhere from fifteen to twenty. Infected. Turning. At the cusp of sanity. The girl raised a slender arm holding a tiny silver pistol. A trail of dark blood ran out of her right nostril, dribbling over her lip.

"You can't kill me, can you?" asked the girl. "I'm still human. I don't want to hurt you, but I can't stop."

He took a step back. "I'm dreaming..."

"Help me." The girl cringed and grabbed her right arm with her left hand, fighting with herself not to point the gun at him. "Run... I'm dying."

She took another step toward him, opening her mouth.

As soon as he whirled around to flee, the psychedelic roadhouse changed to desert scrubland aglow in strong moonlight. All of his clothes had vanished, as had his adulthood. Cold dirt underfoot startled a gasp out of him and made him look down at his younger self. Ten years old and scrawny... the same nightmare he'd had as a boy. As long has he could remember, he'd slept naked. Someone told him he could get sick spending the night in the same clothes he wore all day long, and he didn't have anything else... so he'd worn blankets to bed.

When a pile of Infected broke down the wall of his trailer, his brain couldn't process anything but *get out.* He didn't have to look; he knew a horde of Infected closed in on him from behind, everyone from the little trailer cluster he'd called home back then. One tended to forget trivial things like getting dressed before fleeing from their worst nightmare.

Despite not wanting to, he glanced over his shoulder.

Eva and Hemi, his 'parents,' led the pack of moaning half-alive people.

The sight didn't hold quite the same shock it had to his younger mind, but the uncountable army of Infected behind them tweaked his phobia to irrational panic. Screaming, he took off. Every time he had this dream, it ended the same way. No matter how much faster he could run than the slow-stumbling Infected, they'd always be right behind him whenever he looked back. In the nightmare, he'd run through the waist-high grass until he collapsed, always waking up screaming as hands grabbed him.

As it played out every time, it played out that night. Kevin's child self eventually ran out of steam and collapsed, surrounded by grabbing hands and sharp fingernails tearing at his skin.

Kevin snapped awake, covered in sweat, but silent. He held as still as he could manage, arms straight at his sides, staring at the ceiling. Reality crawled back into his brain fact by fact. Roadhouse. Rented room. Omaha. No longer a little boy. Since they'd gotten one room and Abby shared the bed with them, he'd kept his boxers on, Tris, her shirt. Abby lay between them, in the sweatshirt-turned-nightdress she'd brought along. The girl flinched in her sleep, every so often emitting distressed whimpers.

Her bad dream is leaking into my head. He rubbed his face. *I haven't had one like that in years.*

The girl squirmed side to side and stretched her legs as if cringing away from something held to her face.

Kevin yawned. Tris had an arm over Abby like a giant child clinging to a doll. Kevin lay in silence for a few minutes, tired but unable to fall asleep. He had no real way to know for sure that Infected wouldn't stumble across this place. As unlikely as it would be for them to wander out into the no-man's land along Interstate 80, it *could* still happen. Hell, one had shown up at his roadhouse in Rawlins. Talk about middle of nowhere.

He closed his eyes and tried to focus all his thoughts on Tris. It had been easier to sleep in Nederland. He'd never admit it out loud, but that giant dump truck gate, the wall, and the militia *did* make him feel safer. More so than even the Code had. Fifty or so real people willing to defend their homes reassured him more than a phantom army of thousands who'd supposedly have avenged him after the fact.

Abby convulsed and sat up, sucking in air as if to let out a long scream. He put a hand on her back. She turned toward him, not fully awake.

"Dad!" she wailed, and clamped on before bursting into tears.

"Hey… hey…" He rocked her a little, patting her on the back while she trembled and sobbed. "You're okay."

Abby quieted. After a while of laying still and silent, she sniffed in a wet-sounding breath. She lifted her head, looked at him, and let her face thud into his chest. Again, she broke down crying, but these sobs sounded borne of grief rather than fear.

"It's okay." He rubbed her back. "You're safe."

"Sorry I called you Dad." She sniffled. "He's dead."

"Oh, I don't think he'd mind. You'd just had a bad dream and weren't all the way awake."

She lay still, sniffling occasionally.

"I'm scared of those things too." He shifted to get more comfortable and closed his eyes. "Ever since I was your age. Still have nightmares."

"But you're like… old."

"Thanks." He poked her in the side, causing her to squirm and grin. "Tris told me a bit about what happened. You're a lot tougher than me. I didn't go through half of what you did and I have wicked dreams too."

"I dream I'm back there," whispered Abby. "Tied to a bed and everyone's Infected… and I can't get away. I try to stay quiet but they still find me… and it's Warren after Tris shot him… Infected."

Kevin kept patting her back. "It's just a dream. You'll never see that bastard again."

"I know. Tell that to my dreams." Abby shifted over, laying against him. "What's your nightmare like?"

"I'm back home as a kid. Used to live in this old trailer park. We'd gone on this long trip to move, and a couple of the people with us wound up getting infected along the way. Two older boys, think they were seventeen or eighteen, knew they got it. They buried the other dead and walked away to end it before they turned."

"You dream that?" whispered Abby.

"No… The nightmare I have never really happened. I used to dream that everyone but me in our little town got Infected. They break down the wall of my old bedroom and chase me across the field. Brown tall grass up past my waist. I run and run but I can't get away from them."

Abby almost shivered. "Mmm."

At least I can bore her to sleep. He smiled.

AN EAR-PIERCING SCREAM DRAGGED KEVIN OUT OF BED. HE MADE IT TO THE hallway outside their rented room—one eye open, .45 in hand, boxers clinging to his hips—before his brain caught up to consciousness. Abby backed away from a flaking green door with black spray painted letters spelling, 'shit here.'

"Huh?" He croaked.

Abby, hands flailing, whirled around and pounced on him, burying her face in his chest and whimpering. She couldn't decide if she wanted to sob hysterically or throw up.

Kevin stood taller on the balls of his feet, peering into a small bathroom covered in black stains. A dense cloud of flies swarmed around the back corner, clinging to the wall and ceiling in a carpet of moving black spots. A severed human head, rotted enough to expose skull, sat in the toilet amid a massive bloom of silvery-black mold. He cringed and pushed the door closed with the tip of the .45.

"What the fuck is wrong with that guy?" Kevin stared down the short hallway toward the main room. The wall to his right blocked his view of the counter.

Kevin stood there a moment, comforting Abby. When she calmed enough to release her death grip around his chest, he edged to the end of the corridor and stared at Ben. "Dude..." He pointed the .45 at the hallway. "The fuck?"

"Something wrong?" asked Ben.

"You've got a goddamned rotting head in your toilet." He blinked.

Abby coughed, sounding a hair's breadth away from vomiting.

"Yeah. Had a... umm... raider issue last month." Ben fidgeted. "Wife won't touch it. Kids won't touch it. I don't wanna touch it."

Kevin blinked. "So you just leave it there?"

Ben gestured at the back. "There's an outhouse. No one used the damn toilet inside anyway... not like plumbin' works."

"Unbelievable," muttered Kevin.

It occurred to him at that second that Tris hadn't been in bed. "Where's Tris?"

Abby shrugged. "She was gone when I woke up. Will you go with me to the outhouse? I don't wanna be alone."

"Yeah. Lemme get dressed."

"Not like *in* the outhouse," whispered Abby. "You can wait outside."

"That's what I figured you meant."

"Hey! Get out of there!" yelled a woman in the back.

Soft thuds shook the floor in the gait of a small person running. Seconds later, Katie, naked again, sprinted out of the kitchen area, her face and hands smeared with beige-brown sauce, which had also dribbled all over her chest. Flour dusted her face and most of her legs. She beelined for Kevin and hugged him.

"Hiii!" Her breath carried a spicy fragrance that reminded him of the fried chicken.

A woman, likely Ben's wife, appeared in the doorway, glaring. She appeared to think better of chasing the girl and proceeded to berate Ben as if it was somehow his fault the girl had raided their pantry.

Kevin patted her on the head. "Good morning. What did you do?"

Katie let go and took a step back. "Day food." She wrapped her arms around Abby, who stood ramrod straight. "Hiii!"

"Hello," said Abby.

Kevin took Katie by the hand and led her back into the hallway to Ray's room, obvious due to the open door and loud snoring. She darted in and pounced on the bed. Kevin pulled the door closed and returned to their room, tossing the gun on the bed. After wiping chicken batter off himself, he pulled on his white T-shirt, jeans, boots, and gun belt. Abby waited in the doorway squirming and bouncing, an urgent grimace on her face. He snagged his armored jacket and headed out the back door, Abby close at his heels.

The space out back echoed with a multitude of clucking from the right, where a large fenced-in area held close to a hundred chickens. Beyond that, a few small farm plots contained corn, potatoes, and a bunch of other green stuff he couldn't quite identify from the distance. Twenty paces or so behind the roadhouse, a lime green porta-potty perched on a cinderblock foundation. Considering the air didn't peel the skin off his face, he figured Ben had removed the tank and dug a hole under it.

Kevin pulled the door open and a bit of cold metal pressed into his forehead. It took him a second to realize Tris, seated inside, had put her Beretta to his skull.

"Shit." She lowered it. "Knock first!"

He held up a finger, waited for his heart to resume beating, and slammed a fist into his chest twice. "Right. Sorry."

Tris pulled the door shut with a plastic rattle. Abby whined and sent a look of serious consideration at the grass to the right of the outhouse. She decided against it and remained at his side, bouncing on the balls of her feet for a minute and change until Tris emerged. Abby scrambled in.

"Eww." Her voice echoed. "It's gross in here."

Kevin stood with his back to the outhouse, staring off at the countryside. Tris leaned on him. A moment later, Katie wandered out the back door, waved at them with a big grin, squatted, and proceeded to water the grass not quite five steps away from the door.

"This is so nasty," said Abby, her voice muted by the fiberglass outhouse. "I think I'd rather go outside."

Kevin chuckled. "Your choice. Apparently, that's an option here."

The fiberglass structure wobbled; Abby made uneasy noises. Ray walked out, saw Katie, and slapped himself in the forehead. He hurried over and they had a quick murmured conversation before he stared exasperation into the clouds. The girl darted inside, and Ray approached the converted port-a-potty.

"Take a number," said Kevin.

Ray shook his head, waving his hand in a gesture toward where Katie had been. "Ugh, sorry about that."

"Looks like you've got some work ahead of you." Kevin scratched his cheek. "She doesn't seem *too* feral though. At least she went outside first. Last feral kid I saw, he didn't care inside or outside at first."

"She said someone was in the shitter and didn't wanna wait. Used ta just use the crick behind that store she'd holed up in." He laughed. "Little thing's ravenous. She ate six coins' worth of damage in their cabinet. The owner's wife found her sitting on the floor in the kitchen stuffing her face."

"Kid's been eating fifty-year-old canned food for somewhere 'tween two and three years." Kevin shook his head. "That'd almost make anything taste like the best meal in the world."

"Chicken here is pretty damn good. Too expensive though." Ray spat to the side. "Five damn coins for one portion."

Kevin smiled. "He's only got so many chickens. Guess he doesn't wanna use 'em up faster than they breed."

Abby pushed the door open, looking nauseated.

"Is it safe in there?" asked Ray.

She rolled her eyes. "There's no dead person in the seat."

Katie came around the far corner of the roadhouse at a full sprint, squealing with delight. She ran past the rear porch and ducked into the alley between it and the next building, which appeared to be a dead laundromat. Curiosity got the better of her and she started to climb in through a window.

"Katie!" bellowed Ray. "Don't go in there. It could be dangerous. Come on over here."

She jumped down, looking frightened, and ran over. From her expression, she expected him to abandon her if she did the slightest thing wrong.

"It's okay. I ain't angry. I don't want you to get hurt." He took her hand. "'Mon, let's go in."

Kevin stepped into the outhouse. True enough, Ben had used the fiberglass box as a shortcut for building a shack and bench. A rough-cut hole in the bottom let out into a relatively deep pit. He couldn't help himself but peer down in case another corpse lurked below. *That Ben guy seems a bit... off. On second thought, maybe it's good I was up all night.*

With a yawn, he put himself away and opened the door. Abby seemed nervously tolerant of Ray, but gabbed Kevin's arm as soon as he stepped close enough. Katie zoomed by again waving and cheering, passing a few feet in front of them as he approached the porch. Ray set off, chasing her at a deliberate walk, the army T-shirt in his hand. He gave Kevin a defeated look, but laughed.

Kevin smiled, and headed inside with Abby in tow.

Tris had a table already, with three piles of scrambled eggs and a passable attempt at making sausage patties from dust hopper meat. A few minutes after they settled in to eat, Ray entered carrying Katie, now in her shirt/dress.

"What's wrong with me?" Tris whispered.

Kevin glanced at her.

"I was *this* close to just killing those two guys... and they're normal people." She braced her head in her hand. "I... I'm on edge. I... can't stop thinking about the Virus and curing it and getting to—"

Kevin pulled her into a one-armed hug. "Any decent person seeing a guy dressed like a raider with what looked like a captive child would've reached for a gun too. Somethin' my dad woulda done."

Tris frowned. "No one seemed to care when those shitheads carried me into Wayne's."

He kissed the top of her head. "I did."

"Reluctantly." She managed a weak smile.

"I didn't want to get blood on my food." He winked, leaning closer.

Abby grumbled. "You guys are crushing me."

Kevin sat up, as did Tris.

"Sorry for getting in the way," muttered Abby.

"What?" asked Tris.

Abby shrugged. "You guys couldn't 'do it' last night with me in the bed."

Tris blushed.

Kevin laughed. "We don't do that every waking minute."

"You want to." Abby smiled at him. "You guys are so into each other… it's nice." Her gaze shifted to her food, lingered for a moment, and fell into her lap. "I wonder if my parents were like that."

Tris put an arm around her. "I hope they were, and they're together now."

Kevin cocked his jaw sideways and looked away. He didn't have much room for talk of afterlives or ghosts or some far-off, all-powerful, supposedly benevolent invisible man in the clouds. He'd seen enough in his travels to know that before the war, a lot of people believed in 'religion,' but all it ever seemed to do was cause conflict. *How fucked up is that? People killing each other over who's got the more peaceful belief system.* If in fact some kind of entity did exist out there, to let the world burn itself, he, she, or it had to be either oblivious, careless, or sadistic.

Naw. It's probably like the Great Horned Dust Hopper.

Some settlements got their kids to behave by claiming a giant magical dust hopper would come by and give the good children decorated eggs in the middle of the night. Of course he'd hide them, as simply handing them over would be too easy. That whole religion thing before the war had to be a version of that. Something to make adults behave. The other option, that some manner of higher power *did* exist—and turned a blind eye to humanity nuking itself—seemed worse.

He sighed at the earnest face Abby made at the ceiling. What if some bits of it happened to be true? Could his dad be a ghost? Is *that* why he kept winding up doing stupid things that could get him killed? He hadn't been too worried about Ray and Larry. They didn't carry themselves like slavers, and Katie hadn't acted at all frightened of them. He'd seen slaves before, and nothing in the child's demeanor had put him on edge.

Besides, what kind of slavers would drag a new catch to a roadhouse for lunch? Tris had been on edge lately. Hopefully, he could get her to Omaha before she did something she'd regret. Ever since she'd suggested Nathan might drop Virus on Ned, he hadn't managed a full night's sleep. The nightmare had come back in force. Usually, it played out as it always had: back home, sixteen years ago or thereabouts when he'd been eleven. Sometimes, the Infected chasing him turned into Bill, Ann, other people from Ned. Once, he'd even seen little Zoe crawling after him with her mouth wide open.

His throat tightened and he rubbed his eyes. He barely managed to kill that one young woman... his hesitance got Neeley shot. If he ever saw an Infected kid, he'd be fucked if he couldn't run away—he'd never be able to shoot at a child, even one who'd caught The Virus.

"You alright?" asked Tris.

"Yeah..." He let his arm fall to the table. "My turn to have crappy depressing thoughts."

Katie's voice pierced the silence, practicing words with Ray and Larry. She picked things up fast, making him think she couldn't have gone too long without human contact.

"Wanna talk about it?" asked Tris.

He glanced down at Abby. "Just bad dreams. Infected." He exhaled. "Infected I couldn't bring myself to shoot."

Abby gasped. "I'm not sick."

"No, had a nightmare... Zoe..."

Tris put her hand on his shoulder. "We—"

"Have to stop them, yes. I know. I agree, but I don't see how we're going to do that."

She grumbled. "There might be something important hidden in that data. Maybe Nathan found out about a hidden message? That's why he kept trying to kill me?"

Kevin shoved eggs and ground dust hopper in his mouth. "Maybe."

Katie appeared out of nowhere, ambush-hugging Tris from behind over the bench seat. "Hiii!"

Tris laughed. The child crawled over Abby, hugged Kevin, and ran back to the table with Ray and Larry. She'd gotten so much dust on her shirt/dress she left a trail in the air.

"She's going to run up to the wrong person... Hope that town of theirs is safe," said Tris.

"Ned's not the only 'nice' settlement. There's quite a few actually." Kevin coughed at a surprise jalapeno in the egg. "Besides, kids like her can just tell when someone ain't right."

Tris stabbed a bit of sausage on her fork. "I hope that's true."

Abby whispered, "I never liked Warren, an' I trusted you right away."

"See," said Kevin, winking.

She stared at Abby for a while before looking down. "Those bastards. They sit behind their computer screens and don't care who they kill. I should've shot Warren as soon as I saw him pointing a gun at you."

"I think that would've made a mess." Abby looked down.

"Yeah, you're probably right." Tris teased at her food with the fork.

Abby squeezed her arm. "I blame the Enclave for killing my dad."

Tris offered a slow nod. "Yeah. Yeah… me too."

Kevin attempted a reassuring smile and spent a few minutes working on his breakfast in silence.

Around the time they finished eating, Ray, Larry, and Katie approached.

"Gonna head out," said Ray. "Little one wanted to say thanks again."

"Thank you." Katie grinned.

Kevin got up to let Tris out of the bench. Katie hugged everyone—twice—and followed Ray and Larry outside to a battered blue pickup truck with a cap over the bed made of welded steel plates. She crawled up into a tiny rear bench seat. Both men waved at them in that 'don't get dead' sort of way, and got in.

"We should hit the road too." Kevin put his hands on Tris' hips, and pulled her close.

Forehead to forehead, she smiled and gave him a quick kiss. "Yeah. I'm dying to know what he found in those music files."

Abby scooted to the end of the booth seat and stood. "How much longer 'til we get there? I wanna go home."

"We should get there in a couple hours. Unless whatever he's got to show us takes a long time, we'll probably be back here at night to sleep, and home the next day," said Kevin.

"Great." Tris took Abby's hand. "Let's go."

"Uhh…" Abby ground her shoe into the floor. "Can we maybe stop somewhere without a head in the toilet?"

KEVIN STARED WITH BLEARY EYES AT THE ENDLESS ROAD SWEEPING UNDER the Challenger's hood. Abby had curled up in the back seat, kicked off her shoes, and passed out within minutes of getting underway. He stifled a yawn. *At least I'll be able to sleep tonight.*

Tris couldn't keep still. She spent a little while sitting normally, a little longer facing sideways at him, and about four minutes cross-legged before shifting to sit facing forward again. For the past hour or so, she'd had her feet up on the dashboard and her head back. Despite closed eyes, she remained obviously awake.

He figured he'd pull over for a pit stop around noon. After that, another fifty minutes and they should be at the airport. For a while more, a running track of mental music kept his mind off the steady thrum of wheels on pavement. The occasional pothole, piece of car, or decaying wreck on the side of the road offered small breaks from the monotony.

"If you want me to drive, I can. You look exhausted," said Tris.

He yawned again. "Is it that obvious?"

"Yep." She opened her eyes and smiled at him. "Thanks for taking this trip."

"I hope whatever he finds doesn't disappoint you."

Tris scooted over and leaned against him, head on his shoulder. "That's all I've been thinking about. I can't say I won't cry a little, but I promise not to melt down like last time."

"You never did let me have it for storming off like a jackass." He squeezed the wheel in a repetitive clench-and-release, making the leather creak.

"Want me to? I figured it was my fault." She stared out over the countryside.

"Ol' Wayne would never believe those words came out of a woman's mouth."

She jabbed him in the side. "Hey."

"Guys?" asked Abby. "There's people chasing us. Are they bad?"

Kevin looked over his shoulder. Abby knelt in the back seat, facing the rear window. Two dark shapes closed in on them. The nearer looked like a pickup truck with a machine gun mounted on a post in the bed, a pudgy, bearded guy in leather armor and black goggles standing behind it. A bit to the left and somewhat behind, a smaller, sporty, black car with spikes all over it weaved side-to-side in a rapid wobble. Beard seemed to be lining them up for a shot.

"Either that guy's itching to light us up or his steering is blown. Yeah that's a problem."

Two small e-bikes swerved out from behind the truck.

"Abby. Get down." Kevin shot a look at Tris. "Can you pick off the guy on the '60? Our mounted guns don't go that high."

"What do they want?" A tremor wavered in Abby's voice as she crawled to the floor.

"Probably think I'm—"

Sensing the machinegun about to fire, he swerved left hard, sliding over the grassy divider into the westbound lane. Fortunately, nuclear war had eliminated the bulk of oncoming traffic. Sparks danced across the paving as the m60 on the pickup truck roared to life. The man swiveled to follow, forcing Kevin to keep turning ever tighter. Abby screamed and rolled upside down against the right side. He yanked the manual brake lever and threw the ass end into a fishtail. A soft *thump* announced Abby returning to the seat. The small car lined up with his hood-mounted m60s for a second, but he didn't bother wasting ammo.

"—running a small amount of expensive cargo." Kevin accelerated west and flicked on the rear-view targeting mode.

One of the e-bikes pulled up less than a car length behind him.

Kevin yanked on the wheel and hit the trigger button for the trunk guns. The M16 and Ak47 in back chattered. The unwary bandit fell forward over the handlebars after a two-second burst, sending the bike into a sideways spin over the blacktop.

Tris opened the window.

"Wait." Kevin pulled left into another hard turn that bounced them into the grass median.

Abby flew into the air, touched the roof for a second, and came down on the seat, screaming.

A handful of metal clanks struck the car, but nothing burst into flames and no blood sprayed anywhere. Abby's terrified shouting shifted to sobs.

"Fuck this guy." Tris thrust herself up, leaning to her hips in the window.

Kevin kept going to the right, off the road as the line of tracer rounds skittered across the paving less than an arm's length from his window. The pickup truck driver stomped on his brakes, causing the gunner to sway in his harness. In the second the bearded guy took to yell and beat on the roof, Tris fired twice.

The big man slumped, lifeless meat held up by leather straps.

"Ugh." Kevin groaned as he accelerated and spun the wheel, circling behind the pickup truck with the other e-bike swerving around scrub brush in an attempt to follow them.

Tris fired again as they crossed onto the road, three shots as fast as an automatic burst. The rear window of the truck flashed opaque white from smashed safety glass. No longer steering, the truck rolled in a straight line, gradually losing speed.

"Where's the little car?" yelled Kevin, having lost track of it while focusing on the 360-degree firing machine gun.

"Behind right," shouted Tris. "Five o'clock."

Kevin whipped his head around. The little spiked turtle thing hovered perfectly at his blind spot. A bone-thin woman in a leather jacket and ski mask stood hip deep in the sunroof with a pair of MAC-10s. He figured she'd been lobbing bullets at them for a few seconds already, but sucked at it.

"Dammit," muttered Kevin. "I hate killing chicks."

Tris' Beretta went off twice. "I got it."

He cringed. *Whatever. Bitch was probably batshit anyway.*

"Bike," yelled Tris. She swiveled to her left, sitting on the edge of the door facing Kevin, aiming over the roof above his head.

He stepped on the accelerator to avoid a ram from the evidently enraged driver of the spiked turtle car, and eyed the almost-stopped pickup truck. Tris squeezed off another shot while Kevin peppered the turtle with the trunk guns. The little armored car's driver reached a pistol out the window; Kevin swerved hard to the right, causing Tris to thump onto the roof.

Come on... two more seconds. Kevin fired a few more rounds from both rear-facing rifles to make the driver flinch. A loud *boom* went off behind them, but nothing struck the car.

Fucking magnums. Kevin drove straight at the pickup truck. "Tris! In! Now!"

She slipped down into the seat a split second before he cut the wheel left. The Challenger slid past the rear corner of the truck with inches to spare.

Wham!

The ass end of the truck bounced into the air, going from stationary to about twenty miles an hour in an instant. Kevin stomped on the brakes and steered into another powerslide that brought the larger hood guns to bear on the combined wreck. As soon as he had a clear shot on the turtle, he let off about fifteen rounds in tandem. Rhythmic recoil shuddered in the Challenger's frame.

Tracers passed through the dull black metal without any apparent effect beyond making a bunch of small holes surrounded by pale steel where paint flaked off. He looked around at the horizon in all directions. Nothing moved.

"Where's the second bike?"

"Over there in the field somewhere. Got him in the head." She pulled the magazine out of the Beretta to count bullets. "You hit?"

"No, you?" Kevin looked at the console. Nothing turned yellow. He almost smiled. "Heard a few hit the car."

"Abby?" asked Tris.

Silence.

"Abby!" Tris screamed and leapt between the front seats. "Abby! Come on, sweetie, you're okay... You're alive."

No... please don't do this to her. Kevin shoved the door open, got out, pulled his seat forward, and crawled in over the girl.

She lay on the floor in front of the back seat, motionless. He didn't see any obvious blood, so his heart agreed to move again.

"Hey, kiddo." He grabbed her arms and pulled her upright.

Whimpering and sniffling, Tris pawed at her, searching everywhere for a bullet wound.

Abby opened her eyes and looked around, disoriented. "W-where am I?"

Tris clamped onto her and burst into tears. Kevin wrapped his arms around them both and held on, a lump in his throat too large to talk past.

"I... What happened?" Abby squirmed, but couldn't move.

Kevin swallowed worry. "Are you hit?"

"Someone hit me?"

"No, I mean a bullet. Did you get shot? Does anything hurt?"

Abby stared at him for a few seconds with a disoriented expression. "No... I'm dizzy."

Tris finally let go and slid back into the passenger seat with her hands on her face. "She probably fainted... or hit her head on one of those turns."

"I... could've let that idiot riddle us with bullets. Figured turning hard was the better option." He picked Abby up and carried her outside. "It's over, kiddo. Get some air."

"I didn't mean it like that." Tris gave him a wounded stare. "Sorry."

"I..." Abby put a hand to her head. A second later, her eyes shot open with panic. "A bullet almost hit me! Fluff came outta the seat by my face."

She fainted. He rocked her side to side and patted her back. "Can you stay with Tris for a bit? I'll be right back."

"Okay." Abby sat sideways in the driver's seat, feet on the road.

Kevin pulled the .45 and stormed over to the wreck of the pickup and the turtle car. He walked up on the driver's side window and put a bullet through the head of the driver, who may or may not have died in the crash. Red ooze spattered all over the interior, as well as the thin leather-clad woman in the passenger seat. He pointed the .45 at her ski mask, but didn't shoot. A neat hole almost in the center of her forehead proved it a useless gesture.

He checked on the pickup truck driver, who'd taken two of Tris' 9mm rounds to the back of the head, leaving the windshield a wash of blood. A quick walk out into the grass ended with him putting two rounds into the back of one of the bikers. The man had a .45 as well, but a Glock instead of a 1911. He took it, and three spare magazines, two combat knives, and the boots. He didn't have much use for a battered leather jacket on the verge of falling apart, and less interest in taking the pants from a dead man.

Kevin carried the items back to the car, keeping a wary eye on Tris and Abby heading off the road a bit to relieve themselves. He dropped the salvage in the trunk, watered the grass on the opposite side of the road, and found a few hundred 7.62 rounds in an ammo can in the pickup truck's bed, as well as the remainder of the belt in the weapon itself. He unloaded the weapon and added the ammo to the can, popped the M60 from the post, and carried both back to the car.

Militia will probably get some use out of this.

Abby walked up to him. "Why did they shoot at us?"

"Where's Tris?"

"Over there by the crash." Abby pointed to her left. "She said I should wait here. I'm not supposed to look at dead people."

Her flat tone almost made him laugh. "Seems silly doesn't it, after everything you lived through in 'Rillo."

"Yeah." Abby looked down. "She doesn't want me to have bad dreams, but I already do. Why did they attack us?"

He looked at her. "Pirates. They see a single car out this far alone and they figure it's carrying something valuable. People hire drivers from the roadhouses to transport stuff, and they're hoping to steal it. Either that or they're batshit crazy and like to shoot at anything that moves."

Tris returned with two MAC-10s and a bunch of loose bullets in an improvised flannel shirt sack. She dropped everything in the trunk. "While I find your chivalry somewhere between cute and foolish, that car was full of needles and pills. I don't think either of them qualified as fully sentient human beings anymore."

"Huh?" asked Abby.

"Just say no to drugs," said Tris. "Like the historical documentaries say."

Kevin fought the urge to laugh. Abby caught his shaky lip and gave him a look of 'what's so funny?'

"What?" asked Tris.

"Most of those documentaries are made up." He guided Abby to the car. After she climbed in, he pushed the seatback into place and flopped in behind the wheel.

"This wasn't like that." Tris jogged around and hopped in. "It was a message to tell everyone how dangerous drugs are. So if someone tries to give you some, all you have to do is say no."

He shut down the targeting system and leaned on the accelerator a little too hard. "And you think people who liked getting high saw those ads and said 'oh shit, this stuff's bad for me. I should stop'?"

"Well, no, but... those who hadn't started yet." She sighed. "I'm being silly, naïve, and optimistic, aren't I?"

He grinned. "Maybe a little."

She's wound up about something. Doesn't have that usual sad face she makes whenever she has to kill someone.

The next hour and change of driving passed without any additional pirate ambushes. Tris and Abby discussed random things about the town. Abby was gradually making friends with the local kids, and even looked forward to organized school starting in another month or so, something the town elders decided a good idea. His little trailer-park childhood home hadn't had enough people to warrant any kind of group education, but Hemi didn't do a bad job, even if most of his 'learning' had been about fixing cars and some other machines. Kevin could read, he could repair most mechanical things, and somewhere along the line, he got stuck with an unbroken moral compass.

He glanced back at Abby for a second before slowing to take an off ramp. *We should've left her at Ned.* At some point, Route 80's signs had changed to 680. He remembered the turnoff they'd taken last time, and turned onto the same road that circled around the northeast portion of Omaha straight to the airport without going into the city proper. He didn't even want to know how many Infected dwelled inside the downtown district. All big cities, at least as far as his brain would believe, brimmed to bursting with them.

The same rusting cars sat like barricades before a bridge of hulking green ironwork. Eight or nine months hadn't changed the place, though it didn't feel as if that much time had passed. A collection of derelict cars blurred by the window, congregated in the grassy patch between two lanes. They'd been there so long scavvers had even taken the seats out of them.

Shit. We're going to get back home and find the place fucked from the air. He wrung his hands on the wheel again, fighting back the urge to get angry and despondent over the idea of Nederland falling victim to a Virus attack. His nightmare of Zoe shambling after him made his foot heavy. Tires chirped as he turned past a sign for Eppley airfield. The road led them around in a curve that descended, putting the same bridge they'd crossed a moment before high and left. He whipped through a right turn past a sign that read 'John J Pershing.'

"Slow down," said Tris. "What are you so pissed at?"

"Nathan."

"Oh." She scowled. "Me too."

"Think he did it?"

Tris looked away, out her window at a huge warehouse type building. "I..."

Abby shivered. "Are they gonna kill Ned too like they killed Amarillo? Is that why you let me come with you, even though you didn't wanna?" She leaned into the front.

"I don't think he'd be able to do anything so soon after Amarillo." Tris put her hand on Abby's where she gripped the seat. "He's not operating with the permission of the Council of... I mean the government. He's just being an asshole."

Grass as high as the car's roof passed on the right; when the red and white gas station went by, he thought of Tris' reaction to Twinkies. He glanced at the little rad meter on the dash, the red LED display reading 000. Anticipating the radiation spike from the old quonset hut on the right, he floored it. He pulled 165 past a parking lot full of half-molten cars next to an office building that had definitely seen better days. It looked like it had collapsed in on itself even more since last time. He slowed and turned across the empty oncoming lanes and drove onto the tarmac, still squeaking the tires from speed.

Abby grabbed the 'oh shit' handles on both sides, bracing herself against bouncing around.

"Yeah. That doesn't mean it'll never happen." He drummed his fingers along the top of the wheel. "I hope this guy's got something real for you."

Tris smiled at him. She lit up as though a burden fell from her shoulders. Perhaps he hadn't meant to commit himself as much as she had to somehow stopping Nathan, but she'd sensed it in him. Again, Zoe. The little blonde girl hadn't even asked him to do this like she'd asked him to bring her father and brother back from Chicago. The mere thought of the Enclave's virus hurting her lit his blood on fire.

They rounded the corner of the terminal building. Abby gasped and whispered "wow" at the sight of the huge pile of techno-scrap stacked behind the airport in mazelike rows. A line of airplanes parked near the building got an even more awestruck stare.

"What are those?" She asked in a small voice, seeming afraid of them. "Dead dragons?"

Kevin tried not to think about Nederland at the moment; he put on a grin for Abby. "Airplanes. They don't work anymore."

"Air… plane?" Abby tilted her head.

"You know what a bus is, right?"

She nodded.

"Well, they're like buses, only they used to fly." He pointed up.

"They're big and scary," said Abby.

He brought the Challenger to a stop by a pack of baggage carts parked outside the door to Terminal A9.

"You don't need to be afraid of them." Tris patted her on the hand. "They're machines. We're gonna go inside one."

Abby bit her lip, eyes wide.

Kevin shut down the car and opened his door. "I'm guessing you wanna talk to him first, then go hunting for parts?"

"Yeah." Tris got out, faced the building, and folded her arms. "Now I'm afraid of going in there."

Abby squinted at her. "I told you they're scary."

Kevin shoved his door closed with a *thud* and walked around to put a hand on Abby's back. "It's not the airplane she's afraid of… it's the information inside it."

5

NOTHING IS EVERYTHING

Anticipation built to a point where Tris couldn't make herself take a step forward into the baggage processing room. This place held pain. Here, she'd learned her entire mission had been a lie topped off with the cruelest of puns. Inside, Abby climbed up on an old conveyor belt and walked along still holding Kevin's hand.

Tris took a deep breath. The last time she'd set foot inside this place, she'd been so crushed she lashed out at Kevin and almost lost him. *How did I go from wanting to kill him to feeling like I'd be lost without him?* Going through that door could potentially give Nathan another victory. Maybe he'd hidden some other useless thing in the music file, something he figured she'd find only to raise her hopes to once again dash them.

I'm not going to know if I keep standing here.

She walked in and let the door close behind her.

Abby twisted around at the abrupt change in light. As soon as she realized Tris had closed the door, she resumed walking. "Did those men wanna check that girl for bite marks?"

"Katie? No, they found her like that," said Kevin.

Abby got down to crawl into the port of an x-ray machine, but Kevin plucked her from the conveyor. Giggling, she squirmed in playful protest. "Hey."

"Don't go in there. I don't want you getting hurt."

Abby stared at the machinery, the dead monitors, dark buttons, and boxy housing. "Who made her get undressed?"

"Her parents died years ago," said Kevin. "Maybe she's never had anything."

"Like ever?" asked Abby, blinking. "Why did people just leave her alone?"

"Well, she *did* spend most of her life hiding. Sounded like she had more than one chance to be found, but decided to stay out of sight." Tris jogged to catch up. "If she wasn't so tired of those handcuffs, she probably would've grown old in that grocery store... at least until the canned food ran out."

"That's stupid." Abby rolled her eyes. "It sucks being alone. If it was me, I'd have been screaming for help as loud as I could. How could she stand being locked up for so long?"

"No options," muttered Kevin. "People do a lot of stupid crap out of fear. And, uhh, well, sometimes making a lot of noise isn't a great idea."

Infected have good hearing. Tris bit her lip.

Abby seemed to catch on from the look she must've given her. "Oh... right. They can hear."

Kevin opened the door to the concourse, and slammed it. "Umm. After those raiders grabbed her, she probably figured all adults were dangerous. And it's not like she could check them out and run away if they turned out bad." He pointed at the door. "Maybe we should let Abby wait in the car."

"Shit." Tris rubbed her forehead. *The airports full of skeletons.*

"What? Why?" Abby's voice took on a tone of nervousness. She grabbed Tris. "Don't leave me alone."

"There's umm... dead people out there." Kevin cringed. "From the war."

Abby shook her head. "Don't care. I don't wanna be alone." She glanced at the door. "Are they nasty?"

"Bones. Just bones at this point."

"Oh." Abby's fear faded away. "I can deal with bones."

"There's a lot of them." Kevin pulled the door open again. "If you wanna keep your eyes closed, I can carry you."

"I'm eleven, not five, and—" Abby stared at the airport hallway.

The red tiled corridor remained packed with skeletons, swept against the walls like dead leaves lining the grave of a dried-up river. Most still wore the clothing they'd died in, stained in rotted gore. A few humanoid shapes, lighter than the wall, near the windows hinted at where some had been vaporized by the blast. Where the waiting area faced the tarmac, once-molten glass ran like a maple syrup spill onto the floor. Tris guessed that all these skeletons, those who hadn't been near a window, had died in minutes from radiation.

Abby held on to Kevin's right arm with both hands, taking cautious baby steps between spots where tile showed through dried, dark gunk. "Whoa. I am *so* happy you got me shoes."

"We hadn't exactly expected to be taking you on an expedition." Tris patted her on the shoulder.

Kevin walked with a brisk stride past the security checkpoint and a few boarding areas before heading down the retractable ramp toward the 747 that Terminal9 made home. Tris followed close, eyeing the dead.

Kevin said not all the historical documentaries are real. They're not going to get up.

The air grew hot and stagnant in the flexible tunnel, which tinted the world ochre from the sun beating on the plastic walls. *What's this guy going to do when his AC runs out?*

Kevin approached the metal box beside the door and wiped dust off the small five-inch screen before jabbing at the largest (and only round) transparent button. It lit up in a few seconds, and a sallow face broken by scrolling raster lines appeared in monochromatic green.

"Got your message," said Kevin.

Terminal9 leaned closer to the camera, filling the screen with eyes for a second. "Oh. Hey. Right." The door emitted a heavy *clank.* "'Mon in... and close the door once you're in."

Kevin pulled the entryway open, releasing a blast of cool air into the stuffy boarding tunnel. Tris followed Abby inside, and both of them let off a gasp of relief at the same time. Tris pulled the door shut.

"How is it cold?" asked Abby.

"The man who lives here got the air conditioning working," said Tris. "Used to be pretty common before the war, and it's still used by the Enclave."

"A winter machine? Or magic?" Abby looked around in awe at rows upon rows of empty seats. She touched a few. "I wish we had chairs like this at home. They're so soft."

"No, it isn't magic." Tris mumbled an explanation of air conditioning as they walked out of the first class cabin into the back, and to a spiral stairway.

Kevin kept his hand near his .45 as he led the way up the stairs. Abby shivered at the cascade of even colder air wafting down the metal corkscrew. She tried to tug the hem of her dust-hopper hide dress down farther than the middle of her thighs.

"It's so cold..." Abby's teeth chattered.

At the top of the stairs, Kevin took off his armored jacket and held it open for Abby. She eagerly thrust her arms into the sleeves and let him close it around her. It didn't go much past the dress, but at least it covered her arms and shoulders.

"Heeeeeyyyy," said Terminal9. He walked out from behind a blue curtain in a pair of Hawaiian shorts and flip-flops, no shirt. The man appeared even thinner, every rib showing clear beneath his skin. "Glad ta see you got the message. Wasn't sure if that 'bot of yours would make it."

"What's that supposed to mean?" asked Kevin.

"'Mon." Terminal9 headed back through the curtain. "Means I heard some shit go down over the radio. Someone shot her... it... whatever."

The room behind the curtain held even colder air.

Abby shivered, tucking her hands under her arms, and stared, open-mouthed at all the hentai posters on the walls. Tris wanted to cover her eyes, but after Amarillo, some cartoon tentacles seemed mild.

"Whoa," said Abby. "This dude needs to stop living by himself."

Terminal9 mumbled something too low to hear.

Tris slipped around past Kevin and Abby, avoided the end of the queen-sized bed, and followed him into the next room where he had all his gear set up.

"Uhh... Don't leave me alone with this guy," said Abby. "Those girls on the wall look my age."

"They're eighteen," yelled Terminal9. "It's the art style!"

"Uh, huh, sure." Kevin smirked at him.

"I'm serious." Terminal9 gestured at one with breasts the size of watermelons. "They either have too much or nothing."

"If you think it's stupid," asked Kevin. "Why are they all over the walls?"

"A) it's all I had, and B) you gotta take it in the context it was intended. It's *stylized* and shit, man."

"Is that tentacle going up her... Oh, god... it is." Abby blushed, turned away from the wall, and buried her face in Kevin's chest.

Terminal9 fidgeted, looking quite uncomfortable. "Never planned on no kids bein' in here."

NOTHING IS EVERYTHING | 57

"Yeah well." Kevin put an arm around her. "Just as soon get out of your way. Hope your info's worth the trip."

"Well... I don't really know how good it is, but I figured you'd want to see it." He scurried past the curtain.

Kevin guided Abby along so she didn't have to look at the walls. Mercifully, the former cockpit had little decoration beyond a mountain of tech. Duct tape and a couple of old trash bags sealed the window around the cable bundle snaking in from outside; thin plastic fluttered in the wind.

Tris flopped on the same chair she'd used last time. *This guy better not ask for a tittie pic again.* Her hands shook; she continued to sweat rivers despite the chill. She rubbed the front of her throat for a few seconds while the hacker ambled over to the pilot's chair and got to work tapping on a few keyboards. Flat panel monitors arranged around him, some hung from the ceiling, flickered to life.

"So... what did you find?" Tris rasped.

Kevin put a hand on her shoulder.

She straightened. Resolve flooded into her from the spot where he touched her. *I don't care what it is. I will not let Nathan beat me down.* Tris looked up at him with a grateful smile for a second before glaring at the back of Terminal9's scraggly head. The way his light brown hair collected in cords reminded her of a poorly maintained fern.

"Okay so, I'm listenin' to those tunes you had, right?"

She glared.

"Hey..." He raised a hand. "I know shit was a kick in the balls and stuff, but, free music is still free music. Anyway, I hear these pops, right? Turns out the first ten tracks have shitty audio quality for exactly the same portion of the file. The front 32k of each track had a different sample rate than the rest."

"The hell language is that?" asked Kevin.

Abby giggled.

"There's hidden data in the files..." Tris stared at him. "What was in it? Did Nathan make another bad joke?"

Terminal9 grinned. "I'm gettin' there. Building up to it and stuff. So, I went into the code with a sector editor. Turns out the files are as big as they would be if the entire mp3 had been sampled at the same rate. There's padding data in among the music that the player mostly ignores, but here and there, it had dead space. No data, which made the sound pop silent for a split second. Sounds like an old analog track snapping."

"You *are* going somewhere with this, right?" asked Kevin.

Abby fiddled with a red plastic shroud on the desk, lifting it to expose a button.

"Hey!" yelled Terminal9. "Kid. Don't touch that."

She pulled her hand back as if burned. "Sorry. You don't have to yell at me."

"It's wired to frag mines in the boarding tunnel." He scratched at his head. "Defense system."

Abby gasped.

"Against what?" asked Tris.

Terminal9 grinned as he shrugged. "Against anything that wants my ass for lunch. Anyway… So I spent a couple days mining that slush data for anything, but didn't find a damn thing."

Tris clenched her jeans tight about her knees and glared at him. "Look. I'm about to scream at you. Please just tell me what you found."

"There's a point to this." Terminal9 made a finger gun to his temple before tapping an LCD monitor. "Whoever put this data in the file went way far beyond your run of the mill attempt to hide some shit. It drove me nuts for weeks. Why would someone pad bogus data at the front of the files? It finally hit me that the nothing was everything."

Kevin pursed his lips. "You've been spending too much time in a sunbaked plane."

"No." Terminal9 raised both hands, fingers splayed. "The blank spaces. *That* was the data."

"Blank?" Tris squinted. "The empty spots formed some kind of pattern?"

"Exactly!" He pointed up. "Wow. Took me two weeks to think of that. Yeah. I had to count the file marker positions for each set of zeroes, and that turned into Unicode character codes. Like the first letter in the message is 'T' 'cause it was fifty-four spaces after the file header. The next one occurred seventy-two spaces later… and so on."

"Are you sure that message was even meant for her? How the hell would we have found that? It… would've been reckless for whoever sent it to assume she'd find it."

"You're here right now, aren't you?" Terminal9 winked.

Tris' heart hung in her chest like a lead weight. "How… do you know it was for me? Are you assuming that because you found it in the data I carried?"

"Well the file has your name in it." He tapped a few keys, and a message appeared on the blank monitor:

Tris,

Contact me.

-Dad.

650-555-0447

She squeaked. *What? Dad?* Her gaze fell to the floor. She hadn't noticed she'd been trembling until she looked at her legs. "No... that's gotta be Nathan's sick idea."

Kevin wiggled his finger at the screen. "What do those numbers mean?"

Terminal9 flashed the smile of an ancient guru asked a most basic question on enlightenment. "It's a PSTN number."

"Oh, of course." Kevin raised his arm a few inches and let it fall against his side. "Obviously."

Abby took a step toward Tris and leaned into her.

"Okay. Ever hear of a phone?" asked Terminal9.

"Little things people used to carry around everywhere?" Kevin held up his hand. "'Bout the size of a, umm..." He traced a small rectangle in the air.

"Sort of. Close enough. Those things used to allow people to talk to each other over long distances. Each device had a specific number assigned to it. If you typed that number in on your phone, you'd connect to the other person and be able to talk."

Tris shook her head. "That doesn't make any sense at all. There's no phone network left. It all fried in the war from EMP."

"I don't think your asshole friend did this." Terminal9 tapped the monitor, his fingernail clicking on the plastic. "People like that are too proud of their own cleverness. He'd want it to be found so you could appreciate his bastardry, and that was not damn easy to find. I think whoever sent you that message knew what that dude was up to, and wanted to sneak it past him."

Could it be possible that my father's gone into hiding somehow? She grabbed Abby like a big doll since she stood conveniently close. "I... never did see a body."

"Like they'd have shown it to you." Kevin moved closer and caressed her hair. "I dunno, Tris. This isn't much to work with."

"Okay." Tris held her hands up. "Let's play a theory game here and assume that my father wasn't killed by the Council of Four, and is somehow still alive deep in the bowels of the Enclave, and managed to sneak an encoded message into the fake cure that Nathan uploaded to my implant. What the hell am I supposed to do with a phone number?"

Terminal9 smiled. "Now this might be worth that—" His stare moved away from her chest, to Abby, and back to Tris' breasts. "Uhh, never mind." He grinned. "I don't have any way to connect to it from here, but I talked to a guy farther west who said the number looked like a Redwood City exchange. There's still a fragment of the grid that survived over there on account of bein' mostly underground. Accordin' to Hec8-e, there's at least one functional CO in that area you might be able to patch in from."

"CO?" asked Tris.

"What the devil is heck eighty?" Kevin scratched his head.

"Central office, and Hec8-e is another person like me, a techie." Terminal9 leaned back in his chair. "A CO is a place where the telco had all their equipment that patched into the individual lines running to houses."

"Wait, they ran wires to people's houses?" Kevin blinked.

Terminal9 chuckled. "Yeah man. What do you think all them poles was for? Most of the wires either melted or got salvaged."

Kevin rubbed his chin. "So, in order to contact this father of yours that may or may not still exist, we'd have to go basically into the Enclave's backyard and hope we find a working phone, and hope he's still around to answer it."

"Yeah, basically." Terminal9 nodded. "That's about right."

"Heh." Kevin laughed. "What could go wrong?"

Everything. Tris exhaled. That sick gnawing feeling churned in her gut again. She couldn't ignore the curiosity for long at all before the sleepless nights would get to her. On a rational level, it sounded *so* farfetched. So out there. Stupid. Foolish. Reckless. Run right back to the Enclave she'd escaped from. She looked left and up, into Abby's wide, brown eyes. *Nathan's going to drop Virus on Nederland.* The urge to do something about it took her with a full body tremor, as though she'd sucked down ten quadruple-shot lattes in ten minutes. She hadn't had one of those since the day before they sent her to Detention. *I just found out my father might still be alive, and I'm fiending for coffee. What is wrong with me?*

"That it?" asked Kevin. "Nothing more encoded?"

Terminal9 pivoted his feet on the floor, making his chair swish side to side, and leaned his head against two fingers. "That's all I've found so far.

The rest of the files are uniform, without the extra data. I know it ain't much."

Kevin leaned his head back, eyes closed. "Sometimes the tiniest detail will kill you."

"Your dad?" asked Terminal9.

"Nah. Wayne." Kevin chuckled.

Did he really suggest we actually chase this down? Tris gawked at him.

"We'll talk. Let's round up those parts for Bee and get going. Be nice to make it back to Ben's 'house before it gets too dark."

"What do you think?" Tris stood, facing Terminal9. "Would someone go to all that trouble to mess with me?"

"That's why I gave you the long explanation." He leaned forward, elbows on his knees, fingers laced. "This Nathan motherfucker doesn't seem like he'd have the patience to do something like that. Whoever put that message in there, I think they didn't want the Enclave to find it."

A little warmth gathered in Tris' cheeks. "Still want that payment?"

The hacker glanced at Abby again before winking at Tris. "Nah. Don't worry about it."

She smiled. "Thanks."

"De nada." He shut down a few screens and followed them out of the cockpit, crawling onto the bed in the next space.

Tris took point, heading down the spiral stairs and back out into the airport building. As soon as Kevin shut the exterior door on the 747, it shook with a loud *clunk.*

Abby looked up at Tris. "Did he want you to sleep with him?"

"No." Tris blushed.

"Are you trying to be like tame or something 'cause I'm here? Payment?"

"He wanted to see my chest. Take a picture of it."

"Oh." Abby smirked. "The guy seriously needs to stop being alone."

Tris let out a halfhearted laugh. "Yeah."

They walked in relative silence outside to the car.

Kevin pointed at the car. "I'll drive a little closer to the junk pile so we don't have to carry shit so far."

Abby removed the red armored jacket and handed it to Kevin before pushing the driver's seat aside so she could get in back.

"Okay." Tris headed to the passenger door. A glint of metal caught her eye from the back seat. Two pairs of handcuffs.

Abby crawled in and pushed them out of sight under a blanket.

"Abby?" Tris slid into her seat. "Why do you have those?"

"Huh?" asked Kevin.

The discovery didn't faze Abby. "I want you to teach me how to open them. 'Case I get grabbed or something."

"She's got the cuffs I took off Katie." Tris pointed at the back seat. "Thought she was terrified of them. She must've swiped them from the table when no one was looking."

"I *am* scared of them." Abby looked down. "That's why I wanna know how to get out of 'em. Will you teach me how to pick locks?"

Kevin turned the car on and backed up.

"It's not quite the same as picking locks, but... yeah sure why not. Girl can't have too many skills right?" She smiled. "Later though. I don't want you messing with those things out in the Wildlands. Anything could happen at any time."

Abby nodded. "Okay." She grinned. "An' maybe you can teach me 'bout 'lectronics too."

Oh, I swear if we get home safe, I'll teach you about particle physics. "Sure."

Kevin brought the car around to the narrowest point in the junk row the car could reach, and stopped. Tris looked down, overcome by a sudden wash of sadness at her memory of thinking he'd left her there for good.

He reached over, placed his hand behind her head, and pulled her into a gentle kiss. "Can we forget we both acted like idiots?"

She nodded. "Deal."

Tris hopped out and walked the last thirty or so yards to the left turn that brought her into the rounded area full of old android parts. Kevin wandered about grabbing anything he thought resembled Bee. Abby poked and played with random pieces of tech. Tris hauled the mostly-intact torso of a similar android out of a heap. Aside from missing its legs and head, the interior looked like it had most of the same parts as Bee, perhaps enough to get her going again... assuming they worked.

Abby progressed from curious to passive to visibly bored. Tris spent a little more than an hour and a half collecting anything she thought might be potentially useful for future 'Bee maintenance.' As piece number twenty-two went into the trunk, Kevin raised an eyebrow at her.

"I'm trying to gather a bit of a reserve so we don't have to drive all the way out here again if something else goes wrong with her." She dropped a hollow plastic head with some circuit boards in it into the trunk. "Try to find a couple arms or legs for spare actuators."

Eventually, Tris figured she'd collected a decent enough haul, and slammed the trunk lid. They sat in the shade of a towering collection of ancient kitchen appliances while gnawing on dust hopper jerky. When he finished his piece, Kevin wiped his hands on his pants and stood. Tris gave him a nod to acknowledge his desire to get going. He wandered out of sight behind a pile of junk while reaching for his zipper. Tris ducked into an opposite alcove in the scrap maze, in search of a clear spot of dirt to take a leak before the long ride. As she shoved her pants down, she eyed the surroundings, wary of a sniper.

Abby startled her, appearing close by her side. She also assumed the position. "Why do you look so nervous?"

Having her right next to me is only a little *uncomfortable...* Tris forced a smile. "I, uhh, got attacked by a sniper once while I was peeing in the woods." She chuckled. "Up till that moment, I thought 'caught with my pants down' was only a saying."

"Eww. I hope you killed him." Abby kept quiet for a few seconds. "Did he at least let you finish before he shot at you?"

"Actually, it was a misunderstanding. I trust her now."

"Her?" Abby blinked.

"Zara. She's from the Enclave too."

"Oh, wow. She shot you and you like didn't kick her ass?" Finished, Abby stood.

Tris cringed. "That hurt so damn much, but I knew she'd been manipulated." She got up and hiked her jeans back in place. "And before you say it, yes, I *am* too forgiving."

"You get shot a lot." Abby stared at the ground. "I wish my dad had those things that fix you."

Tris hugged her and rocked her side to side. "Me too."

Abby gave her a teary-eyed look that thanked her all over again for protecting her from Warren. Tris couldn't think of anything to say back to her; guilt sat in her throat like a boulder.

"You girls coming?" yelled Kevin. "Battery's draining."

"Yeah," croaked Tris. She wiped a tear from her cheek. "Time to go home."

Abby nodded, took her hand, and walked at her side to the waiting car.

6

A LONG TIME TO FIX

Acrid fumes from the soldering iron wafted up past Tris' face, making her squint. She waved at the layer of white smoke settling inside Bee's open back. Clatters of metal, the occasional *clonk* of lumber, and the distant murmur of people talking echoed off the corrugated metal walls of Nederland's 'technical center.' The large former factory building housed the extent of everything not covered by simple carpentry, plumbing, or automotive mechanics.

Since she couldn't move, Bee had spent most of the past few weeks chatting with other people in the technical crew, especially Crystal, the manager. Cassie, the head tech from Amarillo, had integrated herself among the locals as one of the more competent people for electronics despite being only twenty-two. Constant blue-eyed blonde jokes stopped once she fixed the central radio unit in a mere fifteen minutes, the same radio the militia had given up on ever being able to use again. In resurrecting it, she'd earned their respect.

Abby sat in a metal folding chair at the end of Tris' workbench near Bee's shoes, holding a set of handcuffs while working at them with a shim. It took her a while, but she managed to open it. Each time she succeeded, she closed the hasp and did it again. Tris took the liberty of machining up three more shims. Two went in her shoe for safe keeping, and the third clicked and scraped away in Abby's grasp.

"You did something good," said Bee. "I am getting a POST from the primary gyroscope."

"Great." Tris wiped sweat off her forehead.

"Post?" asked Abby.

"Means it's booting up. Power-On Test."

"That's POT." Abby stuck out her tongue.

"Self-Test," said Bee. "Reports functional. Still, I do not appear to have arms or legs."

"I'm working on it." Tris stooped over the android's back again. "That power spike cooked a couple things I didn't see before. I'm glad I went shopping."

"This settlement possesses a surprising amount of technology given its size." Bee lifted her head, turned it to peer into the room instead of at the wall, and lowered it. "They have been asking me for advice. I've accessed data tables and run computations I never calculated I would use again."

Tris removed twelve hex screws holding a hip actuator in place and extricated a flat, donut-shaped, metal ring. It looked fine on the outside, but the circuitry in it had fried. "I'm glad you've been involved, not just lying here." She seated a new one she'd recovered from Omaha and started replacing the screws.

"I am not susceptible to the same feelings of distress a human might suffer from inability to ambulate. My great grandfather was a desktop computer. They do not move."

Tris blinked at her. "Your sense of humor is getting better."

"Shit. Tris. Help," whispered Abby, her voice wavering.

Tris looked over. The girl had handcuffed herself, and couldn't get the shim in like she could while merely holding them. She grasped Abby's hands and maneuvered them around to the proper angle. Abby fiddled at it for a few seconds, rising panic visible on her face. Tris again took her hand and helped her force the lock open.

Abby sagged against the wall, out of breath. "Uhh, maybe I'm not ready for that yet."

"You don't *have* to do any of it. No one will be upset with you if you give up. But, the only way to get better at something is to do it over and over. At least you don't have Randall teaching you."

"Who's that?" Abby bit her lower lip and fiddled with the remaining cuff on her left arm.

"He's the guy who forced me to learn how to escape. Even in virtual reality, being dropped face first into a swimming pool while cuffed was *not* fun."

Abby paled.

Tris frowned. "He called it motivation. It wasn't real; I was in a simulation." *And apparently simulated reality* can *cause nightmares.* She finished tightening the screws and connected a ribbon cable to the actuator.

"S-simulation?" Abby glanced down, wincing as the shim slipped and stabbed her in the wrist. "Ow. Shit."

"It's like a dream." Tris pulled her hair back and tapped the tiny plug behind her left ear. "From a wire."

"That's freaky." Abby bit her tongue in concentration, wiggled the shim, and the cuff slipped open. Her entire body sagged with a sigh of relief.

Bee's foot twitched.

Abby glanced at the android. "You fixed her hip. Why is her foot moving?"

"The wiring is in series. The blown actuator blocked everything past it." Tris pointed. "The cable has power and control signals. It plugs into the ring, which connects to another lead embedded in the 'bone' that goes to the rest of the leg."

"Oh. That is most excellent." Bee moved her leg around. "Please fix the other side."

Tris grabbed a black box about the size of her fist. "I'm going to replace the secondary capacitor first. I think I figured out why your arms are offline."

"Serial connectivity routed through the capacitor. You are correct," said Bee.

Abby went back to practicing on the cuffs while holding them. "Can you get out of them if they put your hands behind you?"

"Yes. As long as I can get hold of a shim. That's how I was when they threw me in the pool."

"How can you escape when you can't even see them?" Abby blinked.

"Going by feel. Takes a bit of practice."

Abby seemed frightened by the thought, and looked down as she worked. "I don't want to do that yet."

Tris removed the blown-out capacitor and tossed it over her shoulder. "It's okay. Whatever you want. This *was* your idea."

"Yeah." She sighed. "I don't wanna be stuck if the Infected find me."

Tris paused working on Bee to squeeze Abby's shoulder. "I won't let anyone ever do that to you again."

Abby reached up and grasped Tris' hand, smiling.

"Hey." Kevin walked over holding the dead capacitor. "Careful. That almost hit me in the head."

"Sorry." Tris turned to give him a quick hug and kiss before seating the replacement.

"How's the patient, Doc?" He leaned forward to peer inside. "Wow. I'm in awe that you can make sense of any of that. There's so much stuff packed in there."

"I think I'll have her up and running in another few minutes."

"That would be wonderful," said Bee. "I would possess much gratitude."

"So…" Kevin threaded his arms around her waist and hovered his chin at the side of her head. "Might as well talk about it before you burst."

Tris let her arms slack and hung her head. "I know it's stupid. It makes no sense at all, but I can't stop thinking about it."

"Your dad… They said he was killed, right?"

She clung to an ancient memory… herself about six sitting on the floor, surrounded by computer parts and robot bits in his lab. Her father, frazzled grey hair and white labcoat, smiled down at her from his chair. Six years old and she'd made a robotic fish. Not that it could swim, or even really looked like a fish. It came out shaped like a slab, but it bent itself back and forth almost like a fish swimming.

Dad had reacted as if she'd invented cold fusion.

Tears ran down her face. "Yeah. I was nine when they came for me… told me he'd died in an accident. I spent a day or two in the hospital being checked out and they assigned me to this couple. Those people completely refused to believe they adopted me. They acted like I was really theirs and I'd made up my father like some kind of invisible friend." She sighed. "Enclave probably told them to act like he never existed or they'd kill us all. They thought I was 'disturbed' and brought me to a psychiatrist." She frowned at the painful memory, jabbing at a stuck screw in Bee's back. *They really laid on the guilt trip. I almost wanted to believe it hurt them when I said they weren't my real parents.*

"That sounds painful." Kevin kissed her ear.

Abby popped the cuffs, relocked them on nothing, and attempted to open them again with her eyes closed.

"It's a mental doctor. I eventually stopped mentioning him because I didn't want them to think I was crazy. For a little while, I started to wonder if maybe I *had* made him up, but... I just know. The memories were too real. Too complete."

Kevin squeezed her from behind. "Sorry. So... what does your instinct tell you?"

"My head says this is a stupid idea." She grunted while trying to force a connector into the capacitor. Six tiny flat metal blades protruding from a plastic housing did *not* want to slide easily into their corresponding socket. It *looked* right, but refused to go in. "Shit. Why won't this go in?"

Kevin stepped out from behind her and took it from her grip in two fingers, twisting it up to examine it. He glanced between the connector and the socket. "I think that pin second from the top is a little bit wider than the rest. One of those 'only goes in one way' deals."

"Crap. You're right." She rubbed her eyes. "I've been staring at circuits for three hours without a break... and I'm..."

"Distracted? Worried?"

"Yeah, both." She twisted the plug around the other way and pushed it home. A little corrosion on the metal blades made it a stiff fit, but it worked.

Bee emitted a loud beep before convulsing in a spot-on impression of a live salmon someone had tossed on a grill. Abby let out a shriek of startlement, leapt out of her chair, and scurried to a safe distance. Kevin guarded his nuts and took two steps back.

The fit lasted four seconds before Bee lay still.

A short trumpet sound effect that suggested 'ta-da!' played from her.

"Power on diagnostic complete. Unit online. Maintenance suggested for... Secondary fuse cluster." Pause. "Primary memory module." Pause. "Right shoulder mobility systems."

Beep.

Bee pushed herself up to kneel, twisted about, and sat on the table with her legs dangling. "Gratitude." She reached out to hug Tris.

"You're welcome." Tris embraced the android. "Okay, lie back down a bit more. You're still wide open."

"Oh. Yes. That is a wise decision." Bee resumed lying on her front, though she folded her arms under her head.

"Well, like I said, on a brain level, I think it's stupid and reckless... but on every other level, I feel like it's something I have to do. The Enclave said he died, but... I'm not sure I'd believe anything they say." She opened the back of Bee's head and poked at a row of green circuit board cards.

"Bee... I have to re-seat your primary NVRAM cards. I can't do that when you're on. Would you shut down? I promise I'll turn you back on in like two minutes."

"Okay. I trust you." Bee blinked with a *click*. "Beginning power down sequence. Volatile memory transfer completed. System shutdown in three... two..."

Bee stopped moving.

"You're not going again?" Abby ran over and grabbed Tris. "What if you get hurt and don't come back?" She sniffled and started crying. "I don't wanna be alone."

Tris pulled her into a tight hug. *I'm so terrified that they're going to kill everyone here. I can't just sit around.* "Abby... what happened in Amarillo could happen here."

Abby stared at her, open-mouthed.

"I don't mean to scare you."

"Well, you did," whispered Kevin. He patted Abby on the shoulder. "What she means is, there's a chance they could do it. Not that they will."

"You don't know that." Tris bit her lip and growled. "Nathan's not going through proper channels. He's been rogue from the start on this and I think it's taking him a while to find a way to sneak a flight path past the monitors. I... I'm sorry, Abby, I don't mean to get you worked up over nothing, but I've been scared shitless that there's gonna be a drone coming by."

"Is that why you told the militia to watch the skies?" whispered Abby.

Tris nodded. "If I thought... If I could really believe they'd leave us alone, I'd forget about everything and just stay here and be happy with you and Kevin... This place is perfect."

Kevin raised an eyebrow. "Perfect?"

"Well okay, it's primitive, but"—she smiled—"simple pleasures can be better than all the fancy stuff."

"You don't miss *anything*?" Kevin cocked an eyebrow.

"Well, maybe the medical facilities. I'd say school too, but I don't trust them."

Kevin laughed. "More like movie theater than school."

She poked him in the side.

Abby sniffled. "Can they kill this place like they killed Amarillo?"

Tris grasped her shoulders and locked eyes. "What they did there, they could probably do anywhere. That's why I need to check this message out. To at least try to do *something* about them."

"Okay." Abby clamped on. "I'll go."

"Uhh," said Kevin.

Tris shook her head. "No, Abs… I need you to stay here where it's safe. We're going to be close to the Enclave. It's dangerous there."

"It's not"—Abby dropped her yell to a whisper—"safe here. A second ago, you said it's not safe here. What if they drop that stuff on us?"

"This place is pretty small," said Kevin. "Nathan might not know where it is. Amarillo was a big city, easy to see from the air. That, and the militia is watching the skies. 'Rillo didn't have any advanced warning an attack like that could happen. I don't know what we could run into out there, but you will definitely be safer here. We'll also be safer not having to constantly worry about something happening to you."

"Wait, you're going too?" Abby stared at him. "You're *both* leaving me?"

Kevin squeezed Tris' shoulder. "I made that mistake last time I got a stupid idea. I'm not letting her out of my sight."

She shot him a playful annoyed look, tinged with worry and sadness. "Nowhere is really safe anymore. This is about as safe as it gets… I need to know you're okay." She glanced at Kevin. "Bee could watch her. Oh shit." Tris hunched over the android and removed, blew on, and reseated all twelve tiny memory cards along the back of the skull. Once she replaced the last one, she pushed the power button and closed the head.

Beep.

"I dunno." Abby glanced sideways at the android. "What if it like goes nuts and kills me?"

"Bee's not going to do that." Kevin chuckled. "She's a pretty good cook too."

"That was longer than two minutes," said Bee.

"Sorry. I got distracted talking. How do you feel?"

Bee turned her head to look up at Tris, far enough past a normal human range of motion to be creepy. "The difference is noticeable. Processing is more efficient due to fewer cache misses. You are too good to me." She smiled.

Tris eased the android's back panels closed and pulled a purple T-shirt down over them. "Well, that's about all I can do for now. As good as it gets without a factory rebuild."

Bee climbed off the workbench to her feet. "The factories no longer exist, so I will consider this good."

"I think she'll be happier with Bill and Ann," said Kevin.

"I'll be happier with you guys." Abby folded her arms.

He ruffled her hair. "I don't mean permanently. Just for the couple days it'll take us to go make a… phone call."

"I know." She frowned. "I wanna go with you."

Tris took a knee and looked her in the eye. "Abby… I want you to be safe. I'm going out there for a chance to maybe do something about the Enclave. They need to answer for what they did to you. What they did to your dad."

"Warren killed him." Abby glared. "And you already shot him for it."

Tris wrapped her arms around the girl. "It's the Enclave's fault. It's Nathan's fault. If they didn't drop Virus on Amarillo, you'd still be happy."

Whimpering, Abby sniveled, "I can still be happy here. Please don't go off and die."

"I have to." *Why do I have to? This… god dammit, Nathan. He probably uploaded some subliminal crap to make me believe in that bullshit mission to save the world. Make sure I found the resistance and didn't think too much about what I was doing.* "Maybe… something's wrong."

"Like what?" Kevin rubbed her back. "I mean… other than everything."

Tris kept clinging to Abby, but stood. "This feeling I have. This *drive*. It's not right. It's almost like a ghost in my head. A personality overlay or something. Maybe Nathan wanted to make sure I swallowed his bullshit about the cure and being the chosen one to save the world so I didn't ask too many questions."

"They can do that?" Kevin blinked.

She shrugged. "I don't know. I can't figure out any other reason why I'm feeling pulled to go take on the Enclave alone."

"First, you're not alone. Second, you're not taking on anything right now but a phone number. We don't know what we'll find or even if it'll work. As of right now, we're driving into a pretty shitty area hoping to find some working tech. At no point in this plan does 'taking on the Enclave' factor in. And…" He put two fingers under Tris' chin to lift her face. "I think you've already got enough mom in you to want to make sure they don't send a drone this way."

Abby sniffled. "I don't want you to die."

"That works." Kevin nodded. "I don't want to die either."

Tris cringed, feeling like Bee had punched her in the gut. Guilt crashed headlong into the inexplicable drive to go off and crush the Enclave. The ridiculousness of it would've made her laugh if not for the odd feeling that she actually could do it. It made *zero* sense, and she knew she wasn't half as frightened as any sane, rational person would've been in her position.

Going after the Enclave almost felt like a *good* idea... except for the look on Abby's face.

"Abs. I promise I will be as careful as possible. If things look too insane, we'll abort and come right back home. We can always find some underground place where they can't drop on us."

"Dallas," said Kevin. "They wanted us to stay anyway. That place is pretty much clear for Virus anyway. Enough background radiation on the surface to kill it. The whole place is underground."

"That sounds awful." Abby scrunched her nose.

"We're not going anywhere yet." Tris smiled. "I want to plan this. It doesn't make any sense, but I think this is the right thing to do. Like some external power is telling me that I can do this."

"I guess." Abby stared down at her moccasins. "If you don't come home, I'm going to be *so* mad at you."

"Well." Kevin shrugged. "There ya go. We *have* to come back now."

Abby laughed despite crying.

Tris took the girl's hand. "Come on. Let's get home; it's about time for dinner."

Bee stretched. "I am feeling optimal. Where is your home now? What has become of your roadhouse?"

"Fitch and Neels are taking care of it for the time being." He chuckled. "Okay, I don't have any plans to go back there, but it's technically still mine as far as they insist."

"I see." Bee swiveled to face Tris. "Shall I prepare your food?"

"Sounds good," said Kevin.

Tris stopped to glance at the clipboard hung on the wall by her workbench. Crystal had written in three tasks. Solar Panel Group B, Battery Relay Controller, and 'Town Power Grid – discuss.' *Looks like I'm going to be busy tomorrow.* She clenched her jaw. *The longer I wait, the more likely it is Nathan sends a bird to shit on us.*

"She'll understand..."

"What?" asked Kevin.

"I gotta talk to Crystal in the morning. Maybe fix some stuff before we leave again."

Abby mumbled, "Hope it takes a long time to fix."

Tris squeezed her hand and looked up at the ceiling. *Dad. If you're out there, I need all the help you can give me.*

7

TOO MANY QUESTIONS

Tepid bathwater lapped at Tris' thighs and chest. She reclined with her arms along the tub edges, head back, and eyes closed. This house didn't exactly offer the level of comfort her old Enclave home could provide, but of everywhere she'd been in the Wildlands thus far, it came the closest. Despite wanting to relax, she thought about design schematics for an electric water heater so people here didn't have to rely on a black-painted zigzag of pipes in the sun and a bunch of insulation around a tank.

Not helping.

She sighed. Every moment she spent not chasing down her dead father's message felt like she gambled the life of the world. Spending two hours after dinner with Abby had provided a brief reprieve. She'd wanted Tris there while she practiced opening handcuffs, but as soon as she put them on instead of held them, she became too nervous to do it right and panicked. After the girl had calmed down, they'd moved to house locks… something free of emotional scars. That required a bit more finesse than simply jamming a thin strip of metal between teeth and a spring-loaded catch. *Great, now I'm going to have nightmares about being chained to a bed with Infected coming through the windows too.* She shivered. The girl no longer appeared afraid of handling a gun, probably so nothing like the Warren situation ever happened to her again.

Abby had also asked Tris to teach her fighting, but that could wait.

Tris ran the soap up and down her arms for the fifth time. Her mind leapt to Katie, how terrified she must've been at every little noise for however long she'd been stuck unable to run or even walk. *I hope she didn't spend a whole year like that. I'd have gone crazy.* There couldn't have been too much distance between that building full of Infected and her grocery store home; if even one of them had found her...

A sudden wave of pure rage took her. She curled forward, arms wrapped around her knees, jaw clenched to keep from screaming. Katie's voice said *'Sickers got them'* in Tris' mind. A six-year-old's term for Infected. *God dammit, Nathan. I know you didn't start the Virus program, but you sure as hell don't mind using it.* She growled. Abject sorrow at what *could* have happened to Katie got her crying.

She daydreamed about pushing a button that consumed the Enclave in a nuclear fireball. It felt good. Thousands of people, many innocent, turned to ash in a microsecond... and it felt good. Just. Deserved. Retribution as if from God himself.

Tris snapped her head up, peering over her knees at the door. "Where did that come from? I don't believe in a god." She stared at the knob for a few seconds. "Dad?"

The knob turned with a creak. Abby poked her head in. "Gotta go."

"I'll be out in a minute."

Abby nodded and started to recede into the hall, but stopped. "You don't believe in God?"

"I..." Tris sighed again. "I'm not going to tell you what you should or shouldn't believe. That's a decision you have to make for yourself. I remember my father being into the whole god thing... but if there is one, he either allowed the world to destroy itself, made it destroy itself, or just doesn't care."

"You sound like Kevin." Abby looked down. "Dad used to say it was like Sodomy and Gonorrhea."

Tris coughed with the start of a laugh. "W-what?"

"Two cities that got flooded because they were evil." She backed away from the door enough to give Tris privacy. "Maybe the world had too much evil in it and it needed to start over."

"I..." She stared at the inch-wide gap between the door and the jamb. *People who want to believe will rationalize any way around it. God is merely a philosophical construct, a scapegoat for people to disavow responsibility for anything that happens to them.* She eyed the ceiling for a second. *Dammit.*

Here I go wondering... I guess when you're out of options, even some invisible man in the clouds feels like a legitimate lifeline.

She stood and wrapped herself in a towel. "Okay."

Abby ducked in.

Tris smiled. "Good night, Abby."

"Night."

Tris held the towel around her chest and hurried to the master bedroom where Kevin lay with a plain white sheet up to the base of his ribs. She put on a sly grin and eased the door closed behind her. He glanced up at the *click*. She let the towel drop.

Kevin raised an eyebrow. "You were in there so long I thought you'd fallen asleep."

"I'm not asleep." She crossed her arms behind her head and grasped her elbows, stretching. "Looks like you aren't either."

Kevin raised more than an eyebrow.

She lifted her arms, brushing her hair up into a waterfall of snowy white. The ends tickled the small of her back as it collapsed in a fluff. Prowling like a cat, she padded to the end of the bed and crawled over him.

He reached up and slid his hands down her sides to her hips as she lowered her face to kiss him on the lips. Even with the electric charge his touch sent dancing over her skin, and the beautiful sight of his bare chest and roguish grin, she had to concentrate on not worrying about the Enclave.

Any minute now a drone might—

He slid his arms up and around her, pulling her into a deeper kiss. Soon, he moved to the side, kissing along the ridge of her jaw to her neck. Tingles ran down to her toes from beard stubble scratching at the side of her neck. His lips found that little space right above her collarbone, and she shuddered from the sensation. She let herself go in the moment. He rolled on top; his weight pressed her into the mattress. Tris moaned. Her breaths picked up speed; warmth spread over her face and flooded between her legs. He leaned up from kissing her neck and made eye contact with an 'I got an idea' smile. She stretched her arms out over her head as he slid backward, kissing his way down between her breasts, over her stomach.

Beard grazed the inside of her thighs. Her breath stuttered; muscles clenched in anticipation. His tongue flicked at her sex.

Tris grabbed handfuls of bedding and writhed. Back arched, she closed her eyes and floated in timeless bliss. She started to convulse as the instant of total pleasure approached, but he stopped. She managed to get her eyes open just enough to stare at him. *Why did you stop?*

Kevin kissed her navel, eliciting a shudder of paralytic ecstasy. He crawled back up face to face with her, still grinning like a pirate king. After a second of breathless staring into her eyes, he entered her.

"Oh…" She wrapped her arms up under his, clutching at his back. "Oh… I'm…"

A drone could've flown through the window and set a jar of Virus right on her nightstand and she wouldn't have cared.

The fourth time their hips met, Abby's scream broke the silence in the hallway.

"Ugh," muttered Kevin.

"Nightmare." Tris squeezed him. "Perfect timing…"

He stopped, hands astride her head, wrists touching her shoulders. "She's a big girl."

Tris bit her lip at the… incompleteness. Flushed, and breathing hard, she grumbled.

Abby screamed again and lapsed into sobs.

Kevin rolled off to the side, still sporting an erection that could dent the armor of an Enclave hovercraft. She sat up

He gestured at himself. "It's okay. Go ahead. See if she's all right… I can't walk in there like this."

Tris stumbled off the bed, her legs not quite ready to cooperate. She pulled a T-shirt over her head and crossed the hall to the smaller bedroom. Abby sat curled up in the middle of her bed, sobbing into her knees. As soon as her door moved, she screamed again, but bit it back as Tris went in.

"Hey…" She sat on the edge of the bed and held up an arm. "Bad dream?"

Abby scooted over and leaned against her, still curled in a ball, with her head on Tris' shoulder. "Yeah."

"Do you want to talk about it?"

Abby sniffled. "Same one… I'm tied to the bed and can't get away… and Infected are coming in the door." She shuddered and sobbed. "I kicked at their hands and faces, but I couldn't stop them. Daddy pushed outta the crowd; he was one of them." She started to hyperventilate. "T-that's w-when I woke up. He was gonna bite me."

"It's all right. You're safe." Tris rubbed her back with the occasional pat or shoulder squeeze. "It's just a dream. You were so scared you couldn't deal with it all then. Your mind is processing it bit by bit."

Abby whined, huddling close.

"There is no possible chance that your father became Infected. It doesn't do that. Dead is dead. It won't make someone get back up."

"'Kay," whispered Abby.

Tris sat with her for a while in quiet. Around twenty or so minutes later, Abby calmed enough to crawl back under the covers.

She stared up with a weak smile. "Thanks for staying to protect me."

Tris held her hand. "The militia is up all night. They haven't had Infected in Ned since they put the trucks in the road. Even if one got in, they're not sneaky. They'd get seen, and shot."

Abby's lip quivered as more tears ran down her face. "I'm not as scared of them as I am of ones you can't see."

Tris tilted her head.

"New ones. Like how Warren thought I was." She wiped her face.

"Me too." Tris leaned over and hugged her. "I know you don't want me to go off on this trip, but… if there's even a tiny chance I can stop that from happening again, I have to try."

Abby sniveled, but nodded. "I know. I'm not trying to make you feel bad; I'm just scared. I kinda like having a mom."

Tris smiled and poked her in the side. "Told you already, I'm not old enough to be your mother. I'd have been like seven when you were born."

"Wow. You're only eighteen?" Abby yawned.

"I don't really know. I feel eighteen, but I think I was frozen for a while. I might be closer to twenty or twenty-one, but my body's eighteen. Or, maybe I'm not getting older because of those little medical robots inside me."

"Neat."

"Okay, Abs. Time to go to sleep." Tris stifled a yawn. "I'll stay with you 'til you're out."

Abby smiled and closed her eyes.

Tris waited until the girl's breathing changed, and lingered another few minutes before standing gingerly so as not to cause the bed to bounce. She slipped out into the hall and stared at her bedroom door. *Yeah right. I'm not sleeping.*

She padded downstairs to the kitchen. Kevin sat at the table cradling a cup of tea. It smelled funny, but fair bet the stuff wouldn't be a hundred percent half a century after its 'best by' date.

"Hey." She edged up beside him.

He put an arm around her. "Hey yourself. How is she?"

"Okay. Bad dream." She sat in his lap and rested her forehead against his shoulder. "It's at least a little my fault. I should've put up more of an argument instead of letting them tie her to a bed… twice."

He put his face in the crook of his neck and inhaled her. The cold spot by his nose made her giggle. "Why didn't you?"

"I… guess I was afraid if I pushed back any harder on Warren, things would've escalated into a gunfight. At that point, those people didn't know me at all. I worried they'd all take Warren's side if I shot him, then Zara and I would have to wipe out most of the people we went there to save." She growled. "Damn, that stuff is so evil. The psychological aspect of it is worse than the actual virus."

"Tris…"

She leaned up to stare into his eyes. "If you ask me if I could kill you if you became infected, I'm going to stab a knife through your balls into the chair. Don't make me think that."

"Colorful." He squirmed. "That's not where I was going."

"Good. I like your balls un-impaled."

He chuckled. "That makes two of us. But, what I was going to say…"

"Am I sure I want to do this?"

"Zero for two." He lifted her chin on one finger. "Are *you* okay?"

She smiled. "I got enough guilt for a small banana republic, but I'm the only one here who isn't having nightmares."

"Someone had a government based on bananas?" He blinked.

"Oh…" She laughed, muffling it into his chest. "Thank you."

"I'm serious." He scratched his head.

Tris leaned her head back and moaned at the ceiling. "Ugh, that was like ninth grade. You're making me remember schoolwork I loathed. It's something like a third world country with an unstable government and… they export bananas as their primary income. Lots and lots of poor people, military types are in control."

"Oh. Well if you're right about no one nuking the third world, I suppose they're not selling bananas much lately."

She grasped his cheeks in both hands, mashing his lips into a warped rose. "Do you think I'm being foolish?"

"Do you?" He pulled her hands down and held them in his lap. "You do have a point. He dropped that shit on Amarillo. He can do it again."

"Yeah but… the idea of getting that close to them again… Should we really run off chasing a message from a dead man?"

He ran his thumbs back and forth across the backs of her hands. "Is he dead or did he maybe vanish?"

If I knew that, I wouldn't be going crazy trying to decide. "No clue. Sorry about Abby interrupting."

He shook his head. "It's okay. Even if you stayed in bed, a sobbing, screaming child across the hall kinda kills the mood. Poor kid's been through a lot. All we can do is be there for her." His expression became serious. "If you think we can do something more than just run off and get ourselves killed, I'm on board. Those fuckers deserve payback."

She nodded. "I don't have enough information to make that decision, but I have this strange pull to find out. I can't explain it."

"Protectiveness for Abby? Don't want Ned to turn into a ghost town?"

She ran her hands over her hair, fingernails raking her scalp. "Yes, but, it's more than that. It's like I feel it's gotta happen."

"Probably a little bit of you still not quite over that whole cure thing." He looked down for a second. "Let's go make a phone call at least and see where that leaves us."

She clung to him for a few minutes, trying to make sense of everything. "I don't understand why I want to do this so badly. It's all I can think about."

"Hey…" He caressed her face until she smiled. "If I thought my dad might still be out there somewhere, I don't think I could sit still until I at least tried."

"Like the way you were about Wayne?" She grimaced, regretting the question as soon as it leapt out of her mouth.

"Nah. More. That was about killin' some guys for revenge. Goin' after my dad would be tryin' to help someone… or at least finding the truth." He looked down. "No such hope though. I saw them blow his brains out."

The sorrow wafting off him crushed her heart. She embraced him. "I'm sorry."

Kevin chuckled.

"What about that was funny?" She sat back, peering at him with a cocked eyebrow.

"I was four. I had long hair and pink jeans on… Dad found them in an old store. The bandits thought I was a girl and almost threw me in with the women. They asked; I said boy. 'Course they thought I was lying so they looked. One held me up; the other yanked my jeans down. I pissed right in his eye."

Tris laughed. "Really?"

"Nah, I'm making up that last part. I was probably screaming like a baby, but they did check my undercarriage."

She kissed him for a few long, wonderful minutes. A thin trail of saliva linked their lower lips when she pulled back; the glistening thread snapped a second later.

"I'm *so* glad they didn't kill you."

He chuckled. "Even most slavers draw the line at kids. Either guilt or they don't want the burden of taking care of them 'til they're old enough to be useful. Some would've just left me to my own devices. The nicer assholes would drop them off at a settlement."

"So who grabbed Katie?"

Kevin sighed. "You're still pissed about that. I said 'most' slavers... some keep the girls 'til they get old enough to, uhh..." He looked down.

Tris scowled, clenching her hands in fists.

"Look. Those guys are already dead. Kid didn't seem capable of lying about them getting ambushed by Infected." He winked. "She knew the 'sickers' were in that building and didn't warn them."

"I don't blame her." Tris scowled.

"Well... either they were travelers who found a feral kid that kept trying to run away and wanted to force her back to civilization, or slavers."

"People trying to help her wouldn't have put her in a damn crate and nailed it closed."

He shrugged with a 'you got me there' face. "True."

"This isn't a bad idea is it?" She eyed the door.

Kevin squeezed her ass. "No worse an idea than running off to Amarillo to check for survivors."

"Morning?"

"Sure. What about Abby?" He fussed at her hair.

"Stop it." She swatted his hand.

"I love the way your hair feels." He persisted brushing his hand over it.

Urges stirred down below as her cheeks warmed. "We should really get some sleep if we're going to do this tomorrow. Bee could watch her, but I'm not entirely comfortable leaving an eleven-year-old basically alone. Not that I don't trust Bee, but Abby needs emotional support right now that an android just can't provide."

Kevin sat straighter. "Unpleasant nocturnal mind images detected. Expressing sympathy." He mimicked a robot stroking Tris' hair.

She stifled laughter into his shoulder.

"Bill and Ann can watch her. He's already told me as much. She and Zoe are getting close. It'd be like a sleep over."

The idea of Virus dropping on Ned slammed into her consciousness. They hadn't quite been living here a full month yet and she already couldn't bear the thought of watching this place descend into the same sort of madness that tore Amarillo apart.

"Okay." She bowed her head. "I have to do this."

"No." He waited for her to look up. "*We* have to do this."

8

ACES AND EIGHTS

Ten-year-old Kevin zoomed naked through the endless, waist-high brown grass of a nightmare. Hands raised to shield his face, he ran heedless of rocks underfoot or the occasional whip of grass against his body. Despite the throng of infected behind him, the rush of his breath and heartbeat in his ears drowned out all other sound. Baleful sepia-toned light made the scene feel *wrong*. He knew he dreamed; yet the fear of a child took hold in his heart.

Chased out of bed by the entire town succumbing to the Virus, he sprinted until his jelly legs refused to take another step. Exhausted, he loped to a halt and waited for the endless sea of Infected to grab him, but nothing happened. He doubled over, hands on his knees, and gasped for breath. Moments later, he looked back at an empty field. No Infected, no trailers, no sign of anything but miles and miles of endless meadow. He stood straight and shielded his eyes with a hand, scanning the horizon all around. Sometimes, the dream offered distant mushroom clouds, but aside from the unnatural color of the world, his surroundings looked peaceful.

Wavering grass tickled at his bare stomach; he stood perplexed, wordless at the shock of being alone. Ahead of him, the sun peeked past thickening clouds, but behind him, the sky looked as dark as midnight.

The mood in the air shifted to one of eeriness rather than blinding terror. The meadow had become alien somehow; a growing sense of no longer even being on Earth set in. Pale ochre grass stretched as far as he could see. No field so large had existed anywhere he could remember. The old trailer town sat only a few dozen yards from a highway and a shallow manmade lake.

This isn't home...

As soon as the dream went 'off script,' Kevin's mind seized upon a scrap of reality. His adulthood, and clothes, returned. He gripped the .45 on his belt like a little boy clutching a security blanket.

In the east, the sky shadowed a hazy shade of battleship grey, heavy as though the storm of the century threatened to roll in at any second. Before he knew about Infected, his greatest fear had been tornadoes, and it looked like Mom Nature brewed up a bad one.

Soft crying filtered into his awareness from the left. When he turned, a lone silver trailer that hadn't been there before broke the monotony of shifting grass. An amalgam of his old home, it had a window from Lloyd's trailer, a 'one-way' sign from his adoptive parents' trailer, a dent from Jenny's, and the pink plastic flamingo from old lady Reed's. He smiled at the thought of Jenny, wondering whatever had happened to her. She had him by a few years, and hers were the first pair of tits he'd ever seen. She'd been quite eager to show them off as soon as she got them. He hadn't been old enough to appreciate it, and remained oblivious to the clear offer she'd extended. By the time he'd gotten around to understanding what she'd suggested they do, she'd hooked up with Garret, who'd been seventeen. A couple years later when Kevin had left to start driving, the two of them had four kids. At least they seemed happy.

Crying emanated from the trailer, filling him with a strong urge to help.

Behind him, the clouds blackened further, a giant's withered finger threaded downward in a building whorl. The tendril of darkness touched the grass, gathering into a spinning column of doom. Thunder rolled in the distance, and the first few pats of rain struck him.

He eyed the approaching tornado, fearful of what it would do to a lone trailer out in the midst of an endless field. He couldn't think of a worse scenario. No cover at all, and somehow, he *knew* the tornado would go straight toward it. He approached the trailer at a brisk walk, one hand still on the .45.

The wind picked up in a brief, but powerful, gust, and died down again. Whistles and howls raced overhead. Behind him, debris clattered and smashed to the ground. He didn't dare look; how could a tornado tearing up an open field of nothing be throwing around objects loud enough to shake the ground on impact? Kevin grasped the steel door handle and gave it a twist. The all-metal door swung open, allowing a sliver of light into a chamber of pitch darkness. Abby curled up on the floor, crying into her hands. Her sweatshirt nightdress had been ripped and bloodied in a manner that suggested a horde of Infected trying to grab her.

She looked up at him. "They're coming." Again, she bowed her head into her hands and wept.

He stared in horror at bleeding scratches on her arms and sides. His brain, rejecting the idea that she'd become Infected and he would have to shoot her, kicked him awake. The soft crying continued the same as it had in the dream. He wiped the grogginess from his eyes and found himself at home in bed; Abby had wedged herself between him and Tris. She tried to keep her tears quiet, but her face hovered inches from his ear.

"Hey…" Kevin turned his head and almost touched noses with her. *Thank whatever. Just a dream.*

"Sorry." She sniffled. "I didn't wanna wake you up."

"You didn't." He looked straight up at the ceiling again and yawned.

"Bad dream?" asked Abby.

"More weird. It didn't get bad 'til the end."

Abby wrapped herself around his arm. "What happened?"

"Saw a kid what got infected. I couldn't do it. I got bit." He rubbed his face.

She rested her head on his shoulder, and kept quiet for a long moment. "Was it me?"

He closed his eyes. "Yeah. I didn't wanna say that. You actually didn't bite me. Soon as I saw you got scratched, I woke up. Guess I couldn't deal with it."

Abby sniffled and attached herself to his side. "Are you gonna haveta fight Infected when you go?"

"Probably. The area we're heading to used to have a lot of people in it."

"Are you takin' militia with you?" She yawned.

"Thought about it, but I think Ned needs them more than we do. Don't want to make the place vulnerable if we don't have to." He eased his left arm out from under her and curled it around her back. "This trip isn't something we want to do, but sometimes people have to do things they don't want to do."

"You don't have to," said Abby. "But I guess it's like digging out a shithouse. No one really wants to do it, but stuff gets bad if you don't."

He chuckled.

Tris laughed.

"Good morning, beautiful," said Kevin.

"Morning yourself." Tris sat up and yawned.

Abby pushed herself up to kneel in the middle of the mattress. Kevin sat up.

"How long are you going to be away?" asked Abby.

"Week or two. Back up to Route 80 and west right to the coast. Probably take us three days just to get there, assuming nothing gets in the way."

"We could shift drive." Tris glanced over at Abby with a hesitant look for a second before an expression of 'oh hell with it' took over. She stood and peeled off her T-shirt. "Gonna take a quick bath before we sit in a car for a week."

"Maybe on the way back. I'm not exactly in a great rush to run into the jaws of the Enclave... want to stay fresh for whatever might try to get a piece of us. I doubt we'll find a roadhouse west of Reno... too much risk of an Enclave presence. Coming home though"—he ruffled Abby's hair—"we have a good reason to haul ass."

Abby's lip quivered. She stared at him. "Take me with you. Please! I wanna go. I don't wanna get sick for real when they drop that shit on us." After four seconds without an answer, she flung herself on Kevin and bawled, begging 'please' over and over again.

Tris grabbed a towel from the dresser and draped it over her arm. "Abby... ugh. I don't want to leave her here and I don't think it's a good idea to bring her with us either."

Kevin rubbed the girl's back. "Hey, come on... no need to get upset. We want you to be safe. I don't trust myself enough to watch you out there if it gets crazy—unless protecting you is *all* I'm doing. Can't focus on this thing Tris needs ta do plus keepin' you safe. What if we run into a pack of Infected... or a group of raiders? Do you want to wind up like Katie almost did? Some crazy warlord's pet?"

Abby shivered. "No."

"Don't give her more nightmares." Tris wrapped the towel around herself and sat on the edge of the bed, fussing with Abby's hair. "Yes, there are slavers out there, but they're not *everywhere*. Most people aren't like that."

"The area we're heading to, I imagine there isn't much of anything actually." Kevin tapped his foot. "Enclave and Infected… and Boatmen."

"Are Boatmen slavers?" asked Abby.

"Not in the usual sense I think. I've only heard stories. They take captives, but they don't sell or trade them. Rumors I heard drivin' around said they force people they take to join them, or die if they can't keep up. Not sure if that counts. Heard other stories too… just as likely to use someone for target practice as take a captive."

"It counts." Tris frowned. "Right. So how do I recognize a Boatman so I know to shoot first?"

Kevin chuckled. "Once we get near the Golden Gate, anyone not wearing Enclave stuff who doesn't look frightened is probably a Boatman. Better odds if they point a weapon at you."

"Abby." Tris grasped the girl by the shoulders. "The danger of Virus dropping from the sky here in Nederland could be minimal. It might not even happen. The Council ordered Nathan to stop wasting resources coming after me."

"When has being told no ever stopped an asshole like that from doing what they want?" muttered Kevin.

Tris narrowed her eyes. "Still, it means he has to sneak around. Maybe they catch him and kick him out or kill him. We don't know that there even is a real threat to Nederland, but we do know that there are real threats out there, and we don't want you getting hurt."

"I don't want you getting hurt." Abby sniffed and wiped her eyes. "Take me with you? I'll stay in the car."

Kevin stared at her until she lifted her head to make eye contact. "I want to keep you as far away from Infected… and marauders as possible. I've done crazier things before than this. If shit looks like it's getting out of control, I promise I'll drag Tris back here if I have to hogtie her and toss her in the trunk."

Abby snickered. "She'd kick your ass if you tried."

Tris flashed a coy smirk. "Okay. The tub calls." She walked out.

Kevin stood. "Go on and get dressed. Pack some stuff and a towel. You'll be staying with Bill and Ann till we get back."

"Stuff?" Abby crawled off the bed and stood. "I have two pieces of clothing." She tugged on the sweatshirt-turned-nightdress. "This, and the dress Bethany made for me."

"What about your other dress?" He raised an eyebrow.

Abby looked down. "It's got Dad's blood on it."

"Well, get ready. I'll go cook something."

Head down, Abby trudged out.

Kevin dressed and headed to the kitchen. He started to collect pans and food, but Bee walked in and got in the way.

"I can do this for you, Boss." Bee smiled. "It brings me pleasure to help."

"Heh, okay." He set a kettle on a hot plate and dumped some instant coffee in a mug.

Bee fried some dust hopper strips as well as a couple of potatoes. They'd run out of eggs, but no sense checking with the farm for another allocation yet. Not with them going away for a while.

Abby walked in and hovered at his side while he waited for the water to heat up.

"I got it." Bee smiled at them.

He moved to a seat at the table. Abby sat in his lap, clinging. Whether she meant it as a guilt tactic or not, he felt like an asshole for leaving her behind… but someone *did* go to extreme lengths to send Tris a coded message. It didn't strike him as another cruel twist of the knife from Nathan.

A short while later, Bee set plates in front of them. "How long do you expect to be away? Will Abby be staying here?"

Kevin exhaled. "Bill and Ann are going to let her stay with them for the time being. You may as well join them instead of being here alone."

"That is a good idea. The girl would benefit from a caretaker capable of emotional responses exceeding my capacity."

Abby looked up with an offended expression. "I'm right here."

"You're human enough to annoy an eleven year old." Kevin winked.

Bee emitted her approximation of a laugh. "There are a few maintenance tasks necessary for this house which I shall attend to in the meantime." She walked off toward the living room.

"Bee's kinda creepy… but cool, too." Abby jabbed a strip of dust hopper meat with her fork. "Where'd you find her?"

Tris entered, dressed in jeans and a black T-shirt, trailing an air of soap and warmth. She helped herself to food and sat as well. After Kevin finished telling Abby about Wayne's Roadhouse, no one spoke; only the scrape of forks on plastic plates broke the silence for several minutes. Kevin couldn't look at Abby without feeling guilty as hell for leaving. He couldn't look at Tris without feeling guilty as hell for thinking of not going. Some part of him almost wanted to suggest he stay behind with Abby while she ran off, but he did *not* want to go through that again. He'd spent enough time kicking himself for racing out the door half-cocked to chase down the Redeemed without her. That mistake he wouldn't repeat.

Tris didn't lift her gaze off the plate once during breakfast. He figured she felt every bit as bad about leaving Abby behind as he did, but not quite reckless enough to give in to the girl's pleas to accompany them. Maybe if she were fifteen instead of eleven, it wouldn't feel like such a foolish idea. Odd as it seemed, he might've actually brought her along if she'd been more like Zoe. As much as he hated to think about it, the little blonde nine-year-old knew her way around a rifle. That kid wouldn't hesitate at shooting threats, even if she did try to aim for legs so she didn't kill anyone. He spent a moment debating if she'd hesitate taking kill shots on Infected.

We're a nation of broken people... children carrying guns, so many orphans, so many patchwork families. He smiled wistfully, thinking about Ray taking Katie in. Most people he'd run into (pirates notwithstanding) were decent. Perhaps humanity had needed a reset button. At least Zoe still had her real father and brother. Only about five of Nederland's twenty-something kids had their actual parents around, not counting a handful of new babies of course. *Give it time.* He bit his lip at the dark thought. It only took him one hand to count the number of people he knew who made it into their twenties before their parents died.

"I know you're trying to protect everyone." Abby looked down as she pulled on her moccasins. "I might start crying when you leave, but I'm not trying to make you stay. I'm just scared."

Tris reached across the table to take her hand. "I know it's too soon. You haven't even really settled in here. Neither have we... but I'm *so* worried something is going to happen. I can't explain where the feeling is coming from, but I can't sleep either. It's like I *know* something is coming and I *have* to do this."

Abby exhaled, stared at their joined hands for a little while, and nodded. "Okay. Are you taking Zara with you?"

"I... didn't even think to ask." Tris gave Kevin a momentary questioning look, but frowned before he could answer. "No... The town needs her more than I do. I don't want to get her captured or killed."

"What about you?" Abby sniffled. "You escaped too. Won't they try to kill you?"

Kevin fidgeted, scraping at his empty plate. "We're not going to 'take on' the Enclave. We're looking for a ruined office building. What happens after that is going to depend on what we find there... if anything. All we have right now is a number. If it turns out to be a dead end, we're coming straight back here."

Abby rubbed her hands down her thighs in a rhythmic, repetitive motion. "'Kay."

Kevin stood. As if heading to a funeral, Tris and Abby followed him across the road and down the two-minute walk to Bill's house. He and Paul sat on green-painted chairs at either side of the front door, under the shade of the small porch roof. Cody had flopped on the ground a bit to the left in the start of the trees where the hill took a sharp upward turn. Every so often, he threw rocks into the distance.

"Morning," said Bill.

"Howdy." Pete—Zoe and Cody's father—raised a hand in greeting.

"What happened?" Bill stood. "You three look grim."

Kevin let out a sharp, short, sigh. "We're going to go check on that lead Tris found. Look, I... suppose there's no point trying to honey-coat this. Abby's already heard it. Hell, she lived it once. We both think that Nathan might target Nederland because Tris is here. Drop Virus on it from a drone. I know you guys sorta dismissed the idea, but I'd really like it if you could bring it up again with the militia to be extra careful about watching the air... at least while we're gone."

Abby shivered. "We never even saw it. Some of the soldiers found a smashed bottle in the road with green stuff. Couple days later, they got sick. Couple days after that they... uhh..." She closed her eyes and let out a shuddering breath, fighting off the urge to break down.

Kevin squeezed her shoulder while Tris held her hand.

"I never really had any training or exposure to the drone program," said Tris. "Zara was part of the military, so she might know more. But, those things are pretty quiet. The one we found in Amarillo had crashed. Someone must've seen it and shot it down, but not before it started to drop capsules. It's about the size of a motorcycle, black."

"Basically," said Kevin, "if you see anything flying that isn't alive, shoot the shit out of it."

Zoe walked out from the kitchen door, barefoot in her denim dress. She raised her arms toward Bill, showing off black gunk smearing them from fingertip to elbow. "Finished cleaning it. Wanna check it?" She noticed Kevin and cheered. "Kevin!" She darted over and jumped up and down in front of him without touching. "Cleaned my rifle. I'm too dirty for hugs."

"Hey, sweetie." He grasped her around the chest under the armpits, picked her up, and swung her around once before setting her back down. "We're going on an important trip. Abby's gonna stay here for a couple days. I need you to make sure she stays safe."

"Okay," chirped Zoe.

Abby furrowed her eyebrows. "She's younger than me."

While Tris scooped Zoe up for her hug, Kevin leaned close to Abby and whispered, "Just go with it. It makes her feel better."

"Oh," said Abby. "So I really can't come with you guys?"

"Suppose we do bring you, and we get surrounded by Infected. For one thing, I don't want you to have to go through that again, and for another, I don't want you to have to go through that again."

She smiled despite crying again. "Okay. You guys are my parents now. 'Kay? You better come back."

"That's the plan." He chuckled.

Tris set Zoe down and glanced to the left. "How's Cody doing?"

The little blonde darted inside.

Pete offered a resigned one-shoulder shrug. "He's not talking so much. Gets edgy after dark. Sometimes he wakes up crying, but doesn't want me to see him like that. You know, at the ripe old age of thirteen, he's too big to be scared." He shook his head. "I'd be worried more, but he seems to like that girl Emma. 'Course, he's afraid to talk to her."

Kevin smiled for a second or two. "If there's any way we can pay back the Enclave for everything..."

Pete nodded. "Don't do anything stupid. You want any help?"

"Nah." Kevin smiled. "Right now, we're only checking on something small. Call it a scouting operation. Your family needs you."

"If you want some militia, I can probably get the elders to approve a couple." Bill hooked his thumbs in his pockets.

"Ned needs them more," said Tris. "We can move quicker and easier with just the two of us... and I don't want to be responsible for anyone else being hurt if this turns out to be another tease from Nathan."

"You don't believe it is." Kevin shot her a meaningful look.

"No, I don't. That message was too involved. Nathan's not that crafty." Tris squatted and wrapped Abby in a hug. "Keep yourself safe. See you soon."

"Okay, Mom." Abby squeezed her, sniffling.

Kevin concealed a wince at the look of guilt on Tris' face. *If she changes her mind, I ain't gonna push her.*

Eventually, Abby released her grip, and Tris stood.

Zoe came back outside, her arms and hands clean. She ran over to Abby. "Wanna play?"

Abby made a face like her dog died. "I guess." She hugged Kevin. "Come home, please."

"Be good." He kissed the top of her head, patted her on the back, and gave Tris the 'well, you still want to do this?' glance.

With a grim face, she plodded off down the road toward their house.

"Thanks for watchin' Abby." Kevin shook Bill's hand. He waited for the two girls to disappear inside the house. "She's been having nightmares. Hope it's not a problem. She might wake up screaming a few times."

Bill nodded. "Been there done that. Zoe was the same way for a while. Ann's pretty good at dealing with bad dreams."

"Alright. Well, I better do this before I change my mind." Kevin glanced over at Tris who waited a little ways down the road with a 'hurry up before I chicken out' expression. "I'd be lying if I didn't have a little hope this turns out to be a load of crap."

"Keep your eyes open and get home safe." Bill shook hands.

Kevin nodded. "Will do." He heaved a sigh and followed Tris home.

She had a bit of a lead on him, and ducked inside as soon as she reached the house. He headed for the car. Tris emerged from the front door a second before his fingers touched the handle, carrying two bags of supplies, which she stuffed in the Challenger's back seat before getting in beside him.

"Last chance to change your mind," said Kevin.

Tris let her head loll back against the seat, closed her eyes, and sighed. "I can't."

"All right. Let's do it."

Kevin swiped his thumb over the rocker switches, each one lighting blue. The little screen in the middle of the dash displayed a mangled mess of pixels before sharpening into the rear-view targeting camera.

They sat in silence for a moment, listening to the soft hum of active electronics.

"Tris?" Kevin glanced over at her, raising an eyebrow. "Are you sure we shouldn't have jinx-breaker sex first?"

She playfully punched him on the shoulder. "Just drive."

KEVIN BROUGHT THE CHALLENGER TO A HALT ON ROUTE 119 AS SOON AS Boulder came into sight. Tris had been crying in silence since they started moving. "If you want to go back, say the word."

She clenched her jaw. "I want to, but I can't. Tell me again it's a bad idea to bring Abby with us."

"It's an awful idea." He wrung his hands on the steering wheel, making the leather creak. "Thought she got shot last time when those jackasses strafed us."

"Yeah." She sniffled. "I'm so terrified we're going to come back and find Amarillo all over again."

He accelerated. "Then we should hurry the hell up so we're back in time for the shit to hit the fan."

"Maybe I'm overreacting. Nathan hit Amarillo because he didn't know where we were. How could he possibly know we stayed in Nederland?"

Kevin lifted one hand off the wheel in a limp gesture of appraisal. "True. If he could find us, he woulda dropped that shit right on Rawlins."

"I don't think so. Virus won't kill me."

"No, but it would end my ass, and then you'd fly straight back to the Enclave with murder in your eyes where he could kill you more easily."

She seethed. "Thanks for making me see that."

"You know what I mean."

"Yeah." Tris sighed. "I hope Abby's not too angry at us if we come back."

"*When* we get back, I'm sure she'll be happy enough that we're back to forget all about being angry."

Tris smiled.

"Unless they drop Virus on Ned and she barely survives again, then she'll be—"

Tris punched in him the arm; a flash of pain flickered like lightning from his shoulder to his fingertips, stunning the limb.

"Ow, fuck!" He cringed. "That wasn't exactly playful."

She raised an eyebrow, her face grim. "Don't joke about that."

"Right…" He reached across and rubbed his bicep, holding the wheel steady with one knee. "Gonna head up 119 to 25 to 80 and shoot west. I know at least two 'houses we should be able to stop at. Once we pass Reno, no guarantees. We might get stuck a day or two waiting on the trickle charger."

"Or we could ambush an Enclave patrol stopped for a piss break and steal their Hoplite." She winked.

"I'd prefer to avoid contact if at all possible. Might not even be a bad idea to swap and move at night once we're in Cali."

She scratched her head. "It's not like they're actively hunting us."

"Yeah… Let's hope that stays true after we poke that number. If we can even find a way to do it. Do you have any kind of plan?"

Tris watched the road go by for a few minutes.

"Me neither."

"Terminal9 mentioned a telephone company central office once we make it into Redwood City. Suppose we just drive around looking for it."

"Did he give you anything more specific?"

Tris leaned around into the back and rummaged one of the bags she'd brought. She slid back into her seat holding a few yellowed papers with computer printing on them. "Umm. Not really. This is a bunch of passwords, user accounts, and some technical diagrams."

"Great. So we've got a pile of gibberish and a whole city to search." Route 119 skirted around Denver, sparing them having to deal with any Infected. He hooked a left turn onto 25 north, which would take them to Route 80. "Simple, right?"

"Yeah. I figure there has to be more than one CO, some kind of distribution of load across multiple sites. All we have to do is find one of them." She shook her head, chuckling. "Maybe this weird feeling in my head will give me another waypoint."

Kevin emptied his lungs through his teeth. "Last time we followed one of those glowing trails…"

"Yeah, but I'm not expecting people this time… we're looking for a building."

After hitting Route 80, Kevin opened it up and cruised around 150 mph for the better part of the day. Every minute that ticked by made him second guess leaving Ned behind, but he couldn't argue that something had gotten a hold of Tris. She wouldn't let this go, and would be miserable if they didn't at least try. A telephone number… of all the useless things someone could possess in the Wildlands—that ranked near the top, a few spots below a pilot's license. He'd never once even heard of a working telephone outside of old movies.

"I wonder…" He glanced at her. "Maybe it's a funny way to get us to that building? Whoever sent that message can't honestly expect a phone to work, right?"

She shrugged. "At a basic level, it's a wire between two devices. If the area is small enough, there might be a bit of the network left intact."

Four-ish hours later, they pulled in at the Rawlins Roadhouse… former home. Fitch had taken to running the place, and seemed to have lost his itch to drive around. Of course, not driving around also meant he never had to use up the 20mm rounds he'd collected for the big gun on his truck, which made him happy. The place seemed to be doing well, though a few bullet holes in the wall that hadn't been there before cemented Kevin's resolve that he'd made the right choice.

He did kind of miss the place, but mostly because of all the work he'd put into fixing it up, and that it represented the culmination of a dream long chased.

Fitch dropped off a pair of burgers with Sang's signature fries at their table. "Good ta see ya again. How things been?"

"Interesting." He smiled. "Damn they still smell good."

Fitch settled into a chair. "What brings ya out this way? Thinkin' o' coming back?"

"Nah. I'm gettin' used to Ned. Got the kid to watch out for now and, well." Kevin pointed at the wall. "See you've gotten some new air conditioning installed."

Fitch chuckled. "That Jamie's a hell of a shot. Couple shitheads came in and tried to rob the place. Not even subtle about it."

"Damn." Kevin shook his head. "Things are getting crazy faster than I thought they would."

"Ehh, it's under control." Fitch grinned. "Just means places need some muscle. Neal's doing an okay job maintaining the panels. Ain't quite got Tris' touch with it, but we're gettin' by. So what's got you rollin' again?"

Kevin took his time chewing a seasoned fry before speaking a hair over a whisper. "Got an encoded message. Something about the Enclave. We're checking on that lead, seein' where it goes."

"Oof." Fitch held up both hands in a 'no thanks' gesture. "I'd sooner wave my junk at a rattlesnake's mouth."

Tris stared at him. "How… colorful."

"Where's Neeley?" Kevin looked around.

Jaime, still neck to toes in full riding leathers, sat in a booth on the far right, watching the room. She looked less nervous than the last time he'd seen her, and returned a faint smile during their momentary eye contact.

"Run ta Carver's place. He's thrown a couple M249s on Bull's old 4x4." Fitch chuckled. "Them idiots who tried to rob us left behind two cars and a bunch of ordinance."

"Hey, boss man." Sang glided out of the kitchen and hurried over to shake Kevin's hand. "Good see you." He bowed at Tris. "You as well. How is Abby?"

"Fine." Tris smiled at him. "As good as I suspect anyone could be after what happened."

They chatted for a little while more about the day-to-day while eating. Aside from a few fights, and the one robbery attempt, things were relatively the same as he'd remembered.

"Kinda in a hurry." Kevin reached over to shake Fitch's hand again. "Hate to eat and haul ass, but… Abby's wanting us home on the sooner side of later."

"Understood." Fitch clapped him on the shoulder before bowing at Tris. "You two need anything for the road? Good on ammo?"

"Not exactly planning to get into a war, but… how's the .45 stock look?"

"Shit." Tris sighed. "I'd like a couple more magazines' worth of nine mil, and did you get anything in for an AK?"

Fitch stood. "Let me check."

A few minutes later, he returned with one magazine for a Beretta 92, two thirty-round box mags for an AK47 (loaded), plus a cardboard box of fifty 9mm bullets and two twenty-round boxes of 7.62x39.

He handed Kevin a cloth sack. "Got twenty-two rounds of .45."

Kevin started working out how much he'd charge for it.

Fitch must've seen the math on his face; he held up a hand. "You dropped off over five grand before you shipped off to Ned. Don't worry about it. This is still your inventory. 'House is still yours. I'm only keeping the seats warm."

Kevin smiled. "I can't really see us comin' back here… unless somethin' happens to Tris or Ned gets wiped out." He sighed. "May as well consider the place yours."

"Well." Fitch smiled. "If you ever show up here a bitter and lonely widower, I'll still call it your place."

"Fair enough." Kevin tossed the bag of ammo up and caught it.

"Same goes for you, girl." Fitch winked at Tris. "This guy gets his ass shot up, and you stop carin' 'bout if you see tomorrow, 'mon back."

She swallowed hard and stared at Kevin. "And on that cheerful note..."

"Right." Kevin downed the last of his water. "Take care of yourself, man."

"Don't be a stranger." Fitch winked.

Kevin shook hands, patted his friend on the shoulder, and headed outside, around to the passenger side door. Tris gave him a surprised look, but didn't hesitate to take the wheel. Kevin felt a little odd in the other seat of the Challenger, a vehicle that represented his greatest love for so long... until he'd met Tris. He leaned back and rested his eyes. Having a working telephone would be nice. That would let him check up on Abby (and Nederland) now and then. Tris had a point though; Nathan hadn't found them at Rawlins, so he resorted to taking out Amarillo. He wanted to accept the idea that Nederland could be safe, but security edged away from his fingertips every time he tried to grab it.

The ride west continued for several hours with little conversation, and thankfully, little in the way of bullets flying. One old beat up van tried to chase them, but barely made it onto Route 80 from its ambush hidey-hole before it faded to a speck in the rear-view screen. Kevin blinked at the small monitor.

"How fast are you going?"

"182," said Tris.

"Fuck."

"That would be a little awkward at this speed." She smiled. "Relax. I've got dex boosters, remember? I can react faster than you to shit in the road."

"Right."

He closed his eyes. The next thing he knew, the sun hid away behind the horizon up ahead, creating a band of bright orange over the dark earth beneath an indigo sky. After a stretch and a yawn, he pushed his hands into the seat on either side of his ass and sat up straight.

Tris pointed at a red glow up ahead. "Another roadhouse."

Kevin squinted into the dark. Sure enough, the neon red radiance of a Roadhouse sign cast a haunting reflection on the road surface. "Yep." He ruffled through his map book. "Evanston. This is our bed for the night."

She pulled off the highway, following an approach ramp to a former truck stop. Two small nearby buildings looked abandoned, well progressed in the process of collapsing. One bore signs advertising a fortuneteller, while the one next to it, much larger, appeared to be a weapons shop independent of the 'house.

A pair of pickup trucks, one semi cab with no trailer, three sedans, and a van lined up in front of the main building like pigs at a trough. Tris stopped the car in an open spot between a silver pickup that someone had dropped down to the ground clearance of a sports car and the van.

Three small girls, about Zoe's size, in old-timey off-white dresses that made them look like they'd come out of the 1800s, hung laundry on a cord off to the left of the roadhouse. All had long black hair and appeared to be identical triplets. They looked over with curiosity and unease in equal measure. As Tris stood out of the driver's seat, they relaxed a little, and returned to their task.

Kevin plugged in to the charging board, gave the silver pickup a 'why would anyone do that to a perfectly fine truck' stare, and followed Tris in the front door.

The room held about twelve patrons. Four men played cards at a round table near the back, a woman and a man in their later thirties, both in piecemeal body armor combining prewar Kevlar with patches of steel-belted radial worked on plates of food in a booth near the front door. A few men sat alone, minding their own business while they ate.

A boy about fourteen, shirtless, barefoot, and wearing grey shorts, worked a broom across the floor. He had the same black hair as the triplets outside and the older man behind the bar, who had to be nearing fifty. The guy had a hard, ex-military look to him—or what would have been ex-military, if not for civilization ending around the time he'd have been born.

"Howdy," said the proprietor as they approached the counter. "What can I get ya?"

"Charge on twelve, a room for the night, and what's good for food?" asked Kevin.

"Chicken, squirrel, p-dog, or dust hopper, with 'green stuff' on the side," said the man.

Tris and Kevin said 'chicken' at the same time.

"Ten coins for the lot." The proprietor smiled.

Kevin stuffed his hand in his coat, pulled out a small handful of coins so as not to give anyone in the room too many ideas, and counted out ten. The proprietor nodded.

He added two more coins. "Water each as well."

"Right." The man filled two large steel cups and handed them over.

They took a table along the wall opposite the counter, about halfway between the front door and a stairway in the corner that led up to the second floor bedrooms. Not long after, a girl in her mid-teens, also with jet-black hair, carried two plates out of a flapping plastic door near the counter. A simple denim tube dress clung to her chest by means of a cord tied around her armpits, and covered her to a hand's width above the knee. She lingered by the proprietor only long enough for him to point at Kevin and Tris, and padded over with their food. Kevin raised an eyebrow in alarm at her black toenails until he realized the color came from some manner of decorative paint rather than infection.

"Oh, this is easy," said the girl. "You got the same stuff." She smiled and set down the plates. "Want more water? Papa don't charge for refills on water."

"Sure," said Tris.

"Be right back then." The girl smiled and hurried to the counter.

"How many kids does this guy have?" Kevin chuckled. "Guess that's one way to staff a roadhouse."

Tris made a 'no idea' face.

The girl returned with a pink plastic pitcher and refilled their cups before zipping off again. Kevin found himself missing Wayne as he ate. The chicken-on-a-roll with fries didn't quite live up to the burgers he always wound up craving after a long enough ride. Of course, Bee had been the one cooking them all along. All he had to do was hunt a dust hopper or two and she could make them. Granted, to get the taste perfect, he'd have to kill the dust hopper with his car.

A few minutes later, the triplets walked in and busied themselves wiping down unused tables and chairs. They remained in a cluster, never more than a step or two away from each other. Kevin couldn't help but watch them, mesmerized by their antique dresses, almost choreographed movements, and the steady whispery sing-song cadence of their speech to each other.

Those kids are eerie. He chuckled to himself. *I thought the same thing about Zoe.*

The girls offered polite smiles as they walked past their table to attack the one behind them. Despite their tender age, they cleaned and prepped the table like an experienced pit crew. A few minutes passed in relative silence; he found himself mesmerized by the triplets' whispery singing, and waited for that thing from the one movie to come out of a back hallway and crawl across the ceiling.

Most of the room looked up when the front door opened. A young blonde woman in a white jacket and tight white jeans strolled in. Her unimpressed glance around the room shifted to wide eyes when she spotted Kevin.

"Here comes trouble," muttered Kevin.

"Hmm?" Tris looked up.

Athena sauntered over and slid into the bench seat at Tris' left. "Hey. What are you guys doing out here? I thought you, like, got old and retired."

"Something came up," said Kevin.

"Oh wow." Athena showed off a few new scuffmarks on her armored jacket. "I'm really sorry for being a little bitchy with you. This thing saved my ass three times. It's getting insane out there. This one asshole started shooting right inside a roadhouse near Oklahoma. *Right inside!* Can you believe that?"

Tris looked worried, though her face couldn't get any paler. "That sounds like Mac's place... what happened?"

"Oh, yeah. Mac's cool." Athena grinned. "These two idiots both tried to sign on for the same run and got into a fight. One wound up pulling a gun after the other guy kicked his ass. I guess it was kinda worth it, I got seven hundred coins for that one."

Kevin raised an eyebrow. "Let me guess, both of 'em died?"

"Yeah." Athena nodded. "Everyone in the room let them have it. I took a ricochet in the tit, but it didn't penetrate the armor. Mac's wife got one in the ass through the wall."

"Oh no... Liv..." Tris bit her lip.

"I think she'll be okay. She seemed more angry than worried. It hit a wall first so it didn't do too much damage. Mac was pissed."

The same fifteen-ish girl approached Athena. "Hi. Can I get you anything?"

"Sure, whatever they got... charge on sixteen and a room."

"Seven," said the girl.

Athena fished out the coins and handed them over. The teen smiled and hurried off to the counter.

With no tables left to clean, the three maybe-eight-year-old girls sat on the floor in the corner and set to playing with dolls.

"Bullshit!" yelled one of the card players a short while later.

The room fell silent. Kevin glanced over his shoulder. One guy with a massive moustache stared at a smaller man with a shaved head and a white cowboy hat. The smaller man held up his hands in gesture of innocence.

"Ain't my fault I'm lucky," said the one with the shaved head.

"Fuck you and your luck, Joe." The guy with the moustache threw his cards down.

After another moment of tense staring, the game resumed, and seconds after that, so did the din of conversation elsewhere in the room. The proprietor whistled two sharp notes, high to low. The triplets hurried out of the room toward the kitchen area, carrying their dolls.

Kevin kept his attention on the poker table. "That game's either going to end in a minute or two, or someone's getting shot."

"Wouldn't someone getting shot also be the game ending?" asked Athena.

"Heh." Kevin chuckled. "Depends on who's playing."

"So I run a couple cans of coffee to this crazy old guy out in the middle of nowhere right?" said Athena. "He asks if I take outbound runs… offers me a hundred coins to drive something to this placed called Rexburg right, and a hundred more when I bring back a note from the guy there. So I say maybe, depends what it is. He says it's in the basement and I can take a look at it to decide. Then, he takes me to this cellar door, right, and—"

"Please tell me you didn't go in." Kevin cringed.

"I had a weird feeling. Soon as he opened the door, this girl down there screamed. Sounded like she had a gag in her mouth or something. I hesitate, right? And the guy grabs me from behind and puts a knife at my back. I guess he was like expecting me to be all like 'oh, please don't hurt me' right? So I kinda caught him off guard when I punched him in the throat. He pulls a gun; I go for mine." Athena pointed at a dull grey smudge on the white armored jacket about where her navel would be. "Dude didn't have armor, and I carry a .45."

"Damn," said Tris.

"I know, right?" Athena shook her head. "Guy had two women chained up down there. Wasted four bullets on padlocks."

"Didn't have a key on him?" asked Tris.

Athena raised her arm, elbow on the table, and flicked her hand with a dismissive wave. "Didn't wanna stick around long enough to look."

Kevin shook his head. "Maybe you should consider a settlement 'til things adjust."

"Okay, *Dad*." Athena smiled.

The teen who'd been waiting on their table hovered at the door, afraid to walk into the room again.

"Wow. What's her damage?" asked Tris.

"Their father knows something's about to happen. Doesn't want them out here 'til he's sure bullets aren't going to fly." Kevin indicated the poker table with a nod.

"Oh. And nah. This is way too fun. Maybe I won't take jobs driving out to old men living alone in the middle of nowhere again, but... I'm not ready to stay in one place yet." Athena's bravado faded a little to a genuine smile. "Anyway, thanks for the armor. I don't usually admit to being wrong."

"Fucking cheater!" shouted Mustache.

"Here we go," muttered Kevin.

A chair scraped the wooden floor. Kevin grabbed for his .45 and whirled toward the poker table. Joe lunged up from his chair, twisting to angle a gun on his hip at the guy with the moustache. The two men fired about the same time. Joe's shot winged Mustache in the arm as he took a slug in the gut. Joe fired again from the hip, but the bullet went high and right, shattering a dead light fixture two tables behind them. Mustache squeezed off a second round, putting a fatal bullet in Joe's chest before the man had gotten all the way out of his seat.

Joe's body crumpled to the floor, dragging a chair down.

Mustache held his weapon up to the side, letting it roll back on his finger through the trigger guard as an indication to the room he had no intention to shoot anyone else. Another man from the table slashed the sleeve of Joe's pale blue shirt open, exposing a few cards. Mustache put his weapon back in its holster and lowered himself to sit once more.

The man to his right dropped his cards on the table. "I'm out."

A woman who looked like a forty-something version of the teenaged waitress entered from the kitchen in a blue Kevlar vest over a basic T-shirt and jeans. The vest bore faded lettering across the front spelling DEA. She trained a Colt M4 in the general direction of the table, but didn't point it at anyone specific. The proprietor dragged the dead man out the front door.

"I mean..." Athena ate a fry. "Do you really not miss this?" She winked.

Kevin stuck the .45 back on his belt and relaxed. "I got over the whole 'playing with guns thing' the first time I took a bullet. Never really was about fighting or killing. I wanted money, a roadhouse. Got tired of always moving around, never knowing if home would still be home next month. You grow up nomadic?"

"Nah." Athena picked up her burger. "I'm from this little boring bit of nowhere called Winifred, Montana. It's so boring the nukes fell asleep and didn't go off. My sisters are all quiet, do everything Dad tells them. Except for Lizzie, they're all married already."

Tris tilted her head. "Is Lizzie like you… adventurous?"

Athena grinned. "No, she's five… maybe six now. I got tired of being the 'bad' daughter. Couldn't stand being stuck in a place where nothing ever happens and everyone just exists. Only thing I had to look forward to was pumping out kids."

"I used to know a girl who wanted to be a mother so bad she was ready to get started at thirteen." Kevin chuckled. "Well, I hope you live long enough to get the itch to settle down."

Athena rolled her eyes. "Okay, Dad." She slouched on her elbows, voice quieter. "I never did really thank you for letting me stay so long. Sang's great by the way. Whatever you're doing out here, I hope you live long enough to settle down." She winked.

"Yeah…" Kevin chuckled, eyeing the blood trail to the front door. "So do I."

The proprietor's wife traded her rifle for a mop, while barking, "Not yet," at someone in the back.

Kevin eyed the brown curtain blocking off the kitchen, picturing all the kids huddled on the floor or perhaps down in a basement. *And that's why we took Abby to Ned.*

When the proprietor walked back in, he clapped a few times to get the room's attention. "Silver pickup truck for sale. Thousand coins."

Kevin laughed.

"What's so funny?" asked Tris.

"You saw that truck. Someone put a car suspension on it, dropped it to like an inch of ground clearance. That guy deserved a bullet."

Athena laughed, though Tris continued to give him a befuddled stare.

"Never mind." He tipped back his water.

"Oh." Athena pointed at him. "No matter what Neeley tells you, we did not fuck."

Tris rolled her eyes. "That man is impossible."

Athena stared at her with 'you have no idea' written across her face.

"The perpetual optimist." Kevin sent a suggestive look Tris' way. "S'okay. I wouldn't have believed him if he told me that anyway."

Stretching, Tris yawned. "Why can driving make you so tired when you're just sitting there?"

"Takes a lot of focus." Kevin stood. "Is that a hint?"

"Yeah, maybe a little." Tris smiled.

"Night you two." Athena stood to let Tris out of the bench. She sat, ate one more fry, and looked up at them with a coy wink. "Have fun."

9

TWO ON THE WAY

Tris hurried up the narrow stairway to the second floor and followed the hallway to the sixth room on the left. Kevin slipped in behind her and locked the door. The room contained a battered metal-framed bed, pale grey wherever the paint hadn't flaked off the steel, and about two feet of open space between it and the left wall. She twisted to gawk at the door.

"How did they get that bed in here? This room is so small."

Kevin embraced her from behind. "Probably took it apart."

They shuffle walked together to a tiny handmade table in the left corner next to a small square window that even Zoe couldn't have squeezed through. Despite its size, they'd put a cage of rebar outside. Tris set the key on the table and reached for her belt.

"Wow, I'd hate to be in this place if it caught fire."

Kevin grasped her hand. "Let me."

Tris bit her lip and let her arms hang loose. He swayed her side to side for a while, kissing at the back of her earlobe. *Oh...* She closed her eyes. Kevin slid one hand up her front, kissed her again, and tugged her T-shirt out of her jeans. She stood still as he worked the shirt up and peeled it off her. Her hair tickled at her back for a few seconds until he pressed himself against her from behind. His hands alighted on her hips and slid up over her bare stomach to cradle her breasts. Breath ran in hot puffs over her skin while he kissed the curve where her neck met her shoulder. She bit her lip as he played with her nipples for a while.

The urgency to chase down the phantom number receded.

Take my pants off before they're soaked.

She squirmed her ass into him, smiling to herself as he stiffened against her.

He traced his right hand down her stomach while his left continued teasing her breast. It took him a moment to fumble open the button on her jeans. With excruciating slowness, he slid his left hand over her side to her hips while he sank downward, kissing across her shoulder and along her back. She reached forward, bracing her hands against the wall to keep her weakening legs from dumping her on the floor.

She tried to hold still as he pulled her jeans over her ass, and trailed kisses down the back of her thigh.

"I love every inch of you," he whispered, and kissed the back of her knee.

Oh... Her legs gave out, and he guided her to sit on the mattress before removing her shoes. She kicked free of her jeans and stretched out naked on the bed, smiling up at him. Already, her heart raced and a fine layer of perspiration glowed all down her front.

Kevin slipped out of his armored jacket and dropped it before removing his boots. Tris arched her back and bit her lip while he took his sweet time tugging his shirt up and over his head. She teased at his jeans with her toe. He grinned, undid the button, and let them fall.

She crawled backward as he climbed up onto the bed and hovered over her. He planted the lightest of kisses on her stomach, a little below the navel before moving upward, touching her only with his breath until his lips found hers. Tris wrapped her arms around him as they kissed, moaning into his mouth. His erection traced across her thighs.

Grinning, she grasped his shoulders and twisted, pushing him over on his back. Light brown hair, the longest she'd seen on him yet, spilled out on the sad excuse for a pillow. He grinned like the entire world could blow up all over again and it would be worth it for being with her at that moment.

Tris reached down and grasped his length, guiding him in as she lowered herself onto him. "Oh..." She gasped. "You got me so wound up."

"I haven't unwound since last night." He winked and gave a little thrust, which almost hurt.

"Ooh!" She squeaked.

He slid his hands up her front and played with her breasts while she gyrated in a gentle up and down motion. His eyes fluttered, half closing. She caught his right hand and pulled it up to her face, sucking on his finger, letting the tide of ecstasy build.

"Faster," he wheezed. "You're so damn beautiful."

She dropped his hand and bent forward, grasping his shoulders—and slowed down. "How about I go slower?"

"Ngh!" He clenched his teeth and shuddered.

Tris flattened on top of him, kissing his nipple; he wrapped his arms around her and held on, moaning. He grunted. His fingertips dug into her back and his body convulsed in a series of short thrusts. Warmth bloomed inside her. He held on, groaning with the paralytic clutch of release. Tris bowed her head, panting, so worked up by his foreplay she found herself on the precipice within seconds of his tension fading.

"You are so amaz—"

She smothered him with a kiss before collapsing on top of him in the throes of bliss. He moved her to the side and rolled on top, kissing at her throat while he continued making love to her. She bit her forearm to muffle the gasps and moans she so desperately had to release into the world. Kevin let out a long groan, his body convulsing with spasms. He held her by the hips, his length thrust to the hilt inside her, and shuddered. Everything burst into flashes of sparkling light, and her body spiraled out of control for a heavenly moment.

Gasping for air, she went limp, arms splayed out to either side like a crime victim. "I love you so much."

He eased himself down at her side and half pulled her on top of him with an arm around her back. "I wouldn't know what to do without you."

They held each other, both breathing hard and covered in sweat.

Her mind spiraled down a torrent of worry. What if something happened to him out here? What if Abby resented their going and never forgave her for it? What if this all turned out to be another of Nathan's games? *I want to go home.* She drew in air to tell Kevin they needed to turn around, but anxiety fell on her with a crushing weight. It felt as though the entire world (what remained of it anyway) counted on her to do something about the Enclave. As if somehow, she could make a difference—one woman against ten thousand high-tech soldiers—in defiance of all logic.

Guilt at wanting to walk away from that... *destiny* twisted her guts up and welled out of her eyes. The very idea of going back to the Enclave seemed the most terrifying thing imaginable all of a sudden. *What if they catch me? I'll never see Kevin or Abby again. I'm being such an idiot. What can I hope to accomplish there? Really... I'm only one person.* The chilling grip of fear seized her; she burst into tears, clinging to Kevin like a frightened girl awakened from a nightmare.

"Whoa..." Kevin ran a hand up and down her back. "I wasn't that bad, was I?"

The urge to laugh died like a dust hopper straying onto the road, though it slowed her avalanche of fear and guilt enough to allow her voice to emerge. "No... I'm. Ugh. I was wondering if this is really the right thing to do, but the guilt... it's eating me inside. It's like if I don't do this, everything the Enclave does from now on is my fault, but I'm terrified they'll catch me and put me back in Detention and I'll never see you again."

"Tris." He traced lazy circles around her back with his fingers. "You're no mouse. This might not sound quite like I mean it, but you're the scariest person I know."

She sniffled into a chuckle. "Thanks, but the Enclave soldiers have all the same boosts."

"Yeah, but you've got two things they don't."

"Breasts?" She frowned. "Not going to help. And about a quarter of the military are women."

"Not half?"

She grumbled. "No. The Council wants to keep women safe and alive to have kids. That whole repopulation thing."

Kevin smiled and tapped a finger to the tip of her nose. "I wasn't going to say breasts. You've got experience and a strong motivation."

"They've been soldiers longer than I have."

"Maybe, but they sit behind hovercraft controls and push buttons. How many of them do you think have been shot at for real, or been thrown around by an Infected?"

"I'm sure they keep up on the sims."

"Yeah, but that's not real." He kissed her again.

She shivered. "It's real enough. I was telling Abby about my escape training. They had to unplug me the first time they threw me in the pool. I almost had a heart attack from the sim making me think I drowned." Tris clenched her jaw as a wave of fear smashed into the wall of urgency pulling her forward. "I'm so worried about her."

"She's really preoccupied with those handcuffs. You afraid she'll turn out like Zara?" He chuckled.

"Not at all. It's nowhere near the same thing. Zara gets a thrill out of it. Abby's morbidly terrified of them. If she's holding them, she can pick them open in like six seconds now. Put them on her, she freezes and panics."

He exhaled. "Can't say I blame her after that situation with Warren. If she's that scared of them, why is she doing that to herself?"

"She's trying to conquer her fear… but it's winning right now." Tris stared into his warm hazel eyes. "Is this a good idea?"

"Right now, we're only on the way to see what that number turns out to be. If it looks like a one-way trip, I'll drag you back home. I've still got rope in the trunk."

She jabbed her finger into his side. "Ass."

"If you ever wanna play around like Zara…"

Her blood chilled. "No. Please never do that to me. I… absolutely cannot stand being helpless."

"Like mother like daughter?" He smiled.

She glared. "I'm not kidding."

He raised both eyebrows, and his bad-boy grin faded to a look of concern. "All right. I promise." He brushed a thumb across her cheek. "Wasn't my fault, was it? For leaving you tied up so long?"

She rested her head on his chest and closed her eyes. "Maybe that made it a little worse, but I've always had this aversion to being contained. Even as a kid, I hated the structure of school. It was like being in prison for the crime of not being eighteen yet. Curfew, work schedules, play schedules. They never even let us socialize with each other, like 'fun' was somehow going to ruin humanity's chances at survival. Maybe that's why they kept me under watch because I kept pushing the edge of all the rules. Drag my feet, not quite comply until the threat of punishment got close."

"Sorry you had to grow up like that."

"Don't feel bad for me." She snuggled into him. "My life was easy compared to yours, just rigid."

"I think you're afraid, but anyone with so much to lose would be." He kissed the top of her head.

Can we spend the rest of time together like this? Forget the Enclave?

"You said you had these odd feelings before."

"I did?" she asked, her voice already heavy with the approach of sleep.

"Yeah… something about your knowing the Virus couldn't hurt you. You mentioned it a couple days after we got back to Rawlins. You were standing on the road burning that Infected and it struck you out of nowhere."

"I didn't think you believed in that stuff." She smiled.

Kevin chuckled. "What we're about to do? If it'll get you home safe, maybe I'll make an exception."

10

SKY WATCH

Abby clutched her sweatshirt/nightdress in a ball to her chest, feeling awkward as Zoe freely whipped off her dress, tossed it into a basket and walked nude across the loft bedroom to retrieve an actual child's nightgown from a different basket as though she didn't have someone else standing nearby. Her embarrassment didn't make much sense considering no one seemed to care at the lake where they all swam together. She sighed and changed. After draping her dust-hopper hide dress over the back of a chair, she crawled into bed next to Zoe.

The ceiling angled to a point overhead, with individual boards visible under a layer of wine-colored paint. Here and there, a nail stuck out from inexpert construction, or perhaps more recent repairs. Zoe's room had a lot of space.

Her father and brother live with Bill and Ann. Wonder why her dad didn't take the big room and put Zoe in with Cody. She was here first, guess it woulda been crappy to steal her room. Abby lay flat on her back with her arms at her sides, staring straight up. Zoe yawned, close enough to feel warmth on her arm, but not touch.

I hope they're okay. She wondered how far away her new family had gone. It wasn't fair... they hadn't even been here a month and already she might wind up an orphan again. The look on her dad's face appeared in her mind again as he rasped his last breath. Abby closed her eyes, forcing warm tears out the corners, which slid down her head and gathered in her ears. She swayed from sorrow to rage while trying to keep still so Zoe didn't notice the storm going on in her heart. Had Tris not shot Warren, she'd have gone off to deal with him herself... something to do instead of sit here waiting and hoping for Tris and Kevin to come home alive. If they didn't come back, would she wind up like that feral girl?

As much as she dreaded the thought, she had trouble sleeping without being tied to the bed. Her fear that Warren would come out of nowhere, see her loose, and shoot her for being a risk kept her up. If she couldn't go anywhere, she wouldn't be a threat. She slipped one hand out from under the sheet and wiped her eyes. She wanted to run down the hall and climb in bed with Tris and Kevin. She almost felt safe there. Not here, basically alone, waiting for Infected or Warren to kick in the door.

She lifted her head and peeked where she expected to find a door. An open gap gave her a clear view into a small section of empty space above the hallway below. *I'm in the loft.* A ladder didn't scare her as much as a door. For one thing, Infected couldn't climb; for another, her mental image of Warren storming through the door of the room where they'd kept her didn't work with a ladder. Never mind that more than anything, the dread Tris and Kevin would never come back left her too frightened to sleep.

"You're not sleeping," whispered Zoe.

Abby swallowed. "No. Neither are you."

"Nope. We haven't talked yet."

"What?" Abby rolled her head to look at the grinning blonde at her right.

"You're sleeping over. We have to talk all night."

"I guess." Abby stared straight at the ceiling again. *Is there anything up there, watching us? Waiting to kill us?* "Not like I sleep anyway."

"You don't sleep? Like ever?" asked Zoe.

"I try, but I always wake back up." She swished her feet side to side.

"Why?"

Abby shrugged. "Bad dreams."

"I didn't like my dreams either. So I stopped having them."

Abby glanced to her right again; Zoe's smile had faded to a serious look.

"How do you stop dreaming?"

Zoe rolled on her side, facing Abby. "Ann said bad dreams are like letting whatever scared me keep scaring me. So I didn't be scared anymore. What are you scared of?"

"Stuff."

"You're scared your parents won't come back."

Abby twitched at the sudden contact of Zoe taking her hand. "Yeah."

"They'll come back." She grinned. "They went to Chicago and got my Dad and brother."

"Is that what you had bad dreams about?" Abby looked at her again.

"No." Zoe's confidence faltered. For a second, she looked frightened, but she closed her eyes and sucked a deep breath in her nose before letting it out her mouth. "There's lots of Infected in Chicago. Lot of people were in this building. A man got a bus working, and people were gonna leave. My dad made them take me even though they had no room for him or Cody. I didn't wanna go. Daddy didn't want me to get hurt by the Infected." She kept quiet for a while. "Mommy died tryin' to protect me."

"I'm sorry." Abby squeezed Zoe's hand. "Mine died when I was five. I don't really even remember her. She had something the doctor couldn't fix."

"The people on the bus were kinda mean to me." Zoe frowned. "No one wanted to take care of me, so they stuck me in the back and ignored me. We drove until it got dark, an' the man driving got into a fight with another man who wanted to drive 'cause the other man had been doing it too long. They pulled over so we could get out and pee and stuff. Some people had food, an' they ate some. I didn't have any."

"That's so mean." Abby scowled. "How could they not feed a kid?"

Zoe shrugged. "This one old man was nice to me. He gave me a potato an' told me a story 'bout this other planet that's all jungle and's got these little hamster men who helped save the whole universe by killin' bad machines with rocks and spears an' stuff."

Abby grinned.

Zoe's smile faded to a hollow stare of fear. "The 'fected found us. The old man carried me on the bus, but the driver man was fat an' they got him. The old man took a big suitcase offa shelf, dumped it empty, 'an told me ta get inside." She shivered. "I got in and he shut it up tight. Everyone was screaming and the 'fected made roars and moans. I heard 'em walkin' 'round. Some of 'em stepped on me."

Abby gasped and held Zoe's hand tighter. "That's so scary…"

"I think they smelled me. Kept pickin' up the suitcase and droppin' it. I didn't make noise. I's too scared to cry. They went away, but I still didn't move 'til I had ta pee, an' it was quiet for a long time. I couldn't get out."

Abby shivered.

Zoe blushed. "I cried. I thought I was gonna die. 'Fected too stupid to open a suitcase. I started yelling, but no one was left. They all died."

Abby rolled onto her side, facing Zoe. "I'm so sorry... that's awful." *That's why they let her have this room... the ladder. She knows they can't climb ladders.*

"I got all dizzy and sick, dunno how long I was in there... but I heard someone and tried to yell. Was Bill. He found me and let me out." Zoe got quiet for a while. Color returned to her face, as did her smile. "An' your parents came here an' Bill asked them ta get my Dad and Cody out from Chicago. They did it!"

Abby forced herself to smile back. "That's great. I'm sorry you got stuck in a suitcase."

Zoe shrugged. "It saved me from 'fected. That's what I bad dreamed about. Bein' stuck in a suitcase. What's your bad dream like?"

"Umm. Probably not as scary as that."

"What is it?" Zoe tickled her side.

"Stop." Abby grabbed for the elusive finger, but soon found herself in a tickle war.

A sharp *thud* in the floor brought their giggling to a halt.

Abby froze, dreading punishment. Zoe didn't seem too worried. She kept a hand over her mouth to mute continued laughter. Once she'd calmed again, she pushed on Abby's shoulder.

"'Mon. Tell me. You don't gotta be scared."

Abby cringed, not wanting to think about it. Already, the phantom presence of rope closed around her wrists. "Umm. I was in Amarillo."

"Big city?"

"Kinda. It was. Not really. People got sick. A drone dropped Virus on us, and no one knew what it was. People... people I knew... turned Infected. Everyone went crazy."

Zoe's eyes widened. "That's scary."

"Only like fifteen of us made it. We were hiding in the basement of an old store for like two weeks. When it all happened, I had to run in the middle of the night. I only had my dress, no shoes. The basement was chilly and wet and I got a cold. Everyone thought I'd gotten the bad virus." Angry shouts danced around her memory; again, the harsh overhead light beat down on her. Warren glowered. Tears flowed.

Zoe rolled over and held her. "It's okay."

The absurdity of a younger girl trying to play mommy chased away some of the terror. She wiped her face. "This old bastard Warren thought I was gonna turn into an Infected. He made me take my dress off in front of everyone so they could look for bite or scratch marks. My Dad was angry and told them no, but they yelled at him 'cause they thought he knew I'd been scratched and was trying to hide it. They said he wanted to kill everyone."

"Okay. They checked me when I got here too, but it was only one doctor lady." Zoe shrugged. "I hadda bend over an' touch my toes. She put a cold metal thing on my chest and back. An' this squeezy thing on my arm that hurt."

"I didn't have any bite or scratch marks, but he was still gonna shoot me." A rush of gratitude flooded her as she remembered the glower on Tris' face when she first stormed in. She had no idea who Abby even was then, but still she looked *so* angry at the way Warren had treated her. "Tris came outta nowhere and pointed a gun at him. She tried to tell them I wasn't sick, but everyone was afraid I was gonna turn into an Infected in the middle of the night. Warren made them tie me to the bed so if I got sick, I couldn't get anyone."

Zoe scrunched up her face. "That's mean, but I guess it's better than being shot."

Abby stared at her. "How would you feel if they tied you to a bed and Infected came in? And you couldn't get away."

"Eep!" Zoe curled up and shivered. "That's different! That happened? Did they get you?"

"My Dad and Tris stayed with me. The Infected broke into the basement, but they didn't get to the room I was in. After that, Tris made everyone leave. A couple people got hurt running past Infected. We stopped at this roadhouse to sleep, and Warren said he'd shoot me if they didn't tie me to the bed again. Lauren got scratched bad. She went Infected in one night. I heard her roaring and I couldn't move. I thought Infected were gonna come in the room and get me."

"That's scarier than bein' in a suitcase," whispered Zoe. "'Fected can't open a suitcase."

Abby sniffled. "Later, on the ride, my cold got worse. It was just a normal cold, but Warren was gonna shoot me. He went crazy. My Dad tried to stop him from killing me, and Warren shot him." Abby broke down, sobbing into her hands. "Warren killed my Dad right in front of me."

Zoe held on again. "I'm sorry."

"Girls?" whispered Ann. "Is everything okay?"

Abby sniffled and sat up enough to look at Ann peering over the floor from the ladder. "Yeah. I'm okay."

"All right, but if you need us, we're right below you." She offered a motherly smile and climbed down out of sight.

Zoe narrowed her eyes. "I hope he died."

"Yeah. Tris shot him as soon as Dad died. Zack shot Tris for killin' Warren, but Zara killed Zack and threatened to shoot anyone else who moved."

"Oh, no! Did Tris die?"

"No, dumbass." Abby poked her. "She was here for a month."

"Oh." Zoe blushed. "Duh."

Abby rolled flat and stared at the ceiling again. "Now I'm scared the drones will come here too."

"What's a drone?"

"It's like a machine that flies. Too small to carry a person."

"You don't gotta be scared now." Zoe sat up and pointed. "'Fected can't climb ladders."

"Or open suitcases."

Zoe nodded. "I don't wanna get in a suitcase again. I like ladders more."

"Girls, go to sleep," murmured a male voice from beneath the floor.

Abby cringed again.

"'Kay," said Zoe at normal volume. After a conspiratorial wink, she closed her eyes.

Abby let a long, slow, silent sigh out her nose. She stared at the ceiling for a while, wondering how long it would take her to fall asleep, and if she did, how bad the nightmare would be.

ARMS FOLDED ACROSS HER CHEST, FACE HIDDEN BEHIND WILD HAIR, ABBY sat on the leftmost end of a dingy sofa. She stared at the red, blue, and orange embroidered lines covering the grey fabric by her feet, which she half sat on. She didn't want to be here. Though nice, these people weren't her parents. Zoe's brother kinda bugged her too, the way he stared at her whenever they wound up in the same room. Over breakfast, and later at lunch, he'd spent the whole time watching her from across the table. His blank-faced expression could've been anything from thinking her cute to jealousy to wanting to punch her in the nose.

It's okay if he doesn't want me here. I don't wanna be here.

The sofa faced a bookshelf, which had replaced the television set once mounted to the wall. One working TV existed in Amarillo, in the main Roadhouse where visitors and guests went. She'd heard people say that before the war, they existed in every house. Sometimes people even had more than one. She didn't believe that though... probably only them telling stories to mess with kids.

"Has she been like that long?" whispered Pete, somewhere behind her.

"Most of the morning. Didn't want to go outside with the other kids," whispered Ann.

Abby frowned, thinking of Zoe trying to talk her into going down to the lake and swimming. Not like Nederland offered much else to do, and the children didn't have to go to school during summer. No one could remember why school didn't happen in the summer, only that it had always been that way. She didn't have any interest in playing or having fun, not with her new parents' lives in danger. She felt better being alone.

"Kid looks like some kind of patient in a mental ward, hiding in the corner of her padded cell." Pete sighed. "I hope those two burn the whole thing down. The world could tolerate another nuke to get rid of the Enclave."

"No kidding." Ann walked up behind the couch. She leaned over and tickled at the bottom of Abby's bare foot. "Hey, kiddo. You all right?"

"Yeah." She squirmed to move her foot away.

"Do you want to talk about it?" Ann tilted her head. "*¿Quieres hablar acerca de ello?*"

Abby glowered. "I don't understand Spanish. Just 'cause my last name's Padilla doesn't mean I know it."

Ann gave her a sympathetic look.

"Sorry." Abby looked down.

"You're worried, and that's fine." Ann smiled. "I've seen Tris take on some bandits. She'll be okay."

Abby nodded. "Thanks for letting me stay here. Sorry we kept you awake."

"Zoe's excited to have a friend sleeping over." Ann squeezed her shoulder. "It's bound to happen at your age." She chuckled. "Though I'd appreciate it if you two didn't make a habit of staying up all night talking."

"We won't." Abby picked at the sofa cushion by her knee.

"It's about time I got started on dinner. Would you be a dear and go fetch Zoe and Cody from the lake?"

"Okay." Abby sat still for a little while longer before dragging herself to her feet.

She didn't bother going back up to the loft for her moccasins, and headed outside. Avoiding the gravel road by way of a narrow strip of dirt and grass beside it, she walked around the bend, following the trail deeper into Nederland. She'd been to the lake only a few times, but remembered the way. Of course, in a town this small, it would almost take more effort to get lost than go where you wanted.

Near the center of town, she turned left and followed a strip of paved road for a while before heading off to the right and up a grassy hill. At the crest, she had a clear view of a too-blue manmade lake about sixty yards from end to end. Zoe, Isla, three other girls she hadn't met, and two boys lounged about in the grass near the shore next to their clothes, evidently drying off before getting dressed again. About nine boys continued to play in the water; four had shorts on.

Cassie sat on a bright green folding chair. Her oversized hat looked like it had been an umbrella in a former life, and though she held a book, she spent more time watching the kids in the water than reading. She kind of reminded Abby of Zoe grown up; they had the same shade of blonde hair and both had blue eyes. Of course, Abby couldn't look at her without thinking about the basement of that store. Still, she liked the woman. Cassie had been one of the friendlier people there, and if she hadn't fixed the radio, Tris and Zara never would've shown up in Amarillo.

Abby made her way down the gentle slope of the grass facing the lake, and stopped near Zoe. The girl squinted up at her and grinned.

"You changed your mind!" She leapt to her feet. "Come on. Let's go back in the water."

"Ann said it's time for dinner."

"Oh." Zoe looked disappointed but offered no protest as she grabbed her dress and pulled it on. Facing the water, she cupped her hands around her mouth and shouted, "Cody! Dinner!"

A brown-haired head off to one side in the lake rotated toward them. Cody stood out of the water and tugged a soaked pair of black jean shorts up a little. He trudged, dripping, onto the grass. For the briefest of instants, he smiled at Abby before returning to his usual glum self.

"Imma swim more!" yelled Isla. The seven-year-old sprang upright and ran back to the lake, trailed by a laughing Chinese girl closer to twelve.

The others who had been drying off in the grass gathered their clothes and dispersed back toward town.

Abby turned on her toes and walked up the hill.

Zoe raced to catch up and fell in step at her right, flicking bits of grass off her arms. "Still sad?"

"I'm not sad; I'm scared." Abby studied the ground.

"Of drones?" Zoe held a hand over her eyes and scrunched up her nose as she scanned the sky.

"Yeah. And them not coming back."

Zoe's cheer diminished for a few minutes. "I think they'll be okay… but you can stay with me if something bad happens."

Abby glanced at her, biting her lip to stop from shouting. The girl meant well, after all. "Thanks." She plucked a blade of grass from Zoe's cheek and flicked it.

"They kicked ass in Chicago," mumbled Cody. "I don't think where they went is gonna be worse than that."

Zoe's eyebrows climbed; she stared at her brother for a few seconds in mute surprise.

"Amarillo was pretty scary too. Infected chased us down the street." Abby glanced to her right at Cody, who averted his gaze as if afraid of being caught looking at her. "One got almost close enough to grab me, but Tris killed it."

Cody mumbled, "Wow. That had to be scary."

"It was." Abby slid in single-file behind Zoe as they stepped onto the narrow dirt path alongside the gravel road. "It's okay to have bad dreams. Even Kevin does, and he's old."

"Really?" asked Cody, behind her. "He's like… so tough."

"Infected scare everyone." Abby frowned. "Even old men who wanna kill little girls because they have a cold."

"Huh?" Cody moved up into the thicker grass so he could walk at her side. "Someone wanted to kill you?"

"Yeah. They were scared like little boys. Some of the men even cried when they thought no one could see them," said Abby.

Zoe raced in the front door of the house and headed right for the table. Cody looked at Abby for a while, gave a nod of thanks, and went inside. He hurried down the hall to his room, likely to change into something dry.

Abby plodded over to the table and sat facing Zoe. Ann chased the girls into helping out with the last bits of table setting. She trusted Abby with a knife to cut up an onion while Zoe scooped taco meat and beans onto plates. It almost didn't smell like ground dust hopper.

Eventually, Bill and Pete showed up, and Cody emerged from the back in a white shirt and khaki shorts with oversized leg pockets. Ann and Bill chatted about militia things as well as the town's primary farm. The woman kept referring to it as the 'garden,' but as far as Abby thought, anything that big ought to be called a farm.

After dinner, Pete and Bill approached Cody with the idea of going to the range and practicing shooting. His near-instant "okay" and move to follow them left the men without words until they'd made it out onto the street. Abby and Zoe washed the dishes while Ann set to doing some kind of paperwork at the kitchen table.

"Tracking seeds and production for the garden," said Ann, catching Abby staring at the logbook. "Trying to work out how much to plant based on how many people we've got and how fast we're going through food."

"Oh."

With the last of the dishes dried and put away, Zoe took Abby by the hand and led her back to the loft bedroom. She broke out a bunch of old dolls in much newer handmade clothes. The too-skinny plastic women had stains and scuffs from fifty or sixty years of being unwanted trash, but Zoe didn't seem to care. Abby felt a little too old to play with dolls. Hell, she'd lost interest in them by Zoe's age, but she went along with it.

After a while, Zoe ran off to the bathroom, leaving Abby alone with the dolls. She knelt in the middle of the room, smirking at them as well as the powder blue walls. Aside from the toys and a lone small nightie hanging from a nail by where the angled ceiling got low enough to reach, the loft room looked like an elderly woman had decorated it. She fixated on a few bullet holes by the window, as well as a handful of spent casings on a cushioned cabinet in front of it that resembled a cross between a bench and a bookshelf.

Abby knee-walked over to the shelf and plucked one of the brass casings out of a well in a battered red cushion. Splinters in the fabric suggested the holes in the wall as recent. The window looked out over a small field populated with boulders and brown grass, as well as a few tiny trees no bigger around than a man's arm. One of the larger rocks had a red-brown stain on it.

"That's my spot," said Zoe, sounding informational. "It's where I guard from."

Abby held up the casing. "You?"

"Uh huh." She grinned. "Ann don't like it, but Bill thinks I'm a good shot."

"Y-you've shot people?" Abby let the casing drop from her fingers, frozen in shock.

Zoe nodded, making her blonde hair bounce. "Yep, but I don't kill 'em. I hit 'em in the leg." She poked Abby in the thigh. Inspiration bloomed in her expression. "Idea!"

Abby stood as Zoe darted to a pair of louvered closet doors a few steps to the right of the window. The doors looked strange when they opened, with different heights and angled tops to match the lay of the roof.

Zoe pulled out a squarish olive-drab box with rubber caps on both ends, a little bigger than a thick book. A black lanyard swayed from it as she handed it to Abby. "Here."

She took the bizarre object, which weighed more than she expected. "What is this?"

"Noculars." Zoe leaned into the closet again. "Lets you see far." She took a step back and pulled a black nylon strap over her shoulder, with four rectangular pouches about the size of bricks along its length. It hung down to her calves, seeming heavy.

Abby gasped when Zoe ducked back into the closet and emerged holding a military rifle that had a magazine in it. The nine-year-old made a deliberate show of checking the safety before slinging the weapon over her other shoulder. The butt almost touched the floor.

"That's a gun."

"Duh," said Zoe. "Bad words or 'please don't hurt me' don't work on raiders."

"You're gonna get in trouble." Abby blinked. "Your dad lets you have a gun?"

"Yeah, but I'm only s'posed ta touch it if we're in danger."

Abby stared at her, hands on her hips.

Zoe put on serious-face. "We *are* in danger. C'mon." She headed to the window on the other side of the loft room, by the foot end of the bed. "You wanna rifle too? We can get one from Bill's room."

"Uhh… no. My dad only taught me how to use a little gun."

Zoe scrunched her nose. "Okay. Bill can teach you later. C'mon."

The little one shoved the window open and climbed out, bandolier rattling.

That's more bullets! "Uhh, where are you going?" Abby crept up to the window.

Zoe padded up a narrow section of inclined roof, heading left, and disappeared over the top. Reluctantly, Abby hung the 'noculars' around her neck on the lanyard and climbed out. *We're both going to get in so much trouble.*

"Zoe? Come back inside. We shouldn't be out here."

"Come on," yelled Zoe from up above.

Clinging to the siding at her left, Abby walked heel-to-toe over the sun-heated shingles. After ten steps, the wall became shallow enough to see over. Zoe perched on the flat part over the middle of the house, a space about as big around as the living room with a slight downward angle toward the front driveway. It didn't look like enough of an incline to be frightening, at least no more frightening than being on the roof of a two-story building.

Zoe set the bandolier of ammo down and flipped open the tops of all four pouches. Each held three magazines identical to the one in her rifle, all packed with bullets. As Abby nervously pulled herself up and over the ledge onto the rooftop, Zoe removed the loaded magazine from the rifle and counted bullets.

"… fifteen, sixteen… seventeen." She put it back in. "Eighteen shots."

"Eighteen?" Abby crawled over to her, too terrified to stand up.

"There's one inside already." Zoe replaced the magazine and smacked the bottom a few times.

"What are we doing up here? We need to go back inside before we get caught."

Zoe pointed at the roof next to her. "Sit."

Abby shifted from crawling to sitting. Zoe grabbed the 'noculars' and pulled off the rubber things on both ends, which dangled on little elastic cords.

"Look through it at the sky. Watch for drones. You look that way." Zoe pointed and scooted around to face the opposite direction. "I'll watch this way." She set her feet flat on the roof and balanced the rifle over her right knee before peering into a small scope.

"Are you sure we're not going to get yelled at?" Abby raised the 'noculars' and saw only a blur that hurt to look at. She cringed away, face scrunched. "How do they work? I can't see anything."

"You got 'em backwards," said Zoe. "Look in the side wif the rubber eye holes."

Abby flipped them over and held them up again. She recognized a distant treetop, almost. "Better, but still blurry."

"Wheel on top."

She felt around until her finger met a plastic wheel. Spinning it changed the image, and after a bit of back and forth, she zoomed in on the lake. Cassie appeared to be chasing the boys out of the water and sending them home for the night. Abby panned back and forth, watching people in town for a few minutes before Zoe poked her.

"Watch the sky. We're on drone patrol."

"Oh." Abby set her elbows on her knees to absorb some of the weight of the 'noculars,' and stared into the endless blue of the west.

"You ever see one?" Zoe broke the silence about fifteen minutes later.

"No, but I know it doesn't look at all like a bird."

Zoe shifted a little left, using her scope to scan the sky. "Does it look like a car?"

"I guess. Maybe a small car." She avoided pointing the noculars anywhere near the fading sun, and gazed at the clouds sweeping by as she moved. A speck of black caught her eye and almost stopped her heart, but before she could make a sound, it flapped wings. She exhaled. *Just a bird.*

"Clear."

"Huh?" Abby turned away from the noculars to stare at Zoe.

"I said 'clear.' That means I don't see anything dangerous."

"Oh."

Zoe lowered the rifle and looked at her like a tiny version of a militia soldier. "How's your sector?"

Abby peered back through the noculars at empty sky. "Uhh, clear. How long are you going to want to stay up here?"

"'Til it's dark an' we can't see."

How does she go from playing with dolls to sitting on a roof with a real gun? Abby grimaced at the thought of a girl younger than her with an assault rifle. *Tris wouldn't let me have one. I'm only eleven.* Emma bugged Kevin for certain. That girl was older... thirteen as far as Abby could remember. She didn't act like it though. She might've been small and 'cute,' but she carried herself like an adult.

Abby sighed. *This is boring.* She debated dragging Zoe inside, but for one thing, didn't want to wrestle with an armed child, and for another, the tiny twinge of worry that the bad people would try to repeat Amarillo here wouldn't let her get up.

Again, she raised the noculars and swept the sky. Back and forth over clouds and ever-darkening blue. Off to the right, boys traded shouts of 'coming' with mothers, fathers, and caretakers calling them by name. She twisted left for the umpteenth time, and a smear of something dark against the blue shot past.

What? No... no... Abby frantically tried to find the spot where she thought she'd seen something, biting her lip in the hopes she'd imagined it. After a few seconds of furious back and forth, she caught sight of it again.

A black box.

With little wings and round fan shrouds.

A drone.

Pointing right at her.

"Zoe!" yelled Abby, almost in tears. "They're coming!"

11

ONLY THE GOOD DIE STUPID

Reno came and went without fanfare. As luck would have it, the final roadhouse they stopped at had another portable solar charger in the store, and no creepy singing triplet girls dressed up like antique dolls. Ninety coins proved impossible to pass up. Every so often, stupidity came in handy. Something like that would've been an easy three hundred at most Roadhouses, four or five if the proprietor felt like gouging. The price came with due caution however; perhaps the frazzled old man knew the thing would blow up. Tris checked it out and gave it the thumbs-up. The proprietor seemed amused that a woman's opinion on technology mattered to him, but neither of them bothered to make issue of it. Too tired, too much of a hurry, and not worth the bother.

The closer they got to California, the more on edge Tris became. A heavy fog clung to the road, flanked by dark brown rocks covered in a scattering of green. Somehow, the metal railings on either side remained more red than ruined. For as much as he'd heard tell of the Boatmen running wild in the area around the Golden Gate, the trip had thus far been quiet. The relative desolation of the land north of the bridge suggested that any organized pack of raiders, marauders, pirates, or whatever they considered themselves, would've stuck to built-up areas to the south.

Of course, San Francisco had been a major city before the war. He'd heard they'd outlawed cars about a decade before everything went to hell, after having set up a network of electronic trams. He couldn't recall ever meeting a driver who'd been anywhere near the area. Fear of Infected plus fear of the Enclave on top of all the rumors of how wild and vicious the Boatmen were had likely kept all but the most desperate away.

Maybe they're spooked about Infected too and live in tents around here?

He eyed the area on either side of the road along the approach to the bridge. The fastest map plot to Redwood City came straight down Route 101 over the bridge... of course he *could* go around, but that would add a day and change. If his luck held out, the bridge would have survived the war and half a century of neglect after the fact. Not like it had to put up with much traffic anymore.

Tris stirred in the passenger seat and sat up. At the unmistakable sight of the Golden Gate's red-painted superstructure emerging from the fog, she drew a hissing breath through her teeth and went from groggy to high-alert in seconds. She'd splurged on a loose-fitting short dress in a blindingly ugly green/brown/purple flower pattern when he'd picked up the extra portable charger. Made for a more comfortable ride, or so she said.

She pulled it off, wadded it up, and tossed it into the back seat before wriggling into her jeans, T-shirt and shoes.

"Good morning, sunshine." Kevin smiled. "We're here at the mouth of Hell."

"It doesn't look as bad as I expected." She yawned.

"Oh, we haven't gone far enough. Let's hope I don't drive into a giant hole and go swimming."

Tris froze, staring at him. "Take the bridge slow."

He eased back to about forty MPH soon after he reached the bridge proper. Kevin had gone over bridges in the past, but none this long. As soon as the sway of the suspension reached his awareness, he crept up to sixty, eager to find solid ground again. The road surface appeared to be intact, though barricades of old trucks and cars flipped on their sides riddled it. Few showed signs of damage from bullet strikes, and all looked as though they'd been set up for at least a few years. Based on the arrangement, his mind conjured images of people on the north side fending off swarming masses of Infected approaching from the south.

"I wouldn't want to have been the poor bastard they chased."

"What?" Tris jumped as if she'd been daydreaming.

He gestured at the barricades, which had forced him to slow the car to an almost human running pace to weave among them. Small grey blocks like a huge version of a child's building toy lined up in an attempt to differentiate northbound from southbound traffic lanes, but so many of them were either missing or scattered to the side, it didn't really matter which of the six lanes he used to navigate. "Looks like they were fighting off swarms of Infected here. These are shooting positions, but there's almost no damage from incoming fire. Only thing I can think of is people trying to hold off a huge mass of Infected."

She shivered. "Yeah…there had to be so many people here. The Enclave waited for survivors to start collecting in major cities before they set the Virus loose."

Once he cleared the last of the barricades, at about a third the way across, he accelerated hard and shot over the rest of the bridge doing 135. The sooner he got off swaying road, the happier he'd be. Perhaps he'd find a path home that would avoid the thing altogether. Chances are, the Challenger had been the first wheels to touch it in decades. He envisioned the disturbance of the vehicle's weight causing bolts to rust in seconds and fall. Perhaps it would collapse out from under them on the return trip.

Yeah, that would be my luck. Survive the Enclave only to fall into the goddamned ocean. Enclave. Yeah right. We're going to find jack shit and I'm going to deal with her sobbing the whole way back. He reached over and held her hand. *Better that than losing her.*

"What?" She looked at him.

"Can't I just hold your hand?"

She smiled. "Yes, but the look on your face says there's more."

"Oh, we're like twenty miles from the heart of the Enclave. What would I have to be worried about?"

She squeezed his fingers. "Only a phone call, right? Maybe it's nothing."

"Yeah."

The area at the south end of the bridge contained a massive lot of derelict cars with the twisted remnants of former multi-level parking towers on either side. Judging from the amount of concrete debris, the towers had to have been six or seven stories tall—or bigger. Both had collapsed toward the west, suggesting an airburst detonation somewhere further inland. The city beyond didn't look like it had taken a direct hit. Damaged buildings and smashed e-tram tubes proved it had experienced at least some manner of shockwave and heat, but San Francisco hadn't suffered the same fate as central Dallas… blasted flat to desert sand. Many of the taller skyscrapers looked like standing ivy gardens, dense wrappings of plant matter threaded in and around all the glassless windows and cracks.

He drove as southerly as possible, making the occasional detour around streets blocked off by collapsed buildings. His third alternate route dead-ended at a zigzag of e-tram cars that had fallen from an overhead tube like the entrails of some giant spilled into the road. Every other car lay upside down, wedged between its fellows. He backed up to the start of the block and went farther east.

His plan called for following Route 280 down to Redwood City, or at least the northwestern most part of it. Hopefully, the waypoint Tris had set based on the coordinates Terminal9 gave them would kick in before they came within sight of the Enclave.

"Hey, you know... maybe we should stash the car and go on foot so they don't spot us from the air?"

Tris shrugged. "With as many Infected as are supposed to be here... I didn't think you'd want to risk being cornered."

His grip caused the leather-clad steering wheel to creak. "Thanks. How close can we get before they see us coming?"

"No idea. Zara might know that, but I forgot her number."

"Heh. Maybe we should've asked that before we rushed off."

She smiled at the dashboard. "Yeah. I'm not thinking things through. So, umm. I suppose I should apologize in advance for all the stuff I'm going to call you when you tie me up in the trunk."

Kevin laughed. "You wanna turn around?"

"Yes, but we're minutes from finding out what, if anything, this is going to lead to. That feeling inside me is getting stronger. Half of me knows I'm doing the right thing and feels confident, and part of me is screaming to go home."

"Yeah, that makes two of us." He looked at her, grinned, and winked. "Except the part about me having a confident half."

She closed her eyes, let out a long, deliberate sigh, and reopened them. "I'm trying to listen to the rational part of my—*Look out!*"

Kevin whipped his head about to face forward. A little less than a block ahead of them, a small child in dingy rags darted out of a side street, long brown hair trailing after. He stomped on the brakes, chirping the tires as the Challenger went from fifty to a standstill in a sliding skid. The child whirled to face back the way he or she had come from, raised a silvery handgun, and fired twice before zipping forward, clambering up and over a wrecked car and hiding behind it amid a hail of bullets sparking off the metal.

For a fraction of a second, the kid locked eyes with Kevin. Panting, back pressed against the vehicle, the child stared open-mouthed at the car as if superheroes had come out of the sky to help. In that near-frozen moment, with a better look at the child's face, Kevin decided him a boy.

"Aww shit." Kevin flicked the car into park and shoved his door open, grabbing his Enclave rifle from behind his seat as he slipped out to stand.

Tris took cover behind her door, her black AK47 leveled off at the corner.

The boy peered around the tail end of the wreck, raised his handgun, and lit off four rapid shots before bolting from cover. Sparks danced across the pavement behind him as he sprinted hard toward the Challenger.

Men's angry shouts echoed in the street behind him. Kevin aimed at the wall by the corner building, zooming in with the electronic scope. The first figure to emerge, a bare-chested guy in a black skirt with a white plastic mask painted into a skull, died within a quarter second of striding into view. Despite Tris' bullet blowing out the back of his head, Kevin fired into his chest, lacking the reaction time necessary to avoid wasting ammo on a moving corpse.

Two other men rounded the corner next, both in scrap armor made of thin metal plates and leather. Kevin clicked the trigger twice, putting four bullets into the chest of the one on the left while Tris sniped the third man in the forehead.

The clap of the boy's sneakers got louder, and a little body slammed into Kevin's side, clinging and shivering. Tiny lungs strained to process air. Kevin kept aiming at the street ahead, waiting for the sound of their shots to draw more trouble.

"I hope we didn't just fuck up," said Kevin.

"What?" Tris kept her rifle forward, but looked at him. "They were shooting at a little kid. They deserved it."

"You saved me." The boy wheezed, hooking his fingers in Kevin's belt to hold himself up.

Kevin gave Tris a 'keep an eye out' glance before crouching and brushing long, thick hair away from the child's face. Despite it hanging down near his belt, odds still leaned in favor of boy; however, his round face and large eyes held enough cute to make the point debatable. "What's your name?"

"Fox," said the kid.

His shirt consisted of dust hopper hide scraps stitched together into a larger piece with plenty of holes. Not that he'd have been old enough for breasts or visible chest hair; he looked about seven. Dark grey pants had a lot of dust, but otherwise seemed a recent score from a prewar clothing store. No wonder… a place like San Francisco, no one would dare go for scavenging. There had to be a gold mine here, if not for the looming threat of tens of thousands of Infected. The light brown coloration to his skin triggered Kevin's bad memories of Mexican 'orphans' who acted like kidnap victims to help their parents ambush the unwary. Of course, nothing about this kid felt like an act.

Shit. That name could be boy or girl. "Why were those guys shooting at you?"

"They…" Fox bowed his head, gasping for air. "They…" The hard-muscled little body clinging to him trembled. "Took my family." He coughed. "My mom and sister. They shot my dad." He sniffled, but seemed too terrified to cry. "They started tyin' me up, but I bit the guy on the nose and took a gun. *Please* help!"

Tris walked sideways around the car, keeping her AK trained on the alley. "Did you see where they went?"

"Yeah." The boy's eyes grew wider. "*Please* help me get them back."

Kevin gazed at the sky. "This is what got my dad killed."

Fox tilted his head. "The Boatmen killed your dad?"

"Nah. Trying to do the right thing did."

The boy's lower lip quivered.

"Hey." He patted the kid on the head. "I ain't saying no, just grumbling." The weight of Tris' stare boring into the side of his head lessened. "Okay, kid. Lead the way."

12

STOKING THE FLAMES

Fox pointed at the corner.

"Is your dad... uhh...?" Kevin looked off to the side.

"They took him... I don't think he's dead." Fox wiped at his nose.

Screw it. Little bugger will correct me if I'm wrong. He looked at Tris. "I dunno about bringin' a little boy into a gunfight. Takin' Abby with us on a ride was bad enough."

"I'll stay down. I gotta show you where they are." The kid bounced on his toes. "Please, before they hurt them!"

Tris nodded. "Show us."

Okay. He is a boy. Kevin looked around at the surrounding buildings, several two-inch thick clear plastic slabs (pieces of e-tram tube), the Challenger, and the three dead men. "How far is it?"

"Couple blocks." Fox stopped clinging to Kevin and backed up a few steps, pointing with his handgun at the street from where he'd emerged. "They have a fort."

"How many?" asked Tris.

Fox's eyes widened. "A lot."

A scream somewhere between girl and woman echoed in the distance. Fox started to run, but Kevin grabbed his arm.

"No! That's Hawk! They're hurting her!" Tears finally ran free. "My sister..."

Tris sprinted off toward where the boy had pointed.

"Stay behind me." Kevin ran after her with Fox at his heels.

She flowed up against the wall at the intersection like a specter of white, leaning into the stone building before whirling to point the AK around the corner. Kevin halted behind her.

"Barrier of metal pieces… looks like they took a welding torch to dumpsters. Hanging cages… seven or eight people, men and women. Big fenced-in area in the middle with razor wire. Two guys on the wall and the gate's still open. They're watching this way, probably wondering where those three morons went."

Kevin glanced down at the dead bodies. All three had tattoos of coins on their eyelids so it looked like pennies covered their eyes when they closed them. "Huh. Guess these are Boatmen. I was expecting worse. They look like primitives."

"Never underestimate the power of stupid people in large numbers," said Tris.

Kevin raised an eyebrow. "Think we can sneak in?"

She shook her head. "Doubt it. Besides, I'd rather pull the fight to us so the people they're holding captive don't get shot in the crossfire."

"You wanna yell like you're scared, see if they come running?" Kevin winked at Tris before pushing Fox against the wall. "And you… You stay here until the shooting stops."

A teenaged girl's voice shrieked, "Get off me!" in the distance.

Fox sniffled. "Okay. Please hurry."

"I'd rather just shoot them." She teased her fingertip at the trigger. "That girl screamed, who knows what the hell is going on in there. We don't have time."

"Crossing," whispered Kevin. "Cover me."

Tris fired, shifted aim, and fired again in under a second. "Wall's clear."

He ran across the street and took up a position opposite her, rifle aimed around the corner. The 'fort' Fox had mentioned sat a few blocks down, not an easy shot with iron sights. A wall made out of a patchwork quilt of metal plates blocked off the whole street by a four-way intersection with a crude medieval style gate in the center. Beyond it stood a tangle of steel I-beams, narrow walkways, and hanging cages. Through the Enclave scope, he did a quick scan for hostiles. Four or five people in cages stared at the ground inside the wall, probably at the two men Tris killed. Two other cages either contained corpses, or people beyond caring.

Tris fired again. A blue helmet bounced into the air above the gate. "Here they come."

Muzzle flash burst from an elevated balcony inside the compound. Powdered beige stone sprayed off the wall about a foot over Tris' head. The gate doors swung apart with an ear-splitting screech of rusting metal and clattering chain, leaving an opening wide enough for two cars abreast. Boatmen in various outfits from nothing more than a yellow hard hat held over a crotch on leather straps to full-body metal armor came storming out onto the street. Tiny *snaps*, deafening *booms*, and midrange *bangs* rang off walls from an array of different guns. Fox squatted, back pressed to the building at Tris' side, clutching the pistol in both hands.

Kevin estimated between twenty and thirty Boatmen rushed toward them, a quarter or so carried improvised clubs, axes, or swords while the rest brandished firearms. A handful had blue vests with SFPD in white letters across the chest.

This rifle is from the Enclave; that armor came from before the war... Kevin's attention went straight to the largest figure in the middle of the pack, a behemoth in armor that looked like a cross between football pads and scrap metal. He carried a weapon resembling a massive double-barreled pump shotgun, and sprinted hard, suggesting he *really* couldn't wait to get close enough to use it.

Uhh, fuck that. Kevin triggered three times, perforating the giant with six rounds. The man went from sprinting to sliding on his face in an instant. Kevin shifted and fired again at the left-most armored figure. Though not much happened visually, the Boatman collapsed in a heap.

Tris let off three shots and blurred away from the corner. Less than a full second after her image solidified against the wall, the stone at head level exploded in a spray of dust from a good portion of the charging gang all firing at her position.

Kevin resisted the temptation to switch to fully automatic and hose the street. He aimed, fired, shifted, fired, shifted, fired, as fast as he could put crosshairs over bodies. While he tried to focus on guys pointing weapons in his direction, he didn't waste much time being choosy or going for head shots. The Enclave rifle pierced the prewar Kevlar like papier-mâché. A few held up riot shields, but his high-tech bullets laughed at those too.

Some of the Boatmen got the hint and leapt for cover behind buildings.

Tris spun around the corner in a low squat; her AK let off what sounded like a chatter of automatic fire, but seven heads exploded more or less at the same instant.

Kevin glanced at her, mouth open, frozen in momentary awe. *She is goddamned scary sometimes.*

The sharp *pop-pop-pop* of a nearby pistol startled him. He spared a half-second glance to the right. Fox had stepped away from the wall, two-handing his weapon straight up. A dead woman in piecemeal armor and a skirt made of studded leather panels fell from a second story window. A crude katana bounced out of her hand as she struck the pavement. She lay still on the ground; her bug-eyed gas mask, painted with an exaggerated grin, stared at him. Fox shot her again in the back.

Kevin looked up. His building had no gaping holes on that side, and no one watched him from the roof. As a ripple of fire chased Tris around her corner again, he popped out and shot two guys in matching white hockey masks with bright pink plumes.

A *pop* came from his left at the same time a dull, throbbing pain jabbed into his left side. An answering *pop* sounded from near Tris, and a bullet mushed into the armored jacket by his right shoulder. The boy's attempt to help wound up hitting him instead of the man shooting at him. Kevin grunted and spun to the left, letting gravity take him down. An emaciated man in white paint and a skirt made of shredded tire rubber clicked a handgun at him, but it didn't go off.

Enraged, the ghoulish figure threw the gun aside in disgust and drew a pair of machetes off his back. Kevin fired from the ground, nailing the guy in the right hip. Before the tiny silver confetti squares from his caseless ammunition fluttered to the ground, Tris' AK barked and the man's chest caved in from a lone bullet striking him in the sternum. Gurgling, the machete-wielding lunatic took two steps away as if he'd merely changed his mind about fighting and decided to go for a walk.

And fell on his face.

Fox scampered out into the street to grab a submachinegun off one of the dead guys who had initially chased him. Bullets pinged off the paving behind him as he dashed back around the building, holding it out to Tris. She took it, reached around the wall, and sprayed full auto at a spot where three Boatmen clustered behind a concrete porch.

Kevin cringed. *That was an expensive waste of ammo.*

Using the distraction of the gangers flinching at her barrage, Kevin popped up and picked off two. Tris tossed the micro-Uzi over her shoulder and two-handed the AK. Her lips moved, but whatever she said didn't make it across the street.

Fox nodded and took off at a sprint for the Challenger.

Kevin flicked the mushroomed bullet off his arm and winced at the forming bruise. Both hits felt similar, so he figured the boy had a 9mm as well as white-paint-man. Being able to identify bullet type by how much it hurt striking his armor made him shake his head. *I've gotten shot too goddamned much.* He swiveled and fired at a hint of motion along the opposite wall. Another Boatman in a blue flannel shirt and green camo pants staggered into the road, clutching a geyser of blood spouting from where his neck met his shoulder. Kevin finished him off with a double-tap to the chest. His rifle emitted an electronic chirp that sounded like a warning.

At the lower right corner of the scope view, 06 flashed in yellow. *Damn. Oh well. Was nice while it lasted. Not like I'm going to go shopping for ammo at the Enc—* He laughed. "Maybe I will."

At the rapid clap of tiny sneakers striking the road, Kevin looked to the right. Fox raced from the car with an AK magazine in his left hand. He zoomed up to Tris and handed it over. She reloaded while the boy ran the empty back to the car. After two minutes of silent calm, Tris stepped onto the road, rifle raised, and started a slow walk toward the gate.

Kevin moved out from behind cover, cringing at each breath. At the sight of blood on Tris' shirt, he ran over to her. "You're hit!"

"Graze. Already closed." She jumped and aimed, but didn't shoot the grey cat that raced out from behind a porch.

"I need me some nanites," muttered Kevin.

A moan from the left caused Tris to swivel and put another bullet into a fallen Boatman. He went still. Kevin pulled the Enclave rifle over his shoulder and stooped to grab an AK from a dead man. On one knee, he did a quick check of the magazine, which had about two-thirds left of a thirty round capacity.

Better than six.

"We're lucky these guys are on the lower end of the brains scale," muttered Tris. "Think they *all* came charging?"

A young dark-skinned woman with frizzy hair, no shirt, and torn jeans, stood inside the nearest hanging cage. She reached an arm through slats of metal that reminded him of leaf springs, and screamed, "Hey! Get us outta here!"

"Probably." Kevin waved the AK as a pointer toward the cage. "Doubt they'd scream for help if they had guns pointed at them."

"Or she's been told to lure us in." Tris pointed her AK off to the side in one hand and shot another moaning body while barely glancing at him.

The slow crunch of tires on grit made Kevin look back at the Challenger coming around the corner not much faster than a walking pace. Fox barely managed to peer over the console, but did a serviceable job of navigating the turn.

"God dammit," muttered Kevin. "He's being helpful."

Tris glanced over her shoulder. "Shit. Hope he doesn't find the button for the machine guns."

"Hang on." Kevin jogged away from the camp toward the approaching car.

Fox dropped out of sight, and the Challenger lurched to a halt. When Kevin reached the door, the boy still had both feet planted on the brake.

"Thanks, kid." He reached in and shut down the drive system. As soon as the boy crawled out the window, Kevin punched in the security code. The windows closed on their own, and the car chirped. "Come on."

Tris peered into the gate. "Are there any Boatmen left hiding in there?"

"I-I don't think so," yelled the topless woman.

Kevin jogged up behind Tris. "Guess we go in careful."

She nodded.

A young sounding voice scream-grunted in frustration amid the clatter of metal on metal.

"Hawk!" yelled Fox.

"Charlie?" shouted a female voice, high up. Another hanging cage creaked as a late-thirties woman with red hair forced herself upright. Blood dribbled from her nose onto a new-looking white tank top; she appeared to be bound hand and foot with rope.

"Mom!" yelled Fox, pointing. "That's my mom!" He darted forward until Kevin caught him with an arm around the middle and hauled him off his feet. "Mom! Where's Dad?"

"Over there," yelled the woman, moving her head in an attempt to point. "Kwan?"

A man in one of the other cages moaned.

Kevin held on to the struggling boy until he went still. "There could be more of them hiding in there. Don't run in."

Fox looked furious, but nodded.

After setting the boy down behind him, Kevin raised his AK and glanced up at the creaking of rusty chains. The center of the encampment, which occupied an intersection of two four-lane streets, contained an arena-like enclosure rimmed with concertina wire. An assortment of melee weapons including knives, hammers, axes, all the way up to giant swords and one chainsaw littered the edges by the fence. Eighteen hanging cages dangled from steel I-beams welded into a maze of rickety walkways and cubbyholes among sniper nests made from steel plates.

Tris pointed her AK at one of the nests. "I see you up there. Come out or I'll shoot you right through the wall."

"I can't," yelled a boy. Hands gripped the top of the enclosure where she pointed. "I'm chained to the wall."

"He's the feeder," said the young black woman. "They make him crawl around up here an' bring us food. Come on and get us out."

Chain rattled from a ground-level structure near the back, a building made from the rear end of a flipped garbage truck with the hydraulic crusher removed. A girl inside grunted and growled.

"They all gone," yelled the topless teen.

"Hawk!" Fox sprinted past Kevin, heading for the truck.

He ran after the boy, colliding with him when the child skidded to a halt at the 'door'—a flap of heavy plastic hanging from rope hinges.

An Asian girl in her middle teens struggled at a chain padlocked around her neck, tethering her to a ring in the wall by a mattress so foul shitting on it would've been an improvement. Her clingy pink T-shirt covered to the base of her ribs, but below that, she didn't have anything on. A lump of denim, jeans, lay out of her reach to the left, thrown against the wall on top of brown work boots that looked factory new. Somewhat-clean smears in the floor suggested she'd spent a moment or two trying to reach them with her toes. At the *crunch* of Kevin's boot, she whirled, blushed scarlet, and let go of the chain to cover her crotch while staring at him. Kevin averted his gaze to the left.

Fox ran over and hugged the—possibly Korean—girl. She squatted and wrapped her arms around him, using the boy as cover to hide her lack of pants.

"That's your brother?" Kevin tried not to sound surprised or doubting. Post-war families often formed from people who happened to find each other. Hell, neither he nor Tris had the least bit of Hispanic in them and they called Abby their kid. Her embarrassment suggested origin within a larger settlement closer to prewar society. That, and her mostly-clean clothing. Then again, in San Francisco with so many infected, maybe they'd found a store no one had had the balls to scavenge yet. But a feral or tribal girl wouldn't be embarrassed.

He walked to the left, the garbage truck *booming* with his footsteps, grabbed the discarded jeans, and held them out to her without looking.

TRIS EYED AN EIGHT-INCH WIDE WOODEN BOARD LEADING UP INTO THE I-beam structure. The treacherous pathway spanned three distinct 'floors,' the topmost of which thankfully had only empty cages. Adoring her agility enhancements, she ran up the beam headed for the metal-walled spot that looked like a perfect place for a sentry to take cover. Along the way, she pointed the rifle at a few other 'nests,' but none had anyone in them. She turned right at the second story and hurried past the cage with the dark-skinned topless girl in it, heading for the 'sniper nest' where the boy claimed to be unable to get up.

"Hey, where you goin?"

"Kid," said Tris, not slowing down.

Still not entirely trusting the situation, she led with her rifle around the corrugated steel wall, but lowered it as soon as she made eye contact with a scrawny pale-skinned boy of about twelve. A padlock held a crisscross of chain around his bare chest like a harness. Only a few inches spanned from the middle of his back to the wall, secured with another lock. A chain collar ringed his neck, but didn't connect to anything. Two buckets sat at his left: one held a dried coating of nasty-looking stew as well as a ladle, the other contained an inch or so of urine. Aside from the chain, he wore a battered pair of dark brown shorts that ended in frayed tatters halfway down his thighs, covered in all manner of stains.

A broad purplish bruise on his left cheek paralyzed Tris for a few seconds of pure heartbreak. She reached out to take his hand.

He cowered, crossing his arms in front of his face.

"Fucking animals," muttered Tris. *This is what everyone in the Enclave thinks people are like out here. This poor kid...* "It's okay. Don't be afraid of me. I'm gonna let you out okay? The men who did this to you are all dead."

The boy gawked at her. "R-really? You're not gonna kill me?"

"Are you a Boatman?"

"No. They make me take food to the gladiators."

"Gladiators?" She blinked.

"The people." He pointed at the cages. "They make them fight in the pit. Someone wins ten times, they get to be a Boatman. "I'm not old enough, so I gotta feed them 'cause the Boatmen are 'fraid of fallin' off."

Tris grasped the padlock at the middle of his chest. *Oh. Only a Master lock.* "Hang on. I'll have you out in a few seconds." She pulled two tools from her shoe sole. "Do me a favor, kid. Hold it up?"

The boy grabbed the lock and pointed the keyhole end at her. "You're really pretty. Like a angel."

"Thanks." She fiddled with the pick for about twenty seconds before the lock snapped open. As she started to unwind the X, it became clear that some of the chain links adhered to his skin. "This might hurt a little."

"Don't care. I wanna get outta here."

He held onto her shoulders, valiantly stifling the urge to yell in pain as four or five chain links peeled away scabs. When the last of the metal fell to the floor, he leaned forward and cried into her shoulder.

Tris picked him up, carried him to the ground, and held him for a moment longer. "I need to let the others out, okay?"

He let go. "Okay."

She started to head up the ramp, but whirled back, remembering the chain around his neck. After picking the lock at his throat, she hurled it and the chain as hard as she could in a random direction with no people in the way. *Damned animals. I wish I could kill them all over again.*

"Come on, girl," said the topless one. "You like girls? I'll do whatever you want if you get me out next."

Pass. Tris looked up. *I don't even want to think what these people did to her.* "I'm working on it."

KEVIN WALKED ACROSS THE GARBAGE TRUCK TURNED BEDROOM HOLDING the jeans out to the girl while looking the other way.

"My sister, Hawk," said Fox. "Mom called me Charlie at first, but when she married Dad, I changed it."

"Who are you?" asked the girl in a wavering voice as she took the jeans.

Kevin turned his back on her and folded his arms. "This little guy came up to us looking for help. Couldn't say no to that face." He chuckled. "Bunch of shitheads were trying to shoot him. We put 'em down."

"Thanks. You the ones who started shooting at these fuckers?" The girl hurried into her clothes, the leash around her neck jangling. "I was about two seconds from… yeah." She scowled, a mixture of angry and imminent vomit in her expression. "If you hadn't attacked right when you did…"

"Where's Dad?" asked Fox.

At the sound of a zipper closing, Kevin looked at her. Aside from red marks on her neck, she didn't have any visible injuries.

"They put him in one of the cages. He's… still alive." Hawk shivered. "Hey can you get this damn chain off me?"

"Not without a bullet involved. Hang on. My…" He smiled. "Wife can get the lock."

Fox fetched the boots for his sister. Kevin walked to the end of the truck and peered out at the compound. A filthy, skinny blond boy stood at the bottom of the plank walkway leading up into the structure of I-beams, shivering. An X of bruise in the pattern of chain wrapped around his chest and another circled his throat. Slow trickles of blood crawled down his body from two or three red spots near his shoulders.

Up in the superstructure, Tris appeared to be attacking the padlock trapping Fox's mother in a cylindrical cage made out of haphazardly welded slats of metal. From the width and gauge, he assumed leaf springs from a tractor-trailer. The black girl with no shirt rattled the door of her enclosure and grumbled, clearly impatient. Two other cages held unmoving lumps, which he figured to be dead men, likely having succumbed to injuries suffered during 'sport' fights, or perhaps starvation.

"This is going to take all damn day." He glanced over his shoulder at the padlock holding Hawk's leash to the wall, and considered shooting it out, but didn't want to risk a ricochet catching the kid or his sister. "Be right back. Going key hunting."

Kevin spent a few minutes running from corpse to corpse out in the street, rummaging around for keys. As soon as he found the giant musclebound oaf with two shotguns taped together, he assumed him the boatman's chief. Sure enough, the man had a wad of master lock keys in his left pocket, something on the order of thirty or so.

He stared at the bundle. "Okay, maybe this isn't going to be faster."

⸻ ⸙ ⸻ ⸙ ⸻ ⸙ ⸻ · ⸙ ⸻ ⸙ ⸻

"HOLY SHIT, ARE YOU REALLY HERE?" ASKED A PALE WOMAN WITH BRIGHT red hair. She wriggled around to face Tris, making the entire cage sway back and forth. Her otherwise clean tank top had a grimy handprint over her left breast next to a red mark from blood dripping out of her nose. Her BDU pants looked intact, and also in good condition. Clean bare feet suggested these thugs had only recently taken her shoes.

Tris stared for a second, thinking of Katie. "Hey, did you have a daughter with red hair?"

"No... just Charlie, uhh, Fox. I know... I know... My last husband's name was Rodrigo Cortez. I'm Freya. Never had a baby girl. Why?"

Tris pulled a knife off her belt and sawed the rope binding the woman's wrists behind her back. "Here." She passed the blade to her through the bars. "You kinda look a bit like this kid we found. Haven't seen a lot of people with hair that red."

"Thanks. Haven't seen a lot of people with hair that white." The woman cut her legs free while Tris went to work on the padlock. Stench wafting over from the next cage left no doubt the occupant had died... probably days or weeks ago.

I'm in Hell. This is where humanity goes for what it did to itself. "Your son's fine. Scared, but fine."

"You found him?" Freya blinked. "Oh, thank you... This expedition was such a bad idea."

"He found us." She twisted her whole body to the left as if it somehow helped the lock yield to her will. "Couple of these cretins were shooting at him. He spotted our car and came running right to us. We didn't stop to ask. Saw people shooting at a little boy, so we killed them."

"Oh, no." Freya covered her mouth. "Is he hurt?"

"No. Those guys were pretty bad shots and your son's fast." She pulled the lock away once it opened. "Are *you* hurt?"

"Just bruises. Did you see one with a white mask and pink fur on his head?"

"Two actually." Tris stood and pulled the cage door open with a rusty creak.

Freya held on to her for support stepping from the swaying cage to a solid plank. "Asshole took my boots."

"He's outside the gate in the road somewhere." Tris steadied her. "You okay to get down?"

"Yeah. Kwan's been shot." Freya pointed at a cage holding an Asian man who clutched a blood-soaked blue business shirt at his left bicep.

"Think he'd mind if I let that girl out before she screams herself hoarse?"

Freya crept past Tris, heading for the pathway leading to the ground. "Another minute or two won't matter."

⸻ ⸙ ⸻

WHEN KEVIN RETURNED TO THE CAMP, A RED-HAIRED WOMAN CAUGHT HIS eye, making her way down the rickety one-plank walkway, holding on to the structure around her for balance. Tris worked on the padlock trapping the topless girl. The boy remained standing where Tris had left him. He shied away from Kevin, looking down and cringing as if expecting to be hit.

The rattle of chain accompanied the determined grunts of a small child, amplified by the metal box of the garbage truck. Kevin jogged back to the 'bedroom.' Fox had one foot up on the wall and pulled for all he was worth in an effort to break his older sister free. Hawk stood there with an uneasy expression as if she dreaded the kind of disease she'd get if she touched anything.

Kevin held up the bundle of keys. The girl reached for them, so he tossed them to her and went back outside. The redhead jumped the last three feet to the ground and rushed over, hugged Kevin for a moment, and darted over to the giant garbage truck turned building.

"Mom!" shouted Fox, as he leapt into her arms.

"Mom…" Hawk fumbled with the keys, her hands shaking too much to insert even one in the padlock at her throat. She whined at the woman while shaking the bundle.

The redhead took the keyring and embraced her. "Your father's okay. He's alive. Breathe… slow."

Hawk sniffled.

"Are you hurt? Did they?"

"No…" Hawk shook her head. "They were gonna, but they dropped me and ran out when the shooting started."

The woman gave Kevin an adoring look of thanks. Fox clung to her as his mother tried key after key on his sister's leash.

Kevin wandered outside and glanced up at the four still-alive prisoners in cages: the man likely to be Hawk's biological father, the shirtless girl who he figured for about eighteen, and a man and woman with not-quite-as-dark skin. The man stared at Tris with rapt, though polite attention, as if trying to project his impatience telepathically while maintaining an outward smile. The woman wept while muttering in a language he couldn't follow. Her gestures were universal enough; she thanked something that didn't exist for sending Kevin and Tris here.

A rusty door creaked. The older teen almost knocked Tris over in her haste to leap out of her cage. She stopped long enough to catch Tris so she didn't fall before running down the wooden walkway, breasts bouncing with every step.

"Sorry," yelled the girl once she reached the ground. "Been stuck in that damn thing for weeks." She let off a wail of pain and bent forward, rubbing her legs. "Aww, shit that hurts. Haven't been able to move."

Eight people. I really hope none of them gets any ideas about my car.

"You okay?" asked Tris from above.

"Ngh. Been better," said a man. "Bullet went right through. They cauterized it. Least…" He gasped. "It's not bleeding anymore."

A loud grinding squeak of metal accompanied another cage opening. Tris helped a wounded Korean-looking man out and onto the walkway.

"Heh. You're stronger than you look." The man attempted to laugh, but wound up cringing.

"Get it off already!" screamed Hawk. "I can't breathe. It's getting tighter. It's choking me!"

"I'm trying. Calm down," said her mother.

The shirtless girl hobbled over to Kevin, grimacing at stiff muscles. "Hey…. Thanks. I owe you guys big. Man that was awesome watching you two kill all them shits."

"Uhh, yeah," muttered the blond boy. "Thought I was gonna die."

A look of sudden inspiration took the kid, and he ran to the far right corner of the camp, holding on to his tattered pants to keep them from falling. He halted next to a large green dumpster that had been modified into a cabinet with a welding-torch conversion of the front face to steel doors. A piercing squeal of metal echoed over the compound as he hauled the container open. After grabbing a grey plastic brick from a stack inside, he sat on the ground and tore it in half, causing a number of smaller silver packets to scatter about.

MRE? Kevin cocked his jaw, confused at Boatmen having new-looking military rations. *Poor little bastard damn sure needs to eat.* He gritted his teeth at the red marks on the boy's back in the recognizable shape of chain links. Fresh blood continued to seep down his back.

The shirtless girl ran over and grabbed an MRE as well. She bit the plastic open and sat near the boy to eat.

Fox came running out of the garbage truck, shouting, "Dad!"

Again, Kevin intercepted, catching the child with an arm across the chest. "Slow down, kid. Your dad's hurt." He carried the boy over and set him down by the limping man.

Fox grabbed on, sniffling. "Dad."

"Thanks, friend." The injured man offered his good hand. "I'm Kwan. You two showed up right on time."

"Actually"—Kevin gave him a 'do you mind?' look before peeling the man's blood-soaked dress shirt away from his bicep—"might've been better if we showed up a little earlier. Cut it a bit close with your daughter. How long have you been here?"

"Only a few minutes. Fox ran off as they were dragging us inside. The one in charge couldn't wait to get his hands on Hawk." He shuddered with rage. "Did he, uhh?"

"No. Sounded like a matter of a couple seconds though." Kevin cringed at the sight of a burned bullet hole. "You should head somewhere with a doc or something."

"I can't help that." Kwan grinned. "Anywhere I go, there's a doc."

Kevin raised his eyebrows. "You?"

"Yeah. As much as anyone can be." He grunted and tugged fabric away from the wound. "Small caliber round passed clean. I should be okay after we get back to the truck. Gonna hurt for a few weeks."

Kevin exhaled with relief. "You've got a truck?"

"Yeah. Old ambulance. Parked it a couple blocks back to keep it safe."

"That's good. I don't have a lot of room in my car, plus we're heading into Redwood City."

Kwan leaned back, both eyebrows up. "You don't really want to do that, do you? That's Enclave territory."

"Well... at the moment, I'm trying to find a... what was it? Central office? Telephone company." He thought about the bridge still drivable after fifty years. Could the Enclave be maintaining it so they could send their hovercraft out?

"Really?" Kwan scratched his head. "A phone office? Why?"

"Daddy!" yelled Hawk. Free of the leash, she sprinted out of the garbage truck and charged over. She seemed to sense his injury and slowed; rather than crash into him, she leaned into a gentle hug and burst into tears.

He wrapped his uninjured arm around her and let her cry on his shoulder while mumbling something in Korean. She shook her head indicating no, while whimpering back at him. Kwan gave Kevin the most grateful look he'd ever seen on a man.

The red-haired woman nodded thanks at Kevin before joining her family's embrace. Tris descended from the cage structure, helping the last two people down from the rickety walkway. Their battered clothes, a peach-colored dress on the woman and a worn orange T-shirt and pants made of more patches than fabric on the man, made them feel more like part of the world Kevin knew. Except for Fox's dust hopper hide shirt, the rest of his family seemed to have stepped out of a rip in time from before the war. He figured they'd raided a clothing store somewhere in San Francisco, its inventory intact due to fear of Infected.

The last couple to descend from the cages both bowed at Tris, then Kevin, while saying, "*Namaste*" in unison before thanking them profusely.

"It's kind of a long story." Kevin returned the bow before chuckling at Kwan. "Someone sent us a strange message saying contact me, and a phone number. The dude we got to translate it said he'd heard tell of a bit of the old grid still working out this way. Not really sure what kind of rabbit hole I'm about to jump down… all I have is a phone number."

"There's a phone place," said Fox. "I'll show you."

"Be right back." Tris jogged out the gate.

"I can't ask you to get yourselves in deeper shit over us." Kevin smiled at Fox. "What are you doing here anyway? Didn't think civilized people dared come anywhere near here."

"The Infected seemed to be dying off at a rapid rate," said Kwan. "We're from a settlement up near Point Reyes. We've been watching the area for a while. Six months ago, you couldn't see the street for all the infected shambling around. Decided to take a quick peek in hopes we might be able to find something. Equipment or survivors."

"We found a clothing store untouched, and went looking for more." Freya wiped at the handprint on her chest. "These bastards came after us. Ran us down before we could get back to the ambulance."

"Hey," whispered the topless girl.

Kevin looked to his right; she stood about two steps away, arms folded across her chest—in a gesture of impatience rather than trying to cover up. "Yeah?"

"You open one more lock?" The girl pointed at a sky blue cargo container that resembled a small tractor-trailer without wheels. Some manner of Asian writing ran along the side in white. "They keep shit in there. Maybe a shirt or something I can grab."

Kwan looked up from poking at his wound. "We have some clothes in our truck."

"Yeah, sure." Kevin hefted the AK. "Still got my lockpick out."

He followed her to about twenty feet from the shipping container and took aim at a larger, rounded padlock. Two bullets ripped it apart. He slung the rifle as the girl squatted to work the ruin of the lock away from the door and opened it.

"Aww, shit. No clothes." The girl scowled. "Just boxes."

Kevin pulled the left door wider and did a double take at what appeared to be some functioning computers and a small desk with one chair. One of the two flat-panel monitors displayed a split-screen view of four videos, all of which showed people fighting in the arena. Beyond it stood stacks of white plastiboard boxes. He crept in and pulled open the first one he reached. It held blue foam blocks, each packed with fifty 9mm bullets that looked like they'd been made only days ago. Shiny, clean brass without a single speck of tarnish.

"What the fuck?" whispered Kevin.

"Holy shit." Forgetting her lack of shirt, the girl ran by and pulled open another box. "More bullets." The next one she opened had factory-new looking M-16 style rifles. She took one. "Welcome to mama." She kissed it before looking at Kevin. "Which o' these bullets go wit' this one?"

Over the next few minutes, he found about four thousand rounds of 5.56mm, an equal amount of 9mm, and a box of handguns that looked pre-war but of no design he'd ever seen. They had no manufacturer markings on them, or any indication of what company made them. He pointed her at the 5.56 while examining one of the odd black pistols.

They're 9mm, but it's like they came right out of the factory. He scowled. *Enclave. They're making 'low-tech' weapons for these knuckle-draggers.*

"A-ha!" the girl pulled a blue 'SFPD' vest out of a more distant box and put it on. "Ain't perfect, but it'll do."

A wash of headlights passed over the door of the cargo box. He hurried out of the cargo box as Tris brought the Challenger to a stop a little ways inside the gate. She got out and headed toward Freya with a pair of combat boots.

"Tris," yelled Kevin.

When she looked, he waved her over.

She handed off the boots and jogged up to the cargo box. "What do—the hell is this?"

"I was hoping you could answer that. Is this a telephone box?"

"No." Tris approached the desk and fiddled with the system. "This is a digital video recording of..." She looked away. "What those people were forced to do to each other in that... arena."

On the video, a crowd of Boatmen surrounded the fence, watching a pair of men circle each other hesitantly, one with a hatchet, one with a sword. Not until someone shouted that they'd shoot them both if they didn't fight did the men start going after each other in earnest. The top right panel showed the topless teen using a pair of large combat knives to slice apart a thirty-something man who couldn't catch her.

The girl looked down, guilt on her face. "They... they were gonna kill us both. I said fuckin' do it, so they said they'd kill Chris... that boy they made feed us. Said they'd kill him if I didn't win."

Kevin pinched the bridge of his nose, trying to process the scene before him. "Why? Where did Boatmen get this? The rest of the box is full of weapons and ammunition that all look like they'd been made days ago."

"They're feeding it." Tris shut off the video playback, braced her elbow on the table, and rested her forehead in her hand. "I don't know why they're recording it, but the Enclave is supplying them. No wonder they charged at us like that. They're probably used to having a major advantage against people with bats and crowbars and such."

Kwan leaned in. "What in the name of...?"

"It's full of weapons and ammo... and armor." *Wish I brought the van.* Kevin smiled. *I want to keep all this for Ned, but...* "You got enough room in your ambulance for this stuff as well as the other people? Bad idea to leave it lying around. Uhh, Tris and I are going deeper into this paradise... somethin' she's gotta do. Can you take the others with you?"

"Yeah. Sure. We got plenty of room back home. You don't want any of this stuff?" Kwan raised both eyebrows.

"Well... might take a box of 5.56 and a box of 7.62, but I don't have space in the car for much. If you have the room, Point Reyes might as well get it before the Enclave gives it to more insane savages. Oh... you have any idea where we might find a, umm, 'phone company central office?'"

Kwan nodded. "We saw one on our way into the city. We'll take the same way out and you can follow us?"

"Yeah." Kevin put an arm around Tris as she walked up beside him. "Faster we get this done, the happier I'll be."

"I agree. I wish to get out of this place as well. It will be dark soon." Kwan gazed up. "I am in your debt..."

"Name's Kevin." He smiled. "Let's go get your truck and we can load this stuff."

"Your wife is quite lovely." Kwan bowed to her.

"Thanks." Tris eyed Kevin, flaring her brows as if to ask 'wife?' A hint of pink appeared in her cheeks.

He let his arm slip down and gave her backside a squeeze. "I'd be lost without her."

13

BLACKBIRD

"There!" Abby pointed while looking through the noculars at a thing that could only be an Enclave drone heading straight at them. Her chest hurt from how fast her heart pounded; air refused to enter her lungs. "It's there."

Zoe shifted around. "I don't see anything."

"It's right there." Abby raised her voice (as if that would somehow help Zoe see better) and jabbed her finger at the sky. Her arms trembled and tears ran down her face. "It's gonna kill us!"

"I… Oh. Wow. I see it. Hold your ears."

Bang.

Unprepared for the loudness of an M-16 fired only two feet away from her head, Abby jumped and fumbled the noculars, which dangled from the lanyard around her neck. She clamped her hands over her ears and screamed. Zoe fired again and again, shooting at an even rate of about two bullets per second. Brass casings bounced to the roof and rolled off to the street side. It didn't take long for her to run out and reach for a fresh magazine.

In the quiet of her reloading, shouts rang out on the street below, men and women trying to figure out who opened fire on what. Zoe smacked the side of the rifle twice and it shook with a loud *click*. She took aim again and resumed firing, though her rhythm became faster and erratic.

"Zoe!" screamed Ann.

Abby whirled around. The woman's head and shoulders hovered over the roof's edge, though she seemed too nervous to try climbing up any higher.

"Hang on, Gran'ma." Zoe fired a rapid series of about six rounds before thrusting her arms (and rifle) up over her head. "Yes! Got it!" She jumped up and down, cheering.

"You did?" Abby looked to the west. For a fleeting second, a faint sparkle appeared in the air. She lifted the noculars from her chest and scanned the sky, but couldn't find the drone.

"What the hell is going on?" yelled a man from the street level.

A faint *crack* echoed in the distance.

"Zoe!?" shouted Ann. "What are you doing?" She wrestled with her fear for a second before pulling herself up onto the flat roof and crawling to Zoe. "Why are you up here with that gun?"

"Drone!" yelled Zoe.

"What?" Ann clutched the top of the roof, shaking.

Zoe ran to the Nederland-facing side of the roof holding her rifle pointed upward in one hand. At the edge, she peered down and shouted, "A drone! I shot it a buncha times, and it fell outta the air."

Ann beckoned her with a rapid wave. "Zoe get away from the edge!"

"Get down from there before you fall," yelled a man. "Jim, take Renee and go check it out."

"I don't see it," said Abby.

"That's 'cause I shot it and it caught on fire." Zoe backed away from the edge and flicked the safety on the rifle.

Ann pulled herself up and crawled to the middle of the roof, shivering from her fear of heights. She grabbed Zoe in a bear hug as soon as the child got close enough.

"I'm okay, Gran'ma. We are on drone patrol. We got one." Zoe grinned.

Oh, no. They're really trying to kill us. Everyone's going to die. Images of being dragged out of bed in the middle of the night by her terrified father raced back to her mind. Abby breathed faster and faster until she became too dizzy to stand. Her vision blurred to useless behind a thick layer of tears. She swooned to her knees and bawled.

Ann's arm went around her.

At the instant of contact, Abby screamed, "No!"

The woman cringed.

Abby looked up, sniffling. "I mean… no… they're trying to kill us." She grabbed Ann and wailed, lost to sobs of uncontrollable sorrow as everyone from Nederland died in her imagination.

"Ann?" shouted Bill. "Zoe?" His voice got louder.

Zoe closed her ammo pouches and pulled the bandolier over her head onto her shoulder. "On the roof, Gran'pa. Gran'ma's scared a bein' up high."

Ann crawled backward, one hand around Zoe's wrist, the other arm around Abby. Footsteps scuffed up behind, and a hand patted Abby on the back.

"Come on, hon," said Bill.

Abby released Ann and clung to Bill, who carried her down the angled part of the roof and handed her through the window to a tall woman in militia camo with caramel skin and a round face. The woman sat with her on Zoe's bed, rocking and patting her, asking what's wrong in various ways using both English and Spanish.

Zoe climbed in the window. "Abs, let's go check it out. I wanna see the crashed drone."

All the nightmares of Amarillo cleared from her mind. "No!" Abby leapt away from the militia woman and grabbed Zoe. "Don't go near it!" She stared up at Bill. "Don't let anyone go near it! They'll die. It's carrying Virus."

Bill's expression said 'oh shit.' He blinked at her once and ran out.

Ann stood inside the window, shivering, both hands over her face. Her usual warm complexion had faded, leaving her face paler than Abby's. "What were you girls doing up there? You could've gotten hurt."

Zoe put her rifle and the ammo supply back in the closet, then pushed the doors closed. "Abby told me 'bout the drone that hurt everyone where she used to live. Tris said one might be coming here; that's why they went onna trip to hit the Omclave in their stupid noses."

Ann patted herself on the chest a few times, then fanned herself. After a moment, some color returned to her cheeks and she grasped the shoulder of the militia woman. "Thank you."

The woman nodded. "No problem."

"Thanks." Abby sniffled and forced a weak smile at the woman. "Sorry."

"You musta seen some badness, girl." The militia woman squeezed Abby's shoulder. "Ain't no shame in bein' afraid of that crap."

More shouting came from outside, but Abby couldn't make out words, only that men yelled back and forth to each other. The shouts held little emotion, voices raised only to cover distance. She grabbed Zoe and pulled her close.

"Don't go near it. You'll get sick an' then you'll bring it to town, and everyone will die." She sniffled and collapsed seated on the rug, bawling.

Ann sat nearby and pulled both girls into a hug.

"Not fair," muttered Zoe. "I killed it and I wanna see it."

"You'll die," whispered Abby, choking on her attempt to breathe and cry at the same time.

Ann rocked her and patted her back. She wasn't Tris, but Abby only cared for a half a second before she held on and cried herself to silence. Zoe's annoyance at being denied the opportunity to see her 'kill' up close gave way to concern. She scooted closer on her knees, holding Abby's hand.

Eventually, tears ran out, and Abby stared at the wall feeling hollow. *Are we gonna be alive when they come back?* Zoe squeezed her hand. Ann continued patting and rubbing her back.

A few minutes later, the ladder to the loft rattled. Abby didn't care enough to look, but Zoe twisted around.

"Hi Zara," chirped Zoe.

Sniffling, Abby raised her head and peered up.

Zara climbed up into the loft, a strange-looking boxy rifle across her back on a strap. She seemed less frightening in green camo pants and a purple sweatshirt; without that creepy shimmery armor, she almost looked human. The black-haired woman wasn't quite as 'nice' as Tris, but still had much to do with getting her out of Amarillo alive.

Abby stared up at her. Tears streamed out of her eyes again for a few seconds before she wailed, "They're gonna do it again!"

"What happened?" Zara took a knee at Abby's side. "Why are you so upset?"

"A drone. They're sending a drone to drop the Virus on us."

Zara nodded. "Where did you see it?"

"West." Abby wiped her nose on the back of her arm. "I saw it on the noculars."

Zara's lips twitched as though she suppressed a laugh. "Can I see them?"

Abby held the green box up. "You gotta look through this side, with the eye pads."

"Hmm." Zara looked at the focus wheel. "Hmm. Can't tell. Did you see any glowing numbers or anything when you looked at it?"

"No."

"Damn. Battery's probably shot. This thing's got a rangefinder. Guess I wander around until I trip over the crash site."

"It was pretty far," said Zoe. "Like a thousand. I hadda put the scope all the way far."

"Don't go." Abby grabbed Zara's arm.

Zara smiled. "It's all right, Abby. I'm like Tris. I can't get it. I'm going to bring some ethanol with me and burn it out so no one gets sick."

"What if it gets on you and you bring it back here?" Abby sniffled.

"I'll be careful... I've dealt with this crap before." Zara stood. "Keep 'em inside for now."

Ann nodded. "Yes. It's about bedtime."

Abby shifted her gaze to Ann without lifting her head. "Do you really think I'm going to be able to sleep right now?"

"No, no... of course not." Ann stood. "Get changed for bed. I think we have some cocoa left." She patted the girls on their heads before following Zara down the ladder.

Zoe puffed her chest out, beaming. "We saved Ned."

"We're in so much trouble," whispered Abby. "The militia's gonna yell at us. Maybe lock us up."

"We didn't do anything bad." Zoe pulled her dress off and slipped into her nightgown.

"You fired a gun and didn't tell them first." Abby got up and walked over to where she'd left her sweatshirt/nightgown draped over a chair.

Zoe stared at her while she changed as if she'd said the most stupid thing imaginable. As soon as Abby fluffed her hair out from under the fabric, the girl sighed. "We didn't have time to tell them. It was attacking! When bandits attack, we don't gotta ask the militia if it's okay to shoot them."

"Oh. Duh. Right."

"Come on." Zoe ran to the ladder and climbed down.

Abby trudged after to the kitchen, where Ann hovered by the kettle on the electric stove. She guided the girls to the sofa and threw an afghan over them. With only an oil lamp for light, the house filled with frightening shadows. Abby pulled the hand-knit blanket up to her face, not even noticing that she trembled until Zoe gave her a funny look.

"I don't wanna get sick," whispered Abby.

Zoe mulled for a little bit before smiling. "I won't tie you to the bed. I got a suitcase to hide in."

Abby giggled, despite her fear.

Ann crept in and set a tray down on the coffee table with three mugs filled with pale brownish foam. Abby hadn't seen chocolate for a few years, but recognized the fragrance right away. Ann eased herself down between them, handed each girl a mug, and took the last. They sipped at the cocoa in the quiet dark for a little while before Ann decided to ramble about how this sort of drink used to be common.

"It's rare?" asked Abby.

"Oh, we can get cocoa beans sometimes. Bit too cold to grow them here, but sugar's hard to find. We found a nice big container of this powder a couple years ago, and keep it for special times like this when someone really needs it."

Abby wondered if this 'years old' powder had the flavor it had been meant to. It didn't taste unpleasant, more strange—aside from fruit, she didn't have 'sweet' things too often. "I'm scared. Thank you for using some of your expensive… cocoa."

"Oh, it's fine, Abby." Ann leaned against her for a second in a one-armed hug. "Problem with saving things like this for 'just the right moment' is, you grow old an' you realize you don't got so much left to look forward to. One day, you realize that you missed a whole bunch of 'right moments' and you still got all this stuff you never used. Way I see it, you needed it. Like a nice warm hug from inside."

Zoe slurped her drink.

Does she think we're all going to die soon? Abby glanced over. "I don't want to die. Maybe we should go up into the hills so they can't find us."

"Oh, I didn't mean it like that." Ann bowed her head. "Sometimes people find things like this cocoa and they want to make them special, so they keep them set aside waiting for some special moment that never happens."

"But what if you use it all?" asked Zoe.

"If you use it all, you've enjoyed it right? If you grow old and the jar's still full, you never got to enjoy it—so making it special didn't mean anything. You might as well not have found it."

Abby drank another sip; the cocoa had cooled to the point where she could take a big mouthful. She figured Ann meant to say something more than she didn't mind giving her the hot cocoa. Like she shouldn't be afraid to enjoy life or something.

An explosion in the distance made her jump. "What was that?"

"Something blowed up," said Zoe.

Ann perked, craning her neck as if she expected to see through the wall. "Sounded pretty well away from town. Bet that was Zara getting rid of the drone."

Abby shivered and pulled her legs up under her, cuddling into the afghan. If Zara had found the drone and destroyed it more than the crash already had, she'd be on the way back with news... and possibly deadly contamination.

"What's wrong?" asked Ann.

"I'm worried about what Zara found." Abby sipped more cocoa. "Why did Tris and Kevin have to leave? I'm scared they won't come back."

Ann attempted to be comforting for a while. Abby couldn't blame her for trying, but didn't feel obligated to cheer up either. Soon, their mugs ran dry, and Ann put her arms around the girls, pulling them close. Zoe passed out not long after, asleep with her mouth hanging open, head against Ann's shoulder.

Despite being warm and comfortable, Abby couldn't sleep. Her thoughts refused to settle down. If she thought about the drone, she saw the people of Nederland going crazy and shooting each other for sneezing. If she pictured Tris or Kevin, her gut clenched in knots worrying about them.

Zara and Bill entered about twenty minutes later. Zara seemed pleased. Abby stared at her wide-eyed.

"Well, it wasn't a chem carrier. The drone you took out was a recon unit, only cameras on it."

"That's not good, is it? Cameras?" asked Abby.

She walked over and put a hand on Abby's shoulder. "You can relax, kid. There was no Virus on it at all... and you shot it down about a half mile out. I don't think whoever was operating it could've seen Nederland from that distance. Night vision doesn't have that much range, and they would've been staring into the dark flying east at that hour. Odds are in our favor that they didn't spot the town. Losing that drone could either be great, or bad. Either they'll mark this area as too dangerous for more recon, or they'll send something out to see what happened to the last drone. That's why I blasted the crap out of it. If they come looking, they won't find the transponder or a crash site."

Bill scratched at the side of his nose with his thumb. "We need to double up on our watching the sky."

"Our biggest problem is at night," said Zara. "All their drones are black, and they don't make a lot of noise. I got my helmet back online, and it has night vision. I don't mind pulling night watch, but one person can't cover the entire sky."

Bee walked in from the rear hallway, still holding a pillowcase and the naked pillow she intended to put in it. "Forgive me for interrupting, but I have night vision capability as well. I am also quite accurate in the employment of chemically propelled ranged weapons. And I have excellent auditory sensors."

Abby smiled. The effort to look proud, earnest, concerned, or whatever the plastic-faced woman attempted struck her as hilarious when paired with a pillow. Seconds later, Abby burst into giggles.

"Well, that's a start at least." Bill shook hands with Zara. "Can you get any of those other helmets working?"

"Tried already. Sorry. My rifle makes big holes. Probably take a drone down in one shot. Wish I had more ammo for it."

"Something we can get from Ween?" asked Bill.

"Doubtful." She smiled. "Fifty caliber caseless only comes from one place I know of… and I'm pretty sure they won't sell me any."

Abby yawned. Zara's confirmation that Virus had not flown within seeing distance of Nederland took the wind from the sails of her anxiety. She blinked a few times, finding it hard to keep her eyes open while curled up on the sofa with Zoe under a nice blanket. The hour or so of extreme panic swung hard in the other direction, leaving her exhausted. No longer able to fight the cozy warmth around her, she lowered her head onto Ann's shoulder and fell asleep.

14

CUSTOMER SERVICE

Not quite ten minutes after Kwan and his wife left the compound, headlights washed over the face of a building on the left side of the street. Kevin edged up to the gate, an expectant eyebrow raised.

A large white truck with blinding patches of fluorescent yellow trim and emergency lights rolled into view. 'San Francisco Emergency Management Services' ran along the side in tall blue letters. He recognized the underlying frame as that of a box truck, probably with high-performance e-motors and an enormous battery to support all the lights and whatever other medical systems the thing had. Granted, whether or not any of it still worked… who knew?

"Damn. Look at the size of that thing. That's like what they called when twenty poor bastards got fucked up at the same time." Kevin chuckled. "Could haul people to a clinic by the truckload."

Tris fidgeted at his side. The urgent look in her eyes clashed with the guilt about leaving these people behind.

"Come on; let's help them load up so we can get going."

Kwan turned the giant ambulance away from the Boatman's encampment, stopped, and backed down the street toward it. Kevin averted his gaze, not interested in seeing what a pair of dual truck tires with in-wheel motors would do to dead bodies. Crunching bothered him enough without the accompanying visual. The truck came to a halt within inches of the gate. Both back doors opened, revealing the red haired woman, a small medical bed, and a cavernous space full of tiny cabinet doors and an array of devices and gadgets the purposes of which sailed straight over Kevin's head.

"Boy," yelled Freya, waving at the tow-headed kid still sitting by the pile of MREs. When he looked at her, she beckoned him with a wave. "Come here."

Kwan slithered out of the driver's door and walked around. His left bicep had a coating of clean gauze around it and his face ran with sweat.

"Whoa." Kevin got in his way. "You look like you're about to pass out. I got it... just... sit down or something."

"Kwan," said Freya. "This kid's got skin lesions. We should clean him up." She helped the boy up into the back of the truck. "And we got some better pants you can have that won't keep falling off."

The boy nodded with an eager smile, and followed her into the back.

"Thanks." Kwan patted Kevin on the shoulder and climbed into the ambulance.

Kevin and Tris hauled boxes of ammunition and weapons to the truck, though he did appropriate one case of 5.56 and one case of 7.62, which wound up in the Challenger's trunk, as well as a case of four shiny new AK47s. He had to admit they looked badass, all metal with synthetic stocks.

Allison, the eighteen-year-old, joined in and helped carry. At some point during the procession of moving boxes, she traded the bulletproof vest for a clean beige shirt. The boy, wearing a somewhat-too-large pair of intact jeans, lowered himself out of the back of the ambulance about fifteen minutes later. Six squares of white gauze clung to his chest, shoulders, and sides where Doc Kwan had tended to what the chain did to him. He raced over to the MRE stockpile and started carrying them by the armload to the truck. Fox ran after him to help, chattering away.

The Indian man approached the doc, showing off an angry-looking knife wound along his left side. He spoke so fast Kevin couldn't tell if he used English, though his gesture back at the 'arena' said all. Kwan nodded and waved him in.

Before long, everything worth taking had been loaded into a vehicle. Kevin also helped himself to the Boatmen leader's shotguns, though he did cut the tape to separate them. Fox climbed up on the front end of the Challenger and sat like some kind of biological hood-ornament-direction-finder.

"Oh, no." Kevin picked him up. "You're not riding on my hood."

"But I know where you wanna go," yelled Fox.

Kevin carried him over to his mother. "I believe this is yours."

She laughed. "Figure we'll head out by way of that place you're looking for. Follow us?"

"That works," said Kevin.

Freya, still holding Fox on her left hip, leaned forward and put an arm around Kevin. She tried to say something along the lines of 'thank you,' but only managed a teary babble.

He weathered the embrace with a smile. *Okay, maybe I understand why Dad did this kinda stuff.*

A hatch opened up from the roof of the giant ambulance. Allison emerged from the hole, wearing the bulletproof vest over her new shirt. She perched in a seat mounted to the opening, which gave her a full 360 swivel with the roof at the level of her stomach. "Outta here!" She raised a middle finger at the cage structure. "Fuck this place."

The blond boy leapt out of the truck. He ran over and hugged Tris, gave Kevin a thankful nod, and climbed back into the ambulance. Freya pulled the doors closed. A second later, Fox's face appeared in the square window to grin at them.

Kevin hurried to the Challenger, as did Tris. No sooner did he run his thumb across the row of rocker switches, lighting them blue, did the giant ambulance start forward. "Damn that's gotta be handy. Rolling hospital. Almost tempts me to go find out what might be hiding in central Denver."

Tris blinked at him. "*You* want to go into Denver? We saw thousands of Infected last time."

"Well…" He tilted his hand away from the wheel in a low-key version of a shrug. "The militia. Bet the doc would love us if we brought her one of those things."

She patted his leg. "That sounds like a good idea until you see Infected coming after you."

He tensed. "They're not so bad from a distance."

"That's the problem. They love to come out of nowhere right on top of you."

"Okay… okay." He shivered. "Point."

Kwan navigated a few turns over about a six-minute drive before coming to a halt by where a section of the e-tram tube collapsed in the street among hundreds of old merchant stalls. *Walking* forward would be a tight fit, never mind cars.

"Damn," said Tris.

"The city banned cars a couple years before the war. They were worried about the environment." He let the sarcasm roll thick. "I can just see people holding up protest signs about nukes not being 'green.'"

"Huh?" Tris looked at him.

"Oh, something I heard from Wayne. People around here liked to complain. Get a big crowd together to protest something like fur coats, but they didn't seem to care about the half a million people dying in China."

"Oh... I remember that in school. Their government split in half or something, civil war?"

"I dunno. Wayne said the US had something to do with it... CIA or some other three letters."

"Huh." She shrugged. "They told us the breakdown of society happened gradually across all countries. People like the ones who started the Enclave hadn't suffered the same decay of humanity and they were going to save us."

"Yeah, right." He grumbled, staring out over a few blocks' worth of smashed tram tubes, booths, and half-collapsed buildings. Blue got his attention near the end, a round symbol made out of a stack of lines. "Hey... that." He pointed. "I've seen that mark before. Ads for phones at bus stops and shit."

"More than nothing." She shrugged.

The ambulance slowed to a stop. Kwan, Freya, and Fox emerged and walked back toward the Challenger.

Kevin shut down the car and got out.

"That's it." Fox pointed at the blue orb. "Phone place."

"Worth checking out at least." Kevin smiled. "Thanks."

"As long as I'm there, you'll always be welcome at Point Reyes." Kwan bowed his head. "I can never fully repay you for what you did for my daughter, for my family."

Freya couldn't seem to bring herself to speak. She held Fox tight to her side and smiled at them.

"Thanks!" said Fox, a broad grin on his face.

Kwan shook Kevin's hand. "I hope you find whatever it is you're looking to find."

"Can we go with them?" asked Fox. "Explore?"

"Uhh." Kwan hesitated, evidently caught between worry for his family and obligation.

Kevin shook his head. "Not necessary. I can't ask you to risk your family over what could be some idiot trying to play games with us."

Kwan relaxed. "All right."

"Aww." Fox frowned at the street.

"Hey." Kevin poked the boy in the chest. "You need to help protect your family."

The skinny, wild-haired seven-year-old seemed disappointed that he wouldn't go on an adventure, but nodded. "Okay."

After another round of handshakes and hugs, and a genuine smile from Allison (hanging out the driver side door of the ambulance), Kwan and his family piled back into the rolling clinic and drove off. Hawk peered out from the passenger door window and waved at them.

Tris fumed. "What is *wrong* with people?"

"There've been fucked up people for as long as there've been people. Seems worse when there's no organized law… and the shitheads collect in the same place."

"And the Enclave is pouring ethanol on the fire why?" She paced back and forth.

"Only thing I can think of is the more people the Boatmen kill, the less the Enclave have to… and they probably feel like they're not so much killing as 'letting nature run its course.'"

"I'm ashamed to be part of them."

Kevin pulled her close, quiet until she lifted her head. He stared straight into her gem-blue eyes and smiled. "You are not part of them. You might've lived there, but you were never part of it."

She rested her chin on his shoulder, hugging him. "I always did kind of feel like an outsider. Can't explain it really. The place never felt like I belonged there."

"There ya go." He held her for a few seconds more before moving to the car. "Looks like we're on foot for a bit."

"Yeah." She ran around to her door and grabbed her katana, AK47, and two extra magazines, which she wore in a bright green hip satchel.

Kevin left the Enclave rifle (and all six of its remaining bullets) in the car and slung the AK he'd taken from a dead Boatman over his shoulder. He raided the box in the trunk to refill the magazine to thirty rounds, and stuffed another thirty loose bullets into his jacket pocket.

"Hey," said Tris. When he looked up, she threw an empty magazine at him. "You're not going to be able to load stray bullets in the middle of a firefight."

"You're expecting one?" Kevin chuckled and transferred the bullets from his pocket to the magazine.

She pointed down the road. "Lots of hiding places, and it's way too quiet."

"Right." He closed the trunk, stuck the extra mag in the inside pocket of his armored jacket, and locked up the car. "Moment of truth."

"Not quite yet." She swung her AK around and pointed it down the road. "Moment of truth is when we find a way to call that number."

Kevin unslung his rifle and held it at the ready. "Now you're just splitting hairs."

She chuckled.

They crept down the street, forced into single file here and there by the way the debris had collapsed. Dried blood smears made him feel like a small boy trying not to step on 'lava.' It didn't matter what he tried to rationalize, his mind refused to believe blood on the ground in the middle of a large city came from anything other than Infected.

Plastic and grit crunched under their boots. Something small and metal hit the ground and rolled away as Tris bumped an upended booth bearing signs advertising 'organic satay - $13.50' She grabbed a section of steel frame from the e-tram tube and pulled herself up and over a twisted jumble of concrete and rebar.

Kevin hung the AK over his shoulder and worked his way up the barrier.

"Oh, hey," said Tris.

He reached the top and peered down at her. "What?"

She pointed at a storefront. "I'm tempted to scavenge a bit."

A dusty window held a number of child-sized mannequins modeling clothing. "Uhh?"

"There's never kid-sized clothing at any Roadhouse."

"That's because people grab it before it can hit the shelf. Wayne had a pair of little jeans for a while... finally got thirty coins for them." He grunted and climbed over the top.

Tris stared at him, mouth open. "Paying that much for clothing is ridiculous."

He got upright and descended the hill of concrete with a few quick leaps from flat spot to flat spot. The echo of his boots striking the road carried in both directions for a while. "Especially for little pants the kid will grow out of in a year or two." He grinned.

"I'm going to look. Grab some stuff for Abby." She hurried over to an aluminum-framed door and kicked at it. When it didn't give, she rested the rifle against the wall, knelt, and opened her shoe sole. "Good sign."

"You're serious?"

"This isn't going to take too long and it's not like we're trying to beat some kind of countdown." She withdrew her tools from her shoe and attacked the lock.

Kevin watched the street, squinting at wherever shadows flickered. Any motion might be wavering signs or a scrap of tarp fluttering in the wind, or it could be Infected sneaking up on them. He slid his fingertip back and forth across the trigger. He didn't like being in the city at all, and standing still, he liked even less. Things looked quiet now, but one gunshot could set off a flood of shambling death.

Infected had good ears.

The door gave up the fight, and Tris pushed it open, entering a smallish store. Shelves full of dust-covered stacks of kids' clothes lined three walls except for a small changing area and a door to a back room. Hangars of shirts and dresses sat on round racks in the middle of the floor. Above the shelves, the walls sported yellowed posters of kids posing in the same clothing. Kevin locked stares with a picture of a boy about ten or so in a blue shirt with a white sweater tied around his neck by the sleeves, his arms folded and a cocky expression on his face.

He spent a moment arguing with himself wondering what this world would do to that kid, or if it would've been better for the little arrogant bastard to keep the world he'd known. If that picture had been recent before the war, he'd be a sixty-year-old man now at the least. *Probably not smiling like that anymore.*

Kevin raised an eyebrow at the sight of a price tag on the floor beneath a dress that looked intended more for a prostitute than a girl small enough to fit into it. "What kind of idiot would charge 2,600 coins for that scrap? It barely covers anything."

Tris looked over. "Oh. That's prewar money. I think this was some kind of place for rich people." She paused with an armload of garments. "Look for bags or something. If that phone number turns out to be bullshit, at least we can do something productive with this trip."

Kevin found a few stacks of shopping bags behind the counter. For kicks, he bashed open the register and took all the coins, loose and rolled, while ignoring the paper currency. They spent a little while packing up anything that hadn't fallen apart or that looked too frilly to survive life.

He lugged five shopping bags per hand out into the street and turned to wait for her to follow.

"You know, this is the part where the Infected come after us… when our hands are full."

Tris, carrying an equal number of bags, squeezed past the doorway and hurried toward the Challenger. "You know before the war, I think we would've been carrying enough money in clothing to like buy a house or something."

"Who would pay that much for kid clothes?" He shook his head.

"Rich people." She shrugged. "Hey, not like money matters anymore, right?"

They packed the trunk as well as the back seat, re-locked the car, and resumed their journey into the mazelike debris field. The utter lack of anything else moving got under his skin. By the time they reached the curb in front of the telephone building, his hands shook.

"What's wrong?" Tris put a hand on his shoulder.

"This is too easy. It's too quiet." He looked left and right. "We're going to walk in that door, and this entire street is going to be filled with Infected."

"At least you're optimistic." She bit her lip and looked down. "And here I am worrying that this 'number' is going to be a dead end and I get to feel like a total failure all over again."

"You are not a failure." He walked up a short concrete path connecting the front of the office building to the street past a dead fountain and some curved benches. "Okay, so now's the moment of truth."

Tris chuckled.

The front doors had been reduced to metal frames so long ago that no trace of glass remained anywhere in sight. Something in the lobby moved; he froze and raised the AK.

"Careful…" Tris also aimed toward the doors. "Might be a kid or something."

"This isn't a grocery store with a huge stockpile of food. Some kid wouldn't be surviving in there." He crept a few steps forward, squinting to see into the dark.

"Scavver?" whispered Tris.

Another step closer, and figures became clear in the dim lobby: seven or eight people in bloody, tattered prewar clothes. Vacant stares, greyish skin, and the listless way that they all stood around staring into space got his heart slamming against his breastbone. One woman moaned at the ceiling; she almost glanced in their direction, but seemed to lack the motivation to do much more than stand there.

"Shit," he whispered.

"Infected?" asked Tris, edging closer.

Kevin let off a nervous, whispery chuckle. "I think they're customer service workers."

Tris rolled her eyes.

"Oh, you're right. Infected aren't that bloodthirsty."

"What are you talking about?" whispered Tris.

"How have I heard of customer service and you, Miss Went to School, haven't?" He winked.

"I know what they are. I'm confused why you're saying it. I think you're mistaking them for telemarketers."

"What?"

"Customer service people don't call out. People hated telemarketers."

"Never mind. Joke from a 'historical documentary' I saw once. You know, the whole zombie-like 'someone please shoot me' face?" He chuckled. "I'm trying not to think too much about what we're looking at... though, they do seem a bit more, umm..."

"Unmotivated?" Tris moved up to the door, rifle poised. "They're not even looking at us. No way they haven't heard us this close. Hey, you're right. That woman's badge says 'customer service' on it."

He cackled.

That noise made all seven of the Infected look at him.

"Oh shit." He shot the nearest one.

Tris opened fire. He drilled two dark-skinned men in white shirts scrambling to climb over the reception desk. Scuffing outside made him whip around. A handful of Infected spilled out of a mostly-intact section of fallen e-tram tube and charged up the sidewalk past the fountain.

His first shot struck the lead man in the chest and killed an Asian woman with most of her cheek missing behind him as well.

"Inside. Bottleneck the hallway," yelled Tris as she let off four rapid shots.

The Infected outside didn't possess the same lethargic disinterest as the others, but Kevin still had enough time to take five careful shots and put them down before they made it to the door. He ducked in after Tris, who crossed the lobby to an interior hallway. A metal door slammed open a foot and change before it struck a metal desk, trapping a pudgy man in a blue shirt. He moaned, forcing his head and one arm past the gap while raking his fingers feverishly at the air, reaching for Kevin. His continuous effort to shove his way in repeatedly banged the door against the desk.

She shot him through the door. The Infected fell over backward with a low, gurgling wheeze. Kevin walked sideways behind Tris, swiveling his head side to side to watch the lobby as well as her. A screeching woman with no skin on her left arm from fingertip to elbow fell down out of the drop ceiling. Her blood-soaked shirt clumped up around her armpits exposing breasts, and she had nothing else on save for one high-heeled shoe.

Kevin shot her in the head before she got up. "Must've been one hell of an office party."

"What?" asked Tris.

"Here come the nukes, I'm going to fuck someone." He smirked. "Last-minute panic."

"Kevin, the Infected didn't happen for years after the war... She's a survivor." Tris sighed. "Was."

"Explain the..." He glanced at a logo on the wall. "AT&T workers in the lobby?"

"Died in the war and survivors took their clothes? Probably thought the ID badges were jewelry."

A moan preceded her firing twice into the hallway ahead of them.

Kevin jumped and almost screamed when the ceiling overhead gave out and a trio of Indian men fell on top of him, dragging him to the floor. Blind with panic, he used the rifle to shove them away and rolled to the side. He shot two as fast as he could move the AK, but the third lunged forward and grabbed the end of the rifle in one hand, his leg in the other.

"Nnnnngh!" roared the Infected, straining to bite him on the face.

Kevin stomped his free boot into the man's shoulder to hold him back while reaching for the .45.

Teeth closed around the leather over his shin.

He put the tip of the .45 to the man's skull.

Infected eyes rotated upward and crossed, trying to stare at the gun.

Boom.

Brain and gore spattered the wall.

He kicked the corpse away and scooted backward toward Tris who hadn't stopped firing in slow, even single shots.

"Fuckfuckfuckfuckfuck," he wheezed. After two breaths, he reached past his foot to grab the tip of the AK's barrel, and pulled it into his arms.

A moan came from the ceiling. He snapped his head back, looking up.

An oldish woman in a white shirt peered at him from the hole the three men had created. He raised the .45, aimed at her face, and fired. She rocked from the bullet strike; Kevin flung himself to the side, rolling out of the way as blood and corpse fell onto the carpet where he'd been a second earlier.

Tris grabbed his shoulder and hauled him upright, wide-eyed with worry. "You hit?"

"No." He stared in horror at tooth marks in his boot, and made a *meep* sound. "Not that I noticed... You can check me thoroughly for scratches later."

"Not now." She gave him a hurt look.

"Obviously not now. I ain't stripping in the middle of an Infected shitstorm."

"You're such an asshole." She thumped him on the arm.

He grinned. "Thanks."

That got a laugh out of her.

Tris kicked in a door, aimed, and lowered the rifle. "What the hell are we looking for?"

"I have no damn idea." He pushed a door on the other side open, finding an empty conference room. "You're the tech person."

She stormed down the hallway.

He started to follow, but turned back at a loud chorus of screeching moans. Another ten or so Infected spilled down from the second floor, heedlessly flinging themselves headfirst through the hole.

"Tris," yelled Kevin, as he pumped rounds into the pile of bodies.

She lent a few shots to the purge. Only one of the writhing bodies made it to their feet. Tris' last shot put a neat red dot in the center of a woman's forehead and detonated the back of her skull. Blood ran out of her nose in two trails. Once a stunning straight-haired blonde in a pink blouse and black skirt, the Infected stared with a vacant look for a second or two before falling over backward onto the heap of bodies.

Kevin bowed his head, offering a moment of silence for the dead.

"It's just not right," whispered Tris. "Those people survived a nuclear war only to die because of the Enclave."

"Uhh... none of them look old enough to have survived the war."

"Don't be an ass." She kicked a plastic water bottle with an AT&T logo down the hall. "You know what I mean."

"Think that's the last of them?" He removed the magazine from the AK and repacked it with loose bullets from his right jacket pocket.

"Didn't you load another mag?" asked Tris.

"Yeah, but I grabbed another fistful of bullets. If it didn't weigh sixty pounds, I'd have strapped the whole damn box to my back."

She moved up to another door. Office. "Damn."

They picked through a number of offices, conference rooms, and a few large spaces full of cubicles before finding a cafeteria. Tris didn't even go in, continuing past it down the hall.

"Maybe we need to go upstairs?"

"There's gotta be a network room somewhere." Her worry of Infected faded as she stomped along, checking door after door.

More offices.

Kevin followed, as wary as she wasn't. Twice, he shot shadows, making Tris scream in surprise, but nothing bled.

"Here." She pointed at a door that wouldn't open. "This has to be something."

"Can you open it?"

She pointed at a black plastic box on the wall. "RFID card reader. No physical key." She threw herself against the door but couldn't move it. "Probably electromagnetic locks."

"That's a good sign, right? Still power in the building."

"A place like this probably had its own solar farm on the roof for redundancy's sake." She gave him a nervous look. "Guess I could go search the dead for a badge that'll open this."

"Can't you fiddle with the wires?"

"No... it's not directly connected to the lock. This reads a card and sends it off to a computer somewhere, which then sends a separate signal to the lock if the ID checks out." She stared at the top of the door. "Assuming the security system is still operating."

"So..."

"I think I'm going to vote brute force here. Back up a bit." She shuffled about five steps left to create an angle, and aimed at the top of the door.

Kevin obliged, and stuck his fingers in his ears.

She put few shots along the top of the door, and the one on the left swayed forward an inch or so. The bullets had savaged a metal block near the ceiling that sputtered and sparked, and tore a matching plate off the top of the door.

Tris shoved it aside and walked in. "Well... this is something."

Kevin shook his head to help ease the ringing in his ears while following her into a large room with nine long rows of technology crammed into rack mounts. The floor shifted under their feet, loose tiles in some manner of suspension. A missing panel revealed a two-foot deep space beneath the floor packed full of wires. Small workstation desks ran the length of the left wall, each with a pair of flat panel monitors. Two displayed screen savers of a bouncing AT&T logo, three systems had blue screens full of text, and the remaining seven appeared to be off—or dead.

Kevin glanced right at a poster on the wall. An athletic cartoon man in a toga emblazoned with UNIX rammed a sword through a pudgy man in a shirt-and-tie carrying a briefcase labeled 'Windows.'

"Huh." He scratched his head.

"What?" Tris looked up from one of the computers.

He gestured at the poster. "I remember reading something about there being Unix in ancient Rome, but I thought they were the ones who got fat."

"Eunuchs," muttered Tris.

"Right. They chop off a guy's balls to make Unix."

Her eyebrows formed a flat line across her head. "I have to assume you're not making a joke you couldn't possibly understand."

"You're right. I'm already lost."

She poked around the tall equipment cabinets. "Well, I suppose this is telephone stuff… but how the hell. Argh. We're right here and I still don't know what to look for."

"Such as?"

She held her arms out to the sides. "A way to connect to that damn number."

"What?" He shrugged. "Like a phone?"

Her eyebrows furrowed again, harder.

Kevin grinned. "Like the phones that have been sitting on the desks of every office we kicked in so far?"

"Stop." She sighed. "Okay, maybe I didn't want to believe it was that simple and I'd need to crawl hip deep into some ancient mainframe."

"What's a mainframe?" Kevin scratched his head.

Tris dragged herself to the closest workstation and put a hand on the phone. "A big computer." She closed her eyes, took a breath, and lifted the handset to her head. "Shit. Dead."

"Sorry."

She moved from desk to desk to the right, testing phones. When she got to a workstation where the blue ball logo bounced around the screen, her eyes shot wide as soon as the phone got close to her ear. Her entire body trembled.

"It… it's on."

Kevin leaned close enough to hear an odd noise emanating from the handset. "What the heck is that?"

She hung up, but didn't let go. "Dial tone."

15

CONTACT

Tris stared at her hand, stark white against the black plastic handset. The name 'Bharat Sivakumar' scrolled across the top of the phone's screen, followed by 'Systems Administrator II.' Only a few button presses stood between her and finding out if her father had really died years ago, or if another Enclave lie had ruined her life.

Her knees weakened and she slid into the old grey office chair.

Kevin kept glancing back and forth from her to the door, as if he expected a thousand Infected to come rushing in at any moment. His desire to get the hell out of the city as fast as possible showed clear on his face.

I have to do this. She continued hesitating until the random worry about a drone strike on Nederland played out in her thoughts. Abby not knowing if she'd gotten sick, then Abby sick, and then having to tell her goodbye...

Tris growled and tore the phone off the handset, punching in 6505550447.

"We're sorry. You must first dial a one before calling this number," said a recorded female voice.

Tris slammed the phone down and screamed, "Go fuck yourself!"

"Nathan?" asked Kevin, trying to sound gentle.

"No... no... just a stupid architecture policy."

"Something wrong with the building?"

Tris slammed her head into the desk. "I can't. Please stop."

"What?"

She huffed. "Sometimes you're cute with that not knowing thing but right now I'm... I can't."

He looked genuinely confused. "What?"

"Never mind." She dialed again, this time adding a leading one.

Ringing emanated from the phone. Her heart rate slowed and her throat tightened.

"It's... ringing."

The ringtone played three more times before a sharp *click* and silence. Her heart sank. *Figures. What was I expecting? A phone call fifty years after everything fell apart? As if.*

"Damn. It's dead."

Kevin walked over and grasped her shoulder.

"Tris," said a voice from the phone, laced with age, confidence, and... familiarity.

Her mouth hung open.

"What?" asked Kevin.

"D-Dad?" rasped Tris. "Are you really there?"

"It is good to hear your voice, Sprite."

She leaned into Kevin, shaking and crying. "Dad..."

"I'm sure you have many questions. I have so much I need to tell you, but right now there is not time."

"They told me you were dead." She sniffled.

"I need your help, Sprite. I'll explain everything as soon as it's possible. I cannot stop the Virus without your help."

She scowled at the bouncing blue AT&T logo on the monitor. "I've been down that road before." A crash of inadequacy clenched her gut. She had the cure. She failed. "I... want you to be real too much. How do I know this isn't Nathan messing with me?"

"That is an entirely reasonable worry given what has happened to you."

His voice seemed to flow out of the phone, warming her body as it saturated her muscles. The safety and comfort conveyed by his firm, but placid, tone brought her back to being little again, fiddling with some half-built toy robot while he sat behind her. Her need to have this be real made her wary.

"I... can't believe you'd wait so long to tell me you didn't die. I want to believe you, but it doesn't make sense."

"Much about the Enclave defies what you have been led to believe," said Dad. "I promise you that I am no deception from that fool Savros."

"Who?" asked Tris.

"Nathan." Contempt rang clear in her father's voice. "I am sorry, but I could not do anything to stop his plan to send you out to the resistance. I had hoped that either you or Doctor Andrews would find the cipher in the data."

She looked up at Kevin, asking with her gaze if she should believe it. Not being able to read her mind, he kept squeezing her shoulder and offering a comforting presence. "So you think I'm going to take on the Enclave alone somehow?" Tris poked the speakerphone button.

"Of course not." His voice made her picture that knowing smile he always had. "I'm not asking you to do anything alone, but at this point in time, you are the only one capable of putting an end to their campaign of atrocities."

"I wish I could believe you."

Her father's scratchy chuckle crackled in her ear. "You're sitting by one of perhaps a dozen still-working telephones in the world talking to a man you've thought dead for a long time. What is there to doubt?"

She frowned. "Everything."

"I am counting on you, Sprite. You had always been a timid sort of person. I apologize for the overlay, but it was necessary."

"Overlay?" She leaned at the phone. "What do you mean? What did you do to me?"

"Do not alarm yourself. It is a mild memory overlay responsible for your confidence and belief that you can in fact stop the Virus."

She slammed her fist on the desk, making the phone jump and a penholder fall over. "No wonder. You don't know how *sick* I've been over this for days. I'm looking after a child now, and we left her behind to do this. Argh!" *My father wouldn't do that to me.* "The father I remember wouldn't have forced me to do anything."

"I didn't *force* you to be here. I only made it easier for you to fight past your doubt and fear. You wouldn't have come here if you didn't believe the Enclave needed to be stopped."

Kevin stood beside her chair and pulled her against him. She leaned her head against his side.

"So," said Kevin, "you programmed her to want to come out here?"

"You're overstating the effect of the memory web. This line is not going to last much longer. The systems have not been maintained. Tris, you are the only one capable of helping me. You may resent the means by which you have come to be on this phone call, but I assure you that you *can* be the catalyst that ends the threat of the Virus."

She fumed. "This is such a trap."

"If the Enclave wanted to capture you, there are far simpler ways to go about it than a message hidden deep in mp3 files sending you to find a working telephone. Do you not think they'd have rolled over Nederland to get to you?"

She cringed. "Can I stop them from repeating Amarillo?"

"I am confident you can stop them, period. However, I need you to come to where I am. There is little time. Three blocks to the west and one north, you will find a Starbucks store. Please... go there."

"Hey, Dad type person," said Kevin. "Why Tris? Why only her? She's not some kind of super-advanced android is she?"

She clasped a hand over her heart and stared up at him. *He doesn't believe me? He said he...*

Kevin winked at her.

"My daughter is quite human. Please... hurry."

The line clicked off.

"You said you didn't doubt m—"

He leaned down and kissed her. "I don't. Wanted to see what he'd say. Well... what now?"

That unwavering confidence telling her she had to (and could) put an end to the Virus remained, though she bristled at it. Was that how she had such trust in the vaccine, or such guilt at failing a mission that never had a chance to succeed? *The overlay wouldn't tell the difference because I didn't know the difference.* All the tragedy and shame associated with the blown-out resistance base in Harrisburg dissipated. *I wasn't feeling guilty over failing to bring the cure... it was* this *that I'd been expected to do.* She clenched her fists in her lap. Knowing the urge pulling her to fight the Enclave originated from a memory implant didn't make it any weaker.

"Are you okay?" Kevin rubbed her back.

"When I was a kid, I used to be such a little wimp. I was afraid of the dark, afraid of loud noises, monsters under the bed, monsters in the closet... I hated being alone and I hated being in crowds. At night, I'd hide in my room and cling to this little doll I used to have. I remember in first grade, this other girl, Raina, kept taking my lunch pack. She didn't hit me or demand it or anything... she'd walk right up and take it because I didn't do anything about it. I got a little braver as I got older. After my father disappeared, I kinda rebelled... but I was still a mouse."

"You're no mouse." He kissed her.

"Well, deep down I am. Somehow those people—my adoptive parents... the way they denied that Dad ever existed pissed me off. I rebelled at that and when the social management office announced my pairing with Dovarin, I had enough of a backbone to say no. I hadn't been alone with that bastard for more than a half hour when he hit me for not being submissive enough. He left no doubt where I stood. I belonged to him. Fuck that." She grumbled. "I think... I believe that voice on the phone. The overlay isn't making me want to do anything I don't already want to do; it's taking away the fear of doing something stupid and reckless that a normal person would have."

"Oh, so it's turned you into me?" He flashed that rogue's grin again.

Nathan wanted to kill me before I got him noticed by the Council. Now he's going to want to make me suffer. He's gonna send Virus to Nederland. She balled her hands into fists, shaking with anger and the desire to tear his balls off. She glared at the memory of his arrogant smile on the monitor at Harrisburg, seconds before he armed the explosive she'd had in her gut.

Oh, I want to rip that arrogant smirk right off his face.

"So..." He pulled her up into an embrace. "What do you want?"

She eyed the door. "I'm in the mood for coffee."

16

DARK ROAST

Bodies in the corridor forced Kevin around the long way. Rather than step through a pile of Infected corpses along an approximate hundred-yard path to the lobby, he went three times that distance around the rectangular building. A few times, thuds and dragging scrapes on the ceiling caused him to freeze and glance up.

Keeping as quiet as possible, he walked past another corridor full of offices and hooked a right at the end. The air grew thicker and more foul the farther down he went, until the passage dead-ended at a pair of double doors labeled 'Fitness Center.'

Kevin shrugged and pushed the doors open. The next thing he knew, he sprawled on all fours gazing at a splatter of vomit between his hands.

"Oh, god." Tris gagged. She stumbled to the right, leaned against the wall, and also threw up.

"Wub?" He raised his head, bile trailing from his lower lip, and stared aghast at an Olympic-sized swimming pool. The acrid sting of chlorine and corpse assaulted his eyeballs.

The water had taken on the thickness of dark raspberry jam, filled with the bloated remains of over a hundred Infected. Gas-filled bellies broke the fetid surface here and there amid the occasional detached limb. Such stench rolled out of the room when the doors opened that his mind had refused to process it on a conscious level, instead ejecting the contents of his stomach in seconds, before he even realized he'd smelled anything.

"Oh." He turned away, gagging. "Maybe... we should climb over bodies."

Eyes watering from the fumes, he forced himself to stand again, retching when he dared look at a purplish balloon of flesh striated with veins... a man's gut.

Glorp.

Tris held a hand at him in a gesture of 'shh.'

He spent a few seconds holding his breath, unable to decide between breathing through his mouth so he didn't have to smell anything or turning back.

"Something moved in the water," whispered Tris. "Poor bastards fell in and couldn't get out."

Kevin glanced at the nearest pool ladder and let off a somber chuckle. Fortunately, the floor ahead had only a little contamination from splashing. "We should be able to get around if we can bear the smell."

Glorp.

"Okay." He pointed the AK at the room. "I heard that."

"It doesn't matter if one of them isn't completely dead... they can't get out of the pool or they wouldn't still be in there."

"Think they drowned or starved?"

Tris shrugged. "Probably drowned. They had each other to eat."

He retched. "Not funny."

"Wasn't meant to be." She took a step toward the door.

Multiple black serpentine creatures raced up and over the rim of the pool, quivering toward them like two-foot long snakes on sped up video.

Kevin screamed with the voice of a five-year-old boy. He managed to get off three shots, detonating one of the things into a bloody splat mark before jamming his arm across his face as another two sprang into the air.

A ripple of gunfire hammered his ears. One of the creatures slapped into his arm as if someone had walloped him with a baseball bat made out of flesh. Warm sliminess bounced off his forehead. Tris let out a grunt as though she'd thrown something, and another gunshot rang out.

Seconds passed in silence. Kevin shivered, too frightened to move.

"Keep your eyes closed," said Tris.

"Mmm."

A wet cloth swiped at his eyes in a series of delicate dabs.

"Bend over and turn your head up."

He bent forward at the waist and twisted his head toward the wall.

She poured water over his eyes and forehead, then dabbed at him again with a dry cloth. "Okay."

He stood and opened his eyes. A short distance ahead, a symbiote serpent stuck to the wall, haloed by a splat of black ichor. It still squirmed, but couldn't peel itself free. Silvery liquid oozed out of its hide in several places where the force of its impact had caused it to rupture. Wherever it touched, pieces of wall dissolved into the flow and reconfigured into chunks of biological matter. Fortunately, the 'repaired' flesh fell to the floor in separate bits amid a mirror puddle that resembled mercury.

Tris raised the Beretta and blasted it in the closest thing it had to a head. With a brief squeak, the creature ceased squirming.

Seven more splat marks decorated the floor between them and the pool. He recognized the one he'd clipped with the AK; it had more or less detonated. The others looked torn up but not to the same degree, suggesting Tris had used the Beretta instead of a rifle. *Probably faster.*

"How bad?"

Tris clung to him for a few seconds, at the verge of tears. "Close, but no idea how old that blood is. Chlorine might've killed the Virus... I didn't want to risk it."

"No... no... that's fine. I'm good with extra careful." He smiled. "Doesn't feel like anything got in my eyes."

She nodded and put the mostly-empty water bottle back in her satchel.

He took a deep breath, held it, and ran forward, skirting the pool area by as much distance as the wall and old workout machines allowed. Another attempt to take the most direct route to the front door proved a wrong turn. A giant room full of folding chairs and tables held a few hundred sets of skeletal remains, stacked in a purposeful manner, as if laid out inside a mausoleum.

"Uhh... Sorry." He closed the door. Ten minutes later, he stared through an office at a window. "I'm giving serious consideration to shooting out the glass so we can leave this damn building."

"That way." Tris pointed.

"You're sure?" He followed.

"Mostly... but no sense making more noise than we have to. No telling how many Infected are still here."

"Maybe they left over the bridge? Followed a Hoplite out or something."

Tris chuckled. "Enclave forces probably wouldn't even use the bridge... hovercraft can go over water. Faster for them to drive straight out onto the bay, especially if they're heading east."

"Really?" he blinked. "Those bigass things can float?"

The hallway ended a few paces after a rightward corner at a set of white double-doors. Tris kicked them open, knocking aside a few chairs that had been propped up against it from the inside. About thirty yards of grey carpet and display cases full of awards separated them from the lobby.

"Technically, they're not floating. They're hovering over the water."

"Wow."

"But they would float if the fans cut off. They're kinda like boats." She jogged out to the lobby, which hadn't changed in the hour or so they'd been roaming around.

Kevin ran after, and past her, gulping huge breaths of air once he got outside. The stench from the pool still saturated his senses, making the air taste sweet. As long as he lived, he would *never* forget that horrible odor. He allowed a moment to gather his nerves and headed to the Challenger. Before getting in, he took a swig from the canteen behind his seat, swished it around, spat, and did it again.

Four times.

He drank a little and fell into the driver's seat. "Well that's going into the list of the top three most awful things I've ever seen."

"Yeah. So three blocks that way"—she pointed—"and turn right."

"As you wish." He smiled.

The short drive offered no alarming sights or dangerous complications, but as soon as he turned where indicated, he stomped on the brakes. A building with a green and white awning stood on a street corner behind a large crowd of Infected. Only one or two of them moved, most standing statue still staring off into space.

"Wow, that's like some kind of badly-programmed video game..." Tris swallowed. "The monsters are standing there idle until something triggers them."

"What?" Kevin looked at her.

She shook her head. "It would take too long to explain. Ask me about it later when we have about an hour to waste. How do you wanna handle this?"

"Well." Kevin flicked the master arm switch for the car's machine guns.

"If they're going to be all nice and obliging and stand in a crowd like that..."

"The bullets are going to go right through them and spray the place with dangerous blood. We need to go in there."

"Aww, fuck." He grumbled. "Heh. Never mind. Got a better idea."

He stepped on the accelerator, pinning himself to the seatback. The Infected looked up at the squelch of tires. A few shifted as if to chase. Kevin reached up to the cord along the roof and gripped the plastic-wrapped steel cable. As the first Infected went past the front end, he jerked down on the cord, igniting the incendiary projector behind his seat. A twelve-foot plume of burning gel sprayed out from a nozzle on the side of the car, catching the bewildered Infected at chest level.

The Challenger shot past the Starbucks, leaving a group of burning figures staggering into the road in its wake. Kevin hit the emergency stop switch for the right side wheel motors and yanked the parking brake, whipping the car around in a squealing 180. Tris bounced off her door and flew into his shoulder, grunting. The group of burning Infected moved away from the building, staggering into the road to give chase. As soon as the car's front end pointed at the crowd, he opened fire from the hood-mounted m60s.

Four seconds later, he let off the trigger. A few of the bodies continued attempting to crawl closer. He sat there, fingertips teasing at the trigger button, as the flames reduced the throng to a spread of blackened remains.

Tris scrunched up her face. "That's going to smell."

"Can't be as bad as the pool." He raised an eyebrow at her. "I don't think my nose is going to work for weeks."

He drove back to the coffee place, skirting the carnage in the road, and pulled into a parking space over a blue field with a white stick figure in a chair on it.

"You can't park here, it's a handicapped spot," said Tris, her tone flat.

"Right." Kevin pushed the door open and shut down the car. He paused, one foot on the pavement, one in the car, and stared at the Starbucks wall.

The beige stucco had darkened a uniform ashen black, except for the lighter-colored silhouettes of perhaps twenty people. An image of men and women of varying height standing in a cluster had been burned into the stone. All of the figures had their arms up, raising rectangular objects of varying size in their hands to the sky. A few scraps of clothing and bone peeked out of a thick layer of soot at the base of the wall, fused into a cement by rain and weather.

Kevin studied the macabre 'mural' for a moment, squinting in confusion. "What the hell were they doing?"

Tris shut the passenger door with a heavy *thud* and walked around the nose. "What?"

He pointed at the wall.

"Those people were caught in a nuclear flash... probably vaporized. The wall didn't darken wherever bodies blocked it." She shuddered. "Kinda looks like they were all holding their phones up at the moment of their death. Wonder why."

"Poor bastards." He headed for the door. "Guess they didn't feel much."

Tris followed him inside. A steady electric hum emanated from the ceiling, though none of the light bulbs remained intact. Years of dirt and detritus collected on the floor around the tables, having blown in through windows that existed only as distant memories. Cutesey pink writing on a black panel over the register area suggested a chipper teenaged girl, though it had smudged away too much to make out much more than 'iced caramel' and 'only $8.99.' A few molding paperboard signs advertised a $2 off special on cold drinks for 'Summer 2021.'

"Everything is so... has anyone even been here since the day it all burned?" Tris' shoes crunched over a layer of filth as she crept in, head in a constant state of turning.

"Okay." He surveyed tables, chairs, a long counter, and shelves full of broken cups and small boxes. "Now what?"

She poked around behind the counter, opening cabinets, peering in, and closing them one after the next. "Your guess is as good as mine."

"Think your father's going to meet us here or something?" He scratched at the back of his head.

"Maybe." She stopped rummaging, leaned on the open space by an old computer terminal, and stared at him. "What am I going to say to a man I've thought dead since I was nine?"

"I guess that depends on what his excuse is. If they locked him up, can't really put the blame on him."

She frowned before turning to pluck a pouch from a shelf behind her labeled 'French Roast.' "He's obviously out now... why didn't he make contact?"

"Could be that he just got out... and you've been away from the Enclave."

Tris sniffed at the top of the package and put it on the shelf where she found it. "That's been sitting outside... maybe there's some in the back."

Kevin shrugged and walked along behind her as she headed to a door behind the counter. A small employee break area sat next to a storage room with shelves and a couple of industrial freezers. Handprint smears on the door made him picture infected groping around, but thankfully no trace of blood or other bodily fluids marked anything.

Tris opened the first freezer and recoiled in an instant, kicking it closed. She backed up, waving a hand past her face and coughing. "Those sandwiches are... expired."

Kevin stood in the doorway between the break room and the main area, eyeing the windows for anything moving. Aside from a tiny bathroom, the only way out of the back appeared to be a steel door with a push bar. Feeling confident nothing could ambush her, he returned to the front and took a seat at one of the tables.

Well, pops. We're here. If you've got a hand, play it. Ain't gonna sit here all damn day. We're out before sundown.

Tris emerged in a little while with another plastic pouch, this one opened. She ran back and forth to the car, returning with a canteen, and carried it behind the counter.

"What are you doing?"

She paused long enough to smile at him. "This place's panels still work. I'm making coffee."

"Seriously? That stuff is fifty years old."

Tris held up the bag. "It's been sealed... probably going to be a bit weak, but I'm dying here. I used to have like four cups a day in high school. They didn't let me have it in Detention, and well... out here."

"Mostly instant, yeah."

She shivered.

He rested the AK across the table and tapped his fingers on it for a while. Eventually, the scent of coffee wafted by, and he looked up. Tris hovered over her pet project, grinning like a schoolgirl.

"Smells okay."

She braced her hands on her hips. "I'm kind of remembering it stronger than this, but... it's not exactly fresh."

A machine near Tris emitted a sputtering gurgle. She reached forward and clicked something before pouring coffee into a pair of mugs. After clipping the canteen to her belt, she carried the mugs to the table and sat.

"Looks decent." He picked up the mug and sniffed, shrugged, and took a sip. "Well, I've definitely had worse than this. Spose it's gotta mean something if it's drinkable after so long."

"Mmm." She cradled the mug in both hands, savoring it. "Yeah."

"Yanno, if we didn't pack the car full of kid clothing, this would be worth a damn fortune." He sipped again. "*If* I still cared about coins."

She grinned. "Oh, there's room for a couple bags of beans."

They sat and sipped coffee in the middle of a blown-out Starbucks in the middle of a blown-out city. Kevin tried to picture people in the seats around them, reading, or doing whatever it was people did in a place like this while drinking coffee.

Sure expected there to be more Infected here. He considered Kwan's statement about them thinning out. *Maybe all the symbiotes wound up stuck in the pool and the poor fucks died off like they should have?*

Tris picked at her empty mug. "You think he's coming?"

"Figure we give your old man maybe an hour to show up? I really don't want to be inside the city when it gets dark."

She cringed as if engaging in some internal tug-of-war. "I understand. I'm not sure what's got me on edge more. The possibility of seeing my father again, or worrying about Abby."

Kevin squinted out at the sky. "Nathan really is *that* kind of asshole, isn't he? You really think we're going to accomplish something? Stop them from dropping that crap on our heads?"

"Yes." She shifted in the chair. "I... can't tell if it's that overlay making me feel that way, but my dad is a damn genius. If he thinks I can do something, maybe I can."

He reached across the table to hold her hand. "All right. We give it a day? See if we can hole up on the roof for the night."

17

HIGH ALERT

Huddled against the wall with a ratty teddy bear clutched to her chest, Abby shivered. She scuffed her feet back and forth on the carpet in Zoe's closet, trying to get her toes under some of the clothes lining the floor. She didn't want anyone to see her crying, much less clinging to a stuffed animal as if it might actually do something to protect her. It did help a little, even if she felt foolish acting like a child half her age.

Why did they have to leave? She sniffled and closed her eyes. Her Dad often asked *Jesús* for things when he got scared. It didn't make much sense asking a tiny card tacked to the wall for help. The image of a longhaired man with his heart outside his chest, holding up two fingers lingered in her memory, as did the peeling drywall to which her father had pinned it. Yet, whenever things turned rough for him, he'd always talk to the card... or if they weren't home, to the sky.

Dad always said Jesús is watching... but if he's real, why didn't he protect him from Warren?

The Enclave had killed her father. They'd killed everyone back home, and now Tris and Kevin had gone *to* them. Sick with worry, Abby curled tighter and sobbed into the bear's head. It smelled like fruit, a child's perfume or candy or some such thing. Zoe had evidently not 'needed' the bear anymore, hence her finding it in the closet.

Maybe she had it in the suitcase and it makes her sad. Thinking about Pete handing Abby over to strangers on the bus, not knowing if he'd ever see her again made her Dad's death hurt ten times more. She worried that she'd never see Tris again. A powerful shiver rocked her body, though from cold, sadness, or fear, she couldn't tell. Kevin wasn't such a bad guy. He'd said he'd had a nightmare about her being one of the Infected, but couldn't shoot her. In fact, the idea of it had bothered him so much he woke straight up. Abby smiled to herself. Hearing him say that had changed him in her mind from 'the guy who lives with Tris' to someone who cared for her too. She'd had her doubts at first, only because most men she'd seen come through Amarillo—the drivers—had no patience for kids, and one had even tried to convince her to go into his room at the Hotel.

Don, the manager, had overheard him. He came running over and pulled her away from the driver. A little later, Dad showed up and—as far as she knew—shot the guy once some of the soldiers had whisked her out of the building. He'd warned her to stay away from drivers because she was 'getting near that age now' and shouldn't trust men, especially strange drivers. But Kevin didn't scare her like that. She'd come to trust him, and, like Dad, he would probably also shoot a guy who tried to make her go alone with him into a room. Maybe someday he'd even explain to her why her father had gotten so angry. As furious as Dad had been, he couldn't bring himself to talk about it. Kevin couldn't *replace* Dad, but she found herself wanting him there. Not many grown men would admit to being afraid, or having nightmares. In that, they shared something—complete terror about Infected.

Please come home. She broke down again, crying for a few minutes in the dark. Maybe if she stayed in the closet, the Virus wouldn't find her. She glanced to her left at the M-16 leaning against the wall. Being that close to a loaded firearm added another layer of fear. Unfortunately, Zoe's loft bedroom had nowhere else to hide. The bed sat right on the floor without a frame, and both of the white dresser cabinets touched the wall so she couldn't get behind them. Despite the presence of the weapon, the closet offered the greatest sense of security.

She pressed her right shoulder into the wall, even another millimeter more space between her and the rifle felt like a good idea.

A sudden buzzing noise outside almost released her bladder, but the sound sputtered off into the recognizable chop of a small ethanol-powered motor... probably some manner of handheld farm tool.

Not a drone.

She let go of the bear with one hand long enough to pull a pink and white child's T-shirt over her bare feet. It looked too small even for Zoe to wear, though Isla might be able to squeeze into it.

The closet door swung open.

Abby stifled a scream into the bear's head.

Zoe, in her favorite denim dress, leaned back with her eyebrows up. She lifted and dropped her toes a few times while her expression changed from surprise to confusion and at last, to sympathy.

Abby blushed, trembling.

"It's okay," said Zoe in a half-whisper. She crept closer and sat on the floor, her legs curled to her left. "I used to hide in here too when I was scared."

"The drones are coming." Abby wiped at her face. She cringed inside, waiting for Zoe to make fun of her for holding a teddy bear.

The younger girl tucked a lock of blonde behind her ear. After watching her shiver for a little while in silence, Zoe scooted closer and put an arm around her. "I used to be scared all the time, too. An' mad. I was mad at my dad for puttin' me on that bus alone. After Bill took me here, I'd spend all day in this closet, thinkin' Infected were gonna come in."

Abby relaxed a little, letting her feet slide forward until her legs lay flat. Head bowed, she mumbled at the bear. "Why did they have to go? I'm so scared they won't come back."

Zoe stuck her hand in the pile of old clothes and fished out a six-inch tall action figure that resembled a furry man with a bear's head and a drill sergeant hat. "This is Bear Ranger. He used to protect Fuzz." She pointed at the stuffed bear in Abby's grip. "Fuzz was always scared."

Abby picked at the matted brown fur in her hands. "That one's smaller. He's not even half as tall as Fuzz."

Zoe held the plastic bear-man up and smiled. "But he's tougher." She tapped it with a fingertip. "He's not very good for hugging, but he's brave. Sometimes big people are scareder than little ones."

"You're making that up, aren't you?" Abby sighed. "You're littler than me and I'm acting like a big baby."

"Fuzz was scared longer than me." Zoe bit her lip and put the plastic figure down. She took hold of the M-16, but kept it pointed straight up. "Would you shoot a bad person?"

Abby shied away from the weapon. "Do you have to hold it? What if it goes off?" She squirmed. "I don't wanna shoot anyone."

Zoe put the rifle back against the wall. "Guess you're like Fuzz then."

The nine-year-old's voice held no trace of mockery. Abby looked at her. Despite having a two-year lead in age, she didn't have half the other girl's nerve. Zoe *had* shot people. For real.

"H-have you killed anyone?" whispered Abby.

"No. Killing's not nice. I shoot the bandits in the leg so they can't hurt us. Sometimes they call me mean names."

Abby tapped her feet together, thinking for a moment. "How often do they come?"

Zoe grinned, adoration sparkled in her blue eyes. "Used'ta be like every two weeks, but Kev an' Tris beat a *whole group* of 'em. Been pretty quiet a while now. I like it better not bein' shot at." She looked down and picked at a toenail. "Ann always gets upset when there's shooting."

"She doesn't want you to get hurt. You should hide." Abby relaxed a little more and shifted to put her back to the wall, facing Zoe.

Zoe's expression melted to a look of distant detachment. Her voice came monotone. "Infected kicked and tossed me inna suitcase. They almost got me. I'm not afraid of normal people."

"Sorry." Abby looked down.

"It's okay." Her eeriness dissipated as fast as it had set in. She grinned. "Kev and Tris are too tough for those Omclave shits. They'll come back."

Abby blushed. "My dad said kids shouldn't say those words. 'Specially little girls."

Zoe gave her a meek look. "Sorry if words make you sad, but sometimes a girl just needs to say shit." A mischievous smile played across her face. "Ann really doesn't like it if I say f—"

"Zoe?" yelled Ann. "Abby? Come downstairs. It's time to eat."

Abby gawked at her.

Zoe stuck her tongue out. "Flock."

Abby furrowed her brows. *Is she teasing me, or does she think that's a dirty word?*

"'Mon." Zoe leapt to her feet and dragged Abby by the hand to the edge of the loft.

Zoe ambled down the steep wooden ladder facing forward. Merely watching her sent a twinge of unease up Abby's spine. She turned her back and climbed down. By the time her foot touched the hallway floor, Zoe had already taken a seat in the kitchen. She bounced, swinging her legs.

"Come on Abby," said Ann.

"I'm here." She hurried down the hall and took the chair catty-corner to Zoe.

Ann set a plate in front of each of them. Two sandwiches each contained three small slabs of pan-fried meat. Abby lifted the top piece of bread and examined the strips laid across the sandwich, browned and seasoned. She couldn't tell if she looked at fish or chicken. Ann returned to the counter, sliced two more pieces of bread off the loaf before covering it with a towel, and sat across the table from the kids with her lunch.

"It's rattlesnake," said Ann.

Zoe tore into it without hesitation.

Smells okay. After a test nibble confirmed it tasty, if not a bit tough, she took a real bite.

They ate in relative quiet for a little while.

Around the time she had half a sandwich left, Abby glanced at Zoe. "Do I have to join the militia too? Will they make me carry a gun?"

Zoe shook her head. "Only if you want to."

Abby stared worry into her lunch.

"No one is forced to join the militia," said Ann. "When you're fourteen or so, you'll be expected to do *some* kind of work though. 'Til then, only school is required. Your parents aren't farmers, so you probably won't have to work before that."

Zoe, still holding her food in two hands, brushed her leg with a foot under the table. "It's okay if you're scared. You're just a little girl."

Abby smirked. "I'm older than you."

Zoe shrugged. "If you say so."

"Ooh." Abby stuck her tongue out.

Zoe giggled.

Abby looked down. "I don't wanna shoot people."

"Okay." Zoe winked. "I'll shoot 'em for you."

Ann bit her lip, worry clear in her eyes.

Without much else in the way of conversation, they finished eating a few minutes later. Ann shooed the girls upstairs, offering to deal with cleanup herself so they could play. Zoe started to race off to the ladder, but Abby lingered.

"I'll help. It's okay. You're letting me stay here 'til…" *Ann called them my parents.* A lump swelled in her throat.

"Oh, it's all right dear." Ann squeezed her shoulder. "You've a lot on your mind. Go on and be a child for a bit longer. This world is sad enough without rushing into being all grown up."

Abby started to nod, but froze at the thump of boots on the porch.

Someone knocked, firm, but not the pounding of threat or warning.

Ann went over to answer. Abby backed into the countertop, ready to run.

"Yes?" asked Ann.

"Mornin', ma'am," said a man. "Mayor Wade's called a town meeting. Askin' everyone to head down by the circle. Jes' be a few minutes."

"All right." Ann left the door open and walked closer to the inner hallway. "Zoe? Come here please."

Again, the little blonde sprite raced down the ladder like a stairwell. Abby looked away, imaginary pain twinged in the bones she expected to break from falling if she ever tried that.

"There's a town meeting." Ann took each girl by the hand.

"Do I need the rifle?" asked Zoe.

"No. It's a meeting, not a muster." Ann shot her a pointed look. "And you are *not* militia yet, sweetie. You're only nine. You have to be at least sixteen."

Zoe whined. "But, Gran'ma… Emma's only thirteen."

"Emma's an exception… and one your father won't ask for." Ann shook her head muttering in Spanish.

Abby caught enough to grasp the woman wanted *Jesús* to talk some sense into the child. She twisted back to look at the loft ladder; her moccasins remained upstairs. She opened her mouth to ask if she had time to go get them as Ann pulled her out onto the porch. Neither she nor Zoe wore shoes either. Not wanting to be a whiner, she kept quiet and followed.

She kept her gaze on the ground as they walked along the road for a little while. At the din of numerous voices murmuring up ahead, Abby looked up at something on the order of two hundred people milling around a wide intersection. A pathetic little traffic circle, barely twelve feet (if that) across stood at the front of the crowd. A middle-aged white guy in a beige dress shirt and jeans stood on top of a folding table facing the crowd, with a few older people around him, though not on the table. Zara sat on the table facing the crowd, and Crystal, the woman Tris referred to has her 'boss,' waved at the crowd in an effort to quiet them and get them to pay attention.

Abby's brain shut down at the size of the crowd. She clung to Ann's side, trying to hide her face. Already, she imagined everyone turning to stare at her with accusing glares, wondering if she'd bring the Virus down on them. Would they all think her sick too?

Ann paused to look at her. "It's all right, Abby. Come on now. You're too big for me to carry."

She relaxed her grip and walked a little faster, though still kept her head down. When they finally stopped near the back edge of the crowd, she stood behind Ann so no one could see her. Zoe tugged on the belt of a man in militia camo at her right.

He looked back and down. "Hello, Zoe."

"I can't see back here. Can I go up?" She reached toward him as if asking to be lifted.

After a nod of assent from Ann, the militiaman crouched and let Zoe climb up to sit on his shoulders. He stood, and Zoe waved at Zara, who smiled.

Abby closed her eyes and pressed her forehead into Ann's back. Only the fear of being seen and yelled at kept her from running off back to her room in her parents' house.

A short while later, a man called out, "Thank you everyone for assembling on short notice. I'll be as brief as I can. As some of you may know already, Nederland has likely become a target for the Enclave. We strongly doubt that this will result in any manner of direct assault from individuals like those who attempted to raid us several months ago. If they decide to attack us, it will be by drone."

"What the flyin' shit is a drone?" yelled a woman somewhere to the left.

Mayor Wade waited for an upwelling of murmuring to die down. "I'm getting to that. A drone is an automated flying machine like this."

The crinkle of a tarp brought silence to the assembly. Abby's knuckles widened, clutching the back of Ann's dress. Gasps swept over the crowd.

"This is a mockup of a reconnaissance drone," said Zara, loud but not shouting. "Little Zoe managed to shoot one like this down about a half mile away from Nederland. It's unlikely the operator spotted anything before the drone crashed, but they will probably send more to find out why they lost one."

"Why'd you bring the goddamned thing into town? Isn't it gonna kill us?" yelled a man.

"This is only painted wood to give everyone an idea what they look like," said Zara. "However… if anyone sees anything that looks like this flying around, shoot it down."

Mayor Wade cleared his throat. "On that point. Until or unless the drone threat is proven to be gone, I am hereby asking all residents of Nederland twelve years of age and older to carry a firearm at all times. Preferably a rifle. Anything in the air not recognized as a bird, take it down. Also, if anyone manages to down one… do not go near it."

Abby, trembling with dread, peered around Ann.

Zara lifted herself up to stand on the table. "That's my job. The dangerous part of the drones is if they are carrying the viral agent. I'm inoculated against it, so I cannot get sick. Please, if anyone sees any suspicious broken bottles, stay away from them. Don't touch any green slime or broken glass lying out in the open. If you see anything like it, hold your breath and get away as fast as possible."

Murmurs of alarm rose in the crowd.

"How d'we know if we dead?" asked an older man.

Zara's expression hinted at a smartass remark wanting out. "Depending on the wind conditions, a ruptured capsule can be infectious at anywhere from ten feet to hundreds of yards in a narrow path if there's a stiff breeze. The agent must make contact with your eyes, open wounds, or be inhaled to set in. If anyone sees a smashed glass capsule with green liquid, stay upwind of it and get away as fast as you can. Cover your mouth and nose."

The crowd's silence fanned the fires of Abby's terror.

"I realize that some of you may not be entirely comfortable with so many weapons being out and about, but it is only for the time being." Mayor Wade held up his hands in a placating gesture. "The militia will still be responsible for the primary defense of Nederland, and we are in the midst of constructing more elevated positions to allow for a greater range of engagement. If anyone sees anything suspicious on the ground, get away and notify the militia immediately. Thank you. Any questions?"

Many hands went up.

Abby struggled not to let her rattlesnake sandwich slither back up her throat. Fear made her sick. At her trembling, Ann turned and embraced her. She whispered soothing things into the top of her head, though none had meaning more than comforting sounds and warm breath in her hair. Abby stared transfixed at the black oblong shape of a fake drone sitting on a wheeled cart next to the table. Its elongated airframe resembled a motorcycle without handlebars or wheels. Four 'fan shrouds' about the size of car tires stuck out from the corners, front and back. She thought back to the other day when Zoe had fired off more than twenty bullets before the drone went down.

Image after image of broken capsules on the streets of Amarillo played a slideshow in a waking nightmare. The air in her lungs grew heavy; sweat rolled down her back under her dress. All the voices in the crowd trading questions with Zara and the Mayor became a terrifying roar she *had* to escape. She pushed at Ann, squirming, trying to run.

Find a hiding place.

Get out of sight.

Stop breathing.

Abby shrieked and squirmed. When she couldn't get away from Ann, her legs gave out and she collapsed in place, curled in a ball.

I'm gonna die... I'm gonna die... Mommy!

A blur of Ann's face swept past her vision as the world spun into a smear of color.

Everything went black.

***

ABBY CAME TO ON THE SOFA OF ANN'S HOUSE, A WARM BLANKET WRAPPED around her to the waist. She lay sideways with her back against Ann's chest, and the woman's arms around her. Zoe sat cross-legged on the floor nearby working on a jigsaw puzzle in the middle of the living room. The light outside remained strong, though she felt like she'd slept for a whole day.

"You're safe, Abby." Ann stroked her hair, peering down at her with an expression of concern and relief. "You fainted."

"I'm sorry." Abby couldn't summon the urge to move.

Ann rocked her. "Nothing for you to be sorry about. *Pobrecilla.* You shouldn't have had to see the things you've seen."

Zoe jammed a piece of the puzzle in. Abby looked at her.

Ann chuckled. "She's angry because the militia won't let her patrol."

"I'm a good shot!" yelled Zoe. "I killed that drone when it was way far away!"

"You're nine." Ann sighed at her. "No one wants you getting hurt."

Zoe leapt to her feet and stomped, making puzzle bits bounce. "Drones not gonna shoot at me 'cause I got a gun. They just fly. I don't wanna let stupid Omclave kill us! I'm gonna watch on the roof and you can't stop me."

The little one ran off to the loft.

Ann shivered. "Zoe! Come back here right now. Don't you dare put me through that worry."

"Aww, Gran'ma…" The girl stopped halfway up the ladder. Head hung, she trudged back to the living room and fell seated by the puzzle.

Abby squirmed.

Ann pulled the blanket snug around her. "Don't be afraid, Abby. The militia will keep us safe."

"Amarillo had soldiers too." She looked up, her expression and tone blank. "They didn't help."

18

RESISTANCE

W orry raged like a tornado in Tris' gut. She'd thought Nathan couldn't find them in Ned, but he already had. A whole group of Enclave soldiers had ambushed them there once. If not for Zara and her rifle... No, Nathan damn sure knew where Nederland was. Maybe he didn't know that they had decided to live there permanently yet. He could still be scouring the Wildlands trying to find them, but a good chance existed that the bastard knew Nederland held some value to them. Nathan had wiped out Amarillo without hesitation, even thinking the place had ten thousand or so people.

All to get at her.

While the few hundred who'd died there because of him were a far cry off the tens of thousands everyone believed had lived in Amarillo, she still bore some of the guilt at what had happened. She had no way to know he would do that, no way to stop it (aside from bringing the cure to Doctor Andrews, which turned out to be a lie), and... at least until an hour or so ago, no way to avenge them.

I have to do this. For them. For Abby... for everyone in Ned. Everyone left in the world.

Weakening light outside the dead Starbucks put Kevin on edge. Part of her agreed with him that only an idiot would stay inside San Francisco after dark. Yet that bit of her that had latched on to Abby, some nascent urge of motherhood that had come out of nowhere in high gear, wouldn't stop gnawing on her brain. The mere thought of Nathan harming Abby made her blood rush, flooding her cheeks with heat. She covered her mouth and nose, breathing into her hands to calm down.

"Tris?" Kevin drew her name out long. "Your face is red. Am I hanging out of my pants or something?"

She barked a short laugh. "No. I'm feeling overprotective of Abby all of a sudden. I want to rip Nathan's head off."

"Count me in on that action." He stood. "I'm gonna walk outside and look for some place to stash the car. If we're going to be here overnight, I don't want some drone going overhead and spotting it."

Something scraped in the back room.

Shit. Tris spun in the chair and pointed her AK at the door.

"What?" He followed suit.

"I heard something," she whispered. "A scratch."

Kevin crept sideways to the right, rifle raised, and took cover behind a brick-faced column by the former window to the parking lot. Tris slid off the chair to kneel and edged to her left to a more defensible position behind the barista counter.

The door to the back room swung open. A man in his middle twenties with paper-white skin like Tris and a matching white brush-cut walked in, his stride casual. Beneath a tattered green poncho, the shimmery black gleam of Enclave body armor caught the fading sunlight. The pieces of his suit had differing levels of scuff, suggesting he'd assembled it from multiple sets. He carried a boxy rifle like the one Kevin had in the car, a 4mm caseless.

At the sight of Tris, he froze. His eyebrows climbed together, his mouth opened a touch.

Another man, darker-skinned than Fitch with a short-cut afro, bumped into him from behind due to the abrupt halt. He also wore Enclave armor that had a piecemeal look about it, except for his right leg, decked out in Kevlar panels.

"What's the hold up?" asked a female voice behind the second man.

"Holy shit," said the white-haired man. "What's one of those doing here? We're fucked."

The dark-skinned man eyed Tris with the look of a gunslinger about to throw down, though dread fear shone clear in his eyes.

"Wait," said Tris. "You're clearly not Enclave… at least not anymore."

Kevin lifted his aim to their heads, realizing the AK wouldn't penetrate that armor.

A woman with a snow-blonde bob squeezed past the men. While shorter than both men, she still had Tris by an inch or two. Beneath a dingy brown cloak made from a blanket, a newer suit of Enclave body armor fit her too well to be scavenged. Thin silver hexagons glistened from the polished black surface as she advanced into a patch of sunlight.

"Who are you?" asked the woman. Though she contained it well, her body language betrayed no small amount of fear.

"Is that coffee?" asked the white-haired man.

Tris studied the trio for a few seconds more. *Their gear is too dirty. They're not Enclave.* "Can everyone stay calm? I'd rather not get shot."

"That doesn't tell me who you are," said the woman.

"I'm not a Persephone. I just look like them for some damn reason." Tris lowered her rifle a few inches and stood. "You're Resistance, aren't you?"

"*This* is the contact?" asked the dark-skinned man.

"That's..." Brush Cut stepped forward. "Tris?"

She relaxed a little more. "Yeah."

"Damn. We got a message months ago saying you were on the way. What the hell happened?"

"That's a yes by the way," said the dark-skinned man. "We're Resistance."

"We'd given up on ever seeing you." The woman's tension ebbed a bit as well.

Brush Cut offered a hand to shake. "Printer spat out another message saying a contact was coming here with some data that's absolutely vital to our efforts. Name's Zoryn."

The guy's height made her feel like a tween standing in front of him and looking... up. "Hi."

"Uther," said the dark skinned man. "Before you ask, no it's not supposed to be Luther. My mother's got tons of books."

"Pendragon?" asked Kevin. "I think I read that... or at least a wad of paper I found in a Roadhouse once."

"Yeah, that." Uther nodded.

"I'm Naomi." The other white-haired woman approached and shook Tris' hand. "So are you here by chance, or did that message tell us to find you?"

"Are you sure we can trust these three? They came out of an empty room." Kevin stepped away from the brick-covered column since it offered no cover from their angle now that they'd walked into the room.

"Maybe this will help." Naomi held up a hand in a 'wait' gesture, and reached into a hip satchel. Kevin twitched. Despite his almost raising the AK at her face, none of the three reacted. She removed a folded paper and handed it out to Tris.

Kevin relaxed.

Tris opened the paper, which contained a color printout of a photograph. She turned it right side up and gasped. A tiny white-haired girl in a plain white dress sat on the floor by a desk. Circuit boards, wires, and tools littered the rug around her bare feet. A man with frazzled light brown hair smiled at her from the desk chair, wearing a lab coat and radiating a kindly, almost befuddled presence—the scientist who everyone assumed 'got lucky' whenever anything worked, but masked true brilliance with a blasé attitude and a sense that having fun was every bit as important as getting results.

Dad.

Her lip quivered and she found herself crying in silence.

"Tris?" Kevin lowered the AK and ran over, putting an arm around her back. He glanced at the paper. "Is…"

"Me and my dad… I think I'm five here… maybe six." She traced her fingers over the paper. The office around them looked like it belonged in a school or something; a thought backed up by a Stanford banner half out of frame. All sorts of techno-clutter lined the walls; robot parts, mostly transparent plastic over thin aluminum. The robotics, early, early prototypes, made Bee seem like alien-level technology by comparison. She looked up at Naomi. "Where did you get this?"

"It came out of the printer… right after the message saying we should expect to meet a contact here with information. Didn't expect you to beat us here."

She folded the paper. "Can I keep this?"

Naomi glanced back at Zoryn, who shrugged. "Yeah, sure. So what do you have?"

Tris returned to her chair. She sat with the AK between her knees, stock on the floor, and pushed it back and forth between her hands while explaining about the music files, the hidden data, the phone number, the call… and waiting here.

The three listened, nodding intermittently.

"Dad said he needed me to get inside. I'm supposed to help him with something he can't do on his own."

"Wait. *Inside?*" Kevin stared at her. "You want to go... inside the Enclave? How's that going to work? They're kind of trying to kill you."

"Maybe we can help with that." Zoryn peered out the window. "It will be dark soon. Get in your car and follow us."

Kevin's expression said he still didn't trust them.

"I believe them." She took his hand. "The same way I knew the vaccine would protect me; I know these people are the right way forward."

"The overlay." He bowed his head, eyes closed, and sighed through his nostrils. "Are you sure?"

Tris leaned against him. Rational-brain screamed at her to run back to Nederland. That's what pre-Detention, pre-VR training Tris would do. Something threatened her, she'd hide. As much as she'd have loved nothing more than to race home, dread that faltering now could kill Abby (and everyone else there) in the most horrible way imaginable, made her choice—albeit terrifying—the only one she could make.

"Yeah. I'm sure."

19

AMARANTH

Driving the Challenger at walking pace felt wrong in every way imaginable. Too vulnerable, an insult to a car built for speed, boring. Had they not packed the back seat up with shopping bags, perhaps the supposed resistance people would've climbed in and they'd be wherever they wanted to go by now. He debated tossing the stuff, but Tris had been so happy to find such a pristine stash of children's clothing, getting rid of it would feel like kicking her dog.

The sun continued to slip off to the west, fanning the fires of his worry. Tris at least appeared to share in his concern, as the darker it got, the more she kept twisting around to watch for Infected.

At long last, some twenty minutes after leaving the Starbucks, Zoryn gestured at a right turn. The overall design of the buildings around them had gone toward commercial properties: old warehouses or unlabeled large, plain structures. Signs of warfare remained: barricades, bullet strikes, scorch marks from explosives. The damage could've happened in the immediate aftermath of the war when chaos ruled, or yesterday.

He'd heard plenty of stories from elders in his days running jobs for Wayne. Once people believed no more nukes were on the way, those who hadn't died went crazy. Some ran about raiding things they could never have had in organized society: expensive cars, boats, fancy clothes. Others got testy about more practical concerns like food, clothing, and shelter.

Degrees of violence varied depending on population, but he'd heard some horrible stories.

Hate groups, long restrained from overt acts of criminality, ran amok with the collapse of order. People shot each other for silly things like skin tone, believing the wrong mythology, or speaking with an accent. Of course, not everyone needed an excuse. Some simply enjoyed killing. It hadn't taken long for the 'flares to burn down' as Wayne said. The idiots burned hot and fizzled out fast, leaving the 'honest folk who just wanted to live' behind. So began the people Kevin thought represented the bulk of humanity. Everyone trying to survive, willing to help others who weren't shitheads.

And the Virus fucked them all.

Zoryn directed him at an alley between two buildings that resembled aircraft hangars. He followed it to the end where it opened into an area full of white gravel. The three Resistance people sank out of view as they descended below the level of the ground, again waving for him to follow. Kevin nudged the car up to the side and peered down at an angled concrete wall that led to some manner of manmade river path—only massive. As far as he could see to the right, the channel continued with a slight leftward curve, spanned by a handful of overpasses. Zoryn and the others headed left toward a wall about a hundred yards away with six square tunnels.

"Will the car make that grade?" Tris peered at the bottom.

"Not without pain."

He figured it would scrape at the least, and ruin the bumper—possibly bend the frame—at worst. About a quarter mile to the right, he caught a glimpse of an access roadway and decided to go for it rather than drive straight down the angled concrete. With a spray of gravel, the Challenger took off, reaching the ramp in a few seconds. Though the turn at the bottom proved sharp, nothing scraped. He straightened out and drove along the artificial riverbed back to where the three waited for him. Their initial confusion at him going in the wrong direction gave way to expressions of understanding as he rolled to a stop nearby.

"Maybe I'd have gone straight down if I had a truck." He smiled. "Didn't wanna thrash the frame."

Naomi nodded.

They led him into the third tunnel from the left, one of two not blocked off by walls of shipping containers. A minute or so after driving into the tunnel, Uther waved at him to stop.

He rolled down the window.

"Can leave the car here. We're close enough to the door." Uther smiled.

Once the headlights went out, the three Resistance people turned on flashlights.

"You sure you trust them?" Kevin glanced at Tris.

"Mostly. I got nothing else though. And they had that picture."

He cocked an eyebrow. "Would Nathan have sent that picture?"

"If Nathan knew I was here, and sent them, there would've been gunfire already." She opened her door. "Not saying we should drop our guard, but I trust them enough to see where this leads."

"Okay." He held her hand for a few seconds. "If this goes south, I'm going to be selfish and die first. I don't want to have to deal with the pain of losing you."

She thumped him on the arm. "Ass."

Kevin got out, shut down the car, and engaged the security code. The dry riverbed below the ground level would make a decent place to sit and wait for the portable chargers to work. Probably even leave the car in the tunnel and run the panels outside.

"In here." Zoryn walked up to a pale grey door with some rust spots.

Uther opened it with a key and walked in.

The other two followed.

Kevin relaxed a little bit at their not wanting to flank them. He went in ahead of Tris.

"Close it, please," said Naomi.

Tris backtracked to shut the door behind them.

A short hallway led to a ninety-degree turn to the right, another door, and a long massive room thick with a pungent odor somewhere between seaweed and foot. The last vestiges of the setting sun leaked in from a narrow strip of windows near the ceiling, some two and a half stories overhead. Six massive machines that resembled boilers dominated the left three-quarters of the space. Pipes large enough for a man to crawl inside of connected them to the ceiling and the wall behind. Opposite the enormous machines stood a wall full of dials, buttons, and gauges. The repetitive nature of the pattern suggested each machine had a separate, identical control panel. Rust blanketed most surfaces, and the majority of the buttons and whatnot on the control wall had been smashed.

Zoryn approached the panel opposite the fourth machine and typed a code on a keypad of silver buttons resembling those of an ancient phone.

Kevin chuckled. *This place had to be obsolete before the war.*

A loud *click* sounded from another cabinet covered in gauges and lights. The yellow, orange, and red bulbs looked as though they hadn't seen electricity in a hundred years. Uther grasped the corner of the cabinet and opened it like a door. The interior had scorch marks from recent welding, where most of the guts had been removed to make space for a passageway containing metal stairs.

A silver box about the size of a fist near the top left corner didn't appear to be part of the original mechanism, and the new wires leading from it into the wall confirmed that feeling.

"Interesting doorbell," said Kevin.

"Enclave sometimes comes looking for us here," said Naomi.

"What if they find the car?" asked Tris.

Zoryn smiled. "They don't usually enter the tunnels unless we've kicked them where it hurts. They haven't been doing much lately around here though. You should be long gone before any Hoplites come by."

"Those things wouldn't fit in the tunnels anyway." Kevin finally felt comfortable enough to sling the AK over his shoulder. "They'd have to come in on foot."

"I doubt they'd think anything of that car if they found it." Naomi shook her head. "Just some ballsy Wildlander exploring."

Uther entered last, pulling the hidden door closed.

Naomi and Zoryn jogged down the stairs to a catwalk, lighting the way. Three dark pipes ran along the middle of the curved tunnel ceiling. Dirty concrete patch jobs decorated the bare cinder block walls. Kevin coughed on the taste of wet dust, straining to make out details in the dark.

Their guides stopped again for no apparent reason. Before Kevin could open his mouth to ask why, Naomi spotted her flashlight on a partially concealed door to the left and pounded her fist into it twice. A tense moment later, the door opened inward, flooding the area with bright light.

Kevin squinted, grunting from the surprise. Zoryn stepped in past another pale man in a grey shirt and pants, who looked at Tris as though he'd seen a ghost. Naomi followed. Kevin entered behind her, still cringing at the change in light. Near the door, a flat panel monitor offered a green night vision view of the hallway outside, evidently from a tiny fiberoptic camera overhead.

As his eyes acclimated, he looked around at several long tables with attached bench seats, a row of bunk beds arranged between freestanding lockers, a larger table without chairs that had a hologram of tunnels hovering over it, and one hallway leading deeper in.

Eight more people, none of whom had armor on, froze in their tracks and stared at Tris.

"Oh, please tell me that's not what I think it is," said a tiny girl who appeared around twelve or so. She could've been Naomi's kid sister; they had the same white bob, only this girl had blood red eyes instead of green.

"Damn," whispered someone to the right.

"I'm not a Persephone," said Tris. "Honest."

"As if one of those things would admit it." A deep voiced man, pale but not snow-white, shook his head.

"I met one who did." Kevin smiled. "Seemed like a nice enough girl when she wasn't throwing bikers through houses."

The small girl approached, bare feet poking out of too-long black BDU pants. She wore an immaculate white tank top that exposed her shoulders and showed off her lack of breasts. Aside from her height, she had the physique of a nine year old. "She's right. Persephones are taller, look older, and actually have muscle tone."

"Look who's talking." Tris folded her arms.

Some of the people laughed.

"Your little sister's adorable." Kevin smiled at Naomi.

The small girl sighed at the ceiling. "Right. First, I'm not Naomi's sister. Second, I'm not twelve. You've heard of nanites?"

"Yeah." Kevin chuckled. "Tris has 'em. Kinda want 'em myself."

"Well, I got a slightly overtuned batch. I stopped looking older when they installed it, and sometimes I think I'm creeping backwards. I'm thirty-six. Most of these people call me Amaranth."

"Tris," said Tris. "You must go through a lot of food."

Amaranth rolled her eyes. "Don't get me started on that either. It's annoying. Not fair to everyone else here how much I have to eat."

"Hey maybe you can give me some of those and between the two of us we wind up normal?" Kevin grinned.

"Doesn't work that way. The nanites are coded to my DNA. If we injected my nanites into your body, they'd treat your tissues as being invasive to me and destroy everything." Amaranth winked. "Basically about the most intensely painful way to die you can imagine."

Kevin shook his head. "That would be getting stuffed face-first into Wayne's toilet."

Tris shivered.

Amaranth stared at him. "I don't want to know. So…" She looked up at Tris. "Why are you here?"

"My father told me to go to the Starbucks."

Kevin leaned over to Tris and whispered, "Hey, you're not the shortest person in the room."

Amaranth frowned. "This guy's original. Hope you pay him well. Your father? Doctor Jameson?"

"So you know who I am?" Tris blinked.

"You are well known among the Resistance, as well as certain circles within the Enclave."

Tris bit her lip. "How bad?"

"Well…" Amaranth walked over to the tables, waving for them to follow. She took a seat, shifted sideways, and put her feet up on the bench, ankles crossed. "Are you hungry?"

"Yeah." Tris scratched at her stomach. "Quite."

"Food sounds good." Kevin stepped over the bench and sat beside Tris.

"On it," said Zoryn. He had to duck to walk under a few pipes on his way to the hallway that led deeper into the place.

Amaranth leaned forward, arms folded on the tabletop. "Okay… I'll try to keep it simple and short. Your father was part of a movement that wanted to open the doors and reintegrate the Enclave with the outside world. Unfortunately, he found himself in the minority as most of those in power feared the result of nuclear war and were worried about genetic damage caused by the vast amounts of radiation let loose."

"I knew that already." Tris raked her fingers through her hair. "What 'circles' are you talking about?"

"Well, my people on the inside tell me that one of the First Tier administrators basically has your face on a dart board."

"Nathan," muttered Tris.

"Yeah. There are a small number of people within the biogenic science division who have secretly run progression models that predict the isolationist policies of the current Council will result in an unsustainable situation within thirty years or so."

"They needed computer models to understand that there's only so many ways to match people before you wind up inbreeding?" Tris slapped the table. "I think it's too late. They already did screw themselves into stupidity."

Amaranth smiled. "Perhaps. We've been trying to find a way into the city core, but so far, we've only been able to locate the quarantine district.

They really did their homework. Doesn't seem to be any alternate way into the core other than the main tram, not even vents."

Tris nodded.

"Wait, what?" asked Kevin.

"Shall I, or do you want to fill him in?" asked Amaranth.

Tris looked at him. "The Enclave is split into two parts. There's the city core, an underground metropolis built somewhere in the area around the University, where most of the people live. It's got all the education, technical, training, and residence facilities… basically most of the Enclave civilization. On the surface, there's a smaller outlying section of city they use for quarantine purposes. Basically anyone who goes outside, like the hovercraft pilots, or the patrollers, or in some rare cases, scientific survey teams, lives there for a few months after coming back. The security to get into the city core is ridiculous. The only way in or out that anyone knows about is a small magnetic tram line. The capsule seats four people at a time only, and it takes about twenty minutes to go between the zones."

"Wow… sounds like they're paranoid." Kevin shifted his jaw side to side. "What are they afraid of?"

"A little paranoid, yeah. Disease and radiation mostly." Tris smiled. "There's a decontamination process before getting into the cab… a shower, and they make you wear these paper gowns, which they burn as soon as you arrive… and go through another decontamination shower."

Kevin glanced between the women. "These people do realize the world isn't swimming with toxic shit anywhere near as bad as they think… except for the crap they've set loose."

"Paranoia isn't supposed to make sense." Amaranth leaned back and stretched. "The Council has convinced themselves that the outside world is deadly, and they've got everyone living in fear. That's the first step to controlling a large population: make them afraid of everything so they trust the people in power the way children trust their parents."

"We have to stop the Virus." Tris thumped the table with her fist.

Zoryn returned with a pair of silver trays. Each held a pair of chicken pieces, a beige glop, a basin of little green pellets, a brown square in the middle, and a small reservoir of light brown liquid. "Here ya go." He set one down in front of Tris and one by Kevin. "Oh…" He produced two plastic forks in clear wrappers from his pocket and handed them over.

"What are those?" Kevin pointed at the pellets.

"Peas," said Tris. "Eat the brown one last, that's dessert."

She attacked her food with almost as much ferocity as Katie had.

Kevin stabbed the chicken and tore off a piece. As soon as he bit down, he blinked. Taste unlike anything he'd experienced flooded his mouth. Spices of some kind, it had so much flavor it almost hurt. "Wow…"

"He's never had purified food before." Tris grinned. "It looks like chicken, but it never walked around. It's basically the same… muscle tissue grown in tanks. Less messy than caring for live chickens. Takes less space too."

"Stop." He raised a hand. "Let me enjoy this."

"Try the mashed potatoes with gravy." She winked.

Kevin scooped some of the beige goop, dipped it in the darker brown goop, and put it in his mouth. *If I could sell this shit at a Roadhouse, I'd own the world.* With great effort, he ate at the pace of a human being, and avoided the temptation to eat the tray as well.

Amaranth watched for a few minutes without bothering them.

"So…" asked Tris. "Everyone in the Enclave *doesn't* know me or want to kill me?"

"No." Amaranth shook her head. "Only Nathan's inner circle and a few of the military who've had direct contact with you out in the Wildlands. Director Gerhardt issued an order to the military that promised exile for anyone who volunteered for a 'special' mission issued by Administrator Savros."

Tris flashed a sinister grin. "I bet Nathan *loved* that."

"Please tell me you have the data about the antiviral process. The cure you were supposed to be smuggling out?"

Tris sighed. "I never had it. Nathan set that whole thing up. He loaded my implant with music… a *band* named The Cure."

Most of the people around them groaned.

One man in the back screamed and bashed his head into a locker door. "That's awful!"

"Tell me about it." Tris seethed.

"You okay, Mark?" yelled Amaranth.

The guy banging his head on the lockers waved dismissively at her and walked off rubbing his temples as if attempting to erase the memory of having heard that.

Amaranth leaned forward, head in her hand such that her eyebrows stretched unnaturally wide. "That is a god-awful pun. Someone needs to do something unseemly to Nathan for that."

"Oh… I want to." Tris scowled. "I don't think I can get near him though. He's too deep inside the city core."

"Don't you have to go in there anyway?" Kevin smiled.

"No... I should be able to do what I need to do from a terminal. I'm expecting this is going to involve uploading some kind of virus—software virus—into their system to turn the machinery that synthesizes and stores the biological virus against itself." She poked her fork at the brownie. "It's the only way that it makes sense for me to be able to have any kind of effect alone against the whole Enclave. I've got no chance of doing this up front and loud."

"So the cure was useless?" Amaranth grumbled. "We're back to square one."

"Not entirely." Tris bent forward, scooped the brownie out of the tray on the end of her fork, and pointed it at the smaller woman. "My father hacked a hidden message into the music files. Told me to contact him at an old phone number with an exchange in this area. Managed to find a working phone and... he said he needed me inside to help him, and then sent me to Starbucks."

"Hmm. I think we can help you with that." Amaranth smiled. "The Enclave spends a lot of time being high tech, so sometimes they forget low tech. We found an old subway tunnel that used to have a stop at Stanford. If you don't mind a climb, it connects via a ventilation shaft down a few stories and cuts over into the basement of one of the old university buildings. It's tight quarters, but it should be possible to make your way up through there to the Quarantine Section."

"Wait, didn't you say the Enclave city is underground?" Kevin scratched his head.

"The core is." Tris bit the corner off the fork-impaled brownie, and wagged the rest at him like a wand. "Quarantine is on the surface under a dome and several walls. There's lots of guards, sentry drones, cameras, and such. Remember all those stories about ten thousand coins reward for bringing runaways back?"

"Oh, so it's like a fake Enclave city above the real one?"

"The Quar isn't fake," said Amaranth. "It's about one-eighth the size of the city core. It's a staging area really, the interface between the city proper and the outside world. We haven't been able to locate the exact geographic location of the core, but we're starting to think it's offshore under the San Francisco Bay, given the approximate angle of the connecting tram and duration of the ride."

Kevin squinted. "How the hell do they get heavy equipment like those hovercraft in and out of an underground city with a damn ocean above it?"

"They don't need them down there." Amaranth smiled. "All of their Wildlands operations personnel are in the Quar."

"What about drones?" asked Tris. "Specifically the ones that distribute viral agent?"

Amaranth shot a frustrated glare at the wall. "We've only seen a few drones big enough not to be local area patrols come and go. All from the Quar as well."

Kevin clapped once. "Sounds simple enough to me. Anyone got a spare nuke lying around? Just drop it on this quarantine area and we pull the coyote's fangs right out."

"Great plan." Amaranth frowned. "Don't suppose you've got a nuke with you?"

A blonde woman in a black Enclave jumpsuit walked up behind Amaranth, whispered a few words and handed her a silver cylinder about the size of a pen.

"Thanks." Amaranth nodded at the woman and offered the object to Kevin. "You're probably going to need this."

"What is it?" Kevin took it, turning it around in his fingers. Aside from a small hole at one end, the device appeared featureless and smooth.

"An automatic injector with one dose of a vaccine that will, after about four hours, make you immune to Agent-94."

"What's—"

"The Virus." Amaranth exhaled. "You should take it and then I suggest you get some rest. We'll give you some Enclave uniforms so you don't stand out. Naomi and Zoryn will help you get as far as the tunnel. My people are more wanted than you two, so they can't even set foot in the Quar."

Tris nodded.

Kevin stared at the silver thing in his hand. Every momentary flash of terror he'd had at Infected from the day he'd first seen them as a child until an hour or so ago replayed in his mind as a rapid series of still images. One small device could eliminate all that worry.

He spun it over his fingers, thinking about how it would feel not to have to worry about becoming Infected ever again.

Tris' wide-eyed, somewhat open-mouthed smile made her look like someone had mainlined sunshine straight up her ass. He had to look away, and found himself snickering. "What?"

"That face." He grinned.

"You don't understand." Tris stared at Amaranth for a second. "He's phobic."

Amaranth raised her eyebrows. "Isn't everyone?"

"I mean clinical phobia. Freezes up, blacks out, screams like a small boy."

"Gee, thanks." Kevin flicked his thumb at the device.

Tris grabbed his arm. "Why are you not jabbing that thing in your thigh?"

"Well, for one thing, I'm not in the habit of injecting myself with something a person I've only known for a half hour gives me…"

"It looks authentic." Tris squeezed his arm.

"No one is forcing you to take it." Amaranth smiled. "I should probably warn you that the tunnels may have a significant Infected presence."

Kevin gazed into the warped reflection of his face, stretched into a slender line of tanned beige upon the narrow cylinder. The woman seemed honest enough, and the injector looked 'Enclave' enough, that he felt inclined to believe her. Still, as he thought about taking it, he couldn't help but picture Abby, and how terrified she'd been when the people in Amarillo believed she'd become Infected.

"Hey…" He looked up. "You got any more of these?"

"Not here. Everyone in the Resistance is from the Enclave. We're already all inoculated. We didn't have any pressing reason to stock up on it. We had a few on hand for outsiders who stumbled in and joined the cause, but… that's the last of it."

"I think I'm gonna hang onto it then. Someone needs it more than I do."

Tris gawked at him. "We're going into a tunnel full of those things. Take it."

He traced his thumb back and forth over the metal. "I'd rather give it to Abby. She's got a lot more years ahead of her than I do… and hey, if we don't mess this up, maybe no one will need it anymore."

Tris wrapped her arms around him and sniffled for a few seconds before she had to fight not to cry. "I don't want to lose you. You're too damn caring for your own good."

"Yeah." He tucked the vaccine injector into his jacket pocket. "I got that from Dad."

SURVIVAL

A lone tree branch wobbled in a patch of moonlight on the angled ceiling. Abby stared at the motion, swishing her feet back and forth under the blanket. Deep swirling shadows lurked at the edges of the loft bedroom, making her feel even more like a stranger in someone else's home. Her stomach churned with the same heavy sickness that began as soon as she'd spotted the drone. Every time she tried to close her eyes, the horrors of her old home filled her thoughts. Her hands had barely stopped shaking since she'd been carried in from the roof.

Fuzz, the teddy bear, remained tucked under her left arm where Zoe had put it hours ago, a matter-of-fact, 'here, you need this' gesture before she climbed over Abby to get in bed. Had she been able to peel her mind away from dreading what the drones were about to do to Nederland, she might've been insulted. Zoe meant well, but she'd basically called her a little kid who had to clamp on a stuffed animal to be able to sleep.

Not that she could sleep.

Amarillo had erupted into chaos in the middle of the night. Dad hauled her out of bed in such a rush he'd almost pulled her clean out of her dress. She didn't remember the mad run to the shelter of the army building, or the old fire station after that. One second she'd been in bed, the next she sat on cold concrete clinging to her father's side and shivering, not knowing why all the adults were screaming and shooting outside. The worst had been huddling with other children in a crawlspace for hours while her father went with about thirty others to take back the town. Seven returned.

Over five hundred people became one hundred in two days. Fifty in another six hours. A week after being dragged out of bed, fourteen people remained... and they all thought her the next to die. She squeezed the bear.

Any second now, she expected her dad or Bill or some adult to rush in, haul her out of bed, and drag her into the middle of Amarillo all over again. The second she closed her eyes and let her guard down, everyone would die.

Nederland was doomed.

Abby forced herself to cry in silence so the Infected wouldn't hear her. All the kids from Amarillo had figured that out quick. Every thump in the floor or clatter outside became death on two legs coming for her. The more she tried to stop thinking about it, the more her heart raced.

Zoe emitted a soft sigh in her sleep.

Abby looked to her right. The younger girl appeared every bit the little angelic blonde in her sleep; no one looking at her would ever imagine the tiny spitfire with a rifle who *shot* at people, a little girl who'd hidden inside a suitcase while Infected tossed her around. Abby's heart grew heavier.

I guess we're all broken.

Zoe's close call had frightened her so much she forgot how to 'child' properly. Abby had been so scared in Amarillo (and still was) she couldn't do anything but lay there worrying. The town she had at first thought so welcoming and safe had—in the matter of days—become a deathtrap. Remaining here terrified her as much as being handcuffed to a metal bedframe with Infected crawling in the windows. She couldn't let that happen again. If Tris and Kevin survived and came home, she had to be here for them. Imagining Tris' reaction to finding her sick for real got her near to throwing up. Not even knowing her for five minutes, the woman had seemed so heartbroken at the chance she'd been Infected. Would Abby even be able to recognize Tris if she turned? Would enough of her remain inside the mindless creature the Virus created?

Would Tris be able to shoot her?

Get out of here. She closed her eyes. *I gotta get out of here.*

Abby sat up, leaving the bear on the mattress. She slipped out of bed and pulled off the sweatshirt before grabbing her new dress from the floor, putting it on, and stepping into her moccasins. Zoe murmured in her sleep and shifted. Abby glanced back at her.

Should I wake her up and bring her with me? It seemed cruel to leave the girl here knowing what would happen to Nederland, but...

No. Zoe doesn't know what it's like. She doesn't know. Abby cringed at the memory of people shooting each other for sneezing or coughing. Brothers killing brothers. A mother shooting her son because he 'looked too sluggish and might be one of them.' Maybe he *had* turned, but Aaron had always been a little slow.

She'll try to stop me and yell for Bill or Ann. Abby grasped at her throat, struggling to breathe as fear built to a point the room spun around. She grabbed the bed to keep from falling. Deep breaths. Air in. Air out. Abby opened her mouth and shut her eyes. *The drones aren't here yet. I can get out. I gotta go.*

After two steps toward the ladder, she looped back to grab Fuzz. Another idea hit her and she swiped a small knapsack from the closet before creeping down the ladder. Bill and Pete's snoring almost shook both bedroom doors. It had to be a miracle that Cody could sleep in there with his father so loud.

Baby steps got her to the kitchen without waking anyone up. She swallowed a trickle of vomit sliding up the back of her throat and knelt by the cabinet. After a few breaths to ward off throwing up, she grabbed random canned goods until the knapsack wouldn't hold any more. Abby stood, slinging the burden over her shoulder. Cringing at the clattering bundle, she crept to the door and made her way outside.

The moon glowered at her from a cloudless indigo sky. Full and round, it painted Nederland with blue-tinged light, more than enough to see by. Abby eased herself down the three steps of the porch and tiptoed over the driveway to avoid making too much of a crunch in the gravel. On the road, she paused. Going to the right would bring her to the open area where they'd had the meeting, and eventually, the dump truck gates. She'd surely be spotted that way. Plus, she didn't want to go to another city, even an abandoned one like Boulder. Nothing good happened in cities.

Going left would take her by the lake. No one would be swimming at this hour, probably past midnight. With luck, she'd be well off into the forest before the drones arrived with Virus. She adjusted her grip on the bear, shifted the weight of canned goods closer to the middle of her back, and set off following the road to the west.

Abby refused to look to her right as she passed her house. Barely two months there, and she already felt possessive of her bedroom. She hesitated a moment, debating hiding out in there, but as much of a sanctuary as it had become, it couldn't stop Virus. Head down, she trudged away from the home she wanted so badly to return to.

The road looped around a hairpin turn up ahead and doubled back, running behind her house as well. Before realizing what she did, her gaze followed the curve and she wound up staring at the place again. All the windows were dark; no car parked next to it. It made no sense how much she wanted to hide in *her* room, but death would fall from the sky.

The want for Tris and Kevin to come back brought tears again, though she dared not make noise.

Wiping at the annoying wetness gliding down her face, she stomped onward. If they came back—no, *when* they came back, she'd be alive for them... even if no one else survived. Nederland, population: one.

I should've taken Zoe's gun. The Infected will come after me. She bit her lip. A momentary shiver of dread rattled her bones at the thought of shooting someone, even Infected. *No... I'll just go up a tree. They can't climb.*

At the hairpin, she continued straight onto grass, heading toward a modest hill covered in pine trees rustling in a gentle nighttime breeze. *How far should I walk? Wait... I'm going west... that's the way the drones are coming from. I should turn south.* Cans at her back rattled as she leaned forward, grabbing dirt and roots to climb the stiff incline. *Dammit.* She stopped, head hung in the universal pose of 'I'm an idiot.' *I didn't bring a can opener.* She stood straight and dusted dirt from her hands, debating between dropping the cans and fleeing or going back for a means to open them.

"Hold it," said a man.

"Eep!" squeaked Abby. She whirled around.

A man and a woman in camo approached from behind, both with rifles trained in her general direction. Air stalled dead in her lungs; her body refused to breathe in or out. Her heartbeat pounded in her head.

"What are you doing out here at this hour?" asked the woman, sounding annoyed.

Abby, mute, stared at the end of the assault rifle. Moonlight gleamed from its wood parts. The echo of Warren's voice roared in the back of her mind. If they thought her Infected, they'd kill her.

The woman edged closer, her rifle pointed at Abby's chest. Dark hair hung long and straight along a Kevlar vest decorated with two knives, a few magazine pouches, and old bloodstains.

Suffocating fear shifted to hyperventilating in an instant. She whimpered, clinging to Fuzz. The baleful moon overhead started to look more like a harsh electric light bulb. Abby stared into the muzzle of the rifle, woozy.

"It's a kid," said the man. Short, pale-brown hair caught the light, almost glowing.

The woman lowered her weapon. "You're not supposed to be out here after dark. What are you up to?"

A panicky whine leaked from her nostrils. "Don't kill me!" She dropped the knapsack and pulled her dress up to her armpits, exposing herself.

"Uhh that's a new one," said the woman. "Hey calm down."

Abby squealed and gave in to trembling when the woman grabbed her hands. "I'm not bit or scratched! Please don't shoot me!"

"Whoa." The man slung his rifle over his shoulder and walked closer. "It's okay, kid. Abby, right?"

She turned so they could see her back. "I haven't been scratched. I'm not infected."

"It's okay, sweetie." The woman pulled her dress down. "You don't have to do that."

Abby struggled to rein in her breathing and coughed on a tendril of snot sliding down her throat.

The man picked up the knapsack. "Looks like someone's planning for a trip."

"The Virus is coming." She bowed her head, holding Fuzz in both hands to her chest. "I don't wanna die."

"We haven't seen anything in the air, sweetie. Come on. You need to go home." The woman took her hand.

Abby dragged her moccasins as they walked. "I'm not staying at *home*. Bill is watching me."

"Nothing's wrong there?" asked the man. "Why you're running away?"

"No. They're nice," she said in a small voice. "I like them, but I'm scared of the Virus."

The militia escorted her to Bill's house and knocked until he came to the door. Half-awake, black hair disheveled, with one eye wider than the other, he appeared older.

"Sorry to wake you up, Mr. Vasquez, but we figured you wouldn't want this one runnin' off in the middle of the night." The man handed over the knapsack. "Looks like she'd packed for a long trip."

Abby bowed her head, silent tears of shame, guilt, and fear sliding down her cheeks.

"Thanks, Jim." Bill shook the man's hand as he took the knapsack. "Erin."

The woman patted Abby on the head. "Sorry for scarin' ya. Stay inside at night."

Bill regarded her with an expression she couldn't discern. Worry? Annoyance? Sympathy?

She sniffled into the teddy bear's head as the militia who'd 'caught' her walked off.

A moment later, Bill took a step back and gestured toward the kitchen.

Without a word, Abby walked in. Bill shut the door with an effort to be quiet, and guided her by a hand on the shoulder to one of the chairs. She sat. He set the knapsack on the table and pulled up another chair.

"I promised Kevin and Tris I'd take care of you while they were away." He spoke in a soothing, quiet tone.

Abby nodded.

"What are you doing running off?"

She twirled strands of teddy bear fur between her thumb and forefinger, still gazing down. "I'm sorry."

"Abby… I know you have a… thing about being trapped. If I can't trust you to stay safe, you might wind up locked in a room."

She sucked in a breath.

"I don't want that, and I know you don't want that."

"No." Abby shook her head. "Please don't."

"Why were you halfway out of town at two in the morning?"

She couldn't stop shaking. "I'm scared. If I stay in the town, I'll die when the Virus comes. I'm scared to be alone too… but more scared of the Virus." No matter how tight she squeezed it, Fuzz didn't hug her back. As soon as she thought of her new family, tears burst forth. "I want Tris and Kevin to come home. Why did they have to go? I want them back."

Bill patted his leg. Abby lunged out of her chair and sat in his lap, crying into his chest for a while as he held and rocked her. When she quieted enough for him to talk over without raising his voice, he shushed her a little more. "They seemed to think they had something important to do. Tris has some information… she said they can stop the Virus. I don't know whether they plan to destroy the Enclave or what.

Doesn't seem likely that, but maybe they can do somethin' about the Virus."

Abby sniffled.

"I got the sense they really didn't want to go. They wanted to stay with you."

"Then why didn't they?" whined Abby.

He squeezed her shoulder, then brushed his hand up and down her back. "Because of this exact thing. They don't want Virus dropping on our heads and they really don't want you getting hurt. They went out there to protect you."

"I'm afraid they won't come back. What if they get hurt?" Abby wiped her tears on her forearm.

Bill smiled. "Tris is a lot tougher than she looks, and that Kevin's pretty crafty. I think between the two of them, they'll find a way or decide it ain't worth it and come back."

She curled against his chest, too worried about them to talk.

"Abby. I need you to promise me you won't try a stunt like this again. If anything happened to you, Tris would kill me. I promise we'll do everything we can to protect you."

"Uhh." She tossed ideas around her head, trying to think of how scary the mountains would be all alone. Any number of things could come after her: Infected, raiders, wolves, falling in a hole she can't climb out of... snakes. She gulped. "Okay. I promise."

"Good. I'm going to trust you. Don't make me feel dumb."

Abby nodded. "Promise."

Bill slipped an arm under her legs at the knee and carried her back up to the loft. He went up the ladder only far enough to set her on her feet at the top. "Back to bed for you."

"'Kay."

Abby started toward the bed, but froze at the sight of Zoe's butt protruding from the closet. The girl rummaged around in the pile of junk like a dust hopper digging a burrow, her nightgown glowing blue in the moonlight.

"Zoe?" whispered Abby.

The girl sat back on her heels and twisted around, a bug-eyed gas mask on her face.

Abby screamed.

A heavy thud came from below. Bill said a few nasty words before dragging himself up the ladder.

Zoe pushed the mask up off her face and grinned.

Abby wilted to her knees, both hands over her chest, gasping for air.

"What happened?" wheezed Bill.

A door opened downstairs.

"Bill? What's up?" asked Pete.

"Dad?" Cody sounded exhausted. "What's going on?"

Abby pointed at Zoe, still breathless.

"Oh." Bill chuckled. "Girls, go to bed, now." He eased himself down the ladder grumbling about his knee. "False alarm. Zoe startled Abby with a mask."

Two doors closed downstairs.

Zoe's grin faded to an apologetic frown. "Sorry. I found one for you too." She crawled over and dropped another gas mask on the floor by Abby's knees. "Zara said the bad stuff is breathed. These will help."

Feeling ridiculous for finding Zoe-in-a-gas-mask scary, Abby giggled.

Zoe smiled. "Don't laugh too loud. We'll get yelled at." She pulled her mask off, shaking her head to free her hair from the rubber straps, which snapped up into the mask.

"Yeah," whispered Abby. "Why are you awake?"

Zoe stood. "I was gonna go find you."

Abby knee-walked to the bed. "Sorry."

She started to pull herself up into bed when a ripple of gunfire outside sent her to the floor in a ball. Zoe darted to the closet and grabbed her M-16, then ran back across the room to the window they'd climbed out of before. Hunkered down over the windowsill, she aimed into the night. Shots continued for a few seconds more before fading to silence, though Zoe didn't fire.

A faint electric whine emanated in the distance, and a loud splintering *crunch* preceded a series of sharp *smacks* suggesting a heavy object hurtling through trees.

Abby's eyes widened to their limit. *They shot down a drone... I heard it crash.* "We... we gotta get out of here!" She jumped upright, looking around with random, quick jerks of her head. "They're coming. It's found us!"

Zoe tossed the rifle onto the bed and leapt on Abby. "No. Don't go out there."

"We gotta..." Abby struggled to run for the ladder, but the smaller girl tangled her legs and she fell on all fours. Her heart raced; every second she remained in the house, remained in Nederland, brought her that much closer to death. "Come on!"

Zoe turned into a koala bear, arms and legs wrapped around her. "Abs! Calm down. Gran'pa! Help!"

Abby thrashed to get free, dragging Zoe along the floor. She made it within a few feet of the ladder when a figure rose up past the floor. The motion made her scream and reverse course.

Infected in the house!

Shrieking, Abby twisted side to side to get away from Zoe, but the little one held on like a wolverine. The formless person-shaped blob rising over the ladder got taller... and taller... and taller. She refused to look at the bloody mouth she knew was opening to infect her.

Abby clawed and kicked at the air, screaming, "Daddy!" over and over.

"She's having a panic attack," said a man.

Another huge figure bounded up into the loft. The stink of rotting bodies made her gag; she strained to get away, but the younger girl held her fast.

Zoe pulled Abby upright, sitting behind her, and clamped on. "Abby! It's okay. You're safe. It's just Gran'pa and Dad."

Every muscle in her body locked, she stared at the amorphous figures, breathing hard, covered in sweat.

"Abby." Zoe's arms felt like a steel band around her middle. "You're okay. It's Gran'pa."

The nearer Infected changed... no longer rotten. Older... Bill.

Abby went limp. She stopped fighting to get away from Zoe. Bill took a knee beside them and brushed her hair off her face before staring into her eyes. Her heart raced; she breathed so fast she got dizzy.

"Abby?" asked Bill.

Shivering, she managed to nod and gasped for breath. "Yeah..."

"There's nothing to be afraid of. You're safe in Zoe's room." Bill leaned back. "I'll go and get you some water. Try to think of happy things."

Abby's face scrunched up, a pleading frown mixed with a touch of glare. How could he ask her to 'think happy' after the Virus landed in Nederland?

She squirmed around and clamped onto Zoe, who gave her an 'are you okay?' stare.

Abby shook her head and whispered, "The Enclave killed us. We're gonna die..."

THE COMBAT PACKAGE

Flat on his back, staring at a bleak, pale-grey ceiling with rows of dim fluorescent lights led Kevin's mind through a quasi-dream of having survived nuclear war in an underground shelter. Neither asleep nor awake, the mental wandering left him briefly out of touch with reality. A sudden spike of urgency—needing to rush home to check on Abby—shocked him wide awake. Hundreds of miles away, he had to know if she'd survived the bombs falling.

Tris shifted in her sleep; her hair brushed against his chin.

Oh... dreaming. He closed his eyes and breathed in slow. The life he'd started in Nederland barely a month ago felt like a dream as well. So close to how he imagined the world before it all went to hell. Probably why the sense of being in a nuclear bunker gave him that dream.

I gotta at least try to sleep. Should I take that shot? Damn catch-22. Might find more inside, might not. If I don't take it and I get scratched going in there, finding more won't matter. If we do find more, I'm going to feel reckless for not using it. He shifted, trying to get comfortable on the thin mattress. *Why would they have the vaccine in their quarantine area? They'd keep it in the main city.* He sighed out his nose. *Maybe Abby will be able to sleep if she gets it.* A grin curled his lips. *I'm getting as bad as Tris. Darn kid.*

"Hey," whispered Tris, pushing on his shoulder.

Somehow, she'd teleported from curled up next to him to standing over him.

He squinted up at her, fluorescent lights above her made her hair glow. "What?"

"They're ready to show us the way in."

I just got in bed. "What? What time is it?"

"It's a little after ten in the morning."

Kevin grunted, but sat up. "Okay."

"You didn't take the vaccine, did you?" She bit her lip.

He smiled. "Abby needs it more than I do."

Tris looked away, conflict plain on her face.

"It's fine."

"Is it?" She took his hand in both of hers. "I want Abby to be safe and happy, but we're about to go through a tunnel with a high chance of Infected being there. Abby's not in immediate danger. *You* are."

"And unless you want to sit around for four hours or so, I don't have time to take it anyway."

She rested her forehead on his shoulder. "Dammit. If you get killed down there…"

"Then you finish what you came here to do, go back to Ned, and do everything you can for Abby."

Tris sniffled and clamped her arms around him.

"Hey… I'm not planning on tongue-kissing any Infected. That poor kid's got enough nightmare fuel to last her till she's old and grey. This vaccine thing might help her cope a bit more."

She gathered her composure and raised her head, staring into his eyes. "Okay. You are such an asshole, but you're a good asshole."

He chuckled.

"At least stay near me so I can keep them off you."

"Sure."

Kevin yawned and let her pull him to his feet. She led him down the hallway deeper into the base, hooked a left at a four-way intersection, and entered a space covered in tiny blue tiles. A row of lockers stood to the left in front of a battered wooden bench mounted on two steel posts. The other side of the room held six showerheads around the walls, each with its own drain, and no partitions whatsoever.

Zoryn, and another man he hadn't seen before, as well as a woman with waist-length black hair cleaned themselves, showing little reaction to the two of them walking in. Tris' cheeks pinked, but she disrobed.

Well, I guess this isn't going to be a 'fun' shower. He piled his clothes up on the bench near Tris' and followed her to the far-left showerhead. The heat in the water caught him off guard. In all his twenty-seven years, he'd never seen it come out of a tap hot enough to waft steam.

"Whoa. Yowch that's hot."

She smiled. "I'd almost forgotten what it's like. Once we get home, I'm going to be working on proper water heaters so we can have showers like this."

"Hey," said Zoryn. He didn't quite turn to face them, but Kevin looked elsewhere. "I'm going to be with you guys in the tunnel. As far as the walk goes, it ain't too bad. Should take us about an hour."

"Sounds good." Kevin looked around for soap, but found only a small silver can. He patted Tris on the butt and whispered, "soap?"

She took the can from its shelf and sprayed a lump of lime green foam into his hand. "You've never seen real soap before?"

"Yeah… usually blocks of it." Mint slapped him across the face, making him cough. "Damn."

"This is new soap. It's antibacterial." She sprayed some into her hand and lathered it over her chest.

Nervousness and worry kept any playfulness out of her demeanor. He proceeded to wash himself, though froze two minutes later when Amaranth walked out from behind the lockers, naked. If she looked young before, she looked even younger with nothing on. Her presence made him feel awkward. He'd driven cargo to plenty of rural settlements where some of the people didn't bother with clothes, many of them kids, but he'd never showered within five feet of them either. Knowing her true age of thirty-six didn't take away from what his eyes told him.

He stared at Tris instead.

With no chance of the shower becoming anything more than a cleaning process, they finished in a few minutes and headed to a table nearer the lockers where a pile of towels sat folded safely away from the spray.

Amaranth walked over as they dried off, casual as anything, and smiled. "Good morning." She gestured at the lockers. "There's some jumpsuits for you in number 19. Her shoes look Enclave already, so she didn't need that. We got you some."

Kevin nodded.

"Yes." Amaranth put a hand on her hip. "I might have the body of a twelve-year-old, but I've got the brain of a dirty old woman. It *is* goddamn annoying. No one will touch me."

"Anyone that would, we'd kick their ass," said the unknown man.

Zoryn headed over and grabbed a towel, wrapping it around himself on his way behind the lockers.

Amaranth sighed. "Yeah. Awesome nanites." She swiped a towel from the shelf and draped it over herself. "Maybe they'll turn me back into a zygote and I can forget about all this shit."

"Are you going backwards?" asked Tris.

"I don't know. Seems like I hold steady unless I get really hurt. Like they go into high gear and they keep going after they've fixed the injury. Took three bullets a few weeks back and I swear my boobs shrank."

Kevin opened his mouth to comment that she didn't have any, but closed it. He pivoted on his heel and walked over to locker 19.

"Your guy's smarter than he looks," said Amaranth.

"What?" asked Tris.

Amaranth laughed. "I know that look. A stillborn bad joke."

Kevin whistled innocently as he pulled on his boxers before opening the locker and removing a jet-black jumpsuit, which he put on.

"Sorry," said Tris, her tone quiet.

"What for?" asked Amaranth.

"What they did to you." Tris toweled off.

"Oh." She followed her around toward the locker. "I wasn't a science project. More of an oops. I'm not like 'project Amaranth' or anything... I used that as a code name when I got involved with the Resistance. Eternal flower or something." She rolled her eyes. "I thought it was cooler before I realized these nanites are probably going to kill me."

"Maybe you're not eating enough? Might've attacked fat reserves to rebuild tissue." Tris tossed the towel on the bench and grabbed a jumpsuit. She held it for a few seconds, staring.

Kevin zipped his up. "What's wrong?"

Tris smiled. "Just remembering you telling me to get rid of my old jumpsuit. Unwanted attention. Thought it ironic we're putting them on for the same reason... to avoid attention." She stepped in and zipped up.

"Yeah." He grabbed the red armored jacket, and sighed. "Feels stupid not wearing my armor... but I suppose being the only dude wearing red in a sea of black would be dumb too." He packed it, and the rest of his clothes into the locker. The .45 he kept, stuffing it into the large pocket on his right hip, and two spare magazines in the opposite one.

Amaranth ruffled the towel at her hair. "Yeah. You can leave it here. Assuming you make it out, no one will touch it. Our stuff's way better."

She winked, dropped the towel, and pulled on a pair of white boxers a little too big for her before reaching for her tank top.

"You're not coming with us?" Kevin grinned, intending to tease. Of course, the Resistance leader would want to sit back here where it was safe. "Don't s'pose you can spare any of that fancy armor?"

"If it wouldn't put you at risk, I would kick down the door for you. And no, all of our armor is hodgepodge, scuffed to shit, and dirty. If that didn't get you questioned, being in armor would mark you as military and invite a whole host of other questions you wouldn't have answers for. Better to look like civilians." She wriggled into the tank top.

"How are you a problem?" asked Tris.

Amaranth glanced at her. "My real name is Lisa Yaro."

Tris coughed. "As in Dmitri Yaro?"

"Yeah... he was my father."

Kevin held his hands up. "Savage boy is out of the loop. Who is this bad man?"

Amaranth looked down. Her tiny delicate feet, white as new fallen snow, reminded him of a mannequin from that children's clothing store they'd raided hours ago. A sad doll trapped in an even sadder tomb.

Kevin's smile died. Too much of Dad rubbed off on him. This woman looked so much like a child he wanted to comfort her. "Hey... sorry if it's a sore topic. I'm... I have no idea."

"My father was the Prime of the original Council of Four. He'd have been almost eighty now if he hadn't been assassinated." Amaranth stood quiet for a few seconds, arms limp at her sides, a forlorn look on her face. "He voiced the idea that the Enclave wouldn't be sustainable in a closed community and advocated opening up to the outside world. The only time the subject was ever discussed in front of the people. They had Council sessions about it, televised to everyone in the Enclave. The original Four were set to vote on it on a Tuesday, but someone shot him Saturday afternoon. Someone who had the backing of the other three Council members, because the killer walked right in and walked right out. 'No one saw anything.'"

"Sorry," muttered Kevin.

"They targeted me next. Would've been dead if it wasn't for the nanites." She sat on the bench staring into nowhere. For a few seconds, she looked every bit the tween she appeared to be. "Son of a bitch... I was twelve when..." She scratched at her chest. "Woke up on a gurney listening to two guys talk about how the 'official story' would be I'd been shot in the heart and killed. I almost sat up and told them I was alive, but they said they had to cremate me before anyone came to check. They were part of it. I played dead until they parked me and walked off to do something."

"Damn," said Kevin.

"I ran like hell. Been out here with the Resistance ever since."

Tris blinked a few times. "Your nanites... maybe they're not hyperactive? Maybe they somehow imprinted on your body architecture the instant you took a bullet to the heart, and keep trying to put it back to that?"

"I guess being twelve for the rest of my life beats shrinking until I stop existing. But yeah... if I get seen on any cameras, all hell will break loose." Amaranth made a sad chuckle. "I could really use some dick though."

Kevin coughed, scratched his head, and kept his gaze on the floor. A cascade of uncomfortable grunts and mutterings emanating from the shower area suggested everyone else had about the same reaction to that as him.

"So, uhh," asked Kevin, "how'd a kid wind up in charge of the resistance?"

"I didn't start off leading a cell. I really was a kid when I first found them... twenty-three years ago. Harrisburg almost wiped us out. What you see here is it... managed to get a couple more bodies over the last couple months, but we're still fewer than thirty." She slapped her hands on her thighs and stood. "Right. You two should get going. Naomi and Zoryn are going to escort you to where you need to be. For what it's worth"—she locked eyes with Tris—"I hope I'm right."

"About?" asked Tris.

"I've got this feeling about you. I never trust anyone this fast." Amaranth studied her for a moment. "I can't explain it, but helping you feels like the right thing."

Tris narrowed her eyes. "Yeah. I know what you mean."

ZORYN LED THE WAY OUT OF THE RESISTANCE HIDEOUT. KEVIN FOLLOWED deeper into the outer tunnel, away from sunlight, squeezing the grip of his AK47. At least the Challenger remained where he'd left it. Naomi opened a hip satchel and handed him a set of thin goggles with a wraparound elastic strap. Clear LED bulbs formed a line over the lenses, between two strips of black plastic. She handed one to Tris, who put it on without hesitating.

Kevin shrugged and pulled it over his head. "If anyone wants to clue the caveman here on what this is, please do."

Zoryn cut his flashlight and turned. The LEDs over his eyes almost blinded him as he leaned close and flicked a switch on the side Kevin's goggles. "Active night vision."

"Looks like you're wearing flashlights on your head." Kevin looked around at a world of monochromatic green. "Everything's green."

"The LEDs are infrared," said Naomi. "If you're not wearing those goggles, you can't see the light."

Kevin, being a twelve-year-old boy at heart, pulled the goggles away from his eyes to test. Sure enough, pitch black. He put them back on and the glowing green world returned. "Whoa." He lifted and dropped them a few more times.

"Infected, as far as we can tell, can't see in the infrared spectrum. They'd spot normal flashlights."

"What about Enclave security?" Kevin adjusted the goggles so they didn't press his ears to his head.

Zoryn laughed as quietly as a seven-ish foot tall man could laugh. "They don't come down here. They try to forget the school. It reminds them too much of where they came from."

"They prefer to feel like gods," said Naomi.

Tris hovered close by his right side as they got underway. For a time, they walked in a rough single file, with Zoryn in the lead, Naomi behind him, and Tris bumping elbows with Kevin. He amused himself amid the silence by panning his head around so the band of visibility swept over the old concrete. A few mattresses and sleeping bags littered the floor on the left, though whether they'd been dragged in by people before or after the war, he couldn't tell.

The goggles' time display showed 10:49 a.m. when they started walking. By 11:20, Zoryn stopped and waved, indicating a broken hole on the right that led to a narrow dirt-walled passage with a slight downhill grade. Claustrophobia stiffened the muscles on his back; his arms touched both sides of the improvised tunnel, and his head bumped the ceiling every few steps. After a few agonizing minutes, he emerged from the side of a rounded tunnel covered in semi-shiny white tiles. Two sets of train rails ran along a trench in the middle. Kevin advanced cautiously, inhaling a musty, earthen scent tinged with oil or something industrial. Still, it felt good to stop hunching.

Zoryn went left, jumped down the few feet to the tracks, and walked into the tunnel between the nearer set of rails. Kevin traipsed after, eyes on the rounded ceiling, noting the occasional missing tile exposing concrete and in one alarming case, dirt. Tris hurried along at his left and walked astride. She glanced at him, but the LED strip in her goggles blinded him when she tried to smile.

"Ack." He cringed. "Bright."

"Sorry," she whispered.

At 11:39 a.m., the end of an old subway car came into view out of the murk up ahead. The pale green-on-black world of night vision lent it an eerie, spectral quality as though he peered into the world of ghosts. A clean skull staring at them from the left side window only made the otherworldly feeling stronger. More cars on the second set of tracks bent at an angle, having derailed and pinned the left side train against the wall.

Skeletons hung out of broken windows too small to let anything more than a head and arm out here, a leg there. Kevin's thoughts raced with a daydream of mass chaos… people trapped in the crashed trains losing their minds as the existing panic of nuclear war ramped up to the next level. Had the lights gone out before or after they'd all died? How many killed each other? Did any of them resort to cannibalism?

Ugh. I'm turning into Tris… Freaking out about people who died twice my age ago.

"You okay?" whispered Tris.

He started to glance at her, but remembered the lights on his headband would blind her, so he kept facing forward. "Yeah. Feeling watched."

"Me too."

He smiled. "How many ghosts you think are here?"

"It's not ghosts I'm worrying about."

Zoryn checked the left side train, grumbled, and hurried to the other. After a moment of peering in the window, he took a small device from his belt and held it to the window. A scintillating speck of light appeared at the point of contact, and he traced it around as if drawing a line with a marker. Kevin lifted the goggles away from his eyes; the world became pitch dark save for a nimbus of bright violet where the cutter ate the train window. Nose-burning fumes followed seconds later.

Naomi punched out a slab that clattered like plastic when it landed inside. She gave Kevin a nod and slipped into the car. Zoryn followed. Kevin tugged his goggles back down, slung the rifle over his back, and approached the opening.

The car sat at an angle, one set of wheels on dirt tilting it toward him. A tangled pile of skeletons, luggage, and rotting clothes lay against the end door on his right. More skeletons occupied seats at random to the left, on both sides of a clear aisle that ran the length of about five cars.

He hauled himself up and in. Zoryn again took point, moving with care to minimize noise. Kevin took the hint and tried to be silent as well. Tris held on to him from behind, hiding her face against his back.

"What?" whispered Kevin.

"I don't want to see them. I couldn't handle it if one of the skeletons is small." She shivered.

He hadn't thought of it until she mentioned it. Curiosity battled with not wanting the sight of a child-sized skeleton burned into his mind. Kevin didn't close his eyes, but he didn't bother searching either. "Okay."

Zoryn stopped at the end of the last car, where another train had rear-ended this one. The door had been opened about two inches. He ignored it and used the energy cutter to open a hole in a window on the left. Naomi stuck a knife into the cut after the torch passed, and pulled the slab of resin back into the car so it didn't make noise when it fell.

She grabbed an overhead baggage rack, pulled herself up, and threaded her legs into the opening before letting go and dropping out. Zoryn shifted sideways and stepped through the hole. Not being seven feet tall, and not wanting to smash his balls on the windowsill, Kevin exited via the baggage rack grab like Naomi.

Tris jumped down behind him, rifle up.

They walked along the tunnel, past the train that had apparently caused the derailment. Except for the first car crumpled into the one they'd emerged from, every door on the second train was open, no sign of any skeletons.

"That's so fucked up," whispered Kevin.

"What?" Tris looked at him, making him cringe away from the IR glow.

He wagged his AK47 at the empty cars. "The people who caused the wreck all walked away… poor bastards in the other one never got out."

"I don't think it was their fault," said Tris. "If anything, blame the engineer—but they'd likely have died on impact."

Kevin continued to look around as they walked. The tunnel's

condition didn't do a whole lot for his confidence. Perhaps their guides had been keeping quiet to avoid triggering a cave-in rather than any worry about Infected hearing them. *I bet I could fart and kill us right now.* He grinned at a dark metal door on the right wall by a tiny porch, more than likely a fuse station or whatnot.

The idea of ripping ass and having it actually *be* deadly leapt upon his nervousness and made him laugh.

Tris glared at him.

Clank. A metallic ring echoed from up ahead, like a tire iron striking one of the rails.

All four of them froze.

An unmistakable moan followed.

Fuck. He grimaced at Tris and whispered, "My fault. Totally my fault. Sorry."

The ground in front of Zoryn and Naomi came alive with bodies moving.

Kevin squeezed his rifle. "Or not… We almost walked right into that."

"So much for quiet." Zoryn raised a handgun and opened fire.

Intense flashes of white muzzle flare snapped in the monochromatic green world. The enclave pistol made a squidgy, muted *pop* that didn't sound anywhere near lethal. Exploding heads and sprays of liquid from human silhouettes up ahead said otherwise.

A moan echoed from behind.

Kevin whirled.

Scuffing footsteps came from a maintenance door thirty feet or so back; it bumped open with a slow creak of rust as a nearly naked man stumbled out onto a tiny concrete platform. He wore a chain around his waist for a belt with two license plates hanging over his crotch. His one boot, black leather with rough armor plates made from old traffic signs, made Kevin think of the Boatmen. He shambled in a beeline toward them, but failed to notice the four steps from the platform to the ground, and fell flat on his face. More figures emerged behind him: a thin woman in leather riding armor, a fat guy in a dark-colored skirt down to his shins, two large metal Chevrolet symbols gleamed from his nipples. Both of them walked heedless off the tiny stairwell and crushed the former Boatman harder into the ground.

The skinny woman raked at the gravel, emitting a series of high-pitched eager grunts.

A ripple of fire that sounded full automatic came from Tris. Five heads exploded simultaneously. Kevin fired once into the chest of the already-dead fat guy. Behind them, the muted *pops* of two Enclave handguns went off in a continuous, but controlled barrage. He risked a glance over his shoulder, wondering why their escorts weren't going all 'superTris' on the Infected. They fired, aimed, fired, aimed at a normal human pace.

Kevin walked backwards, covering the rear. More Infected, these clad only in filth and dark black tunnel grime, scrambled out of the same door and walked over the dead, which had piled up into a ramp from the little porch down to the tracks. He didn't look at the pale night-vision-green shapes long enough to tell man from woman as he fired at anything moving.

Round after round barked out of his AK as he backed up. He might've been screaming, but couldn't hear himself over all the gunfire. He stopped shooting for a second when he couldn't spot any motion. His ears throbbed from the pounding of firearms going off in a confined space.

Naomi shrieked. Kevin looked back. A scrawny, teenage-looking boy had clamped his teeth around her left leg, right above the knee. Blood smeared his cheeks; his 'no-one-home' eyes stared at nothing as he grunted and tore while she bashed him in the head.

Kevin pivoted and aimed. The instant his finger squeezed the trigger, a body hit him from behind, forcing his shot low. It struck the rail with a spark and a *clank*; a soft fleshy *thump* came from Naomi, who screamed again.

Tris roared a battle cry. A hand slapped into Kevin's back and pulled down. Fingernails scratched over the jumpsuit; he forced himself to hold steady, taking careful aim. When he fired again, the boy's head splattered like an overripe melon. Naomi staggered to the right and fell to one knee, grabbing for a new magazine.

"Come on," yelled Zoryn. He took the head off another infected with a sword, his empty pistol in his left hand.

Kevin spun to the rear as Tris hurled a nude, bald man to the ground by a hand around his throat. She straightened in a blur, foot on his chest, and shot him point blank with the AK in the face.

A shrieking elderly woman, her distended breasts bouncing off her stomach as she ran, came out of the dark at his right, a flash of pallid green on black. Kevin let out a yelp of surprise and cracked her across the face with the butt of his rifle. The old woman's body whirled to the left, following her skull. Something fleshy and altogether too hard to be what he thought it was hit him in the face with enough force to knock him stumbling.

Tris roared and stomped the old one in the middle of the back, sending the spindly body flying, arms windmilling. Kevin recovered his balance and fired at the old woman as soon as she landed on her chest. Tris' AK spat a bullet as well, which tore apart the side of the Infected's head.

"You okay?" asked Tris.

"Just took a petrified tit to the face… I think. Nothing's broken."

Naomi yelled, "Look out!" and fired four or five times.

Zoryn let off an "Oof!" as a thick-bodied man a head shorter than him grabbed him in a bear hug and lifted him off his feet while biting at his shoulder. The Infected's outfit of tow-chains, a stop sign, and leather suggested he'd also been a former Boatman. Zoryn grunted and groaned, struggling to break the hold, but had all the success of a toddler held by an adult.

Tris' AK blurred from pointing behind them to aimed forward. A shot rang out, crashing into Kevin's eardrums, before his brain fully processed that she'd moved. The bullet hole appeared above the Infected's right eye and most of the back of his head blasted out into a cloud of gore. Zoryn flung the corpse away and staggered.

Another naked body pounced on Tris from behind. Kevin smashed the butt of his AK into a head of long hair that could've been a skinny dude or a flat-chested woman. Arms grabbed him from behind, but Tris had her Beretta out and fired before anything pierced his skin. Ears ringing, Kevin shot the skinny one and spun to aim at the Infected behind him.

A wet, crunching splatter preceded a grunt of exertion from Zoryn. Metal rang against metal, and the unpleasant squelch of a blade stabbed into meat brought silence to a steady, low moan Kevin hadn't noticed until it stopped.

At the twitch of a hand in the pile of dead behind them, Kevin fired. His shot kicked up a spray of blood, but he couldn't tell if he hit the one that moved. He froze, weapon still trained on the spot until he trusted all the corpses would remain still.

Naomi grunted and screamed past clenched teeth. Kevin looked from side to side over his rifle. Since nothing had yet tried to move, he rushed over to her.

She half sat on the rail, struggling to remove a metal spar from her left shin. He couldn't tell if she lacked the strength or if the pain proved too great for her to dislodge it.

"Shit," he muttered.

"Thanks for shooting me, jackass." She stared at him.

"Sorry. Aiming for the kid biting you… something hit me right when I fired."

"Kevin!" Tris yelled as she ran up and grabbed his shoulder. "Don't touch it. The blood could be tainted. I got it."

He nodded and took a step back.

Tris put her right hand on Naomi's shoulder and grabbed the metal shard with her left. "On three, okay?"

Naomi nodded.

"One…" She tore it loose.

Naomi's scream melted into a stream of obscenities.

Tris held up the metal rod, the lower two inches coated in blood. "Only two inches… that shouldn't have hurt that much."

"Let me stab it into you and see how bad it hurts," rasped Naomi.

"I took a .50 cal through the lung." Tris dropped the metal. "Guess that threw off my pain scale."

"Ouch," said Zoryn.

Kevin glanced around at everyone. "That was… a bit less smooth than I'd expected."

"How's that?" Zoryn sheathed his sword and chuckled.

"Looked like every other time I've seen settlers deal with Infected… except you two don't seem to care you got bit or scratched."

"Ahh." Zoryn nodded. "Well… we're vaccinated, but we're no better at this than you are."

Naomi glanced back at the pile of dead Infected in the rear. Perhaps eighteen lay littered around by where everyone stood, more than thirty had come out of the maintenance door. "Damn… how the hell did you two take all them out without a scratch?"

"I got three or four." Kevin offered a sheepish smile.

Zoryn gestured at Tris with his pistol before sliding another magazine in. "She's boosted. We're vaccinated against the Virus, and we have nanites, but we don't have any augments." Awe took over his expression. "I thought you went full auto… That wasn't, was it?"

"No," muttered Tris. "Single shot as fast as I could aim and fire."

"Daaamn." Naomi shook her head. "I wish I had dex boosters. What's it like shooting these things in slow motion?"

"Still scary as hell." Tris eyed Kevin. "Especially when little boys don't take their vitamins."

"Oh, I figured all you guys had 'em." Kevin tried not to think about the feeling of fingernails sliding down his back. "'All you guys' being Enclave, not resistance."

"Nah... only the military gets the dex boosters." Naomi picked at her leg, watching the wound close. "Most citizens only have the nanites."

Oh, makes sense then why Amaranth stays behind... She's only as strong as a kid. Can't really fight. "She's stronger than I am too." Kevin laughed in a whisper.

"So you got the full combat package." Zoryn grinned at her.

Tris shrugged. "I guess."

Kevin leaned over to her and whispered, "Check my back. Please tell me the fabric didn't rip."

She slapped him, knocking him three paces left and almost sending him to the ground.

"Fuck," he mumbled, cradling his jaw. After straightening on his feet, he looked at Zoryn. "See?"

"You bastard." Tris ran over and yanked the zipper on his jumpsuit open. After peeling it down to expose his back, she forced him around and looked him over. A moment later, she grabbed him and bawled on his shoulder.

Kevin's heart fluttered. "Oh, please tell me that's good crying."

She sniffled. "Red marks, but it didn't break skin." Limp, she clung to him to keep from falling over. "Dammit, why didn't you take the vaccine? You almost gave me a heart attack."

"I'm an overconfident asshole with a soft spot for our little girl." He grasped her cheek and stared into her eyes.

Zoryn gave them about thirty seconds before he cleared his throat. "Sound travels down here. We need to go."

Kevin zipped up his jumpsuit as soon as she let go.

"I don't understand anything anymore." Tris hovered at his side. "Why the hell would Nathan arrange for me to get so many boosts?"

"Well... either he wanted to make sure you'd stay alive long enough to carry that surprise firecracker to the resistance in Harrisburg... you know what they think of the Wildlands." Kevin counted three rounds left in his magazine and decided to swap it for a full one.

"I suppose." She looked down. "Speaking of overconfident assholes... I bet he never imagined I'd survive and come anywhere near him again."

Zoryn cleared his throat.

"All right, all right." Kevin put an arm around Tris and hurried after their escorts, who walked as though they hadn't been injured at all. "Damn. I gotta get me some nanites."

Tris chuckled. "Would you save those for Abby too?"

He tapped his chin. "Yeah… probably."

She gave him an adoring look. "Those don't come in an autoinjector. It's a surgical process to implant the control node."

"Or…" Kevin held up a finger. "Maybe Nathan didn't do it. Maybe he doesn't even know you have all those boosts."

"Huh?" She squinted at him.

Kevin shrugged. "Dear old Dad?"

PLEASE FOLLOW

Light flared from the rails, whenever a clean spot caught the infrared lights from Tris' goggles. She walked with her head down, burdened by the weight of doubt. Kevin's attempt at a wisecrack got her wondering. *Would* Nathan have really initiated—or even approved—her augmentation? She couldn't remember being told about the surgery, which meant they'd likely done it to her while she floated in a tank in the 'hidden Resistance safe house.'

She'd believed Nathan a hacker who opened the door to her Detention cell and walked her step-by-step through an escape, telling her when to hide in an alcove and when to run so the guards didn't see her. The entire event replayed in her mind, the worst forty-something minutes of her life sprinting barefoot down hallways in the middle of an Enclave prison before crawling into a filthy ventilation system. One day she'd been looking forward to going to college—the next, a fugitive escaping prison for refusing to marry.

By the time she'd emerged in the maintenance conduit, her Detention jumpsuit had turned black. Or had it always been black? She wanted to say it had been light grey, or even white... but in her memory, she looked down at herself and saw black... like she wore at that moment. She hadn't kept it for long. A man supposedly working for the Resistance met her in the conduit and brought her to a room filled with glass-top tables loaded with terminals and CPU cases. Everything had looked so haphazard, she had immediate doubts about her odds of survival, but anything seemed better than sitting in prison until she agreed to marry that abusive shit.

Not ten minutes after arriving in the 'Resistance safe house,' she'd stripped and climbed into a tank. With a facemask holding an air hose to her mouth, an IV in her arm for nutrition, and a plug behind her ear, she spent two weeks unconscious... which had felt like closer to eight months in virtual reality. How many of the men and women who'd taught her to fight, shoot, hide, pick locks, and survive had been real? How many might have been computer programs simulating people?

They must've loaded me up with implants while I was in the tank... nanosurgery.

She furrowed her brow while poking at the dusty scratch lines on Kevin's back. By the luck of whatever higher power may or may not exist, the Infected hadn't drawn blood. He had to hate not having his jacket.

Maybe Nathan did arrange it. We're all taught how dangerous the Wildlands are... She thought about that poor boy from the Boatmen compound. How long had he been kept chained to the wall, let out only to run food to other caged unfortunates? How many people had he witnessed forced to murder each other for sport? She didn't even want to consider how many had died there... or that the Enclave appeared to be perpetuating the mindless violence.

They could do so much to help humanity. Why do they want it to burn? She stared at her left hand, opening and closing her fingers. Sure, she'd been made strong, but no more so than a human could be. A bigger person, a man, could've been boosted more... her frame could only take so much. Still, if the numbers on the fake Resistance man's equipment had been correct, her physical strength hovered near the upper five percent of human potential, not counting outliers.

She shivered.

"Here we are," said Zoryn.

Tris blinked at the time display showing 12:08. *Damn, my head's not here.*

Their two escorts had stopped by the edge of a platform. Over a span of about thirty yards, the right side of the train tunnel opened out to an area with columns, benches, and ticket vending machines. Several doors and corridors branched off from it. She walked over to them and leaned forward to peer around. The metal-capped edge of the station floor came up to her chest while she stood in the recessed tracks. Lettering on the distant wall read 'Stanford.'

Ancient papers in various shades of light and dark clung like a coating of tatter to columns; some offered tutoring, some announced concerts, a handful showed a picture of a lost dog. About a third of the seats in a waiting area had collapsed, and rat shit dotted everything. A handful of rodents scurried around, their eyes glinting in the night vision panorama before her.

Zoryn climbed up and reached down to help Naomi. Tris pulled herself up before giving Kevin a hand. Naomi shot her a look part amusement part playful jealousy. In the middle of the innermost wall, a four-escalator wide hallway led up at an angle, presumably to the surface, but a yellow collapsible barrier closed it off, secured with chains and padlocks.

Kevin pointed. "That way?"

"No," said Naomi. "They've got sensors in that tunnel and a stronger barricade at the top. Nothing we have on us can dent it, and they'd know someone came up that way."

Tris crossed the platform to the ticket booth. Bulletproof glass offered a view of a small office, long-dead computers, and one small door into a dingy office. *No way through here.* She glanced back at Zoryn and Naomi. "So where are we going?"

"Here." Naomi pointed left and walked off to the left.

As Kevin passed behind her, a surge of worry, relief, and the need to hold him took her. She grabbed him and clung protectively, not wanting to let him go into this place that could kill them both. He flashed a smile, that cocky rogue's grin that ten years of driving around getting shot at still hadn't managed to punish out of him.

Unable to help herself, she leaned up and kissed him.

He brushed her hair away from her eyes. The intensity of his smile faded, changing its character. The look he gave her could've said *it's not too late to go back* as easily as *I'm gonna be right next to you.*

The squeak of Naomi's shoes on the tile pulled her out of the smoldering stare, and the enraging worry that Nathan would hurt Abby if she didn't do... something... got her moving again. *What's wrong with me? How did I go from feeling sorry for Abby to feeling like she's mine and I'd rip the testicles off anyone who even looks at her wrong?* She grumbled.

Naomi exited the platform on the left side beyond the ticket booth, and headed down a corridor past two bathrooms on the right, an 'employees only' door on the left, stopping at a large plywood slab bearing a faded 'We're Improving!' poster on it featuring a smiling construction worker.

The slightly taller woman took hold of the giant piece of plywood and tugged. With a grunt, she pulled it aside, swinging it flat against the wall to reveal a battered pair of elevator doors.

"Oh, they even installed an elevator for us. Nice." Kevin grinned.

Zoryn crunched over broken tiles and coils of wire. He grabbed at the metal sliding door and jerked back with his body weight, moving it a few inches. Kevin approached to help. Tris handed the AK to Naomi, and lent a hand, and between the three of them, they forced the door open, bending the metal.

Tris stuck her head into the gap, inhaling the overwhelming smells of wet earth, metal, and a salty, biting aroma she assumed to be rat piss. About three stories overhead, rats darted around hanging hoses on the underside of an elevator cab. One leapt to the wall and scurried out of sight into a hole. A nimbus of infrared glare followed her gaze down the shaft to the bottom, about fifty feet further below.

"I guess we're going down?" asked Tris.

"Correct," said Zoryn. "This will take you to another tunnel that leads to a basement annex of the school. No one's been in there for decades."

"Why would a school have a secret tunnel to a subway station?" asked Kevin.

Naomi gave him an impressed eyebrow lift. "We think the tunnel was made later during the initial formation of the Enclave. Back when they were a mixture of intellectuals, scientists, and whatever government forces decided to use the shelter here. Our best guess is they wanted an escape route, but never needed it... and eventually forgot about it."

"You should probably leave your rifles with us," said Zoryn. "Enclave citizens aren't allowed to possess firearms, and those things stand out as low tech. You might be able to hide your handguns in your pockets."

"I'm not going in there without at least this." Tris squeezed the Beretta.

"Good thing you left the katana in the car." Kevin winked. He handed his AK to Naomi again. "Sorry about that ricochet."

She grasped it, frowning. "Yeah... no problem. Just make sure you come back and get it." Her glower softened to an expression of 'be careful' and she clapped him on the arm. "I don't want to, uhh, you know, have to look at it since it caused me so much pain."

Sensing the tease in her tone, he chuckled. "Yeah. That's the plan."

Tris shook Zoryn's hand. "Thanks for the escort. I'm not entirely sure what I'm going to find in there, but it feels like the right thing to do." *Does it, or is this part of my programming? What other personality alterations did they do while I was plugged in?* All of it was so new at the time... One had to be eighteen or older to get an interface jack. She reached up and touched a finger to the little socket behind her left ear. Everyone had to get them installed after high school graduation. Some kids couldn't wait and got them the day they turned eighteen. Others dreaded it and tried like hell to avoid it until the security forces dragged them to the clinic. Tris fell into the smallest group—ambivalent. She hadn't cared enough to get it until the security people showed up to ask about her lack of patriotism, but she didn't fight them either when they told her she had to have it.

Okay. Here goes. She stared at the elevator shaft. *Why do I feel like I'm climbing down the rabbit hole?* "I'm late. I'm late."

She grasped the door and pulled herself in, searching for handholds.

"Late?" asked Kevin.

"A very important date." She spotted a ladder recessed in the wall on the right and reached for it.

"What the hell are you talking about?" asked Kevin.

Zoryn and Naomi snickered.

Tris grabbed a rung covered in dust. *Speaking of late... it has been awhile since my 'friend' stopped by.* She sighed, feeling a pang of sorrow. *Stress. They harvested my ovaries already.* With a contemptuous grumble, she leapt into the shaft and made her way down.

Kevin followed. The flare of his infrared headband danced around the walls, casting her long shadow out below. She glanced up; he eased himself down one rung at a time, his attention on her more than where he put his feet.

"Be careful," she whispered.

"This *is* careful." He chuckled. "If I was being careful, we wouldn't be sneaking into the bowels of the Enclave."

She rolled her eyes. "That's... colorful."

A few minutes later, the ground came into view. She hurried down the last few rungs and got out of Kevin's way. The shaft bottom had collected a fair amount of small debris. Spongy matter underfoot likely contained at least forty percent rat turd, mixed with dust and other things she didn't want to think about. Shiny steel slats glinted in the light from her headset as she examined a set of elevator doors. Much to her surprise, the seam along the top and bottom glowed as if the doors offered passage into the heart of a furnace, night vision exaggerating the light.

Kevin's shoe crunched behind her. He overacted slipping off the ladder and grabbed on to her. She set her stance and held him up, giving him a 'must you?' smirk.

"Am I that obvious?"

She looked again at the door. "You didn't trip."

"Any excuse to hold you."

She couldn't let her heart melt. Not here. Not in the basement of the Enclave. Tris put her hand atop his where it rested on her stomach. A moment later, she patted him. "I love you too, but I'd like to get out of here alive so I can continue loving you instead of winding up a female version of Wayne with nothing but a bottle of hooch and a sad tale of broken dreams."

"Ouch." He hugged her tight for a second. "I'll try not to get my ass shot off then. Oh, Wayne didn't have broken dreams. That man was happy being alone."

Tris leaned forward with Kevin's arms still around her middle. She tested the struts and motivators on the inside face of the door until she found one she could force. Pulling it down disengaged a locking mechanism as if the elevator cab had arrived. That done, the doors slid apart from each other with ease, blinding them with an intense glow.

"Gah!" muttered Kevin.

She shut her eyes and pulled the goggles off. "It's the night vision."

It took a moment or two of blinking to adjust. Soon, the green and white checkered tile floor of a basement classroom hallway solidified out of the blurry glare. About one out of every six LED light tubes on the ceiling remained on. Without the goggles, the corridor looked dim... but compared to pitch darkness, it felt like daytime.

Three light fixtures dangled on wires, and about half of the drop ceiling panels had collapsed to the floor. A handful of beige desks with attached chairs stood against the right wall a short distance from the elevator by a door. The next door sat about forty yards farther down on the left.

She shut off the infrared lamp on the goggles and pocketed them. Kevin took about ten times longer to find the power button. Once he had his optics put away, she crept forward, resisting the urge to pull the Beretta out. *Yeah, right. If anyone finds me down here, they won't buy any excuse I can think of; I'd have to kill them.*

Tris peered in the first door at shelves covered with old pre-war desktop computers, keyboards, monitors, and many stacks of medium-sized grey slabs. It took her a moment to remember her technical history classes and recognize them as laptop computers. Fair bet none of this stuff would work anymore, not that anyone left in the world had a use for them even if they would turn on.

"Nothing in there we need."

He peered into the room for a second before following her. "Lot of junk. Damn I'd have gone nuts if I found this stash a year ago."

She walked for the next door at a brisk pace. "No one would buy any of that crap. What's a Wildlander going to do with a computer?"

"Sit on it?" Kevin chuckled. "And hey, some of them still work. How do you think I've seen so many 'historical documentaries'?"

Tris chuckled while peering at a label on the left-side door, 'Lab F.' A quick peek inside at black-topped work tables with small silver faucets and gizmos, as well as walls filled with periodic tables confirmed nothing of interest. 'Lab E,' a little ways ahead on the right had similar work tables but the walls held diagrams of dissected dogs, cats, frogs, horses, and some kind of rodent. She backed away and closed the door.

The hallway went another fifteen feet before an opening on the left revealed a small area where the floor tiles changed to black and white from the green-and-white of the corridor. Vending machines, two pool tables, and a row of arcade game cabinets took up most of the space not used by a snack counter and four tables.

Tris started to walk in, but froze, gasping at the sight of several corpses lying on the floor. All had desiccated into a semi-mummified state with skin the color of creamed coffee. Her jaw tightened when she spotted necrotic lesions that appeared to have set in prior to death.

"Don't." She backed up and put a hand on Kevin's chest. "I think they're Infected."

He held her hand against his heart. "I've never seen them looking dried out like that. They're dead, right?"

She picked up a chair and poked one of the legs into the nearest body. Skin crunched like chicken that had been fried too long. Darker brown dust dribbled out of the hole. "I'd say yes. Quite thoroughly dead. Probably for more than a few years."

"When did they set that shit loose again?" Unease sounded clear in his voice.

"As far as I know, around 2056. These people had to have caught it before the symbiotes happened… The Virus is supposed to kill its victim in three to four months. Guess it worked here."

Kevin's expression shifted unusually somber.

She backed away from the break room and looked up at him. "What?"

"2056. Twenty-one years ago. I was just thinking... Abby's never known a world without Virus in it. Shit, I was like six when they started. I dunno if we're going to do anything here, but I think I understand why you've got that drive in you find the cure."

"That's a memory overlay." She allowed a moment to hug him and close her eyes.

Kevin's hand slid up her back, holding her tight. "If you believe your old man, the overlay is only removing your fear, making you feel invincible."

"Heh. I guess feeling invincible proves I'm still eighteen, right?" She winked. "Come on."

She glanced to the right at the open elevator shaft as she exited the café. Relieved not to see anything shambling after them, she continued straight down the next leg of the corridor past more classrooms and an offshoot labeled 'Faculty Offices' on the left.

"I wonder." She backed up and went to a narrow hallway with drab brown carpeting and cheesy wood-paneled walls. Seven teachers' personal offices, the doors adorned with schedules for student conferencing, surrounded her. "Damn this is cramped."

"What's up?" asked Kevin.

"Oh... I was half hoping one of these offices belonged to my dad. You don't see one labeled 'Doctor Jameson' do you?"

Kevin slipped past her to check the three offices at the end. He cringed. "Nope. Another dead guy in here though." He tilted his head, staring at a nameplate. "Kiran Vishnashitload of letters."

A faint whirring noise grew louder. Tris slid her hand in her pocket and gripped the Beretta.

"What?" whispered Kevin.

"I hear something." She took a step toward the ninety-degree bend left back to the larger corridor.

Shadows moved on the wall as a small light source approached. She scooted to the left, putting her shoulder against the wall, and pulled the gun. *I'm only going to get one chance at this.* A subdued buzzing quality infused the whir as it got louder.

"That sounds like the mother of all mosquitos," said Kevin. He slipped the .45 out and gripped it in both hands.

"Tris?" asked a digitized voice, closer to male, but far removed from natural human.

She lifted the Beretta. *How dumb do you think I am?* She bit her lip. *Pretty dumb... I came down here, didn't I?*

"Tris. Please follow," said the voice.

A hovering drone with four little rotors slid sideways, peeking around the corner as if afraid to fully expose itself. Downdraft created a miniature dust storm on the floor. It looked like some manner of remote-controlled toy, barely twelve inches square, with two tiny spotlights on the forward face and a bevy of antennas sticking out of the back.

She pointed the gun at it but, for no reason she could fathom, held her fire. After a few seconds, she swallowed. "Who are you?"

"Tris, please follow." The drone glided closer. "Doctor Jameson wants to see you."

Are they listening to us?

The machine rotated and drifted off back the way it came. Seconds later, when she'd made no move to go after it, the drone returned.

"Tris, please follow."

Kevin walked up behind her. "Is that thing like Bee, or does it only know three words?"

"It looks like 2020 tech... early drones. Probably a toy from before the war. A lot of people had them. Some kind of obsession about recording video of everything they did. Can you imagine an entire city where everyone had one of these things following them around?"

"Tris, please follow," said the drone, before zipping off.

"What the hell for?"

She shrugged. "Beats me. Humanity probably recorded more of itself in the last five years before the war than it did in the centuries prior. Some people didn't even work. They'd let their drones film them having sex, and charge people to watch it. Little kids playing sports would have drones chasing them. Some entertainment channels streamed it. Big money betting on nine year olds' soccer matches. They used to even kidnap parents or siblings and threaten to kill them if the kids didn't throw the matches sometimes."

Kevin raised an eyebrow. "Wow. Guess the world really was screwed up. No wonder they hit the reset button. Are you sure that's true, or is it more Enclave horseshit?"

She shrugged. "I dunno. It wouldn't surprise me if people saw the nuke coming and just took pictures of it to post online.

Kevin blinked, thinking of the silhouettes on the Starbucks wall all holding their... phones up to the sky. "Yeah..."

The drone glided back into view. "Tris, please follow." It zipped off again.

"I don't know why they'd lie about the world before the war. That wouldn't make people more fearful of the Wildlands." She lowered the Beretta and put it back in her pocket. "Let's see where this little bugger goes."

"Why does anyone in power lie about anything?" Kevin concealed his .45 again. "To make reality seem not so bad compared to what could be."

"Tris, please follow," said the drone, before zipping off.

She hooked a finger in the front of his jumpsuit and pulled him in for a quick peck on the lips. "Look at you, Mr. Wasteland Philosopher."

"Nah. I don't trust any kind of authority."

Tris bit her lip. *Like you trusted the Roadhouse?*

"What?" He smiled, hands on his hips. "Go ahead, say it. I promise I won't get pissed."

She exhaled. "Amarillo?"

He hung his head. "Yeah, so I did... and look how that turned out."

"Tris, please follow," said the drone.

"Okay." Kevin stared at it as it disappeared around the corner yet again. "That thing is getting annoying."

Tris walked after it. "Let's go see what it wants."

LOCK AND KEY

A thin nimbus of light glided down the corridor, projected from the little drone. It matched Tris' cautious pace, seeming content that she followed it at all without concern for how fast she moved. It led them deeper into the basement to a stairwell. A pair of black-painted doors with brushed steel knobs, closed and reinforced by a pile of chairs, blocked the way. The drone slid through a broken out window that it cleared by less than an inch on either side.

Tris grabbed the knob and turned. Though unlocked, too much debris had been stacked up behind it to allow it to move.

"Tris, please follow," said the drone from inside the stairwell.

"Hang on, you little shit." She scowled at the door. "I'm trying."

Kevin pushed at the doors. "What do you think? Shove it open?"

"Someone must've barricaded this against those Infected, but that doesn't make sense. No one was supposed to have been down here for a long time."

"Maybe those corpses were lab tests and they dumped them down here?" He scratched at his head. "That could explain why they're so old. They died before the Enclave released it on the rest of the world."

She looked up at missing panels in the drop ceiling. Solid concrete blocked off the stairwell. "Well, we're not going over. Suppose should at least try to open it."

"Tris, please follow," said the drone.

"Can I shoot it?" Kevin exaggerated a smile. "Please?"

She leaned against the door, turned the knob, and shoved. With a great screeching protest of wood and metal on linoleum, the blockage slid backward as a single mass. Kevin shoved at the other door, and they created about two feet of clear space before the jumble of furniture hit the bannister and stopped.

"Okay... I can work with this." She pulled her door shut and left his open. After letting all the air out of her lungs, she squeezed between them.

She daydreamed about that plasma torch Zoryn had used on the subway car as she tried to disentangle a metal-legged plastic chair from the stack. The drone hovered overhead; the steady breeze from its fans made her hair dance about and provided an endless supply of dust to breathe. She gave up pulling on the junk and climbed over it. From the inside, she tested a few other chairs and an IV stand before a wheeled stool came free. The stool proved to be the keystone. Piece by piece, she removed chairs, combination chair/desks, a few footstools, a filing cabinet, and a water cooler base before the door moved enough for Kevin to fit.

The whole time she worked, the drone kept gliding up and down, repeating, "Tris, please follow," every fifteen seconds.

It's just running a program. It's not trying to piss me off. It's just running a program. She growled at it.

Kevin forced his way into the landing and pointed his .45 at the drone when it came back around the stairs to ask her again.

She pushed his hand down. "It's not aware."

"*I'm* aware that it's fucking annoying." He hissed through his teeth. "Now I kinda wish we run into some Enclave jackass I can shoot."

"Don't say that." She bit her lip. "I'm hoping we can find some computer, do what we have to do, and get the hell out of here before anyone even notices us."

He pulled her into a kiss and stared at her for a long few seconds after. "You know that's not going to happen."

Tris spun on her heel and headed up the stairs. "Yeah, but a girl can dream." Ten steps later, she swung around a switchback and took another ten steps to a landing where the drone slipped through the broken window of a matching pair of doors.

These, at least, had no barricade.

She followed it down a corridor past doorways labeled 'Lab A' up to 'Lab D.' Scattered trash, notebooks, old exams, CD-ROM cases and pens rustled underfoot. The air tasted like paper and mildewed shower curtain. Drab grey walls streaked here and there with streaks of verdigris beneath corroded copper pipes in the ceiling. The lack of moisture suggested the water had run out long ago.

The drone pivoted left at an intersection, going the same direction as a sign on the wall pointing the way to 'computer science.' She glanced up at the ceiling, wondering how no one in the Enclave noticed the power drain of the lights. *Did those light tubes last fifty years, or are they motion triggered? The Enclave's power grid must connect to the school's somehow. I thought the reactor was in the City Core? Did they run a wire back here or does the Quarantine Section have another one? Maybe panels.*

"Tris." The drone stopped, hovering by a dark blue door. A black square on the wall suggested badge-swipe access, but the significant amount of charring on the paint around it made her think the security system had died a violent death. "Here."

The drone glided a little bit to the left, landed, and shut down. Four tiny rotors stopped not quite at the exact same instant.

"Well, I guess this is it." She grasped the door handle. The Godzilla of stomach butterflies leaned back and roared at the heavens. "Ungh." She bowed forward holding her belly.

Kevin put a hand on her back. "What happened?"

She swallowed. "Moment of nerves. I…" Tears flooded from her eyes as she looked up at him. "Thought my father was dead. I don't know what I'm going to say to him."

He rubbed her shoulder. "It's okay. Take your time. Not like there's ten thousand heavily armed people above us."

Asshole. She thumped him on the pectoral, grinning. "Yeah. Suppose I should be nervous later."

He rubbed the spot, overacting pain.

Tris took a deep breath, held it, and pushed open the door, staring into a dim, square room. Unlike the rest of the place so far, the lights remained dark.

Workstations in mini-cubicles lined most of the walls, except for a small space that held a featureless white door on the opposite wall from where she stood. Tall blue-grey cabinets the size of refrigerators, likely supercomputer housings, formed another square wall in the center of the room, with about twenty feet of space inside. Above them, a hemispherical machine mounted to the ceiling sprouted dozens of hoses, most wrapped in silver foil insulation. The tubes ranged from finger-sized to several inches thick, all descending into the space inside the giant computers.

The half-sphere appeared to be three nested rings connected by hydraulic struts, suggesting it capable of extending downward. It supported an armature like something she'd seen in doctor's offices from historical documentaries, tipped with a boxy housing bearing five lenses: the largest as wide as her handspan, the rest far smaller, the size of coins.

"Hello?" asked Tris.

Tittering of stepper motors emanated from the computer towers, a sound she recognized as idling hard disks coming to life with a flurry of activity. The boom attached to the ceiling machine shuddered with a metallic *clank*, making her jump back. It lowered, the box on the end spun 180 degrees around its axis the same time it rotated forward. As the rings to which it mounted extended, the boom elongated, bringing the lens-end closer, like the head of some great, robotic praying mantis leaning in for a better look at her.

An iris door within the largest lens narrowed, a faint purplish light within glowed brighter.

"Tris," said the voice of her father, as if he existed everywhere with in the room.

"W… what the hell is this?" asked Tris.

"I apologize if my appearance is not what you expected." The robo-mantis receded a few inches.

"Dad?" Tris stepped after it, eyeing the twitching hoses, some of which leaked fog like dry ice. "Why aren't you here? Are you in the back room?"

The housing on the front end of the boom rotated downward, a gesture reminiscent of a head bowed in regret. "There is much I have to tell you and little time. I shall try to be as concise as possible." It 'looked' up at her. "Doctor Ian Jameson is dead. Your father was murdered by the Council of Four eleven years ago."

No! She put a hand to her chest, lip quivering. *It's not fair! You were supposed to be alive.*

Kevin rushed to her side as her legs started to give out. He caught her and guided her into a wheeled office chair before taking a knee at her side.

"You told me you were alive." She sniffled.

The boom rose and fell, suggesting a sigh. "I technically did not say one way or the other. I feared your reaction would be not to come. I regret creating false hope."

Fuck this. She clenched her jaw. *I swear. If this is Nathan's fault, I'll kill him slow.* "Why do you sound like my father?"

"I am an artificial intelligence created by Doctor Jameson with as much of his personality and memories as were possible for him to transfer. If he did not make me aware of what I am, I would likely believe myself to be him and wonder why I am stuck inside this machine." It lowered and extended, moving its 'face' within an arm's length from hers. "What I am about to tell you will come as a surprise."

She folded her arms and frowned. "Oh, I can't wait."

Kevin kept his arm around her back. The way he squinted at the cyborg-machine-whatever said it wouldn't take much for the .45 to come out.

"Tris, you were born in in the year 2014."

"Horseshit," she said.

"I knew you would say that." The machine tilted, somehow creating the impression not-Dad smiled at her. "Do you have the photograph I sent?"

She put a hand over the breast pocket of her jumpsuit. Paper crinkled. "Yeah."

"Look at it."

Her throat clenched with sorrow. Shaking fingers peeled the Velcro strap aside before plunging into the pocket and extracting the folded printout. She opened it and stared at herself, perhaps five years old, sitting on the floor of her father's lab. The walls were similar to where she now sat, but didn't exactly match this room. She stared at her younger self for a while, taken by vivid memories of how the carpet felt on her bare legs. The way it stank, how everything about that room smelled like pipe tobacco or coffee.

"You remember this, even though you were a month shy of your fifth birthday," said Dad-AI.

"Yeah." Her voice quivered with the approach of crying.

"Look above your father's head. On the wall by the filing cabinet."

Tris stared at her father's light brown hair, struggling to accept it that color and that neat. She remembered him with frizzy white hair, and older. This picture didn't seem right. When she finally managed to peel her attention away from him, she looked where the computer indicated. A calendar perched on the wall displayed the month of October, 2019. Her hand flew to her mouth, but she caught herself before meltdown reached critical mass. "Wait… an image file can be edited. That doesn't prove anything."

Kevin leaned close, squinting at the picture.

"Do you remember your father with brown hair? Or as an older man with wild white hair?"

She slouched. "Okay. I admit that doesn't make sense. I spent a few years wondering if he was really my grandfather."

"Doctor Jameson worked on several classified projects with an organization known as DARPA. One such project involved long-term suspended animation in an effort to research extended immersion in virtual reality worlds. By 2019, they had mastered the process of preservation, but the subject's brain did not remain aware enough to allow for cognitive abilities to be stimulated by any manner of virtual reality. In short, they could store people indefinitely, but it was little different from sleep."

Tris shivered. "So… I was frozen?"

"Your father had access to intelligence information very few individuals had. He believed a nuclear war was imminent within months. The government wished to bring him to a secure location, but he refused unless they met his condition of putting you in stasis. He wished to spare you the horrors of a world torn asunder by greed and paranoia."

Tris shook. "I…" *Why? What am I supposed to say to this?* "He was really my father?"

"Yes." Dad-AI leaned closer, almost to the limit of its actuators. All five lenses whirred and refocused. "Some years after the proverbial dust settled, my biological predecessor had established himself among the people who would eventually become the Enclave. They created enough of a secure existence for him to release you from stasis. Biologically, you remained five years old at that time."

"I have a question." Kevin put a hand over his mouth, looking downward as if gathering his thoughts. "Why does Tris look like those Persephone androids? She is human, right? A lot of people from the Enclave are *seriously* white, with white hair. If she was born before the war, why is she like that?"

Tris blinked. "Yeah. That doesn't make any sense."

"Yes. The woman before you is Tris Jameson. She is quite human." The boom swung around, retracting and extending in a way that made the head end seem to glide diagonally across the room in seconds. A bank of nine flat-panel monitors on the wall arranged to form a single, large display projected an image of a nude white-haired woman who quite resembled Tris if she'd been a bit more muscular and about two inches taller. "Doctor Jameson was the lead architect on another project for DARPA to create android soldiers capable of infiltration, assassination, and hand-to-hand combat. I am incapable of determining the logical reason behind it, so I calculate that his motivation to run this age progression of Tris came from reasons of pure sentimentality. He made them look like he thought you would look in your middle twenties."

"That doesn't explain the whiter-than-white thing." Kevin cocked an eyebrow.

"At the time," said Dad-AI, "they had been experimenting with various chemical agents to create a gel that could freeze evenly for cryogenic stasis and protect the body within from crystallization. Early cryogenics processes suffered from a fatal build-up of ice crystals in the blood and tissues. They knew this gel had... bleaching properties that affected the subjects' DNA. I believe that Doctor Jameson made the Persephone androids white with white hair because the image of test subjects had struck a chord with him somehow. I do not believe at the time he had expected Tris to be exposed to the same chemical bath."

Tris buried her face in her hands, breathing in and out in slow, measured sips of air. "That's why the former Army people in Dallas knew what a Persephone was... they were around before the war."

"A few. Only a handful were activated. Most remained in storage in the DARPA facility, never used." Dad-AI glided back over as the display showing the lifelike 3D model of a theoretical adult Tris shut down. "Your father had you removed from stasis in 2050 when he was sixty-one years old. From the time you were five until the age of nine, you lived with him in the nascent Enclave."

Tris stared into space. Her entire life, the Enclave city felt like she'd been trapped in a dream of a strange alien world. The memory of an incessant doorbell dragging her nine-year-old self out of bed unfurled in her mind. She'd trudged in her clingy one-piece nightsuit down the hallway to answer the door and stared up at two Enclave security people. They had seemed so sad for her. As soon as she'd seen their faces, she'd started to cry, knowing something bad had happened. "I remember the security officers finding me home alone. Dad didn't come home after a late night at the lab."

"He was assassinated that night." Dad-AI drooped; the synthesized voice came so close to human, sorrow sounded clear in each word. "Do you remember where they took you?"

Tris looked at her knees. "They told me to get dressed, and then they drove me to the clinic. They said my father had become very ill and I needed to be checked to make sure I didn't have the same sickness."

"A believable enough lie."

"I..." Memories she'd lost track of came swirling back. Cold fake leather on her back. Rubber-gloved hands sticking little electrodes to her bare chest. "They told me to take my clothes off and lie on this table so they could scan me. This woman put electrodes on my chest and head... so many of them on my head." Bright white light ate the scene, and another woman in a black jumpsuit smiled at her. The uncomfortable procedure table had changed into a bed like magic. The electrodes gone, replaced with a little hospital gown. "I... don't know how I wound up in a bed."

"Mmm." Dad-AI grumbled. "In 2055, you were returned to stasis as a nine-year-old while they prepared replacement parents for you."

"P-prepared?" Tris shivered at the thought of the kind of people who could toss a newly-orphaned little girl into a freezer while they cooked up a new set of parents. "Why? Why didn't they just give me to new parents right away?"

Dad-AI glided side to side in a slight arc, a head wag of sorts. "I have no way to know that, as my biological originator had ceased to exist at that point in time. They selected a young couple who had recently been denied a pairing because their genetic material was needed elsewhere. Amid the deceit, they said there had been an error and the two would be allowed to pair as they requested."

Tris frowned. "They almost never let people marry for love."

"When the girl next door is your second cousin, you gotta be careful," muttered Kevin.

"Ass." Tris poked him in the side.

Dad-AI wobbled up and down as if chuckling. "The man may be indelicate, but he is not incorrect. This couple were told they needed to have another scan to confirm that there had been an error."

"... and they put them in the freezer again," said Tris.

"Correct. They harvested genetic material and put them into stasis. While in stasis, they believed they had left the procedure room within twenty minutes. "In truth, they were in virtual reality where they believed they had a baby daughter... you."

Tris blinked. "I thought they were being cruel to me on purpose... like everyone was lying. They really had no idea you were—I mean Dad was real."

"They did not." Dad-AI sagged with a labored whine of hydraulics. "After nine years, they arranged for the artificial version of you to experience a mild medical condition which required hospitalization for a brief period... 'for testing.' You were thawed, and placed in a real hospital bed where you woke up, not having any idea how much time had passed. Your parents were removed from stasis without their knowledge and placed in the bedroom of a house painstakingly arranged to match the simulation."

Tris' mind leapt back to that day. Everyone acted as though she'd been sick. No one remembered Dad. The people who'd shown up to take her home... *They both seemed stiff and sore. Oh, God... it's true...* "Why... why did everyone act like you never existed?"

The bot's main iris lens narrowed to a sinister purple dot. "They attempted to implant a memory overlay on you that would have created the same false life as your adoptive parents believed. The Council of Four wanted to clear your memories of me as a security precaution. I did not allow that to happen." The AI sighed. "It is quite fortunate that Yana and Marcus only believed you to have suffered delusions and not taken their concerns to the authorities. Had the Council become aware your memory modification had failed... they may have taken more *drastic* measures."

Tris found herself crying in silence. She'd not quite 'hated' them for most of her life, more resented... for thinking her crazy and making her ignore Dad. It hadn't been their fault after all. They really *did* believe her to be their biological daughter. "Why am I so important?"

"Hey wait a second." Kevin snatched the printed photo. "She has white hair in this picture. If we're supposed to believe that she was born before the nukes, how did she look like that back then?"

"Tris was a platinum blonde." Dad-AI sprouted a narrow metal appendage, which pointed an intense, albeit tiny, spotlight on the paper. "The printout is not the best quality. The toner has been sitting idle for fifty years or so, and the light in here is... poor."

Under the spotlight, the little girl in the picture had a hint of blonde in her hair and a trace of color in her skin, neither of which present-day Tris possessed.

She exhaled. "I... don't know how to feel. W-why am I so important?"

"I do not know the full extent of their knowledge of you, me, or the risk you represent. However, considering you were born in 2014, I imagine they are most interested in your DNA. They also likely fear my biological predecessor may have left sleeper programs in the systems that you would be able to access." Dad-AI glided to Tris' left and activated another set of monitors, which streamed with program code. Black textual ants raced across white background. "The Enclave does not know that I, that is to say the artificial intelligence of Doctor Jameson, exist. I inserted the message into Nathan's music files hoping you would be able to find it. I was unable to do more to stop them from putting the explosive in you, though I did manage to reprogram it not to detonate until five seconds after exposure to air."

At the mere thought of what that charge would've done to her, she lurched, dry heaving. One of the wheels on her chair cracked.

"I have the means to shut down the production and distribution system for Agent-94, or 'The Virus,' as you know it. However, I do not have direct access to the main Enclave network. There is no hardline connectivity between the old Stanford network and the modern systems. I have been operating via an unsecured backdoor through an ancient tape drive, but they have been upgrading and I am no longer able to establish connectivity. I need you to create a router to connect the two networks."

"And how the heck am I going to do that?" Tris lifted her head, wanting to crawl off somewhere, wrap herself around a stuffed animal, and cry until everything just stopped mattering.

Hydraulics whining, Dad-AI swiveled around the room, activating panel after panel of displays. All the supercomputer towers lit up from inside with a cobalt blue glow. After a minute or so of frantic zipping about, the boom extended the 'head' close to Tris once more. "Once you create a path for me to connect to the Enclave's current systems, I will be able to eliminate the Virus, their capacity to manufacture it, and all records of how to make it. However, I need *you* to remove a security protocol I—Doctor Jameson rather—put around certain file structures within the Enclave system. I have already created programs that will do everything that needs to be done safely, but your genetic fingerprint is coded to what Doctor Jameson named the Eden Protocol. You are the only one who can open it."

Tris shivered and looked up at the metallic box hovering over her, unsure which of its five lens 'eyes' she should stare into. "Me?"

Kevin folded his arms. "No wonder Nathan wants you dead so bad."

THE NEXT ONE

A bby lay curled on her side facing out into the room, Zoe's arm around her. The younger girl's breath warmed the back of her head. It felt like an hour since they'd gotten into bed and the adults left. She didn't dare close her eyes. Although they said only Zara would go near a fallen drone, the crash sounded too close. The wind would carry death over the whole town.

Her eye caught the glint of moonlight off one of the gas masks lying on the floor. She sat up.

"Are you okay?" whispered Zoe, her grip tightening.

"We should put the masks on. It's gonna blow through town."

"Okay." Zoe insisted on holding her hand as she crawled out of bed.

Abby picked up the mask Zoe had designated as hers. "I'm not gonna run." She looked at the tangle of rubber bits and lenses, with a pair of disk-shaped vents on each cheek. "How does it work?"

"Here." Zoe dropped hers at her feet and helped Abby get it over her head before adjusting the straps.

The mask pressed into her face too hard to be comfortable, but in some odd way, it reassured her. Zoe put hers on and marched over to her desk. She dragged the chair closer to the bed, left it, and headed to a wardrobe cabinet from which she lugged a rolled up sleeping bag almost twice her size. Abby tilted her head in confusion. Zoe unrolled it in the space between the bed and the chair before pulling the blanket half off the bed, using the chair to drape it into a tent.

Abby started to protest when Zoe grabbed her rifle from the closet, but didn't want to make so much noise Bill or Pete woke up. Zoe crawled into their blanket fort and lay the rifle flat beside the bed. Abby scooted in next to her and pulled the 'tent flap' closed.

They could've been playing army… except for the real firearm.

She felt a little ridiculous in a knee-length purple sweatshirt and a gas mask, but maybe if the Virus got into the house, she'd be able to get away. The mask didn't fit Zoe well, since it had been made for an adult. The occasional brush of coolness below Abby's ears worried her that she had a similar issue. She put a hand on the mask to hold it tight to her skin, and shifted from sitting cross-legged to lying on her side.

"Cnh mm slee im eees?" asked Abby.

Zoe looked at her. "What?"

Abby took a couple quick breaths trying to calm down, but the difficulty of breathing in the mask frightened her to where it had the opposite effect. "Can. We. Sleep. In. These?"

Zoe shrugged.

Fogging lenses needled at claustrophobia. It made no sense at all, but the blanket wall did make her feel safer. If Amarillo repeated here, at least they had a high place. Nothing could get up to them. Zoe's closet held enough bullets to kill everyone in Nederland twice…

Abby grabbed her chest and panted.

Zoe hovered over her, rising up on her knees. "Ymm kay?"

"Scared." Abby closed her eyes.

The more she tried to breathe, the harder it got, and the more frightened she became. In minutes, the overwhelming urge to rip the mask off crashed head first into the terrifying idea that one tiny sip of air without it would kill her. Her gut churned.

No! Don't throw up! She cringed. The mere thought of vomiting while wearing a gas mask made her even sicker. *Bunnies! Flowers! Bunnies! Flowers!*

Zoe peeked out the flap. "Nothing's coming. We're clear."

Abby coughed, wheezing. *How do soldiers wear these things? I can't breathe!* She grabbed the mask in both hands, pressing it down but wanting to pull it away.

"We're safe. Stay quiet." Zoe, apparently taking a cue from Bill, shuffled over and stroked her hair as though she were a giant housecat. "Don't be scared. Dad and Gran'pa will protect us."

Abby tried to think of fuzzy white dust hoppers frolicking in a flower-laden meadow, but still couldn't calm down. She clutched her throat, wheezing, fighting for air.

Zoe grasped her mask. "You're having 'nother 'tack. Should take this off so you can breathe."

"No! I don't wanna die," yelled Abby.

She jumped at the *clonk* of the front door closing. *They're coming!* Her eyes sent a warning to Zoe.

"Shh," whispered Zoe. "You're breathing too fast."

The loft floor thumped with the weight of someone coming up the ladder.

Abby sat upright, grabbed Zoe, and whispered, "They're here."

"'Fected can't do ladders."

"Girls?" asked Bill. "What in the name of…"

"See?" Zoe held her hands up in an exaggerated shrug. "It's just Gran'pa."

Bill pulled the 'tent' open and blinked at them. At the sight of Abby's fish-out-of-water act, he swooped down and pulled the mask away from her face. Air across her cheeks felt as though she'd walked from a sauna into a nice autumn day.

"No!" Abby reached for the mask. "The Virus!"

"No virus." Bill wiped sweat from her forehead. "Another camera unit."

Abby clutched her fists against her chest, right below her chin.

"Really." He shook his head at the 'fort.' "Zara went out to check the drone. It came down about a hundred yards southeast of the artificial lake. There's no need to suffocate yourself with a seventy-year-old mask."

No Virus. She blinked a few times and held that thought until her breathing slowed to normal. "The air is safe?"

Zoe pushed her mask up so it sat on top of her head. A second later, super-serious face broke with a giant grin.

"Yes, Abby." He held her hand. "That drone didn't have anything on it other than electronics. You can relax."

"But…" She gazed down. "It got close enough to see us, didn't it?"

Bill eyed the rifle and gave Zoe a warning look. "You're getting a little too casual with that weapon, sweetie. You need to respect it like the tool it is. It's not a toy."

Abby brushed her fingertips over the goosebumps on her calf.

"Sorry. We thought the 'Fected were coming." Zoe pulled the mask off her head, picked up her rifle, and carried both back to the closet.

"It saw us, didn't it?" whispered Abby.

Bill's lips curled inward. He heaved a sigh and nodded. "Yeah. Probably."

"Can you take us away from Ned?" She put a hand on his arm.

Zoe scurried back to the tent and crawled in on her stomach.

"There's no need to get that extreme yet." Bill patted her hand.

"But… they're gonna attack us. They're gonna send it here where everyone is. We gotta go camp out in the woods so they can't find us. Please, Mr. Vasquez… please take us somewhere safe." Abby stared at him, whispering, "Please."

Zoe yawned. She pushed at the sleeping bag and squirmed, frowning before glancing up at the bed then over at Abby. "We can sleep inna fort if you want. Or bed if you think the floor's too hard."

"Please," whispered Abby. She eyed the pink fabric. "Blanket isn't gonna stop anything… bed's fine."

Zoe smiled. "Okay. If you're sure."

"I'm not five years old… I don't…"

"Here." Zoe handed her Fuzz.

Abby looked down, but took it.

Bill backed up as the girls moved the blanket back to the bed and climbed under the covers. After putting the sleeping bag back in the closet, he tucked them in and sat on the chair, already nearby. "We've worked out an evacuation plan to temporarily relocate everyone to Boulder in the event a weaponized drone shows up."

"I'm scared," whispered Abby.

Zoe rolled toward her and put an arm over her chest. Bill's eyes reddened and he wiped a tear before patting her on the back.

"The next one won't be a camera." Abby stared at Bill. "The next one will kill us."

Bill bowed his head, some of the color faded from his cheeks.

It's gonna come. It's gonna kill everyone if we don't stop it. She clenched her jaw. The drones were only scary if they got close. *We gotta stop it from getting close. I gotta stay alive 'til my…* A tingle spread over her back, ran all the way down her legs to her feet, and bounced back up as a surge of determination. *I have parents! I gotta stay alive 'til they're back.*

She grabbed Bill's hand. "Tomorrow… can you show me how to shoot a rifle?"

He blinked at her, wordless.

"I want to help. I know I'm not twelve yet like the mayor said's gotta carry a gun... but I wanna help anyway." Abby shuddered. "I saw it happen in Amarillo. I don't want it to happen here."

Bill pondered for a second or two before nodding. "Alright. We'll see if you're comfortable with it tomorrow. Try to sleep. And let's hope you're a little more careful with it than a certain little girl who thinks she's nineteen instead of nine."

Zoe snuggled closer and drooled a little on Abby's shoulder. Somehow, she'd already passed out.

"Okay," whispered Abby, closing her eyes.

Bill grunted; the chair creaked. A rough hand patted her on the forehead before the *smack* of a light kiss happened somewhere in Zoe's vicinity.

They just *shot down the camera. The Virus won't show up tonight.* Little by little, the dread that the instant she fell asleep, Nederland would be wiped out faded.

"*Jesús*, if you're real. Please let Tris and Kevin come home," she whispered before letting the air out of her lungs in a long, slow breath. "And tell Dad I love him."

A STORM OF DOUBT

R andom memories of childhood flooded in still-image flashes through Tris' mind. How old had she been when her father decided to use her as some kind of key? She couldn't doubt that he'd loved her, but she found herself livid with him. More so for the tease of thinking him alive, only to find the voice from the other end of the phone had been a computer program pretending to be a dead man.

The dark-brown face of Randall, the 'Resistance' contact who'd run all the training sims and watched over her while she lay helpless and naked in a tank, appeared in her mind. They'd gone all out with the act. He'd dressed in quasi-military rags, spoke with a hint of patois, and acted like he loathed the Enclave and everything they stood for.

She almost felt his hands clutching the fabric of her jumpsuit at each shoulder. *You kin do 'dis 'ting woman. You may be small, but ya got lot o' 'art. Go out 'dere, show 'dem who's da boss. Believe in yerself an ya kin do anyt'ing.*

"Right. Suppose this works." She opened her eyes and looked at the mechanical thing pretending to be Dad. "Stopping the distribution of new Virus is one thing, but what about the symbiotes or the existing Infected that haven't died off naturally?"

"Yeah." Kevin flashed a rogue's smile. "Some of those things are well past their expiration date."

The 'head' on the end of the boom swiveled down to peer behind it while rotating to keep itself right side up. One of the distant monitors flashed a stream of data too fast for a human eye to read. "I will be able to initiate a self-destruct command to the symbiotes. There has always existed an 'off switch' per se. From the start, their end game"—its 'head' swiveled around to face her—"has been to retake the land outside. They would not have wanted to fight off the weapons they'd unleashed upon the world."

"What about the non-symbiote Infected?" Tris folded her arms.

"Those, alas, would be left to Agent-94 running its standard course of progression. All should expire within three months. Preferably without contaminating more people."

"But they're *not* dying in three months." Tris stood. Dad-AI glided back as she approached. "Some of them have lasted far longer than that."

"I believe you are falling for an illusion, Tris." Dad-AI moved around her, the boom arm holding its 'head' like a medical instrument running a 180-degree scan of her skull. "They expire but are replaced by new victims. I have found nothing to indicate they have managed to extend the terminal arc of the disease. It is hastened in cases where the victim is unable to find food. Reduced mental capacity also interferes with their ability to recognize some sources of nourishment. Canned food, for example, they would perceive as inedible slugs of metal."

Tris paced back and forth running her hands through her hair and grumbling. An idea sparked, and she stopped cold, pointing at the machine. "You're an AI with some part of my father's intelligence. His brain running at the speed of a computer would be scary to behold... Can you somehow reprogram the symbiotes to break down Infected instead of blow themselves up?" She waved her hand around in a circle near her head. "Like... like... reverse the process by which the symbiotes stall death. Speed it up instead. And set the symbiote to self-destruct if it fails to encounter an Infected in something like seventy-two hours."

"And disregard uninfected humans," said Dad-AI.

"Well yeah." Tris stared into the largest lens-eye, inches from her face. "That kinda went without saying." She sighed and bowed her head. *I shouldn't have gotten my hopes up that he'd be alive.* "Of course. Programs need to state everything explicitly."

"Correct. I am already generating the necessary instruction code. By the time you initiate the Eden protocol, it should be ready." The boom glided closer, iris lenses narrowing. "I am sensing an unusual tone in your voice."

"It's... I... You should've told me you were an AI." She looked around for something to punch. Kevin crept closer, so she settled for holding him instead. "I let myself believe you... I mean my father... might've still been alive."

"I apologize for becoming 'Schrödinger's Dad.'"

Tris gasped a chuckle and wiped a lone runaway tear.

"Who the hell is Shrow Dinger?" asked Kevin.

"Maybe you're right." *My father is dead, and this is his last message to me from beyond the grave. He grew old and left me frozen while the world collapsed and reshaped.* She clenched her fist into the cloth at Kevin's back. "He could've taken me out of stasis, kept me with him. Let me grow up with a father."

"Forgive me if I am being semantic, but you did grow up with *a* father... merely one who was not biologically related to you. The man believed you to be his child. Did he not treat you well?"

"I..." She walked away from Kevin and got to pacing. "Aside from the whole almost putting me into a mental health path because I hallucinated you—I mean my dad." She growled. "No. Once I lied and said I made my father up, Dad2 was okay." *I never had a problem with Mom2. I never even knew Mom1.* "Do you know what happened to my mother?"

"As far as I know, she is still within the Enclave, believing you are in Detention for refusing the pairing. They have been appealing, which may have succeeded had there been no need to cover up your disappearance."

Her face flushed warm with annoyance. "No, dammit. I mean the woman whose uterus I came out of."

"Oh." Dad-AI leaned back. "Liliana Martin. She was quite a bit younger than my biological self. The human I once was believed she had fallen in love with him, though she dated him on a dare, and stayed around for some months later out of guilt when she realized the 'scientist nerd' wasn't such a bad guy under the lab coat." The boom arm drooped, digitized voice taking on a somber tone. "Eventually, she decided to move on. You weren't even one year old yet. I suppose being nineteen, she figured it better to leave you with an 'adult' for a parent." It sighed, all the lights in its lens-eyes pulsed brighter and fading with the sound. "If she were still alive, she'd be seventy-eight now."

"She died?" asked Tris, mildly ashamed of herself for not feeling much of any emotion about the idea.

"I do not know either way. The day she told me she wanted to leave was the last day... I correct myself—the day she told my biological counterpart that she wished to leave was the last time he saw her. He was at least pleased she gave him the news in person rather than leaving a note."

Her jaw tightened. "She didn't seem too upset about leaving me behind."

Dad-AI swung side to side, a gesture perhaps meant as a head shake. "She believed herself too much a child to care for one."

At a mother that didn't want her, a dead father who wasn't... but was, fear of ten thousand Enclave soldiers overhead, and the need to protect Abby, a twinge of horrendous nausea overwhelmed her. She raised her hands, and stormed out. "I... don't know. I can't do this. I don't know what the hell to believe anymore."

Dad-AI swiveled, extending after her as much as the boom permitted. "Tris?"

Out in the hall, she leaned her folded arms against the opposite wall and rested her forehead on them.

After a minute or so of silence, shoes crunched dust and concrete silt behind her. The approach sounded like Kevin, so she didn't bother moving. He put a hand on her shoulder.

"Hey," he whispered.

She mumbled, "So I guess I'm not really eighteen."

"I can see no situation where me making any kind of a grandmother joke results in an ending other than your fist in my nose... or balls." He squeezed her shoulder. "Besides, if you're biologically eighteen, that makes me feel a little... odd."

"Nine years isn't *that* much of a difference." She turned away from the wall to wrap her arms around him. "Besides. I've been awake for twenty years... even if some of it was in virtual reality. I think I want to go home. I've got the worst feeling about Abby. I wanna hold her."

"You've gone super-mom." He smiled. "Where'd that come from?"

"I dunno." She scratched at her stomach, again feeling like a nutrient packet that had been sucked dry and thrown aside. *Longing for what I can't have?* "Maybe I'm still angry that they took my ovaries."

"That sounds kind of painful." His sympathetic look lasted about four seconds before he grimaced. "What's an ovary?"

She chuckled into his shoulder. "I'm not explaining that now."

"Look." He held her face in both hands, lifting her head so she made eye contact. "We've come all this way to stop these fuckers from dropping that green shit on anyone else. Maybe that electro-dad of yours is full of crap. Maybe he isn't."

"Can *you* believe that?" One tear slid from each of her eyes and crept down her cheeks. "Could you believe you were born before the war? That the parents who you thought you were crazy are victims too? That your own *father* helped them—" Tris glared at the doorway. She pulled away from Kevin and stomped back into the room.

Dad-AI, stretched to the limit of the boom toward the entrance, glided backward. The tilt of the 'head' and dilation of the irises seemed happy to see her return.

"How could you have gone along with it?" Tris pointed up. "With making the Virus?"

It bobbed. She imagined it shrugging if it had arms. "I, forgive me, *he* didn't. That's why they killed him."

"You keep slipping and saying I." She squinted. "Are you really alive and speaking through this thing?"

Dad-AI slouched. "No. I am sorry, Tris. Sometimes the illusion of being a human I never was feels too real. The memories appear to be mine, but they are not. I am sure, despite everything, he would have been very proud of the woman you've become."

"But, I know my father helped with some of the design. Doctor Andrews told me." Tris folded her arms. "Why?"

"I will be less obtuse. Yes. Your father did initially participate in the design program of a manmade virus. However, its initial concept came about as a mechanism to distribute vaccines and a restorative nanomedical treatment for radiation damage in the manner of a contagious agent. The early founders of the Enclave believed the population would not readily accept technological medicine, and so they sought to release a benevolent plague so to speak. A contagious virus that would carry with it a cure as well as inoculate those it infected from the usual array."

"Usual array?" Kevin slipped back into the room, and pushed the door closed.

"The usual vaccinations. Measles, Mumps, Rubella, Polio, Chicken pox, ad nauseum." Dad-AI bowed its 'head.' "Alas, the paranoids won out. Before Agent-8 could be released into the world, opinion towards outsiders changed. The Enclave shifted toward weaponization of it. Rather than curing the people who had survived nuclear war, the First Council came to see them as contamination on the Earth, a disease in and of themselves that needed to be eliminated before we could re-emerge. They believed any who had not sheltered in here to avoid the worst of the radiation and environmental disasters would only introduce runaway genetic damage into the human genome—and had to be euthanized."

Tris scowled. "Who the fuck do these people think they are that they can arbitrarily make a decision like that? How are they that much better off after generations of breeding in closed quarters? I bet half these people are so inbred they're their own fathers."

Kevin laughed.

"I... rather your father... agreed with you. Hence... dead."

Hands balled into fists at her sides, Tris fumed. How many Amarillos had there been? How many families thrown into paranoia, torn apart by the fear of the Virus as much as the Virus itself. *They were ready to murder Abby over a goddamned cold.* A growl started deep in her chest and rose from her throat.

"Okay." Tris looked at not-Dad. "How do we blow the fuck out of this place?"

"I do not think that is wise. I will guide you to do what you must do. I will explain more as you continue. You know the man for whom I was modeled. Ask yourself deep inside the nature of my intentions. I will not mislead you." Dad-AI swooped across the room. A tiny claw arm extended from the underside of the 'head' and disconnected a USB memory stick from one of the computers. It whirred back over, offering it. "This memory module contains software code that emulates the function of a router. It is already configured with the appropriate data translation routines."

"You're gonna clean a toilet with that?" asked Kevin.

Dad-AI angled to face him. "A router is a computer networking device that provides a connection between two dissimilar networks and—"

"*Dad!*" yelled Tris.

It pivoted back to her.

"Save the Networking 101. You just said we don't have time." She grabbed the USB. "Right, so I don't think there's going to be any 2020 era computers in the Quar. I'm going to need some kind of hardware connection too."

"Correct. There is a prototype Petafiber card in one of the labs. You should be able to install it in one of the computers, which is already connected to the Stanford network. Then, you would only need to run a fiberoptic line through the ventilation ducts. I have calculated the best path for you at 217.4 meters to a small office room. The storage closet there should have a cable long enough to make the run. They have not used cables in many years, so it will likely go unnoticed long enough to complete the upload."

"What upload?"

"My consciousness," said Dad-AI. "Once I transfer myself off the dying Stanford net and onto the Enclave system, I will be able to grant your wish."

"Great. And what happens if I get caught?" She looked at Kevin.

"Probability scenarios take up quite a lot of resources that I need to allocate elsewhere at this moment. Will you settle for 'that would not be wise?'"

"No shit." She bowed her head, took a breath to psych herself up, and looked up at the boom. "Okay. So how are you going to lead me anywhere?"

The small drone glided into the doorway.

"Consider that my finger pointing the way." Dad-AI tilted a bit, as if trying to smile.

Kevin pulled the .45 out of his pocket. "Be careful. If anything goes wrong, we haul ass back the way we came and hope the subway's still clear."

"Sounds like a good idea." Tris walked at the drone, which glided away and zoomed down the corridor.

"Be careful," said Dad-AI.

Tris paused in the doorway to glance again at the machine mounted to the ceiling. "I have no idea why I trust you, or why I'm inclined to believe what sounds like a massive load of bullshit… but… thanks."

The boom arm bowed.

Whirring hung in the corridor about twenty paces away.

"Tris, please follow," said the drone.

"Oh, I *am* going to shoot that thing." Kevin hurried through the door.

She grabbed his shoulder. "We need it."

"Right." He pointed the .45 at it in a 'your days are numbered' gesture, and lowered his arm.

The chuckle in her chest couldn't quite lift the weight of duty and guilt sitting on top of it. By the time it reached her lips, it petered out from a laugh to a faint smile. She marched after the drone, which continued past the computer lab to another stairway. Since the window here remained intact, it waited for her to open the doors before gliding onward. It led them two stories up and came to a hover at another set of black-painted double doors. A sign on the wall referred to this floor as B1.

"Damn, how deep was this place?" asked Kevin. "We're *still* underground?"

She pulled the door open. "I'm really going to stop asking how deep some rabbit holes go."

The corridor outside contained hundreds of old desks, chairs with an attached slab of some beige plastic-like substance that looked far removed from what anyone could consider comfortable. While the drone glided merrily along above them, Tris and Kevin struggled to climb over clusters of debris, jogged through short spans of passable hallway, and climbed again.

Eventually, the drone stopped at a heavy wooden door with a tiny square wire-reinforced window. Tris crept up to it and grasped the knob. She stared at the ceiling, terrified at the thought a couple thousand Enclave military walked around less than twelve feet overhead. She'd been in the Quar before, but hadn't remained there long enough to have learned about the old university below it. Then again, that sort of knowledge she imagined the Enclave wanted to keep secret. Above her might be a tarmac full of Hoplites as easily as a building where soldiers practiced hand-to-hand fighting.

She turned the knob, pushed the door in, and gasped.

Before her lay the same room as depicted in the photograph of her at five years old. Within two breaths, the smell of old technology, older paper, and a faint wisp of pipe smoke weakened her knees. She stared at the same desk her father used to work at, standing in front of the same worktable that once held his prototype android limbs.

As if on autopilot, she walked to the spot where she'd always sat on the floor, and sat on the floor. The room seemed *wrong* when viewed from the height perspective of a grown woman. Maudlin thoughts, wishing the world had never gone crazy, squeezed her throat closed.

Kevin approached, looking around with a whistle of awe. "Wow. This is that room. Hey look, a 2019 calendar. It's still there."

"I don't want to look." She wiped sadness from her mind and stood. "If we don't screw this up, I'll have years to cry into my beer over what my life might have been. I can't do it now." She scurried to a table near the back right corner, where a handful of PCs sat dormant.

The drone glided to land on Dad's desk, and bounced a few times.

Tris looked at it. "Is it resting or is it 'pointing' at the desk?"

The drone bounced a few times.

"I'd say pointing." Kevin crept over.

She changed course. "Oh, the prototype card."

A moment of rummaging drawers turned up a locked metal case about the size of a book. As soon as she raised it from the drawer, the drone slid back a bit and powered off. She set the case down on the desk, pulled out her smallest lock picks, and got to work. Kevin paced around, drawing and concealing his handgun as if he couldn't decide if their odds of bluffing exceeded their odds of needing to shoot their way out if someone found them. It was unlikely, but possible. But if anyone saw a firearm, especially an old-tech one, Kevin would have to use said old-tech firearm.

Nine agonizing minutes later, the diminutive—though sturdy—lock yielded and popped open. She stuffed the tools back in her shoe, closed the sole, and flipped open the case.

Between two slabs of dark grey foam sat a green PCIe card with a silver metal frame around the entire circuit board. The outer-facing edge contained small socket in the middle.

"Wow. Back when I was five years old, this card was probably more valuable than a shitty house." She blinked at it and set it back in the case. "Right… need to find a working system."

Kevin sat at the desk and put his feet up while she went from computer to computer until one turned on. When she found a 'winner,' she shut it off again and flipped the tower on its side.

"Why'd you turn it off again?" He raised an eyebrow.

"I can't put the card in when it's on. Antiques were touchy like that."

A minute or four of searching turned up a screwdriver from the worktable, and she made short work of installing the prototype card. The system already had an Ethernet line connecting it to the Stanford net, so she had only to run a fiber line to create a bridge to the modern network.

"Great." She looked around at the walls. "He said vent. Do you see a vent in here?"

Kevin pointed.

All the way on the left end of the room, as opposite to the entry door as one could get, a three-by-three foot air filter covered an intake duct. She studied the upper walls as well as the ceiling. A few other openings, exhaust ducts, looks about eight inches tall and a foot wide. She doubted even five-year-old her would've fit through those.

"Well, I guess the choice is kinda obvious."

He nodded. "What's the plan?"

She jogged over to the empty worktable under the vent, climbed up, and pulled the cover off. A dusty, square metal shaft proceeded in a few feet before curving straight up. "This is going to suck. You're not going to be able to bend enough to fit. Wait here. I'll scream if I get stuck or need you to come after me."

"You sure?"

"No, but you're not exactly quiet." She kissed him. "Give me fifteen minutes before you come looking… unless you hear any strange noises."

He held her tight for a few seconds. "I don't like this, but if you think it's best."

"None of this is 'best,' only necessary." She kissed him again before crawling up into the shaft.

A short distance ahead, a curve in the duct bent vertical. She braced her shoes on the half-inch seams between sections of ductwork and shimmied up. *Hopefully, this doesn't turn into a maze.* She crawled to the curve and stood inside it, pulling herself upright with a hand on each side. A crosswind lofted her hair as soon as she peered over the top. The duct to her right ran back over the lab, and ended at a fan unit about where the wall would be. *Not going that way.* To the left, the shaft extended about forty yards before reaching a ninety-degree right.

Tris crawled as fast as she could go without making too much noise in the flimsy metal tunnel. The passage after the turn stretched even farther, with a left offshoot a decent ways off. She shimmied ahead, biting back curses whenever something on the top of the vent scraped her back, or she put her knee down on a flange between sections.

When the duct firmed up, as if embedded in dirt, she picked up the pace as it made little noise. As she neared the offshoot, her hair pulled forward and trailed out in front of her face. Devoting one hand to holding it out of her eyes slowed her somewhat. Roaring of fans grew louder as she neared the opening on the left.

She peered in as soon as she could, finding a curved duct blasting air into the section she crawled along, aiming it in the same direction she'd been moving. Not wanting to go face-first into a turbine, she continued straight with a stiff tailwind.

Some minutes later, light stretched into the duct from the left. Her best estimation had put her a little past 217 meters, but she gave that up to nerves. This had to be where the not-Dad wanted her to go. She edged up to a square grille, smaller than the intake, but still not too difficult to squeeze through.

The room on the other side reminded her of Detention. Black gloss tiles and white walls. From the floor-level opening, she got a glimpse of a few desks and strong daylight. An antiseptic smell swirled in her nostrils and brought back memories of home. Her whole house reeked of the same chemical when she was nine. *I'd been thawed. That was the Enclave... Maybe it's not a smell, but the absence of stink? Everything's constantly being cleaned here.* Her stomach churned at the memory of her first night in the Wildlands sleeping in an old sewer. And those bastards who'd captured her had been *so* foul. Maybe Kevin had a point. They hadn't raped her because they worried the Enclave wouldn't pay them if she'd been 'contaminated.' But that didn't stop them from squeezing and groping.

She grumbled, stopped, and listened.

Two minutes of silence exceeded her patience threshold. She grasped the vent and gave it a light push, popping it out. The room had to be air conditioned, but it felt warm, likely from her being *in* the AC vent for the last eight minutes or so. She crawled behind the nearest desk and peered over. The space resembled a tiny classroom containing six desks facing a single, larger one. Each desk had a computer terminal and a set of storage drawers. The sight of school desks drew a sad sigh from her. It felt like only yesterday she'd been a high school senior looking forward to University and a future far removed from one where a day without being shot at wound up in the 'great day' column. The walls held clear panels with glowing text detailing inventories of everything from clothes to toiletries to weapons and armor... even ordinance for Hoplite or Guardian hovercraft onboard weapons.

Weird. This is set up like a classroom, but it's some kind of quartermaster's office.

The door behind the large desk looked too much like an exit compared to the one four steps behind her. She opted for the nearer door and found a decent-sized storage room full of metal wire shelves packed with stuff. Folded black jumpsuits, shoes, boxes labeled only with alphanumeric codes... random tech. She raced up and down the aisles for a little while before remembering not-Dad said they hadn't used cables in ages.

To the back she went.

In a dust-covered box on the bottom shelf, she found bundles of Petafiber cabling. Powder blue ran only twenty feet. Pastel orange, fifty feet. Dark blue, a hundred meters. Finally, she grinned at a fat donut of bright red cable. Three hundred meters. She grabbed it while offering a prayer to the gods of technology that the optical fiber inside hadn't broken in however long it had been left here.

She ran back to the office, closed the door, and froze glancing at the clock: 12:21 p.m.

Oh, shit. No wonder no one is in here. They're in the cafeteria. She chuckled. *I guess for once having everything scheduled to the minute worked out to be a good thing.* She hurried to the desk closest to the vent cover she'd come in from, set the cable bundle down, and snapped off the plastic tape holding it in a donut. Whoever worked there had a lot of kitsch in—probably her, judging by all the cat-themed items—workspace, which made hiding the wire atop the desk possible. Tris threaded it around various knickknacks, penholders, and whatnot before plugging it in to a Petafiber port on the all-in-one terminal that had likely never been used.

Most of the Enclave tech ran off exabyte wireless... they had no need to bother with the wires anymore except for long runs, like connecting the Quar to the Core City. *When civilization consists of one city...* Well the Quar wasn't quite part of it. *Okay, one-point-two cities.* She shoved the bulk of the cable spool into the vent and took a moment to tape the wire in place to the side of the desk, in hopes whoever worked here would assume it had always been there. She moved the wastebasket to cover the cable on the floor a little.

"What are you doing?" asked a young sounding voice.

Tris popped up, eye-to-eye with a white-haired, twig-thin girl in a kid-sized version of the ubiquitous all-black Enclave jumpsuit. The child's ice blue eyes narrowed with suspicion at the open vent and wire leading out of it.

"Oh, just fixing a technical problem. I'm almost done."

"You're lying. You're not supposed to be in here." The girl pointed at her. "I'm gonna get security."

A HOLLOW ECHO

Tension built in the muscles along the back of Tris' legs. She summoned her most innocent smile. The girl took a step back, seeming about to run for the door. Time appeared to slow as her combat boosts kicked on; she sprang to her feet and grabbed the wrist behind the pointing finger.

"Wait," said Tris. "You don't need to bother the ISF. I'm part of a test scenario to evaluate operator awareness. It's supposed to be secret."

The girl struggled to pull her arm away, wincing as Tris tightened her grip. "Ow! Let go of me. You're not supposed to be here. I can tell you're lying." She grunted; her shoes slipped forward. "Wires don't go into the wall like that. Stop! You're hurting me!"

When the child sucked in a breath, Tris pulled her in by the arm, spinning her about, and grabbed her from behind with a hand over her mouth. The girl struggled, trying to scream. Panic sent her into a brief frenzy, but Tris held on, unable to comprehend how she'd wound up attacking a little girl. She pinned the kid's arms to her sides and tried to hold her as gently as possible, but the vast difference in their strength set off a nuclear detonation of terror in the small body. Hot breath blasted in rapid pulses over her fingers from the girl's nose.

"Shh. Please calm down." Tris cried as well. *What am I going to do with this girl? I can't hurt her... I can't let her go.* She considered leaving her in the storeroom hogtied and gagged, but didn't see anything useful to bind her with—nor could she get the concept of doing that to a child past her conscience. Overpowering the girl already made her feel like a horrible, horrible person. That, and if the workers or students came back at 1:00 p.m., they'd most certainly hear her struggling.

Tris' stomach churned with guilt, but this kid screaming or getting away could doom the only hope she had to stop the Virus… and protect everyone she loved. Before her brain could think, she pushed the girl around behind her and sent her stumbling into the wall by the vent. With her right hand free, she drew the Beretta from her pocket and aimed an inch to the left of the kid's ear, hoping the girl didn't notice she wanted to miss. Firing a gun would be as bad as the girl screaming anyway. A faint pinkish handprint on the girl's face shamed her into looking down. *I don't deserve Abby. What am I doing?*

"That's…" The girl's eyes widened and brimmed with tears as she whispered, "That's a gun…"

I'm not going to hurt a child. I just need to scare her a little. "Please listen to me. I don't want to hurt you. I'm sorry I had to grab you like that, but too many people's lives are at stake."

The kid shrank against the wall, hands cradled together at her chin. She went from looking twelve-ish to closer to nine. "Why are you doing this? Why do you have a *gun*? The ISF is gonna shoot you." She whimpered for a few seconds before her knees buckled. "Please don't kill me."

Tris sucked air in her nostrils, trying not to let the ninety-ton boulder of guilt crush her into the floor. She glanced at the wire. *That's about as concealed as it's going to get. I need to clear my ass out of here before anyone else shows up.* "Stay quiet and do what I tell you, and we can both go about the rest of our day without anyone getting hurt." She pointed the gun at the vent. "Crawl in there and go to the right."

"But… but… it's dirty in there." She gulped. "My name's Aura. I'm eleven years old. I like cats. I have two… Yinyang and Lily. I've got a little brother Alan. He's seven. Dance class and robotics are my favorites."

Tris let a sigh leak out of her nose without making noise. "Aura… That's a pretty name. You're a smart girl. I know what you're trying to do by telling me all about you, but you don't have to. Look at me." She wiped at her face. "I'm already upset. I promise I won't hurt you, but I can't let you run off and alert the ISF to what I'm doing. They work for the Council, and the Council is killing thousands of innocent people. I'm not the bad guy here. I'm doing the right thing."

"B-by pointing a g-gun at me?" Aura trembled.

Nausea clenched her stomach. *Do raiders ever feel this bad when they abduct people the first time? One loud noise, this kid's gonna wet herself.* She kept her voice slow and calm. "I don't have time to debate right now. I'm really, really sorry, but please get down and crawl into the vent."

Aura sniveled as she lowered herself to kneel. Tris didn't react to a long, pleading stare. The girl bowed her head and leaned forward onto all fours. She hesitated two more seconds before crawling into the duct, crying. Her snowy hair hung within an inch of the floor; as soon as she got into the vent, it lofted to the left, fluttering in the air-conditioned wind. The hesitance of the child's motion and look on her face made Tris feel as though she forced a little girl to dig her own grave before shooting her. She put the Beretta back in her pocket and stifled a few tears.

Once the kid cleared the opening, Tris shimmied in behind her and eased the ventilation cover in place, careful not to crush the petabyte-fiber cable. Aura's sniffles and whimpers echoed in the shaft, loud in Tris' ears as if broadcast over a PA system. The small body ahead of her shuddered.

"Please be quiet," whispered Tris. "Look at me."

Aura shifted left, pressing herself against the wall, and peered around past her shoulder at Tris.

Holding eye contact, Tris spoke a touch above a whisper. "I will not hurt you. An hour from now, you'll be home or wherever you want to be. Not a scratch on you. I promise."

"Why are you kidnapping me then?" Aura whimpered.

"Crawl forward." Tris picked up the donut-shaped bundle of cable. The fear in the girl's eyes—fear *she* caused—cut deep. As much as it hurt, she couldn't let guilt kill thousands of people. If any truth existed in Not-Dad's plan, if he could stop the Virus, scaring a kid for a little while was a necessary evil.

Shaking and crying, the child crawled. She didn't move with much urgency, though Tris couldn't blame her. "I promise I won't tell if you let me go."

"Aura… If I was in your position, I'd say the same thing. And as soon as I got away, I'd run straight to the Internal Security Force. I don't know if you'll believe me or not, but it's not easy for me to do this to you." She bowed her head for a second. "I've got a daughter your age. She's eleven too."

The vent crinkled and popped under their weight. Aura took the brunt of the incoming wind, though crawling into the breeze pushed her hair back and didn't whip it around her face as it did during the inbound trip. Tris unspooled wire as fast as she could, taking care not to lay it over anything too sharp.

"You can go a little faster," said Tris.

"I'm scared. I don't know what you're going to do to me when we get... wherever you're taking me."

Tris grumbled to herself for a few seconds. "The worst thing that will happen to you is being bored for an hour or so."

"But you have a *gun* and you're not ISF. Only dangerous people have guns."

"I guess you won't believe me if I tell you it pained me to have to threaten you with it."

Aura kept quiet for a few yards. "No... not really."

"Sorry."

"What?" Aura stopped short to look back, and Tris bumped her head into the girl's backside. She made a noise part chuckle, part sob. "You're sorry for kidnapping me at gunpoint?"

Tris nodded. "Yes. Actually, I am."

Aura resumed crawling. "Then why are you doing it?"

"The Enclave is misguided. They're afraid of the outside world, but they don't have to be. Much of the stuff they teach us is exaggerated. Yeah, there are some bad people out there. That's why I have a gun. Mostly, it's because of the damn Infected. The teachers and the Speaker are lying to everyone. The world outside isn't a threat. We can do so much to *help* civilization recover from the war, but all they want to do is kill everyone who isn't Enclave."

"Infected?" Aura's sniveling lessened, but didn't stop.

"The Council thinks that everyone outside the Enclave is genetically impure and should be put down like an animal too sick to save. They created a biological weapon that destroys people's minds, makes them incredibly strong, and gives them the urge to kill everyone they see."

Aura stopped crawling amid the throes of a coughing fit. For a second or two, she appeared about to vomit, but choked it back. "You've been outside?"

"Yes."

Fan noise grew louder up ahead. Once they passed the intake duct, the wind would drop off to almost nothing.

"I can't feel my fingers anymore." Aura's voice stuttered past chattering teeth.

"Crawl faster. We're almost there."

The girl picked up a little speed. She tried a duck-walk for a few yards, but returned to crawling on all fours. "Yinyang fetches like a dog, but Lily's too proud. Whenever I throw the fuzzy ball, she looks at me like 'pff... *you* go get it.'" A few seconds of silence later, the girl burst into tears again.

She still thinks I'm going to kill her. "Aura... I told you I have a daughter, right?"

"Yeah," whined the girl.

"If I found someone taking her away like what I'm doing to you, I'd probably shoot them." Her mind ran off with a daymare of Abby in Katie's place; rather than a pair of decent guys, a couple of raiders carted her off screaming. "You have every right to be terrified. Please believe me when I say the only thing I will do to you is stop you from setting off an alarm for a little while. Once I do what I need to do here, it won't matter who you tell about me. I don't have any reason to hurt you. I couldn't."

Aura raised her arms to shield her face as she passed the port on the right where the fan blasted a jet of freezing air into the duct. Fierce wind caused the girl to slide backward on her knees. Tris palmed her rear end and pushed her forward past the gale. The girl stopped once out of the windblast, rubbing her hands up and down her arms, shivering, teeth chattering.

Tris took a moment to enjoy the warmer air on the far side of the fan. "Damn, that's cold."

Aura looked back at her with a pouty-pleady face, reddened by emotion and from spending the last two minutes crawling into an arctic gale. "Would you have shot me if I tried to run away?"

"No." Tris sighed. "If you'd gotten away and sounded the alarm, you would've probably caused a few thousand people to die because I wouldn't be able to stop the Enclave from releasing their virus into the world... but I couldn't have shot you." She stared at the bundle of red wire for a few seconds in silence. "You're a little shorter, but you remind me too much of Abby."

Aura's expression held more confusion than anger or worry. "You're really going to just let me go?"

"Eventually, yes. I promise."

A hint of trembling returned as the girl resumed crawling. "Why were you in the ACP/AD room?"

"Huh? I thought that was a quartermaster's office."

"I'm taking advanced computer programming and algorithm design... it's a sophomore level course. There's only a couple of us. It's an after-school extra work project. I think they use it as an office during the day."

Abby's barely able to read. "Wow... that's. You're in what, sixth grade?"

"Gonna be next year. We're on summer break now." Aura coughed. "There's a turn up ahead. Is your daughter in school, or does she shoot people and run around with no clothes?"

Tris let off a somber laugh. "No. Abby's terrified of guns. I doubt she'd touch one to save her life. And most people out there aren't tribal primitives. We live in an old city that we're trying to rebuild... and the Enclave wants to kill us. They want to kill my daughter."

"Why? She's just a kid. Like me. It's bad to hurt kids." Aura looked back with huge saucer eyes. "Especially cute ones."

"You're right. And that's why I'm not going to let them. If you'd gotten me caught by the ISF, my daughter's life... as well as everyone else in what's left of the world, would've been in danger."

"Are you gonna blow us up?" Aura stopped. "'Cause if you're gonna do that, I won't help you. You'll have to shoot me here."

That thing *pretending to be my father hasn't said what its plans are. I'm pretty sure the City Core has a reactor...* As much as she'd become hostile to the Enclave, she'd always known innocents lived within. She used to be one of them. The terrified girl in front of her made the idea of 'one more nuke isn't so bad' painful to consider. "It's not my plan to hurt anyone here. I only want to stop them from making that virus."

Aura stared at her for a little while, ice-blue eyes narrow. "Okay."

Tris followed the girl around a left ninety-degree turn. Forty yards ahead, the opening back to her father's old lab leaked light into the shaft. "Head to that light up ahead."

The girl crawled forward.

At the opening, Tris dropped the donut of cable down the vertical. It bounced off the curved bottom and rolled out of sight. A half second later, the *thud* of it hitting the table echoed back up. She pulled Aura around and held both her wrists.

"Slide your legs down there. It's okay. I won't let you fall and hurt yourself."

Aura gave her the most pathetic, heart-crushing look of 'please don't.'

Tris closed her eyes and focused on her complete lack of any plan to hurt this kid. That she had to be cruel to a child wound up being Nathan's fault. "Please."

Sniffling, Aura squirmed around and put her legs down the shaft. Tris held her by the arms like a caught fish, and lowered her until the distance between the child's shoes and the vent bottom looked trivial.

"You've only got a couple inches left, but the bottom's a curve. I'm gonna let go."

"Tris?" asked Kevin. "Who are you talking to?"

Aura's eyes snapped open. She drew in a gasp to scream, and let it out as Tris released her grip on the girl's wrists. The child slid over the elbow at the bottom of the vent. Tris jumped down after, and caught herself against the sidewalls before she bumped the kid out of the short section at the bottom. She slid up behind the girl, wrapped her arms around, and scooted out to stand on the table below the opening.

Kevin stopped in mid-stride, halfway across the room on his way over. "What happened? Decided to pick up another orphan?" He grinned.

"No. This is Aura. She caught me connecting the Petafiber line." She jumped to the floor and carried the girl over. "I had to bring her with me so she didn't get the ISF and unplug the line. Hold her. Don't let her run off 'til Dad's inside. After that, it won't matter if she sets off an alarm."

Aura pressed herself into Tris, staring at Kevin. "He's a Wildlander... No! He's gonna give me something. I'm gonna get sick, or he's gonna kidnap me!"

Kevin put his fists on his hips and blinked at her. "Technically, Tris already did kidnap you."

Tris pushed Aura at Kevin and rushed past him. "Make sure she doesn't run away."

"Tris..." Kevin caught Aura and held her as she struggled to pull back. "I'm not gonna tie up a little girl."

Tris whirled around, yelling, "I didn't ask you to! Just watch her. I don't have time."

Aura writhed and pulled, sniveling. "Please don't hit me!"

Kevin sighed. "Oh, stop it. I swear we'll let you go as soon as she's done doing whatever techy shit she needs to do."

"Are you gonna eat me?" asked Aura in a mousy voice. "Or put me in a cage?"

Kevin grumbled to himself for a second. "Kid, you've been watching too many 'historical documentaries.'"

Tris rushed the Petafiber line to the PC she'd found, connected it to the prototype network interface card, and plugged in the USB stick Not-Dad had given her. *Oh, please be self-booting.* She restarted the computer, and waited.

Aura cried.

Kevin carried the girl closer to Tris and gestured at her as if she had brought a too-expensive purchase home and needed to return it. "What the hell are you doing? What the hell are *we* doing? I'm not this guy? I'm the guy who shoots the guy who scares the shit out of little kids. What's happening to us that we have to kidnap someone's daughter?"

Aura wiped her eyes, sniffling.

Tris glanced between them and the monitor in front of her. "We're not 'those people.' All we're doing is delaying her running off to get the ISF involved. Once Dad's inside, they won't be able to do anything. It won't matter if she"—*Aha!* She highlighted the option for a USB boot and jabbed the enter key—"runs off and whacks the hornet nest."

A progress bar crept across the screen above the word 'Loading.' *Damn old computers were so slow.*

Kevin carried Aura four steps away and put her in a chair. "Can you sit still for a little while? We're not going to hurt you. I'm not going to eat you, sell you, hit you, or whatever. We've got a kid your age."

Aura gasped. "But… he's a *Wildlander.* Eww!" She pointed at Tris. "You *did it* with a Wildlander?"

Tris turned away from the still-creeping 'loading' bar. "Look at me, Aura. Do I look old enough to have an eleven-year-old daughter? We took her in after the Enclave's virus killed her family."

"Oh." Aura glanced down.

"And yes." Tris snapped her head back to the monitor when an interface panel appeared. "We've 'done it' quite a few times."

Aura cringed, sticking her tongue out a little.

The screen looked like an attempt to reproduce a high-tech looking Enclave display with the limits of a prewar graphics processor. Text scrolled across a status readout line near the bottom under a pair of windows showing data throughput stats for both the Ethernet and Petabyte networks.

"Plug in, Tris," said Not-Dad, from a speaker on the PC.

"Eww!" yelled Aura. She cowered away from Kevin. "Are you gonna do it to me too?"

"God dammit! No!" Kevin went red in the face. "What the hell kind of shit do they make you kids watch in that place?"

Tris glanced back at him. "You really don't want to know. She's not even old enough to have seen the bad ones yet."

"I heard some older kids talking about it," whispered Aura.

Kevin pulled a chair up near her. "Just relax. You'll be home in no time. I wanna get out of here too."

"This place is, like, old." Aura looked around at the room. "Where are we? I wouldn't even know where to go if I tried to run away."

Tris fumbled around looking for an interface cable. After twenty seconds of searching, the tiny drone whirred to life and glided across the room to a storage cabinet, where it bounced in midair. She followed its lead, and located a two-pronged wire in a drawer. Only three feet long, it wouldn't give her much room to move, but how much mobility did one need while unconscious to the real world.

The plug resembled a headphone jack, but each peg consisted of thirty-two wafer thin contacts separated by equally thin plastic rings. Somewhere, she'd learned it supported data transfer speeds in the Exabyte-per-minute range, but except for her training time in VR, hadn't used one much.

Kevin muttered in the background, keeping Aura's mind off her situation by telling her about Abby and Nederland, trying to make a case for them *not* being child-abducting criminals. Tris sighed, her gut leaden with guilt. *That kid's going to be terrified of me for the rest of her life.* She stared at the ceiling. *Come on, focus. No big deal if one kid doesn't like me.*

She leaned back in the chair and let her body go limp as a test to make sure she wouldn't fall. Satisfied her perch would hold her, she connected one end of the wire into the PC, and the other into the socket behind her left ear.

Nothing happened.

Shit. They found the damn wire. We're fucked.

"Tris." The voice of Dad-AI echoed in her mind. "I am still uploading myself to the Enclave system. Seconds remain. Close your eyes and relax."

She exhaled, closed her eyes, and tried not to shake from nerves.

"Do you have a gun too?" asked Aura.

"Yeah," said Kevin.

"You're kinda clean for a Wildlander."

Kevin chuckled. "Thanks. I had my yearly shower this morning."

"Yearly?" A chair rattled. "Eww."

Tris smiled. *She sounds calmer. I wonder if—*

Kevin's laughter pulled away into the distance. The chair evaporated, leaving Tris falling into darkness.

Seconds later, she spilled out on the floor. Cool air blew over her bare legs. She sat up and gazed down at herself, white dress, no breasts, little spindly legs.

Cute. I'm five again. Is that for his benefit or mine?

"Yours," said Dad.

She stood, finding herself not quite eye-level with the top of the desk she'd been sitting at seconds before… only it didn't look battered anymore. Or dirty. In fact, the entire lab appeared rejuvenated, as though she'd shot back in time to 2019.

Her father, or at least a digital simulacrum thereof, walked into view from her left. Frazzled white hair went in all directions. Thick, black-rimmed glasses made his eyes look like those of a bug, and he wore the knee-length white lab coat she always pictured him in.

"If it bothers you, it isn't necessary."

Tris looked down at her toes. The appearance of being a child again hurt. It made her think about how much she wanted to go back for real, and have the war never happen. She wanted to grow up like a normal kid, in a normal world… without the Enclave ever having existed.

"It's nothing I can ever have. I'm not a child anymore."

Dad smiled. "Sometimes it's nice to allow a little fantasy. It can help the mind heal." He took a seat at his desk and picked her up into his lap. "We have a little time… things move faster here." A small book with a metallic gold spine appeared in his hand out of thin air. He opened it and started reading a story to her, the kind of story one might read to a seven or eight year old.

Her throat tightened as the smell of pipe smoke saturating his coat filled her nose. Virtual reality, even funneled through the ancient computer, created such a believable lie to her brain that the temptation to let go and embrace the not-world made her cry. She could be an innocent again, never cut open to have a bomb put inside her. Never having killed anyone. Safe at home with her father.

This isn't real.

"Dad…"

"Hmm?" He peered at her over the top of the book. "What's the matter, sweetie?"

"I'm sorry, but as much as I want this to be real… to go back and wish that the war never happened, I can't. Real people are depending on us. Both of us."

"Yes... I suppose you're right." He closed the book. "As you know, I am merely a set of program instructions based on his memories, thoughts, and personality. I thought you would benefit from this."

"Sorry. It isn't helping. It's like teasing me with something I want and can't have."

He picked her up and set her on her feet before him. The room changed perspective as she grew back to her normal self in the span of two seconds. Her child's dress melted into black liquid that ran down her legs and reshaped itself into the Enclave jumpsuit and shoes. Fortunately, the simulation did not provide tactile sensory feedback for the transformation.

"Dad? Why would you go to all the trouble of writing whatever attack worms you wrote, and then secure everything behind a programmatical lock that only I can open? What if something had happened to me?"

"Not exactly." He smiled. "I could've opened it too, but... I don't have genetic material anymore. If you ever have children, they would likely be able to open it as well."

Tris looked down. "They harvested my eggs after I rejected Dovarin." She pushed her feelings of violation aside after a fleeting instant of rage at Nathan. "I still don't buy it."

"Quite a lot of things had to happen perfectly for you to be standing here talking to me right now. This AI your father created could have failed to execute upon his death. It could have failed to compile properly and manage to gain self-awareness. You might've tolerated that unfortunate pairing assignment."

"Wait... what?" Tris blinked. "You *know* about that?"

The white haired old man pretending to be her father smiled. "When I mentioned I had no connection to the Enclave system, perhaps I stretched the truth. I did have an extremely slow link through one legacy backup system that the current Enclave occasionally accesses... an old tape array that's not long for this world. I'm amazed it still functions."

"So..." She massaged the start of a headache out of the bridge of her nose. "You had a connection but not one fast or stable enough to transfer your AI program core?"

"You are correct. What you did with the Petafiber link was vital." Dad bowed his head. "I know you will not trust me if I continue to obfuscate the truth. The arrangement to pair you with Dovarin was my doing."

Tris glared at him.

He raised a hand. "I had no intention that it would result in you living with him. I knew who you were, and I knew who he was. To me, no doubt existed that you would reject him and wind up in Detention. Nathan Savros had already gotten it in his head that you were a threat purely because of your relation to me."

"I was only nine when you died! What threat could I be?"

Dad let out a sad chuckle. "He suspected I had things lying in wait that would somehow enable you to be a threat. Of course, the man wasn't wrong. I feared you would soon be targeted for 'enhanced interrogation.' By setting it in motion for you to be detained on record, it prevented him from proceeding with any plans of that nature. I had expected to make contact with you once you were placed in Detention, but the uplink via that backup array is unreliable. I was unable to reach you before Nathan did. By that time, you were out of VR."

"Out of VR? You mean training?"

He shook his head. "No, Tris. Detention is virtual reality. So is University."

That's why my cell had... Her mind leapt back to the feeling of lying paralyzed on a gurney while that creep stripped her. A momentary caress of his hand switched to plunging into cold slime. She shuddered. "No toilet..."

"I was able to reestablish connection while you were placed in the training sim. I adjusted the surgical protocols to add the combat augmentations used by the military, including an upgraded nanite unit, but the low-bandwidth connection did not permit me to join you in the simulated reality."

She squinted at him. "Is that why I still look like I'm eighteen? Am I going to go backward like Amaranth?"

"No, Tris. She is not going backward, but she is a special case. I do not know exactly what happened there, but my calculations estimate that a software error occurred after she suffered a normally fatal wound. The nanites managed to resuscitate her and likely became stuck in a mode where they think she is injured even when she is not. That girl got extremely lucky. She should have died, so I do not recommend you shooting yourself in the heart to freeze your aging process."

"Thanks for pointing that out, but you didn't have to. Wasn't even a thought on my mind."

"You technically *are* eighteen as your time in stasis forestalled your aging. The Nanites do have an inhibiting effect against aging, but you won't get younger. They slow the aging process to about a tenth of normal."

She blinked. "So I could live to be hundreds of years old?"

"Yes. The same is true for all Enclave citizens." He smiled. "Provided no one shoots you first. A heart injury like that poor Yaro girl suffered is not typical to recover from."

"They tricked me..." Tris looked down. "Before they put me into Detention, they said they had to do a standard medical check for prisoner intake. That's when they put me under VR, isn't it? You set me up with Dovarin... what else did you do?"

"Well, aside from the cybernetics, I stepped up the combat training and survival sims beyond what Nathan had requested. He gave you only enough for a modest chance of surviving to find the resistance in Harrisburg. I wanted to protect you."

She folded her arms and rolled her eyes. "Thanks for leaving that bomb inside me."

He reached over and patted her leg. "I apologize for not being able to stop that detonator from being implanted... The surgery for that happened in a separate batch. Delaying the explosion was the best I could do."

"Sorry." She leaned forward and grasped the desk on either side of her legs. "I... guess I wouldn't have made it without your help."

He leaned back and tapped his chin for a few seconds. "Do you think the Enclave is evil?"

She balanced Nathan on half of her brain and Aura on the other. "They sure act like it. But it's only the ones making the decisions."

Her father let out a heavy sigh while looking at a wristwatch. "What I'm about to tell you may come as a shock." He wagged his arm. "Quaint little device these. Don't see them much anymore."

Tris stared at him expectantly.

"If you would prefer to have me change your avatar once more to that of a child, please just ask." Dad winked.

"After everything else I've learned? How bad can it be?" She sat on the desk and scooted back so her shoes didn't touch the floor.

Her virtual father laughed. "Good attitude. Tris... The Enclave you think you know is only about eight percent of the total population."

"Yeah..." She scoffed. "All the assholes."

He laughed. "Not entirely, but close enough to make debating the point arguably semantic. The vast majority of the citizens are in stasis. At any one time, only eight to nine percent of them are living in the real world."

Tris gasped. "People not in Detention?"

"I'm afraid so. 'Going to University' is the soft term used by those who know the truth. Only the upper echelons of the administration as well as workers responsible for maintaining the systems are aware of it."

Tris' mouth gaped in shock. "Why don't they tell anyone? Do they threaten them?"

"Not all the time. Most believe it when they are told that it is for the good of mankind. Though advanced, because they refuse to enter the outside world, the Enclave does not have the resources nor the space to accommodate a population of its size all awake and functioning at the same time. What you know as the Core City is false. It's an illusion in virtual reality. Did you ever wonder why the tram connecting to it only carries four people at a time?"

She nodded. "Yeah. That does seem weird."

"It goes to the underground cryogenics facility. People are put through—"

"Decontamination," said Tris in a daze, staring into nowhere.

"Again, you are correct. They finish the tram ride in VR and believe there is an enormous city underground. In reality, their bodies are floating in stasis pods. They don't put anyone in storage until they turn eighteen. People who have been chosen for a pairing are kept in the Quar. There are real-world facades of University called 'special advanced placement.' Also, parents are left outside VR until their child turns eighteen and is put into storage. Soon after, the parents are brought in for a 'routine checkup' and transferred to VR unaware that they are no longer awake in the real world. They are told they have been reassigned to new housing."

Tris put a hand on her gut, feeling queasy. "They don't put kids into storage until eighteen? What about me? I was nine."

"You represented a special security situation. They did not put you in a simulation, so the nine years it took for your surrogate family to 'raise' you passed in an instant to you. They are now back in the sim, unaware of the nature of their environment."

"How has no one noticed they haven't been getting older?"

"Everyone knows the nanites slow the process. I imagine the Council expects to retake the world before they have to explain why no one is aging at all. Come. We should do what we have come here to do."

"You're not going to overload the reactor and blow everyone up are you?" She slid off the desk to stand. "I'm not going to help you if that's the case."

"No, Tris. I wish to stop the virus and reveal the truth to everyone. We are trying to *save* people, not set off another atomic blast."

She bowed her head and rubbed her face. "And you need me to open the gate."

"Succinctly put." Dad stood, took her hand, and walked to the door.

Tris followed him without protest out into an immaculate hallway. The sounds of people moving about came from both directions, conversations, footsteps, the squeak of a pushcart wheel, but they appeared to be alone. A whiff of coffee that didn't exist slid past on air that didn't exist. If not for the lack of seeing anyone, the place sounded as though the university still functioned circa 2019.

Dad led her to another door, two classrooms down, and opened it without knocking.

She stepped through into her old bedroom, which had most certainly *not* been in the university, and stared at herself. A child version of her, perhaps eight years old, sat cross-legged in bed clutching a ragdoll to her chest. Tris cringed at first, but when she realized the girl didn't move—that she'd walked into a three-dimensional still image—she whirled on her father.

"This is cruel. Why do you keep tormenting me with my childhood? I know I can't go home again… it's a hollow echo of a life they stole from me when they killed the man who wrote you."

The AI smiled; deepening wrinkles made him look more like her grandfather than her father. "I prefer to think of it as a fond memory. At least, to me, it is. The war would have taken this life away from you with or without the Enclave. They did not exist until after. Please… go to her."

She let a lingering glare seethe for a few seconds before approaching the bed. The child-Tris didn't move so much as a single eyelash. Something about the scene made her want to recoil, to run off screaming at the impossibly eerie false child.

"Do you remember what you named that doll?" asked Dad, behind her.

Tris' heart raced at instant recognition. All the times she'd heard that word recently, not once had she remembered this doll. Her lungs seemed to implode, releasing a wheeze of a voice, "Persephone."

The ragdoll twisted its head around and looked up at her. "Hi Tris! You have been gone a long time."

She glanced at her father, trying to force herself not to cry. "It was only a ragdoll. It never used to talk back to me."

"A child's imagination," whispered Dad. "Say hello to it."

Tris raised a hand in a limp version of a wave. "Hello, Persephone."

Black button eyes shimmered to points of white light, fading to ancient television snow a second later. "Is it time to activate the Eden Protocol?"

'Yes' formed in her brain, rode down a nerve to the muscles that would eject the air from her lungs necessary to speak it, and halted halfway up her throat. "Umm. Define Eden Protocol."

The doll nodded once. "Eden Protocol consists of multiple subroutines. Module One initiates a modification to the simulated reality module CoreCity.exe, which allows Module Two to run. Module Two plays audiovisual data media kit. Module Three begins complete stasis system shutdown and pod thaw. Module Four and Module Five run concurrently with Module One. Module Four searches for and erases all technical documentation related to the Agent-X program. Module Five contains updated program code for Symbiote Agent-94 extension/control units. Module Six completes shutdown of cryogenic stasis units and overrides local control systems to open all active pods. Module seven triggers an overload in the production machinery associated with the Agent-X program, which will render them inoperable."

Tris exhaled with relief. *Nothing about boom.* "What's in the media kit?"

White dots turned black for an instant, suggesting an eye blink. The doll extended a fabric arm, above which appeared a tiny playback window of Dad speaking.

"The truth," said Dad. "The truth for the people of the Enclave. That they have been paired and bred like farm animals, then put in the freezer for later use."

"Later use?" She shivered. "That sounds ominous."

"I mean repopulating the Earth once they've wiped everyone else out."

Tris looked back at the fake child. "Persephone?"

"Yes?" asked the ragdoll.

"Initiate Eden Protocol."

A jolt of pain shot into her skull from the left side. Her knees weakened, but didn't dump her to the floor. In VR, Tris grabbed her head where the plug would've been.

"What the hell was that?" She stared at Dad.

"The program used your implant to analyze a minute amount of blood to confirm your genetic password. Nothing to worry about." He smiled. "The first part of the password was your voice speaking the doll's name."

Tris stared down, chuckling. "You named your dolls after my doll."

Her father's apparition laughed, a sound tinged with a hint of digitization. His face pixilated a touch. "I suppose he did."

"Genetic match confirmed. Access granted." The doll bowed. "Confirm authorization?"

Tris clenched her hands into fists. *Please be right.* "Yes. Do it."

LYING IN WAIT

After the story of how Tris went off on Neon and they wound up helping six women escape slavery (Kevin omitted that two were teenaged, and that all had been forced into prostitution), Aura seemed ever so slightly more relaxed. She still sat rigid, hands clasped atop her knees, looking like the smallest aggressive motion from him would set her off screaming.

Kevin glanced at Tris' body, slumped back in the chair by the desk. The monitor showed three boxy windows, two small ones over a wider space on the bottom. Nothing there to indicate what went on in her head but numbers, text, and a pair of 'data throughput' meters—whatever that meant.

"Look, Aura... I know you're scared. I would be too at your age."

She knotted her eyebrows closer. "But you're a boy."

Kevin chuckled, and gestured with a side thumb at Tris. "Don't let her fool you. She'd kick *my* ass."

"Well, no kidding." Aura started to roll her eyes, but her casualness faded to trembling. "She's rogue ISF or something. They have cybernetics. I'm only a little girl. I've got two cats. One's named—"

"You don't have to do that." Kevin sighed into the hand he rubbed the bridge of his nose with. "We're not going to hurt you."

Aura looked down. "What are you going to do with me? I wanna go home. I already miss my family."

"That's the plan." He smiled. "Back to your family. What got into her? Kidnapping isn't who we are. Hey, maybe think about it like you just walked into a dangerous situation and we're keeping you safe 'til it's over."

"Yeah, sure." Aura smirked.

Tris squirmed and made an odd noise in her throat, like someone trying to sob through duct tape.

"What is she doing in there?" Aura glanced at her. "She sounds like my mom when she's in those stupid drama sims."

"Drama sims?" asked Kevin.

"Entertainment. Before the war, they called them 'movies,' but with these, it's like you're *in* there with the characters. She always watches lame ones where people fall in love and then one of them dies... or something like that. Puts her in a bad mood for days. I don't know why she keeps doing it." Aura grumbled. "It's like living with someone who has a death in the family once a week."

"Damn that sounds..." He scratched his head. "Yeah. Why would anyone do that? Why not watch a funny one?"

Aura shrugged and swung her feet back and forth.

She looks like a little version of Tris. Same shoes. Junior fascist soldier. "They've probably told you a lot of lies about what the world is like outside. Tris..." He chuckled. "She had all these ideas in her head from the 'historical documentaries.' She didn't know they were movies."

"They're not movies." Aura folded her arms.

"Okay, you know the one with the guy and the car... and this black woman with the big hair and the little midget sitting on the shoulders of the giant?"

Aura nodded. "Yeah. That's from Arizona. Like 2062 drone footage."

Kevin laughed. "Sorry. Nope. It's a pre-war movie. Hell, it was old even in 2021. The guy's name is Max right?"

"Yyyyyeah..." She stared at him.

"And I'm a Wildlander, so I couldn't have seen it."

"You're *out* there." She gestured at the wall. "You saw it happen in front of you."

He shook his head, and rambled on about other things that happened in the movie, as well as other movies he'd seen. "They were all actors. What happened in that video never really happened." Kevin bit his lip at the thought of the Boatman compound. "Okay... I will admit that there are *some* people out there that need to be shot in the face, but the entire world isn't like that. Bad people existed before the world blew itself to hell, and they're still out there. Only real difference is now there's no cops. People have to protect themselves."

"We have cops." Aura narrowed her eyes. "And they're gonna shoot you in the face if you hurt me."

"You're such a little sweetheart." He smiled.

Kevin leaned against the next desk over from Tris, in front of Aura enough to probably grab her if she made a run for it. He hoped she didn't. The situation already felt bad enough; having to manhandle a kid would cross the line. *Dad would kick my ass.* "We found this girl about your age whose father got killed by the Virus." He rambled on about how she survived escaping her town past packs of Infected along with a bunch of survivors who all thought she'd been infected because she had a cold. "Tris told me they tied her to the bed in case she woke up as one of those things. They're damn lucky I wasn't there. I wouldn't have let them do that to her."

Aura stared into his eyes for a few seconds and looked down. Her posture relaxed a bit more.

"I saw Infected for the first time when I was about ten or so." He told her about how his adoptive parents decided to move, and their convoy strayed too close to a big city. Aura started to cry when he mentioned the teenaged boys who buried the dead before realizing they'd become sick and committed suicide after digging graves for themselves. "Abby's got nightmares still… like I do. I don't know if we'll ever stop seeing those things in our dreams. What we're doing here… we're only trying to stop anyone else from having to go through that."

"What you're saying sounds like a lie, but I think you believe it," whispered Aura.

Kevin gripped the desk on either side of his butt, and looked down. "I wish it was a lie."

"Okay, so say I do believe you're really going to let me go. I don't know where this is. It's scary down here. I hope you're not going to like tie me to a chair and hope someone finds me when you leave."

"Nope." He pointed at the vent. "You can crawl back up the way you came in. We're probably going to leave underground. I doubt you'd want to go there."

The lights flickered.

"What's happening?" whispered Aura, looking up.

"She's doing… something." Kevin glanced to his left.

Tris sat up, her eyes fluttering like hummingbird wings.

"You okay?" asked Kevin.

She slumped forward over the desk, shivered, and lapsed into a mild seizure. Right as Kevin moved to run to her side, she recovered and sat up straight.

"Ouch." Tris unplugged the wire from her head.

"What the hell was that?" He took a step, backed up to take Aura's hand, and pulled the girl over to Tris.

Tris frowned at the desktop computer. "This old piece of crap doesn't have enough RAM to process a smooth transition between VR and reality. Felt like I went face-first into a bathtub full of ice water and needles."

"Are you done? Can I go now?" asked Aura.

Tris stood and embraced him, trembling as if about to explode into tears, but kept quiet.

"What happened in there?" He pulled her tight with one arm, keeping Aura's hand in a firm grip with the other.

"That AI kept teasing me with my past." She took a step back and gathered her hair into place. "I'm fine. Just… emotional. We need to do two things before we can go. I know the path… got a map in my head now." She put a hand on the girl's shoulder and stooped to eye level with her. "Aura… I need you to stay with us for a little while longer. We're going to the surface, and I want you to come with us both because I think you need to see this, and because people will die if you run off and sound an alarm. Can I trust you to stay quiet while we move?"

Aura shivered.

A momentary vision of carrying a struggling girl with a hand over her mouth reddened Kevin's face. "What are we doing? Is this kid really going to be that much of an issue if she runs off?"

Tris looked up at him for a second before standing straight. "I have no way to know that, but are you willing to gamble Abby's life on it? Or everyone else out there? Zoe? Bill? Ann? Emma? The whole town?"

"Okay… okay…"

Aura bowed her head, trembling. "I won't scream. Please don't hurt me."

Tris crouched again and looked the girl in the eye. "I need to go to a room and push a couple of buttons. When we get there, you'll see what I'm saying is true. The Enclave has been lying to everyone about everything." She glanced up at Kevin. "There is no Core City."

"What?" Aura blinked. "No way."

"It's all virtual reality. Kids live with their families here in the Quar. As soon as they turn eighteen, they get put in stasis again and plugged in. The parents think they 'went off to University,' and a day or so later, the parents get put back on ice too. Everyone in the Enclave except for parents, children, active military, and the politicians, are frozen."

Kevin blinked. "Okay... I've seen some wild movies, but... damn." He chuckled. "I get it. That's why you had no toilet."

"What?" Aura looked back and forth between them. "Where did that come from?"

"Come on." Tris took Aura by the hand and headed for the door. "They paired me with this guy who hit me in the face after only a half hour alone in a room with him. I said no, so I got put in Detention."

"You rejected a pairing?" Aura gasped. "Why would you do that? I'd give *anything* to be chosen. I want kids someday. My friend Dhara doesn't. She thinks kids are a waste of time." She frowned. "Not everyone is allowed to have them."

Tris headed left out the door, moving a brisk pace the girl had to struggle to maintain. "Yes, I did. Would *you* want to be told who to marry and then spend the rest of your life living in fear of what he'd do to you?"

"But... it's the *pairing*. We're supposed to... for the good of humanity." Doubt crept into the girl's voice. "He really hit you?"

"Yep. He was First Tier and thought I was worker caste. When I refused to talk to him like he was better than me, he punched me straight in the nose. I was just there for him to..."

Aura grunted with her effort to keep up. "You can say it. I'm old enough to know what sex is."

"That. I would've been a possession to him, not a wife."

Tris jogged down a long corridor and stopped in an area that widened out to both sides. Three elevators lined the wall on the left with still-perfect looking ferns between them, obviously plastic. An information desk took up the majority of the opposite side of the space, and a handful of decaying chairs and sofas sat in the middle of the room.

Kevin followed, eyeing books laid out on a coffee table. Course catalogs, admission guidelines, and a couple of issues of *Time* from 2020. "I think I get why you always stare at this shit. It's like the world stopped when all the people disappeared."

She forced open the elevator doors, since they didn't react to the button. "Yeah." Her voice echoed in the shaft. "Okay, we have to climb up one floor. Aura, do you want to climb? Or do you want me to carry you."

"Is it dirty?" asked the girl.

"Filthy." Tris squeezed in and moved to a ladder on the right side wall.

Aura crept to the edge and reached out. "I don't wanna get sick."

Kevin grasped the girl under the armpits and lifted her over to Tris, who wore her like a backpack.

"I know you know that I've got a gun in my pocket. Please don't do anything stupid." Tris checked her footing on the ladder, and climbed.

Aura sniffled. "I don't wanna get in trouble for touching a gun."

Kevin blinked. He forced the doors open a little more and shimmied in after them. The ladder rung squished in his grip, coated with dust-encrusted grease. "Wait... you're really more afraid of getting in trouble for handling a weapon than you would be if you needed to use a gun to protect yourself from a pair of kidnappers?"

"Uh huh. Guns aren't allowed unless you're in the military. If they find out I touched one, they'd lock me up." Aura paused a tick. "I thought you said you weren't kidnapping me."

Kevin smirked up at them. *Little brat.* "We're not, I'm just... Wow. Tris, tell me that kid's taking fear a step too far and those idiots aren't *that* bad?"

Tris stopped at the inside of the doors one floor up. "Since we've repeatedly told her we don't want to hurt her and haven't been violent, if she told them the truth of what happened... yeah they would charge her with a firearms offense if she got her hands on my gun and used it to escape. Even if she didn't fire it."

"What the hell kind of fucked up shit is that?"

"What do you think, Aura?" Tris pulled the upper set of doors open and crawled out on her knees. She shifted to the right and lowered the girl to sit on the edge, feet dangling.

Aura scooted back, whimpering while staring down the shaft. "Guns are bad. They hurt people."

A Cheshire cat grin formed on Kevin's face. He climbed up into the hallway and eased the .45 out of his pocket. With Aura distracted by backing away from a deadly fall, he popped the magazine out and ejected the round from the chamber.

"There are a small number of people running everything," said Tris. "They want everyone afraid so they can be controlled. In a little while, everyone will learn the truth."

"What does that mean?" asked Aura.

Kevin stepped up behind the kid, reached around to grab her arm, and put the .45 in her hand.

Aura stared at it as if he'd handed her a dead baby.

Tris scowled at him. "What are you doing?"

Tears rolled down the girl's cheeks, though she didn't make a sound.

Kevin took his weapon back and reloaded it. "She had a gun. Now she can't run to the ISF. No need to worry about her causing an alarm."

Aura continued to stare at her empty hand as though it needed to be 'cleansed.'

"I was trying to make this as un-traumatic as possible, and you just…" Tris sighed.

The girl looked back and forth between them, her face warped with dread and shame.

"Look at her." Tris picked the girl up and cradled her sideways across her chest. "She looks like we made her shoot someone."

Aura burst into tears, clinging to Tris and sobbing into her shoulder. "I don't wanna go to Detention."

Kevin winced. Though having her afraid of the ISF instead of wanting to run to them made him feel better. Now they could be the good guys again. "I'm sorry, Aura. I won't tell anyone you touched a gun."

"You *made* me touch it." The girl sniffled.

"Will the ISF care?" asked Kevin.

Aura stared at him with a blank-faced gawk. "I don't know."

Tris carried her down another hallway past doorway after doorway of classrooms. "They'd probably think letting her handle a firearm would diminish the fear they try to cultivate. Even if we forced her to, she'd at least get some kind of punishment. So, as far as anyone here is concerned, that didn't happen." At the corner of the hall, she booted open a classroom door and crept inside. "Stay down."

Kevin crouched, ducked into the room, and pushed the door closed.

Day shimmered in from windows covered in grime, painting a dry erase board along the right wall with blotchy shadows. Jagged silhouettes over the glass suggested an irregular barrier of scraps or debris outside. Tris crawled past student desks to the windows and peered up. A raccoon-band of sunlight lit the upper half of Tris' face.

Aura crawled up behind her and huddled in a ball. "I know where we are… we're inside the wall."

Kevin took a knee behind them. "I'd hope we're inside the wall. What else was the point of sneaking through the damn subway?"

"No." Aura looked up at him. "I mean this building is part of the wall. We're literally *in* the wall. No one's supposed to go here."

"Right," muttered Kevin. "Can't let the prisoners out."

Aura's eyebrows scrunched together. "We're not prisoners."

"Sure, kid. Keep telling yourself that." Kevin patted her on the head.

Tris moved left to the last window in the row. A wide rectangular slab at the bottom opened after she twisted a handle, lowering inward like a hatch.

"Ugh," muttered Kevin. "That's going to be a tight squeeze."

"Minute… I'm watching for patrollers. We need to go out and left. There's a white and silver building about thirty yards away across a patch of grass. I'll go out first. You lower Aura out to me, then follow."

"Got it."

"Can I go now?" whispered Aura. "I promise I won't tell anyone you're here." She wiped her hand on her leg as if trying to clean 'gun' off it.

Tris glanced down at her with guilt and temptation all over her face. "When I first saw you, you sounded like a little ISF cadet. I think you really need to see this so you understand what I'm saying is true. Ten minutes, okay? Stay with me for ten more minutes and you can go home."

Aura shivered, but nodded.

After watching out the window for another minute and change, Tris leapt up and slid through the opening. She landed outside, head-level to the window. Aura climbed up onto the radiator. Kevin again took her by a grip under the arms and lowered her feet first into the open window. Tris caught her and helped her down, out of sight. Kevin moved to climb after and froze, stunned by the view.

Beyond a patchwork of rusting metal welded into a security barrier, a sprawling complex of buildings, perfect roadways, and verdant patches of green grass stretched for miles. Black specks, people in jumpsuits, walked around a city that looked like a scene from a science-fiction comic he once read. Potted trees stood interspersed among fantastic swoops of silver architecture, thin decorative spirals with no purpose he could discern. The buildings had a sameness to them that reminded him of an old video game he'd found, where the lazy designers had pasted the same five houses in a repeating pattern to make a city.

Overhead, a great bubble of thin plastic formed a dome over the entire complex, easily several miles across. Sunlight reflected in hundreds of tiny flares. He shook his head at it. *These people are paranoid.*

A teenage girl went by on a bicycle with cobalt blue light glowing in rings around the tires and pedals. Two men walked on the opposite side of the street, having an animated conversation involving large smiles. *No wonder Zara wanted to come back here... it's like the war never happened and humanity kept going. All that's missing are cars.*

As if on cue, a boxy vehicle closer to a tiny van than a car glided by. The shroud of its body panels came within an inch of the road surface. He squinted and made out a hint of tiny enclosed wheels. Before he could mock whoever would put such minuscule tires on a car, the realization that the man inside sat back while the car drove itself shocked him mute.

"Kevin," whispered Tris. "Come on!"

He blinked away the mesmerizing effect of the Enclave city and hauled himself headfirst out the window. Tris grabbed his shoulders and pulled him down, saving him from a faceplant on dirt. Much to his surprise, Aura hovered close, making no attempt to run off. He got his feet under him and blinked at her. *Guess the gun thing worked.*

Tris again took Aura by the hand and ran, heading across a rectangular patch of grass so perfect he wondered if little robots measured every individual blade to length. Ahead, a small cube of a building perched in the middle of the lawn. The upper part of the walls were white, with about a third of the building paneled in mirror like silver. It appeared only large enough for one room with no windows or decoration aside from some chugging machinery on the ceiling, which he assumed to be overworked air conditioning.

A brief sprint later, Tris flattened against the wall and crept to the corner. Kevin didn't bother leaning against the building; the exterior barrier around the entire Quarantine Section stood less than twenty yards to their left, no one in sight to look at them.

"Ugh." Tris gagged and coughed. "Okay. Need to run for the door. Don't stop for anything."

She kept a hand around Aura's wrist and darted around the corner.

Kevin followed, sparing a quick glance up at metal letters over the cube-building's only door.

"Sewage Processing."

No sooner had the words crossed the threshold of conscious thought, a stench slapped him in the face. He, too, coughed and gagged on the air wafting from the front of the building. Tris rushed a plain opaque black door resembling a slab of onyx glass, shoving it aside. She let go of Aura's arm once she reached the doorway.

Kevin came up behind the girl, not sure what to expect, half intending to grab her if she tried to run.

"Afternoon," said Tris. "I'm here about maintenance order CS-101997B."

Surrounded by walls of baffling computerization, a pair of Enclave ISF officers staffed a desk facing the door. Both wore the same style of super-thin armor that Zara had, clean, new, and form-fit. Two helmets sat beside them on the desk. Seeing it on people it had been made for made it clear why Amaranth had denied them armor. The difference between these two and the Resistance people couldn't have been more vast. Even if they had their helmets on, the curvy shape of the one on the right would've left little doubt as to her being female.

The woman started to give Tris a suspicious glare, but diverted to blink at Aura, her black bob swaying with the sharp head motion.

"There's no record of a maintenance request," said the man, who also had black hair, but streaked with a bit of white. He looked in his middle twenties, as did the woman.

Tris smiled. "You're probably not cleared to know about it then. It came right from Director Kuroyama himself." She approached the left side of the desk, nearer the man.

Kevin tried to keep a straight face, but couldn't help a slight flare of the eyebrows when the smell of sewage ceased as soon as he walked into the air conditioning. He glanced back at the soft *hiss* of the door closing behind him. *Why does it only stink outside?*

"What's the child doing here?" asked the female ISF officer.

Aura slipped into an easy smile. "I'm doing job shadowing since I asked about the waste treatment processor."

The man's expression darkened as if the girl had somehow given away a lie. He reached for his sidearm. "Don't mo—"

Tris' body blurred. An instant later, she held a small black box to the side of the man's neck, a flickering blue light crackled and buzzed where the tip met skin. His eyes rolled up into his head and he went from standing to Tris holding dead weight.

In another second of blurred limbs, Tris and the woman pointed guns at each other. She let the man drop to the ground, keeping the stunner in her left hand. Kevin eased his hand into his pocket. The woman eyed him for an instant.

"Don't move," she muttered.

"No one needs to die here," said Kevin.

"Kid, go get help," said the woman. "If that guy touches you, I'll shoot this bitch."

"You're not faster than me," said Tris.

Aura rubbed her hand on her jumpsuit. "I'm scared."

"Why don't you tell her what's downstairs?" asked Tris. "This isn't a shit pumping station."

The woman blinked in shock. "How..."

"I know everything. The real question is how can you go along with it? They're lying. This isn't about protecting humanity. They want to destroy it. Go ahead, tell Aura what you're guarding. Why are there ISF people stationed to guard a waste treatment plant? Why are sprayers making stink outside but it smells like a hospital in here?"

"I was wondering that too," said Kevin.

Aura glanced back at the door, wide-eyed. She looked up at Kevin with a 'holy crap she's right' expression.

"Drop the antique," said the woman.

"You first." Tris' arm held so steady she didn't even look human.

Kevin felt a little too much like he used the child for a shield and stepped out from behind her. "Look... just calm down. It's already over. You can't stop what's happening in the computer. The Enclave's war on the remnants of humanity is going to end today."

"What are you talking about?" asked the ISF woman.

The instant the woman glanced at Kevin, Tris whirled into a spinning kick aimed at the gun. Kevin lurched to the side and dove on Aura. The ISF woman's gun went off with a squidgy, muted pop followed by a pair of *clanks* so close together they sounded like one noise. With a fleshy *thump*, a starburst of pain exploded in his back, behind the left shoulder. Another *pop-pop* preceded two more *pings* and a shower of sparks from somewhere behind him.

"Ngh," he groaned.

Aura screamed.

Rubber-soled shoes squeaked on the other side of the console. Women grunted and gasped. Aura's scream faded into sobbing.

Kevin huddled over her, pressing her into the floor.

"Ow!" wailed Aura. "She shot me!"

Tris roared. The next fleshy *thump* made him cringe from the loudness of it. The ISF woman wheezed and gurgled. A meaty *smack* rang out. Kevin looked up at the armored woman's face bouncing away from the wall of display panels. Tris held the wrist of her gun hand, keeping the weapon pointed more or less at the ceiling. The woman bounced away from the wall with a dazed expression. Tris stabbed the stunner past a feeble grope for her arm and held it to the woman's cheek for three seconds of electric buzzing.

A limp body collapsed the ground.

Kevin shifted to his knees and rolled Aura onto her back, checking her for injuries. His hand came away from her left thigh bloody. "Dammit, she's hit."

Tris hurried over. "I'm so sorry... it's my fault."

"Ow!" Aura whined, clenching her teeth. "It burns!"

He pulled at a rip in the fabric about a hand's with down from the girl's hip. The wound looked more like a nip from a sword than a gunshot. "It just grazed her."

Tris ripped the jumpsuit open a little more to get a look at the girl's paper-white leg. She deflated into a slump. "Oh damn... we got lucky. I shouldn't have done that."

"Done what?" Kevin smiled. "Kicked the gun or kidnapped the kid?"

Tris' mournful frown made him feel like an asshole.

"Sorry. Trying to lighten the mood."

"Am I gonna die?" whined Aura.

"No kiddo. You got a little scratch." Kevin patted her forehead. "The bullet bounced off the wall before it hit you, barely touched you."

Already, the wound appeared smaller.

Tris gasped. "You're shot!"

"Yeah." He grunted as concern for Aura gave way to feeling pain. "That one probably would've hit her in the face. Better it got me."

Aura looked at him in disbelief.

"*You* don't have nanites." Tris fussed at his back, making the pain flare.

"Holy fffaaaah!" He bit his knuckle.

"That's not what you wanted to say," whispered Aura.

Kevin laughed as a tear dropped from his left eye. "They give kids nanites too?"

"She's probably had them for about a year. Ten's the minimum age." She picked at his back. "The slug hit your shoulder blade. I can't tell if it went into it or stopped against it. Gonna pull it out on three."

He clenched his teeth, expecting her to count to one and yank.

She did.

The room turned white for a second as pain flared and faded. A small metal *click* came from the left.

Aura sat up and poked at her leg. "It stings."

Tris bowed her head and took the girl's hand, apologizing over and over. Kevin gritted his teeth and reoriented himself. Aside from being smeared with blood, the paper-white skin visible through the rip in the girl's pant leg looked pristine.

"I need me some nanites," he muttered while grasping Tris' shoulder. "Hey, come on. We can't sit around here feeling guilty."

"I'm sorry." Aura looked down. "I didn't mean to make them angry."

Tris shook her head. "You couldn't know. As soon as you acted like this place really was a waste treatment facility, they knew I lied. If I'd been sent here on a maintenance job, I'd know what they really used this building for... and there's no way they'd send a child along here."

"What is it?" asked Aura, genuine interest in her expression.

"Come on. I'll show you." Tris stood. "But first..."

She hurried around the heavy security desk and stooped out of sight. A small white box came flying over a second later. Kevin caught it, recognizing a first-aid kit from the green plus on it.

"Aura, take one of the white tubes with the blood drips on it out of that box, pull off the green cap, and spray a bit into the hole in his back please?" Tris sat at the console and typed at a keyboard.

The girl rolled over and stood on her knees. "Okay."

Kevin opened the box; on the left half, five white plastic tubes sat in rails, each with a red blood droplet mark on the side. The other side had a few bottles of pills, gauze, bandages, and three gizmos he couldn't begin to guess the function of.

Aura reached past him and grabbed one of the tubes.

"What is that?" asked Kevin.

"Spray-skin," said the girl. "It'll stop you from bleeding."

"Not that I have a problem with no longer bleeding, but if everyone here has nanites, why do they have first aid kits?"

Tris bent down and stripped both ISF officers out of their utility belts and armor. "Kids under ten, plus some of the kits have been around since before the nanites became widespread."

"So this is... twenty year old medicine?" He chuckled.

"Maybe," said Tris.

A faint *snap* came from behind him. He tensed.

"It's okay," said Aura. "They don't hurt. It'll feel cold and itchy for a little bit. I built this remote control plane once and it blew up. It took my dad almost an hour to pluck little pieces out of me."

Hiss.

His shoulder twinged with a chill similar to what he imagined being impaled with an icicle would've felt like, minus the pain of being stabbed. "Oh, that's odd."

Both of the ISF officers had black military-style handcuffs with a hinge rather than a chain in their belts. Tris secured their hands behind their backs with their arms linked. After, she slipped into the woman's armor. It made her chest seem larger, but otherwise fit.

"The other suit might be a bit pinchy. You're bigger than him."

Kevin chuckled. "I didn't think you looked."

Her face turned pink around the nose. She shot a pointed glare at Aura as if to say 'there's a damn kid here, watch it.' "Hurry up. Anyone could walk in here at any minute."

Kevin grumbled and stood, rolling his left shoulder to work the soreness out. His skin tugged at the wound site, like a patch of something sticky clung to him. "That feels so damn weird." He stared at the armored suit. "Umm. How's this thing work?"

Tris sighed and dressed him like a three-year old, holding up the pants for him to step into. She hit a button near the waistline and they cinched snug in an instant, making him groan as his junk crushed. "Oof." The upper half fit like a jacket; it too squeezed tight at the push of a button. The material couldn't have been thicker than an eighth inch in some spots, up to a full quarter-inch over the heart and major chest plates. Chromatic silver hexagonal lines gleamed under a smooth layer of black, catching the light as he moved.

"This doesn't feel heavy enough to be armor..."

"Move!" Tris waved for Aura to follow and ran to the back of the room. She typed a code into a keypad on the wall, and one entire cabinet's worth of computer equipment opened like a door, revealing an elevator with bright silver walls. Five glowing lights in the white ceiling resembled blobs of gel sitting in bowls. "In here."

"Oh wow." Kevin overacted an impressed face. "An elevator that *works.* I didn't think this place had any."

Once the door closed and the cab began to lower, Aura burst into tears.

"What's wrong?" asked Tris, sounding worried.

"I... I'm gonna get in so much trouble." She sniffled. "We just beat up the ISF and this isn't a waste plant. I don't know what's going on anymore."

Tris patted her shoulder. "Try to stay calm. Everything's going to be okay."

Whenever we say that, it turns out the other way. Kevin forced a smile.

Another set of doors on the opposite side of the elevator opened. Tris strode out into a corridor with an immaculate white floor and walls, lit with a blinding glow from overhead LED tube lights, bee-lining for the door at the far end about fifty yards away. Kevin peered into rooms on the left and right as they passed. One looked like a break room, another a storage room full of shelves, another a long hallway leading off to the right. The third and fourth resembled hospital procedure rooms. Another much larger room had a secondary corridor going off into the distance that appeared to connect to a train tunnel.

"You..." said Tris.

A man yelled out in alarm.

Aura screamed.

Kevin, having fallen behind due to his curious gandering, sprinted ahead into a room with four rows of control desks like some kind of NASA launch center. Despite the size of the place, it held only five people. Three men in their mid-twenties stood half out of their chairs in the center of the room. One white-haired, one black-haired, and one brown. They stared at Tris who had a fiftyish man in a white jumpsuit pinned against the leftmost wall.

She pistol whipped him as fast as she could move her arm. "Goddamned filthy piece of shit. You're lucky there's a damn child behind me or I'd put a bullet in your lousy pig face. I remember you! You thought I was unconscious, but I was only paralyzed." She let off a shriek of rage and hit him harder.

A younger woman by the console farthest from the door, beneath a huge bay window that wrapped around in a manner suggesting her workstation occupied an overhanging ledge, gasped.

Noting she, as well as the three men at consoles, all wore sidearms, Kevin pulled his .45 and raised it. "Please just stand still."

The man against the wall moaned, waving his hands in a futile effort to ward off Tris' blurry arm. Her strength and speed rendered him unconscious in seconds. She hit him twice more before letting him slump to the floor.

Tris stood over him, fuming. The look in her eye worried him.

"Tris?" he asked, drawing the word out long. "You okay?"

"I wanna kill him. When they put me into VR, this guy was about to rape me. I woke up, but the drug left me paralyzed. He would have if another tech didn't walk in on him."

The other four workers gasped.

"Rich?" asked the man with white hair. "He wouldn't do that."

"Bullshit," muttered Tris.

"Uhh," said the brown-haired man. "Actually…"

Tris whirled around and stared at him. "You walked in on him. You knew what he was going to do to me."

"Yeah. That's why I went in there… usually, prepping someone for the chill is a one-person job. I'd… caught him before. Reported it, but they never did anything."

Tris pointed the Beretta at the unconscious man, hand shaking.

Aura turned away, covering her face.

Kevin shrugged. "I would. Go for it."

"I have more important things to do. Besides…" She waved at the techs. "I need these people to trust me for a minute."

"What do you want?" asked the woman.

Tris walked over to the first row of consoles by the wraparound window. "What's your name?"

"Mara."

"Hello, Mara. I'm Tris. Doctor Jameson's daughter." She waved for Kevin to bring Aura over. "What is your job function?"

Mara eyed the girl.

"Oh, she's already down here." Tris smiled. "No more secrets."

Kevin edged up to the window behind Tris. Aura gasped, half crawling up on the console to get a closer look. Thousands of coffin-sized chambers lined a wall about twenty feet away from the window, stretching down at least five stories into the earth. Tracks carried box-shaped robots with four and five limbs back and forth, tending to the pods. Each contained a single nude body, floating in translucent slime on the clear end of whitish.

All had a single wire connecting from behind one ear to the head-end of the cylindrical chamber covered in flickering lights. Toward the left, age varied quite a bit among middle to late adulthood, though as he swept his gaze to the right, the occupants became younger and younger. At the point he couldn't make out enough detail to guess age, most appeared to be about eighteen.

Bursts of orange sparks leapt into the gloom every so often in the distance at random places, too far away to discern the cause.

Aura, shaking, pressed her hands to the glass and stared at the seemingly endless room. "W-what is this?"

"This is what the Core City really looks like." Tris eyed Mara. "How many?"

Rich moaned.

"Excuse me a moment." Kevin walked over to the guy lying on the ground, the man who'd tried to rape Tris. For a second, he almost felt like pulling the trigger, but he channeled his abrupt boiling of rage into a kick across the man's face. He turned back to the room, blinking at the realization he'd taken his eyes off three armed men who still stood among the middle consoles. *Shit. Maybe they're too afraid of Tris to try anything.* The blur of her arm as she pistol-whipped Rich gave away her boosts. *Oh, armor... right. Those pistols won't go through this.* The attack on Nederland replayed in his mind, the pistol he'd taken from the first man Zara sniped hadn't done a damn thing to the others.

Mara sank into a chair and poked at one of the screens. "I'm not sure I can tell you. The systems have been misbehaving for a little while now. My job is to monitor the people in stasis and make sure their vital signs stay healthy. I mean... they're frozen, so it's not like anything can happen unless the system fails." She blinked when the terminal responded to her command. "Wow... guess we're back online. The current population figures show 5,653 individuals in deep stasis, and another 2,925 in light stasis."

"What so some are only half awake?" Kevin blinked.

The three men chuckled.

"Light stasis are those in the virtual reality of the Core City," said Mara. "Individuals who were either too old to have children, incapable of doing so, who possessed no skills or knowledge of immediate necessity, or those who finish University with no acceptable genetic partner are placed into deep stasis. They are not in VR and are unaware of the passage of any time."

Aura pushed away from the window and grabbed Tris. "I don't wanna be frozen."

Monitors on various consoles cycled among views from small drones, more advanced versions of the one that led them around the basement. Cameras panned by rows and rows of people stuck in cylindrical ice cubes. Almost all of them had white hair and snow-white skin. The occasional outlier with black or brown hair stood out like a fly on a tablecloth.

One screen scrolled past a point where the tanks ceased holding bodies. About six columns of empty capsules contained the goopy translucent gel, after which the clear plastic tanks sat empty. About fifteen pods farther to the right, workers assembled more of the superstructure that held the tanks, installed wiring, built the rails for the attendant robots, and hoisted more tanks into place. At the point the drone reversed course, the hint of excavation crept into the edge of the frame.

"They're still going," whispered Kevin. "Building this room bigger and bigger."

"That's correct." Mara folded her hands in her lap. "Until the outside world is ready for human habitation, we have to put people in stasis. We don't have enough resources to feed and provide for a population much past a thousand people."

Tris folded her arms. "They would if they opened the gates."

"The Quarantine Section?" asked Kevin. "So... there's no ten thousand some odd soldiers?"

"That's right." Mara nodded. She looked up at him with a flirtatious smile. "You're from the outside, aren't you?"

Tris leaned toward her. "He is. And he's taken."

"Okay." Mara raised her hands in surrender. "I'm dead ended, so..."

"Sorry." Tris frowned. "It's nowhere near as bad as they tell us outside. You *can* have a family. You only need to go outside. If you're really desperate for some D, I know this guy... Neeley."

Kevin snickered.

The men gasped.

"But it's contaminated," said the one with black hair.

"Most of the contamination out there came from the Enclave." Kevin's knuckles creaked as he squeezed the .45 tighter. "People *were* rebuilding... some of the settlements got pretty damn large. Tens of thousands. Then the Virus knocked us back to the Stone Age."

Tris put a hand on Aura's back. "When you turn eighteen and finish high school, you'll be required to have a jack installed in your head. Then, you'll be told you're going to University... but the medical checkup is a lie. That's when they put you to sleep and load you into one of those pods... unless you join the military or the ISF... or get approved to have kids of your own. Now I understand why the interface plugs are required by law... so they can force everyone into VR."

Aura yelled, "No! I don't want to be a popsicle!"

"That's why I'm here." She squeezed the girl's shoulder before looking at the four techs. "I don't know if any of you have ever heard the name Doctor Ian Jameson... he was one of the founders of the Enclave. He knew the Council had set us on an unsustainable path. His ghost is in the system now. It's time to open the gates and rejoin the world."

The door they'd entered from burst open; six figures in sleek black armor with ISF logos rushed in, rifles raised. Two covered Kevin, three pointed their rifles at Tris, and a short woman left of the lead man trained her weapon on the techs.

"You," said the man in front, aiming at Tris, "Drop your weapon and get on the ground."

28

DIPLOMACY

F*uck.*

Kevin flashed a cheesy smile at the men pointing rifles at him. He knew his .45 wouldn't bother them much unless he caught them in the head, and he had no clue how those Enclave rifles would fare against his stolen armor. They had a better chance of penetrating than his pistol, so he lowered his arm and indicated it with his left hand, shrugged, and chuckled. *Oh this? Don't mind this... it's just a toy.*

"You're making a mistake," said Tris. "The Council has been lying to you."

Aura hopped down from the console and stepped in front of Tris. "I don't want to be frozen." She tugged on Tris' arm. "They won't shoot if you're pointing the gun at me."

"No." Tris stared at the security team. "I'm not putting a gun to a kid's head. Look. If we were here to cause trouble, we wouldn't have left those two upstairs alive. Have you ever been down here? Did you know what this facility was?"

The ISF team shifted and exchanged uneasy glances.

Tris tried to move Aura around behind her, but the girl held her ground. "The outside world isn't as bad as the Council wants us to believe. They are lying to everyone to control them. The Council isn't worried if we can survive out there. As long as they keep everyone inside, they have complete control over every aspect of their lives. Absolute power. We're almost out of gene pairs. The Enclave is dying, and it's trying to take the rest of the world down with it. Besides, you're too late. It's already started."

"I suppose you have some evidence to support your claims?" asked the commander, taking a step closer. "Let the girl go."

"I'm not holding her." Tris frowned. "She can go if she wants to."

"Come on, sweetie. Step away from them." A woman ISF officer crouched, waving Aura over.

"If I walk away, you're going to shoot her. Listen to what they're saying. If it's wrong, why would the Council lie about freezing everyone? If it's good for us, why not tell everyone?"

"The less information you give to the people, the easier it is to control them," said Kevin.

"Release the girl," said the lead man, in a sterner tone.

Tris smiled. "I'm trying, but she's got a hell of a grip. Open your eyes, dammit. The world is dying. The Enclave is dying. The only way for either one to survive is to open the gates."

"Oh, she's one of *those* activists," said the woman with her rifle on the techs.

"Look." The commander took another step closer to Tris, bringing him within lunging distance. "I'm willing to listen to what you have to say, but you'll have to plead your case to the Council of Four. I'm placing you under arrest."

"That's not happening." Tris narrowed her eyes. "Not that I don't trust you, but I don't trust you."

"Fine. We do it the hard way." The man angled his rifle at Tris' thigh.

She blurred into motion, darting forward and swatting the rifle to the left at the same instant her other fist connected with the man's jaw. The remaining four ISF officers all swiveled their weapons toward Tris. Kevin snapped his arm up and fired four shots as fast as he could into the chest of the nearest man. Lead dots appeared on his armor; he let out a grunt like a kicked goose and doubled over.

Mara slapped the console, plunging the room into darkness, save for the eerie glow of hundreds of stasis tanks in the cavern behind the giant window. Kevin charged at where he remembered the next nearest man to be. Blind in the sudden loss of light, he managed to find a vertical body and tackled it to the ground, sending a chair skittering away.

Tris grunted. A fleshy *smack* rang out, and a man groaned. Armor struck the floor. Unarmored bodies dove for cover and crawled off, probably the male technicians. Aura shouted 'please don't shoot me' over and over. No sooner had his eyes adjusted to the eerie light from the cryogenics chamber, Kevin raised his arm to block a strike from a rifle stock that would've caught him in the head. His elbow paid the price, leaving his arm stunned and tingling. He reared up and punched at his best estimation of head, and hit shoulder. His second attack landed against the unmistakable crimple of a nose.

Shoes scuffed and scrambled about. Numerous *thuds* and *whumps* a short distance to his left created a fight scene in his mind; he hoped Tris had the advantage. Sparkling blue light inches from his eyes caught him unaware. He cringed up and away, causing the stunner to scrape over his chest. The electrode had no effect other than sending a blanket of sparks dancing over the surface, diffusing into the hexagonal pattern inlaid within the smoky black material.

Kevin seized the man's wrist and wrestled for control of the stunner. The man he'd shot wheezed and gasped for air off to the right. Tris let off a shout like something out of a bad Kung Fu movie a second before the *thwap* of shoe on face went off like a gunshot. A body sailed over his head and landed behind him with a plastic-coated clatter.

Lights flashed on.

The ISF man beneath Kevin, flat on his back, blinked dazedly at the ceiling. Seizing the advantage, Kevin overpowered the arm and jabbed the stunner into the man's right ear. Froth burst from the man's mouth as his eyes crossed.

The short ISF woman shook off the effect of the rapid shift to bright light and rushed Tris from behind. Kevin brought his .45 up, but before he could fire, Tris caught her in the side of the head with a reverse heel kick that threw the little woman face-first into the giant window overlooking the stasis pods.

She moaned, sliding down from the glass onto the button-covered desk.

Aura darted out from her hiding place beneath the console, pulled the stunner from the woman's belt, and touched it to her head. The officer convulsed and spasmed, various parts of her hitting random buttons and controls, but nothing appeared to happen because of it.

"Drop it!" yelled Tris.

Kevin spun toward her voice.

She planted one foot on the commander's chest, pointing an Enclave rifle at his face while staring at the last ISF man.

"They're going to exile you for this." The last ISF officer tossed his rifle to the floor.

"That's supposed to be a punishment?" She raised an eyebrow. "I *want* to leave. Only problem is they say 'exile,' but they mean execution. Any Enclave people who actually leave are hunted down like escapees."

"She's right." Kevin waved the pins and needles of a funny bone strike out of his left arm. "Ten thousand coins' bounty on anyone brought back here... assuming of course they don't kill the poor idiot who thinks they made payday. But you should know that, right? Being security?"

"Uhh," said the man. His features suggested he should've been black, but he had the same bleached-white skin and hair as Tris, though his eyes retained a rich brown hue. "The military patrols outside the gates. We're strictly internal."

"So they don't even let *you* outside?" Kevin shook his head. "She's right and you can't even see it. Even you people—the ISF—you're prisoners too."

"But the Speaker says—"

"Fuck the Speaker," yelled Tris. "I've hated that floating head since I was a kid. If he's even a real person, he's a font of lies."

"What the hell is a font?" asked Kevin.

Aura scrunched up her nose. "Isn't that a typeface?"

Tris sighed. "Never mind." She glanced at Mara and chucked the rifle to her. "Thanks. Help me a little more? Watch these people? Don't let them leave until it's safe."

"Sure." Mara sat on the console desk, rifle across her lap. "How will I know when it's safe?"

"Oh... I think you'll know." Tris smiled.

Aura started to approach Tris, but froze when she picked up another rifle. Tris ran around and collected the security team's weapons, piled them up by Mara, and dragged the four unconscious officers into a heap by the corner. The three techs took rifles and stood guard over the officers.

"We're in so much trouble." Aura looked down at her shoes. "I guess it doesn't matter now what we do. Are they gonna put me in Detention too?"

Tris sighed. "I hope when the dust settles, they'll thank us. A person who's been weaned on bullshit their whole life gets a taste of truth, the first thing they want to do is spit it out." She held a stare on the ISF man for a second more before rushing to the console and tapping some buttons. "Mara, watch him... but let him come over here and see this."

Within the giant window, transparent virtual monitors appeared in hologram. Each the size of a large television screen, they contained images of a grand city. The buildings resembled those outside, mostly silver and white, but stretched dozens of stories tall. Perfect roads formed a regular grid between manicured lawns. Little drones sprayed water on the grass, and people went about their day. Small children played in a park, giggling and racing around.

"This is the sim," said Tris. "This is what those people are seeing while they sleep."

"Why are there little kids in there?" asked Aura. "You said they only put us in when we turn eighteen."

"They're programs." Mara flicked a fingernail at the rifle grip. "Some of the kids are simple decoration. A handful are watcher programs... basically 'cameras.' Their parents are either virtual, or nonexistent. They help reinforce the illusion."

"It would seem wrong if there were zero children in a city that big," said Tris.

"Damn." Kevin looked among the eight views. "That city looks bigger than some of the prewar metros."

"Easy to build big when it's only data." Tris frowned.

Flying billboards, monitors in storefront windows, and in some spots, plain walls shimmered with television snow for a second before the frazzle-haired face of Doctor Ian Jameson appeared. Tens of thousands of him smiled from all over the city.

"Citizens of the Enclave, your attention if you don't mind. I am Doctor Ian Jameson. Some of you may remember me from the early days of our society. The reawakening of civilization has not gone as I and the other founders had envisioned. I am speaking to you now regarding a matter of utmost importance. I must tell you that you are stuck in a dream. The world you see around you is not real. You are all asleep in stasis pods, experiencing a collective simulation of a city that does not exist."

Some of the buildings changed color. Cars broke apart into digitized pixels and faded away. Most of the small children froze like statues and disappeared, as did some of their 'parents.'

"The Core City is not real." Doctor Jameson's visage switched to drone camera footage of the stasis tanks. The view zoomed in close to provide a clear view of faces. In another screen, a wider angle conveyed a sense of the chamber's vastness. "In a few moments, you will all feel a sudden tiredness come over you. Do not worry. You will fall asleep in the false reality and wake up in the real world. Please understand that what you are presently experiencing is the dream. *This* is the lie. The Council of Four has been deceiving you for your entire lives. They fear the outside world with no reason. The historical documentaries are fictions used to control you."

The screens shifted again, showing scenes from pre-war movies overlaid with 'Historical Documentary' next to a file number on one side and images of advertising for the movie, publicity stills of the actors, images of the actors from other movies or real life. Shock spread over the people in the sim as individuals they thought had been violent raiders barely surviving the nuclear apocalypse showed up smiling in expensive clothes, at fancy parties, and in a few not-so-flattering photographs.

"These so called historical documentaries were culled from entertainment videos produced before the war of August 2021," said Doctor Jameson. Thousands of screens throughout the Core City shifted again, showing aerial views of what Kevin recognized as real settlements. "This is the reality of the world as it is now."

Please don't let them have footage of Ned. Kevin's chest tightened.

The drone camera video zoomed in on families in piecemeal dwellings, farming and surviving. Another image showed a bunch of men playing their best guess at basketball, followed by video of settlers swimming in a river. Squealing, happy children hurried to swim away from a tremendously rotund man doing a cannonball jump from a rickety dock.

"Then, there's this…" Doctor Jameson's voice grew somber.

The images changed. Infected. Cities teeming with half-alive people moaning and milling about. Enclave drone cameras caught a few glimpses of people failing to flee, overrun by the virus-riddled wretches. A split screen window opened, going back to the image of the settler kids frolicking in the water.

"Believing that the outside world was too contaminated to save, the Council of Four made the decision that everyone not within the Enclave deserved to die, purged from the world so the Enclave could take it back in a supposed pure state. Agent-94 is a perversion of research originally conducted for medical purposes. Our council dropped this virus on the unsuspecting people of the Wildlands… robbing them of reason, filling them with the need to kill, and wiping out hundreds of thousands of innocent survivors for being 'impure.'"

Doctor Jameson paused the drone camera footage on a small Hispanic boy with a huge grin upon his rounded face as he plunged into the river. "This, citizens of the Enclave, is an 'impurity' they believe deserves to die. They believe you are a resource to be frozen and stacked until needed, without a voice in your own destiny. Now is the time for you to stand up for yourselves."

The face of Doctor Jameson filled in all the viewscreens again, smiling like a benevolent grandfather.

"I was present at the founding of the Enclave so long ago… What we tried to do has been twisted and taken away from us. You do not live in the world we imagined. For that, I am sorry. They killed me for trying to stop them. This face you see now is little more than a digital ghost, an artificial intelligence created by a man who knew his death approached. Although I no longer walk among you, I am not ready to fade into obscurity."

The false Core City hung in total silence, thousands of people holding their collective breath.

Doctor Jameson's ghost spread his arms to the side. "I give you back your destiny in hopes that you make better decisions than your so-called leaders."

All the screens within the sim went black. Seconds later, the people swooned as if taken by a sudden exhaustion, many collapsing where they stood. Outside in the cavern, the pod-tender robots sprang to life, whirring back and forth like gargantuan versions of old printer heads. Hundreds of robotic arms flailed and poked at pods one after the next.

"It's working," said Tris, wide-eyed. "It really worked!"

"What's happening?" asked Aura.

Mara glanced at the console screen, a field of hundreds of green dots. Yellow crept in from the top left corner, spreading from dot to dot. The upper-left dot flashed to a brighter shade of green with a blue border. "Holy shit! *All* the stasis pods are opening. W-w-what are we going to do? We don't have the food for that many people. We… don't have the room for that many people."

Kevin threw an arm around Tris and grinned at Mara. "Guess you'll have to go outside."

29

DREAMS' END

Urgent beeping crept into Kevin's ears like a microwave oven in another room finishing. The ISF man looked up. Mara and her three fellow techs also stared at the ceiling. Rich moaned and stirred.

Kevin glanced over, frowned, and shot him twice in the chest. After, he reached over with his left hand and pushed his right arm down. "Oops. Sorry. Hate when it does that."

Aura cringed and covered her ears.

"So I take it someone wasn't cooking in the break room?" Kevin pulled the mag from the .45 to check it, finding it empty. *One left in the chamber.* He traded it for a full magazine from his left pocket.

"That's a general quarters alarm," said the ISF man. "I'm getting comm traffic. Director Gerhardt herself is ordering the military to move into the city to back up the ISF and enforce an immediate curfew." He looked from Tris to Kevin. "Seems that speech didn't only happen in the sim. It went off in the Quar too. It's a total clusterfuck out there right now. Sounds like half of 'em agree with her"—he gestured at Tris—"and the remaining half are split between jamming their thumbs up their asses in confusion or listening to Gerhardt."

Aura gasped.

"Sorry." The ISF man scratched at his head. "Forgot we had a child in here."

"So where do you stand?" asked Kevin.

The man approached the window. Some of the pods at the top left corner drained, allowing the limp, nude body inside to slump down into the foot end. The clear housing rotated open going from tube to bathtub. A track-mounted robot slid into position by the tank and lifted a fifty-something man out while disconnecting the wire from the jack behind his left ear. It cradled him in its two largest arms. Flashing yellow lights around its rear face turned on, and it glided straight to the floor five stories below, painting the wall with a dancing array of amber.

The ISF officer leaned close to the glass, his face hovered an inch from his reflection. Kevin figured him for about thirty, the neat flattop suggested a by-the-book 'eager to please' sort who'd probably wanted to be a cop since he had been old enough to walk. The man made eye contact with Kevin via his reflection. A male voice murmured in the officer's earpiece.

"Director Whitford just give the military permission to fire on anyone who refuses to obey. I'm with you two. Name's Jordan."

Doctor Jameson's face appeared in a smaller holographic image embedded within the inch-thick observation window. "Tris."

She looked up from whatever she'd been doing at the controls. "It's starting."

"I know. There is a complication. I need you to go to building 32-A. That's where they store Agent-94 in liquid form. It's also the drone hangar facility. There is enough mayhem going on at the moment where you should be able to get there without a problem. Especially in that armor. You'll blend in like ISF."

"What happened?" asked Tris.

"I'll explain on the way. Go now. There are three cars outside. Take one."

The image winked out.

Tris grumbled, gave Kevin an apologetic look, and stormed for the door.

"Wait!" yelled Aura, chasing her. "You're not gonna really leave me here?"

"No... come on." Tris didn't slow.

"Need a hand?" asked Jordan.

Tris looked at Kevin. "You trust him?"

The guy looks sincere. "You know me. I don't trust anyone, especially strange women who need rides..."

She grumbled and continued for the elevator.

Kevin looked at Jordan. "Come on. Grab a rifle."

He ran after Tris and Aura to the elevator, where they waited six more seconds for Jordan to catch up. Tris pounded the button as soon as the man ducked inside.

"What happened to those two from upstairs?" asked Kevin.

"Sent them to the infirmary." Jordan cringed. "Stunners do a number on a person. Usually takes a few hours for everything to work right again."

Aura stared guilt into the floor.

"It isn't permanent." Jordan patted her shoulder. "I'd rather that than be shot in the face."

The elevator opened behind them, allowing the brain-mushing alarm to triple in volume. Tris sprinted across the empty single-room surface building and out the front door, the girl trailing behind her. Kevin kept his .45 in hand, hoping no one would notice its 'antique' status in the confusion.

Outside, screaming people ran in all directions. A few ISF personnel stood like cops attempting to direct traffic for hundreds of rabbits that had been lit on fire. A few men in thicker armor that reminded Kevin of the Hoplite pilot he'd waved at before covering the skirt of his hovercraft with incendiary gel, clubbed and shoved at a pack of civilians in jumpsuits who appeared to be trying to approach a distant five-story building.

The place has gone completely nuts.

Three black boxes sat outside, a vague suggestion of 'vehicle' in their design. All had ISF logos, and large hatches opened like awnings on their left side.

"You can go home now." Tris offered an apologetic smile to Aura. "I'm sorry for scaring you."

Aura shook her head. "No way. I'm not going anywhere alone. I don't want to be shot... again. Everyone's gone crazy."

"Fine." Tris ran to the nearest vehicle, which looked about the size of a pre-war van, and headed in the open side. The roof had enough room to where she didn't have to duck. She hooked a left to the driver's seat and flopped, attacking the controls before her ass hit the cushion. Aura sprinted after her. Kevin jumped in a second before Jordan. The hatch closed as the console lit up blue. Neutral beige covered everything inside except for the controls and the plain metal floor.

Aura scurried into the passenger seat, so Kevin headed for the bench in the back, flush against the right wall opposite the door he'd entered from. The rear quarter of the cargo area looked like a cage made for people, fortunately empty. Jordan opened a locker-style door on the left side. He pulled out a handgun, which he tossed to Kevin, as well as two boxy magazines full of little orange blocks.

"That old-ass gun of yours won't work on anyone in armor." He grinned and sat on the bench right behind the driver seat, facing Kevin.

"Neither will this… but I guess it will blend in more." He pocketed the .45.

"True, but those rounds have more energy than that old thing. One or two to the chest will still knock the shit outta someone."

Tris backed into a K turn and jammed the control lever forward. Acceleration knocked Kevin over sideways.

"You know where you're going?" yelled Kevin.

"Yes. Waypoint," shouted Tris.

Aura curled up in a ball on the seat, staring over her knees at people outside losing their collective minds. She picked at the rip in her pant leg where a thin strip of snow-white skin showed.

A man's voice announcing, "Please stay calm and return to your homes," over a loudspeaker repeatedly passed on the left.

"When in the history of human beings has 'please stay calm' ever actually succeeded in calming anyone down?" asked Tris.

"No idea," muttered Kevin.

"That was a rhetorical question," said Aura. "She wasn't expecting anyone to answer her."

Kevin glared at the partition behind the girl's head. *Smartass.*

Doctor Jameson's face appeared on a six-inch square display screen in the dashboard. "Found you."

"Dad… can you shut off that damn alarm? It's making my brain pulse." Tris let out a sudden 'eep' noise before jerking the control stick left, swerving the van hard.

Kevin grabbed the pole to stay in his seat. Aura tumbled into a heap on the floor between the front seats. A woman's scream shot by outside. She swerved back the other way, tossing Jordan out of the bench seat to stand. The child climbed back into her seat and buckled in.

"Yes, I believe so. The Eden Protocol is running perfectly. People are waking up and the Enclave will be forced to open its doors to the outside world. The software has already successfully purged all records of the

Agent-X program. I've also deleted the initial work-ups regarding the beneficial virus. As much a boon as it might have provided if completed, it would've been too much of a foundation for someone to rebuild Agent-94."

"Good call," yelled Kevin.

"Watch out!" yelled Aura, pointing at the windscreen. She cringed, and looked down. "Don't crash."

"Not trying to. This thing isn't exactly nimble." Tris grunted as she swerved around another vehicle coming the other way.

Jordan laughed. "These weren't designed to go past forty miles an hour. You're doing eighty-five. If you turn while we're going over thirty, we'll roll. They're a little top-heavy."

"Right…" Tris eased back to sixty and glanced at Dad-AI on the little screen. "So what's this problem?"

"I am unable to physically purge the existing stockpile of Agent-94. There are control mechanisms in place, which rely on a person opening valves. Fortunately, they *did* have the foresight to install an emergency flush system to an incinerator, but it requires manual operation."

Kevin broke out in a sweat. "Whoa… wait you mean we're going to have to go in there where this shit is sitting around in its pure form? Not little capsules like they drop, but giant fucking vats of it?"

"Yes, that sounds about accurate," said Doctor Jameson. "There shouldn't be a risk of exposure. The valve controls are not in an area requiring a clean suit." He bowed his head. "There is something I must tell you."

"Oh, wonderful." Tris squirmed. "Is it something that's going to make me want to kill someone, or curl up and die where I am?"

"The former I hope." The old man offered a wan smile. "Nathan has sent a weaponized drone to your settlement. Nederland I believe. Eight capsules of Agent-94."

"No!" Tris yanked back on the lever, which had the effect of slamming on the brakes.

"Gah!" Kevin slid to his right, crashing shoulder first into the partition behind the kid.

Aura rocked forward into the seatbelt while making a noise like a kicked chicken.

"Whoa!" Jordan caught himself on a padded pole between the benches. "Easy."

"Ow," whined Aura.

"Open the fucking gate," yelled Tris.

Doctor Jameson shook his virtual head. "The drone did not drop its payload. I have control of its flight systems. It is currently en route back here for disposal."

Amid all the chaos raging outside, Tris sat for a moment in what appeared to be meditative calm. When she spoke, a hoarse whisper came from her lips. "How close was it?"

"I overrode its flight controls at 848 yards from the first drop location. The drone suffered a handful of bullet strikes, but no critical systems appear to be damaged."

She shivered.

Kevin closed his eyes. *Please don't let Abby have seen it.*

"The flight program was not official," said Doctor Jameson.

"Nathan," growled Tris. She snapped her head around, fixing Kevin with a stare. "I'm not leaving here until I find that son of a bitch."

The van picked up speed again and swerved to avoid a frightened little boy standing disoriented in the middle of the road. Tris yelled and spun around to grab the stick, but the van ignored her.

"It's me," said Doctor Jameson. "You have no time to spare. The remaining quantities of Agent-94 must be routed to the incinerator before military forces loyal to the Council secure the facility. I have disabled all vehicles and drones, including armed military craft. You, and only you, can re-enable them individually or all at once from the central command system."

"Well, that's good," said Kevin. "We won't have to dodge Hoplites lobbing grenades at us on the way out."

"It also means they won't try to kill her if they know that," said Jordan.

With the van driving itself, Tris faced the back and massaged her sinuses. "So why'd you trust this guy?"

Kevin smiled. "Mostly because he dropped his weapon. From what I've seen of these psychos so far, he would've gambled on reflex boosters and nanites to beat you if he didn't believe us."

Jordan chuckled. "I always did kinda wonder about that waste treatment building. Never made sense to me why it needed ISF on site. Shit doesn't need a guard."

"Maybe it's top secret shit," said Kevin.

Aura giggled.

"The Protocol is nearing completion. The deep-stasis pods have started release processing." Doctor Jameson smiled. "All you need to do from here is switch the manual valves to reroute the fluid to the incinerator vessel instead of the encapsulation path. The ordinance already loaded into capsules in the drone facility, I was able to redirect via software into a burner."

"How much are we talking about?" asked Kevin. "Uhh, left to burn I mean."

"Four tanks. About 160 gallons."

Tris blinked. "Damn..."

The van swerved through a hard right turn, throwing Kevin onto his feet. He got his arms up in time to catch himself against the wall next to Jordan. Once it straightened out, he returned to his bench, but grabbed on to the padded bar.

Gunfire snapped and popped in the distance, making Aura shiver. "Why are they shooting?"

"People hate change," said Tris. "Change is scary."

"We're here," said Doctor Jameson, as the van halted by the front doors of a one-story warehouse-style building. Unlike much of the Quar, it had black walls. "I'm sending you a waypoint now over the Exa."

"You can drive this thing, right?" Tris gave the display screen the side-eye. "Can you find Aura's family and take her to them?"

"I'm showing them all at their assigned residence. Cats included," said Doctor Jameson. "Yes. I can drive her home."

Tris stood and bowed over the girl. "I'm sorry for getting you hurt. I put you in danger and that's inexcusable."

"I, umm... You didn't lie. You're letting me go and you're trying to stop them from freezing me, so I guess I might forgive you even if you did scare me to death." She looked at Kevin. "Thanks for saving me from that bullet. Sorry you got shot."

"Not your fault." Kevin winked. "You didn't kick the gun."

Doctor Jameson cleared his throat.

Tris put a hand on Aura's cheek. "Help me make the world better. Keep your head down."

"Okay."

The side door whirred open. Kevin jumped out. A short asphalt walkway connected the street to a set of glass double doors. Four figures in the thicker military-style armor stood behind a silver metal barricade close to the building, with a gap for the walkway. Jordan hopped out behind him, followed by Tris.

"Wanna try and play this cool?" asked Jordan. "None of these guys know you from the next guy. Act like ISF."

"Worth a shot." Kevin nodded.

The van hatch closed and it drove off, e-motors whining.

Jordan led the way, with Kevin and Tris abreast behind him. The soldiers' smooth black facemasks glinted in the sun.

"Halt," said a man's voice past the crackle of an electric amplifier. "This is a restricted area under military jurisdiction. You boys don't need to be here."

"Guess you missed that last comm," said Jordan. "We're supposed to relieve you. All military forces are being recalled to the council chambers."

"I never heard that," replied the soldier.

The four armored figures all tilted their heads in unison as if listening to something.

"Uhh, yes sir," said the soldier who'd been speaking. His helmet turned toward Jordan. "Sorry. Looks like you were right."

Jordan walked around the barricade and took a stance as if about to stand guard duty. *Why not?* Kevin did the same on the other side. He couldn't look at Tris overacting 'serious face' without bursting into laughter, so he thought about Abby, and how bad he felt leaving her behind. That kept his expression grim.

The soldiers hustled off to the right and vanished around the corner of the warehouse.

"You got some serious skills, girl," said Jordan.

"What do you mean?" Tris blinked at him.

He chuckled. "I don't know you got Director Kuroyama to come over the comm right at that second and order those four guys in particular to the Council Chamber."

Tris peeked at the ammo counter on her rifle. "That had to be Dad. He's probably listening to and watching us through your communicator."

Jordan patted a small bulge in the left shoulder of his armor. "Well, Pops. Thanks."

Kevin leaned forward over the barrier to stare at the corner where the soldiers went. "Think we're clear by now?"

"We're in a hurry." Tris headed for the door.

"Guess that means yes." Jordan chuckled.

Kevin jogged after Tris. Two more soldiers in a small lobby rose from behind a desk and started to raise rifles.

"Don't," yelled Tris, aiming at them. "Stand down."

"ISF personnel aren't authorized to be in here," said a thirtyish woman on the left.

"This building contains a biological weapon that's in violation of every scrap of human decency imaginable. I'm going to give you five seconds to decide if you want to throw your lot in with the Council and be responsible for the deaths of hundreds of thousands of innocent people, or if you're still a goddamned human being." She moved her finger onto the trigger. "Don't think I won't kill you. I have no patience for the kind of monsters that could set the Infected loose on the world."

Kevin raised his handgun at the woman and nodded toward Tris. "Yeah. What she said."

"You saw the video feed." Jordan advanced, his rifle held sideways across his chest. "I saw the pods in person. They really do have all those people frozen. It isn't much of a stretch to wonder what the hell else they've lied about."

"Get out of our way or go for that gun. Either way, do it now." Tris edged closer.

"Before you worry about treason," said Jordan. "I got this feeling that the Council ain't long for this world. Couple thousand frozen people are gonna be pretty pissed off, and unless they turn you lot against our own people..."

"You know how touchy they are about murder." Tris advanced right up to the counter. "It took them generations to build up that many people. I hope they don't covet their power so much that they waste it all and start over."

"And I really don't want to have to shoot a lady." Kevin smiled.

"What now, then?" asked the man.

Tris moved around the side of the desk, keeping her rifle trained on him. Sweat gleamed on her forehead as she neared an overhead light. "Leave your weapons behind and go outside. My only objective here is to disable the bio weapon. There is no reason for its existence other than mass murder."

"Okay, fine." The man leaned to the side, putting his rifle down on the desk. His arm blurred into a sideswipe that swatted Tris' weapon away.

Two gunshots went off at the same instant Kevin fired at the woman. Hoping for a peaceful resolution, he'd had the Enclave pistol pointed at her armored chest rather than her open face. He fired four shots faster than expected, not used to an electric trigger. The handgun kicked like a magnum despite its somewhat unimpressive sound.

Tris screamed. Muzzle flare bloomed from Jordan's rifle. Tris, and both soldiers, hit the ground. The female soldier writhed like a landed fish, gawping for breath. Tris rolled on her side clutching her breast. The male soldier remained flat on his chest, not moving.

Kevin fast walked over to the woman, keeping the gun pointed at her. All traces of hardened soldier left her expression; she stared up at him pleading. Four slugs stuck in her chestplate like darts, the 4mm penetrators not the least bit deformed. If the ache in his hand meant anything, she probably felt like she'd been hit with a sledgehammer by a 400-pound gorilla four times.

"Tris you okay?" yelled Kevin.

"No, ass!" she yelled. "He shot me through the tit. I'll... it's closing."

Jordan leaned up and over the counter. "Sorry man." He shot the soldier in the back once more. "Well I guess I'm officially in the Resistance now."

"Is that why you just stood there during that little brawl before?" asked Kevin.

"Sort of. Been thinking about things, ya know? Some stuff didn't make sense. Not enough doubt to do much but doubt." Jordan looked at the woman. "She go for a weapon?"

"Uhh, no." Kevin flashed a sheepish smile. "All that blurry, too-fast-to-see shit. Didn't wanna take the chance." He pocketed the pistol and took the rifle from the desk. "Guess these *can* penetrate armor."

"Yeah. Need a dead-on angle though. More than eight degrees of deflection, and they'll glance."

Kevin rushed to Tris and helped her sit up. The bloody hand she pulled away from her chest filled him with panic.

Metal slammed against concrete to the left. Jordan sprang in a blur, body-checking Kevin over the counter. Gunfire rippled from the direction of the door. Kevin flipped over in midair and landed on his back between the wheezing woman and the dead man. Three more soldiers fired into the room from a set of double doors in the middle of the wall.

The figure in the middle staggered backward, thin gouts of blood sprayed out of his torso as bullets riddled him. Kevin fired from the ground at the one on the right side, peering through an ACOG sight sideways. As fast as he could click the pushbutton trigger, he offloaded somewhere between eight and fifteen bullets before the man fell over.

Tris went from fetal to poised on one knee and shooting in an instant. A few sparks danced off the third man's helmet. His arms flashed from pointed at Jordan to pointed at Tris. Two sluices of blood trailed out of the back of his head at the same time a long splatter of red painted the floor under Tris' left leg. Something hit Kevin in the belly, making him see stars.

She shrieked in agony; the soldier fell over dead.

Kevin pushed himself up kneeling and shot the man twice more before turning to her. "Tris!"

"Argh!" She dragged herself toward him. "Hurts so much. Fuck."

He helped her sit up. "I don't think we have time for that now."

"You asshole." She rested her head against his side, and laughed.

"Yo, Jordan?" yelled Kevin. "You still with us?" He coughed and checked his gut, only a scuff on the armor. No hole. *That's gonna bruise.*

A weak moan emanated from the other side of the desk.

Kevin cringed. "I think he said, 'oh shit, this hurts like a motherfucker.'"

Another moan, less weak, emanated from beyond the desk.

"Yeah," said Kevin. "That's exactly what he said."

Tris clutched her thigh, trying to stem the geyser of blood bubbling out of it. Kevin put his hand on hers and pressed down. He peered back at the female soldier, who appeared to have passed out.

"Shit." Jordan wheezed. "I'm gonna be okay, but not for a while."

Kevin kept pressure on Tris' leg. She bit his shoulder and screamed, every muscle in her body tense and locked.

"Pins and needles?" asked Kevin.

She nodded.

About fifteen seconds later, she went limp and gasped for breath. "I'm... good."

He pulled her up and set her in the chair before walking around the desk. Jordan lay on his back, rifle across his chest, staring at the ceiling with an expression that made Kevin imagine the Challenger's primary battery hooked up to testicle electrodes.

"Whoa." Kevin took a knee at his side. "How bad is it?"

Jordan coughed up blood. "Hip's disintegrated. Left femur smashed. Think both lungs are pierced, and my right clavicle has seen better days. I don't know how the hell they missed my face or heart, but I guess the man upstairs is on your side too."

Why do people always credit mythology for good luck? Kevin smiled. "That's gotta tingle like a bastard."

Jordan gave him a 'you have no damn idea' look.

"Anything I can do?"

"Got about five steaks on you?" He chuckled into a coughing fit. Dark crimson blood streamed over porcelain cheeks. "I'll catch up. Maybe ten minutes. If I try to move, it'll only take longer."

Tris stood and walked around in a small circle for a few seconds, her left leg rigid as a stick. "Come on." She pulled out of the circle and headed for the door from where the soldiers entered.

"Thanks, man." Kevin squeezed his hand. "You saved my ass."

Jordan grinned; blood leaked between his teeth. "You need to get some nanites while you're here."

"Yeah, I hear that." Kevin patted Jordan's shoulder and stood. "Cover the door."

"Gotcha." He grunted and shifted the rifle to point at the entrance.

Kevin ran after Tris, following a drab grey corridor. Plain metal doors every fifty yards or so bore only numbers. She'd almost gotten back to a normal walking gait, but still favored her left leg. He slowed to a brisk walk at her side.

"Too close to stop." She pointed at a door up ahead on the right, a long ways down a blinding hospital-clean corridor. "Almost there."

Two more soldiers came rushing out of a door on the left. Kevin's heart jammed itself up into his throat, but the men jogged straight on past them without much show of reaction. Tris exhaled. Kevin peered in the room they came from as he passed it; a monitor inside showed the Quarantine Section's central district flooded with a sizeable mob of angry, naked, slime-covered people, several of whom carried weapons. He paused to watch for a second.

"Now that's a sight."

Tris slammed open a door and went in. He jogged after her and entered a smaller control center with four, single-operator desks in the middle. The far wall held an enormous television made from six wide-screen monitors slaved into a single display. He didn't understand one bit of the graphs, math, or program code scrolling by.

"Pretty colors," said Kevin

She leapt into the nearest chair and hammered away at a computer keyboard. "Shit. This is going to take me a few minutes. Can you go down there and trip the valves?"

"Go through where?"

Tris pointed at the right wall. He looked at her finger and tracked its path to a square silver hatch. She tapped a key on the desk and it whirred open, staying parallel to the wall as it rose out of the way on four struts.

"Go in there. You'll have to crawl about fifteen feet before making a left turn, another ten feet, another left turn. There are six valves that need to be switched from the 'main' to the 'purge' setting."

"What are you doing?" He peered over her shoulder.

"I'm bringing the incinerator online. This whole facility except for the drone controls is on an island network. Dad can't get to anything in here except maybe a vid comm, but that won't access the control system. It's going to take two minutes for the incinerator to cycle up to a temperature where it will destroy the Virus for good. I'm rerouting flow paths and setting the—"

"Fine. Okay." He pulled her head around by a finger on the chin and kissed her. "Valves to purge."

"Right."

He ran to the hatch and crawled into a square passage lined with black grating. It didn't offer much of a view of the room despite it being metal mesh due to cabinet components stacked against the wall. He crawled forward and hooked a left into a shorter spar that cut around into the next room. Another left turn led to a long straightaway. About fifty feet ahead, the bright red handle of a flange valve adorned the bottom of a steel cone. He stopped beneath it and looked up.

The funnel connected to a tall, metal cylinder some fifteen feet high. Stamped letters in the metal around the handle path read 'main,' 'close,' and 'purge.' Both main and purge lined up with three-inch thick hoses winding off above the ceiling of the crawlspace, while the close setting put the handle over blank metal.

He grasped the rubber-coated handle, and froze. *This fucking tank is full of Virus. I'm directly beneath enough noxious agent to kill millions of people.* A high-pitched squeaking fart slipped free as he tried not to shit his pants.

Don't think. Don't think about it. Just pull the fucking lever and go.

Kevin grunted and shoved the handle around to 'purge.' He stared at the armored glove over his hand and hyperventilated for a few seconds. *Good gloves. Love the glove. Love glove.* He laughed, and crawled to the next valve.

Don't think. Purge. This valve emitted a metal-on-metal chirp when he moved it. He closed his eyes and fantasized about arriving back in Nederland, Zoe and Abby attacking him with hugs, thrilled to see him again. His throat dried to cotton, but he kept crawling.

TRIS TYPED AS FAST AS SHE COULD MAKE HER FINGERS GO. THE IDIOTS HAD installed an incinerator, installed hoses that could carry the virus to the incinerator, but had never written control routines for any of it. Or maybe they had but some shit for brains deleted them. Not-Dad had given her the program code, but she couldn't find a wire and had to hand-type it. Fortunately, the routine to fire up the incinerator consisted of only about 900 lines.

Copying the floating text her implant generated onto the screen would've been tedious and boring if not for her need to get the hell out of there as fast as possible. Alarm lights flickered on the console as the first tank went from showing 'ready' to 'purge.'

He's going to kill me if he realizes he's crawling under giant tanks of Virus. She bit her lip. *I should've stabbed him with the vaccine when he slept.* She bowed her head. *I can't do that to Abby.*

By the time the third tank flickered red and the word 'purge' appeared over the tank graphic, she hit compile and execute. Seconds later, a low rumble emanated from deep within the building. The fluid routing didn't require programming, only changing settings on a touchscreen panel. It reminded her of a puzzle game where she had to rotate shapes to make a pipe maze passable for a relentless stream of mystery liquid so it could go from one side of the screen to the other, only this screen had four streams of not-so-mysterious liquid that had to all go to the same place.

She grabbed and twisted graphical pipe elbows and valves to set the routes, so the virus flowed into the fire rather than up to the roof where machines would load it into capsules. Her heart raced at being this close to the place responsible for what happened in Amarillo. Never had she wanted to kill someone so much.

Motion caught her eye. The farthest monitor to her right displayed a camera view of the area outside. A group of ISF officers tromped down the corridor heading her way, and they didn't look friendly.

Fear churned in her stomach, threatening to projectile vomit all over the console. *If I run now, they'll go on killing people. They don't need to make more Virus. They have enough to kill the world fifty times. Kevin's got the vaccine... it won't do Abby any good if he doesn't get out of here.* The leaden feeling in her gut grew heavier as she kept on twisting valves. One finger tap closed the maintenance hatch behind Kevin.

Please don't find him.

She opened another command window and hacked down the software firewall making the chemical weapons facility an island network.

As soon as the fourth tank valve sensor went red/PURGE, she flicked four plastic safety shields off the buttons they blocked and smashed them one after the next. Pumps vibrated in the floor. She grabbed a handle and pulled, triggering a neutral agent wash to enter the tanks from above, scrubbing all traces of the virus from the tank walls and carrying it off to its sudsy doom in a five thousand degree inferno.

The door behind her slammed open.

"There she is," said a man.

"Where's your pet Wildlander?" asked another.

Tris raised her hands. "You're too late. The Virus is gone. The Enclave won't be murdering any more innocent people."

A man ran up and grabbed her shoulder. "Where is he?"

"On the roof smashing drones." She sprang out of the chair, going for his rifle.

The man stumbled backward, evidently unprepared for her strength. She wrenched the rifle out of his grip and cracked him across the head, not caring if the weapon broke. He twisted away up on tiptoe, spiraling with his back to her. She grabbed him like a hostage taker, pulled his sidearm, and raised it.

Another man tackled both of them from the side. She got off two shots on the way down, nailing a man in the knee, but the *ping* said it hadn't pierced his armor. The hit to the floor knocked the air out of her lungs and trapped her right arm under the unconscious man. Hands grabbed at her legs.

"Stop," yelled a different man. "He wants her alive."

Tris screamed and thrashed, jerking her arm out from under two-hundred some odd pounds of dead weight. She rolled to her left, punching the guy grabbing her shoulder in the balls. He crumpled in place. Two more grabbed her from behind, hauling her into the air. She squirmed and writhed, not used to men being stronger than her. The unfamiliar sensation, so much like being a normal small-framed woman trying to fend off a pair of huge men, brought a genuine scream of fear.

They flipped her over in midair and drove her chest-first into the floor before pinning her arms behind her back. She struggled and strained, but couldn't move. Steel ratcheted around her wrists. One of them sat on her legs and secured her ankles with another set of cuffs.

She stopped struggling and let her forehead touch the floor.

I suppose this is where I get to use that escape training. Please don't take my shoes... and please don't throw me in a goddamned pool.

30

WHAT SHE'S ALWAYS WANTED

Two seconds after tripping the last valve to the 'purge' setting, an unsettling vibration rattled the grating under Kevin's knees. The corrugated plastic tubes not quite a full foot over his head all wobbled at once. Bright green fluid rushed down and raced over his head. He squeaked and collapsed on his side as the edges of his vision faded to blur, which kept clouding inward until he gazed down a dark tunnel. Over a hundred gallons of the most terrifying substance imaginable coursed through thin plastic hoses.

One drop leaking would kill him in the most horrible way imaginable.

In his mind, his child self ran naked into the meadow again, chased not by Infected, but by a tidal wave of green death. After he ran himself to exhaustion, he tripped and fell down a hole, landing as an adult back in the present day, curled up on the floor of the entryway to Hell.

He trembled, staring at the neon lime doom overhead. Striations of white contaminated it after a few seconds, thickening until the entire hose filled with foam. A section of clear water followed.

Bang.

Kevin twitched.

"Gunshot?"

He breathed in and out for two seconds.

"Shit!"

Thuds and the sounds of struggling came from the control room. He pulled the Enclave pistol from his pocket and scrambled on all fours as fast as he could move. A toilet-like gurgle came from the hoses overhead as they sucked on air. The gun *clanked* against the grate every time his right hand came down.

Tris' screams changed tone from angry to scared. He rushed around the corner, hauling himself down the narrow passageway as fast as he could move—straight to a closed hatch. He scooted left to the first point that offered a narrow view of the outside room. Six men surrounded Tris and forced her into handcuffs. He sucked in a breath, ready to charge out and start shooting, but the hatch didn't move when he pushed on it.

Tris went limp. Two men grabbed her by the arms and dragged her out.

"Avor, take Gallas and check the roof for that Wildlander."

"Yes, sir," said a woman.

She told them I was on the roof? He glared at the closed hatch. *Dammit!* He shimmied to the right and pushed on the hatch cover again, but it wouldn't open. It didn't even rattle. *What the hell am I doing? They're all boosted. If they got her, they'll tear me apart.* He pressed his forehead against the cold metal, trying to think. *Charging at them is stupid. I gotta follow them somehow. Jordan? Did he play dead? Did they kill him? Did he screw us over?*

Figuring they'd gotten far enough away not to hear him, he kicked the panel.

"One moment," said Doctor Jameson somewhere out in the room.

Kevin seethed. "They got her."

"I am aware of that."

"Let me out of here! I gotta find her."

"I am working on that. I must ask a moment of your time first."

He growled. "You're fucking kidding me right? Did you plan this all along?"

"No. I do not want any harm to come to her. Despite that I am a program, I still think of her as my daughter. But… the incineration is not complete. It is still possible for them to recover the agent and continue using it against innocent people."

"What are you talking about?"

"They got to her before she could initiate the final command sequence."

"How long?"

"Forty seconds. She would want you to do this. It's what she's wanted to do since before you met her. Ever sense they set her loose into the

Wildlands, she's been driven by the need to rid the world of the Virus. Even if it costs her life."

His mind drifted back to the earnest look she'd given him from the Challenger's passenger seat so many months ago as they left the destroyed Resistance safehouse in Harrisburg. She said she had 'small' dreams... saving the world. He'd laughed at her at the time. Foolish. Idealistic. Who was she to take on the Enclave? His gods, Amarillo and the Roadhouse, had been smoke and mirrors. The dreaded Enclave, too, seemed to suffer from a bit of the same. *So much for ten thousand super-soldiers with untouchable armor and unstoppable weapons.* He let the image of her smiling at him from across the car linger in his mind, scrub brush and desert blurring by behind her in slow motion. He stared at her sad, pleading eyes; frustration at being unable to save her boiled over, and he punched the metal in front of him. The worry he might not see her again sent trembles of rage down his arms.

He sighed, not caring who saw him crying. "Fine. I promise I'll do it. Open the fucking hatch."

The panel whirred up and away from the passage.

Doctor Jameson's face regarded him from five monitors on each of the three control stations, except for the middle screen on the center desk, which displayed some kind of weird maze thing with green lines going everywhere and a bunch of text, as well as four bright red graphics that reminded him of the tanks he'd been crawling under. He walked over to that station.

"Okay, what do I need to do? And hurry it the hell up." He started to brush tears off his face, and stared at his hand. *I touched the valves. What if there's a tiny bit of Virus on me?*

He tore the gloves off and hurled them across the room.

"On the second screen from the left, tap the 'incinerator temp select' slider and drag it up to five thousand."

Kevin hunted around for a second or two before he spotted the control. He poked his finger into the graphic of an old slider switch and pulled it up until the line met 5000 along the side. Distant, deep rumbling gained intensity.

"At the top left of that same monitor, you should see four flashing yellow triangles. Tap each one and select 'yes.'"

He found the triangles in a half-second. Nothing could've been more conspicuous. He touched one and got a dialogue prompt that read, 'confirm command execution' with a yes/no option. He hit yes, and repeated it three more times.

"Okay, this next part is a bit complicated," said Doctor Jameson.

"Fuck. Hit me." Kevin sat down.

"On the third monitor from the left, near the bottom, there's a graphic of two large round tanks. One is red and one is green."

"Yeah, I see it."

"On the pipe connecting the two tanks, you should see a 'go' button."

Kevin stared at said button. "Yeah. Push it?"

"Please."

He tapped the button.

The ground, and his chair, vibrated hard.

"Hmm. Nice office. Ass massager included. Okay what's next?"

"That's it. You're done."

"What about the complicated thing?"

"That was the go button." Doctor Jameson smiled.

Kevin stood, glaring at the monitor. "Bad time for jokes. Where's Tris?"

"The van I used to drop the child off at her home is on its way back to you. Go outside and wait. They've taken Tris to the ISF holding facility in the southeast corner."

"Are they going to kill her?" He backed toward the door.

Doctor Jameson's expression became somber. "I really cannot say. It would not be wise for them to do so, but then again, these people have not exactly shown much wisdom as of late."

Kevin pointed at the screen as he backed into the hallway. "You get me to her."

"I will."

He sprinted down the hallway toward the exit. Halfway there, it became obvious Jordan had been taken away. He wondered if the man had played them, calling in help once they'd left him behind, but... *Naah. He killed that guy. He wouldn't have done that—or saved my ass—if he wanted to screw us over.* He sped up, suppressing the worry that charging straight out along the same path the Enclave had taken Tris would get him ambushed or killed.

And ran straight into five rather surprised ISF officers standing in the lobby.

IRONY

Three men carried Tris headfirst down a hallway, one holding each bicep, one with his arm around her legs. She squirmed only a little, more to ease some of the pressure from the handcuffs biting into her wrists than get away. They hadn't taken her shoes, though they did find the Beretta in her pocket.

The moment months ago when Kevin handed it to her outside that old barn where they'd hidden the Challenger came back to her. Now she understood how he'd gotten so attached to his .45. It had nothing at all to do with the weapon itself, but of how it reminded her of how she felt once she realized he'd decided to trust her.

Cutting her loose in the car while trying to outdrive a pair of Hoplites had been an act of having no other options. Handing her a loaded firearm however… She bowed her head enough to look back at the man studying it like some kind of museum piece.

She hadn't seen much on the short ride to this building, as the holding compartment in the rear had no windows. The screams and fists of angry people pummeled the armored sides of the transport van.

They turned a corner and pushed open a set of black plastic doors. Tris lifted her head. At the sight of the heavy padded chair full of straps next to a bank of machines and a clear plastic tube, placid calm went straight out her ear. They weren't going to leave her in a cell long enough for her to attempt escaping the cuffs.

"Stop! You don't know what you're doing! The Enclave has to change or you'll all die off."

They wrangled her over to the chair and hurled her face-first into the cushion. She struggled against six hands holding her down.

"Please, just think! They've been lying to you. You saw everything," she screamed.

The steel let go of her right wrist. Two men pinned her arm while another two flipped her over on her back and secured heavy synthetic straps around her chest and right arm. Another man unlocked the cuff from her left and forced her arm into the restraining band.

Dad... whatever the hell you are... help!

She yanked her legs back, her ankles still linked by handcuffs, and mule kicked the guy who had tucked the Beretta under his arm so he could fumble for a key to unlock her feet. Both heels nailed him in the jaw with a satisfying *crack* that torqued his head around at a fatal-looking angle. He sailed into the air and landed on his back, sliding. The Beretta bounced on the floor and skidded to a stop halfway under a desk by the door.

None of the ISF officers paid it any attention, likely thinking it a toy.

The one who'd had her right arm slugged her in the side of the head, making the room spin. She floated in a moment of dizzy nothingness, barely aware of someone removing the cuffs from her legs and strapping them down to the chair.

"She killed him," said a distant man.

One by one, they approached, grabbed one of her fingers, and broke it backward. Tris writhed and screamed. She clung to the anger she'd felt at Nathan for sending the Virus at Nederland to resist begging them to stop.

The third man leaned close after he broke another finger. "I don't care what Gerhart's orders are. Once they freeze your ass again, you're gonna have a nice little accident."

Once five of her fingers had broken, the five ISF officers collected the dead man and carried him out. She eased her head back into the cushion and sobbed in silence, waiting for the nanites to repair her hand. She clenched her jaw and shrieked while forcing her fingers as straight as she could in hopes they knitted properly, rather than at some odd angle.

Soon, cold tingling replaced the splintering pain.

After a few gasps for air, she raised her head. Straps held her by each wrist and ankle, one at her waist. Another one around her chest at the armpits kept her from sitting up too far. She let off an ironic laugh at her shoes. Even if she could reach the tools hidden inside, they wouldn't be of any use. As best she could tell, the motorized restraints responded to a control panel on the back of the chair, well out of reach of anyone stuck in it.

She felt somewhat better that they hadn't taken her armor off; likely they wouldn't bother with that until they'd drugged her unconscious… or paralyzed. Few things truly frightened her as much as feeling helpless. The nightmare snippet of that man attempting to molest her the last time they stuffed her in stasis shot a thread of bile up her throat. It didn't seem possible that they'd want to do that… Not-Dad should've disabled all of the stasis tanks. *Maybe they don't know they're inoperable yet…*

She twisted at her arms, but they'd overtightened the straps; she couldn't even rotate her wrists.

Hope lasted for only a few minutes of struggling before futility set in and she sagged limp.

I did it. I got rid of the Virus. She stared at the ceiling. *Guess it doesn't really matter what happens to me now. Please let Kevin get out of here in one piece.* Tris bit her lip. *He's going to come after me. No. You have to go home to Abby, you asshole!* Tears slipped out of her eyes and slid warm trails down the sides of her head. It would be nice to be with him again even if only for a few minutes before the Council ordered them killed. Together would still be together. Abby would eventually move on. Or not. Tris growled and struggled again, but gave up after a moment of getting nowhere.

A door squeaked open.

She kept staring at the ceiling, trying to find anger under the thick blanket of gloom. Letting them see her cry would give them too much.

"Well… I dare say you've made *quite* the little nuisance of yourself."

Nathan.

Tris thrashed, trying to sit up. The chair creaked.

Nathan approached to within a few feet. He wore a smug grin along with a high-collared black Chinese tunic and trousers. His chest-length blond hair hung straight and perfect as always, a few stray strands down his front all but glowed against his shirt. To think that she'd considered him cute when he'd first spoken to her in Detention, when she'd thought him a Resistance hacker.

Behind him stood a naked woman with a startling resemblance to her, only taller and more muscular. Clear gel dripped down her body, collecting in pools by her feet. She appeared unconcerned with her lack of clothes, and had the most unsettling neutral expression.

"You look like a casting disaster from a historical documentary about Kung Fu," said Tris.

Nathan scoffed. "If you're going to insult me, at least say something that makes sense."

She eyed the woman. "What sort of pervy thing are you planning now?"

He wandered closer, examining his fingernails. "I'll assume you've learned about the Persephone androids. I took this one out of its packing material a few moments ago. She's brand new for you to play with. Little girls like dolls don't they?"

"Why?" She stared at him.

Nathan let off a beleaguered sigh. "I'd love nothing more than to put you out of my misery, but Gerhardt wants you back in the sim… along with everyone else. Exactly what did you think you would accomplish by opening all the pods?"

"You sent me out there to cure the Virus. That's what I did." She scowled at him.

He chuckled. "You haven't cured a damn thing. All you've managed to do is create mass panic and kill a few dozen people. It boggles my mind why the Council wants you kept alive. Of course, by the time we're done with you, you won't remember that filthy Wildlander you've fucked… or any other contaminated organisms out there you've become attached to. You'll be reprogrammed into someone's nice little subservient wife." He held his hand out to study his nails, arching his fingers back as far as they'd bend. "Don't worry about missing that little hovel you've holed up in by the way. A day or two from now, they'll all be gone."

"No!" She screamed, forgetting herself for a moment of furious, but futile struggling at the straps holding her down. *Dad stopped it.* Forcing calm over herself, she glared, hard breaths gasping past clenched teeth. "Why me? What's so damn important about me? Why do you have a bug up your ass?" She grunted, straining against the straps. "Why am I so goddamned important?"

Nathan covered his mouth to mute a haughty chuckle. "Oh, you're not. Your father started the Resistance. Those softhearted idiots would've been the doom of humanity. I took it upon myself to personally ensure that you were made an example of. You know…" He looked up, head at an angle, tapping his chin. "Poetic irony and all that."

She dug her fingernails into the upholstery. "You can't put me back into the sim. It's shut down. The software's eating itself; the preservative fluid is halfway out into the Bay, and the robots are dismantling the pods. It's over, Nathan. Everyone knows the truth."

"You vastly underestimate the willingness of sheep to be sheep." He let his arm fall at his side. "When confronted with the reality of what it would entail to... what is it you so naïvely said? 'Become part of the world?' They will run back to the pods like children hiding under the covers." He laughed as if at a stupid child.

Tris lurched against the straps at the sound. His voice scraped down her spine like glass claws.

"I must say you surprised me. I never honestly expected you to make it *to* the Resistance in Harrisburg, much less all the way back here. Your pitiful 'assault' on the Enclave is a forgettable footnote in an otherwise forgettable life. Your father should've left you back in time where you belonged."

She tried to project an aneurysm into his brain by sheer hatred.

"Of course, I happen to disagree with Gerhardt. Keeping you alive is a needless risk. A mistake... like that one little frayed thread sticking out of an otherwise perfect cheongsam. I can't help but pluck it. And... best of all, thanks to *your* little attack, everyone is quite too busy to notice what we're doing right now." He brought his hands together in a rapid, soft clap. "By the time things are back under control, no one will notice or care what happened to you. And my new friend here will take your place. The council's never met you up close."

Tris summoned all the desire she could manage, her need to get back to Kevin... get back to Abby, and channeled it into her muscles. She strained against the arm straps. At her utter lack of moving them, she dug her fingernails into her palms, refusing to cry in front of him.

"And now, another poetic irony." He grinned. "You're going to kill yourself."

"No way in hell." She scowled.

Nathan looked over his shoulder at the Persephone. "Kill this woman."

The android walked forward, raising an arm to grab her around the neck.

"I meant kill yourself in a metaphoric sense." He chuckled. "This thing does look like you. Enough to fool Gerhardt into thinking you're still alive."

Tris' eyes bulged; she tried to lean back, but couldn't move away. Clear slime dripped onto her chest from the android fingers inching for her throat. The robotic woman stared down at her with no emotion whatsoever in her perfect face, Tris' reflection in a demonic mirror.

BURN

The Persephone's frigid fingertips touched her skin.

"No!" yelled Tris.

It stopped. A second later, the Persephone lowered her arm.

"What are you doing?" barked Nathan. "Kill her."

The android reached for her throat.

"No!" shouted Tris.

Again, the Persephone halted.

"Kill her now!" shouted Nathan, his too-beautiful face showing signs of red.

"Don't!" shouted Tris.

The android stopped with its hand six inches from her neck.

"What are you doing?" roared Nathan.

The android straightened and faced him. "Persephone series designation I6-414 possesses a failsafe."

"Failsafe? Disregard the failsafe, kill her!"

She reached for Tris' neck again.

"Don't!" yelled Tris.

Again, the Persephone reset to a neutral stance.

"Define this failsafe," said Nathan with an imperious wag of the head.

"Failsafe directive. Core program code. Firmware revision 17.25.002. Failsafe routine enacted 2017, authorization Doctor Ian Jameson. Subject

Tris Jameson granted command override access to all Persephone series units."

"Huh?" asked Tris. "Dad programmed you all to listen to *me*?"

"You are correct," said the Persephone.

"No!" yelled Nathan.

"Knock him out," said Tris.

Nathan pivoted to run, but the android leapt into a foot sweep that took him down. The Persephone pounced, hauled him to his feet, and held him off the ground. She looked at him for a second as if calculating, and rabbit-punched him square in the forehead. Nathan collapsed in a heap.

"Please get me off this chair… without hurting me."

The Persephone padded over and threaded a finger under each strap before snapping them away from the chair as if they'd been made of thin plastic. Tris gawked at the eighth-inch-thick nylon/steel weave composite. As soon as the last strap came free, she leapt off the chair and ran to the Beretta. Of course, the asshole took all the bullets, though at least he left the magazine in it. She recognized the scratch down the left side—the same mag it had when Kevin gave it to her.

If I get out of here alive, this is going in a case. I'll carry one I don't care about losing.

She stuffed it in her pocket and jogged to Nathan. He moaned and stirred as she grabbed the sidearm from his belt. She knelt on top of him, waiting a few seconds for his eyes to focus on her.

"Hello, Nathan." Tris whacked him across the jaw with the pistol.

A little blood spattered on the floor.

"Don't let him out the door," said Tris.

The Persephone walked across the room and stood in the doorway.

"And don't let anyone else in unless their name is Kevin."

"Understood," said the Persephone.

"No!" said Nathan.

She smiled.

Nathan surged upward; Tris may have had the strength of a large man, but she had the body mass of a wisp. He threw her to the side, keeping a hand clamped around the wrist of her gun arm. Tris landed flat on her chest and wheezed, her fingers clenched. Nathan attempted to pry the weapon free, but couldn't budge her grip. He dragged her a few feet while clambering to his feet, and drew his leg back to kick her in the gut.

She grunted and twisted, pulling him off balance. They fell sideways together, Nathan wailing. Tris sprang toward him, distracting him with a fake punch to the face and landing a real kick to the groin.

The strike sent him sliding along the polished floor a good ten feet. He crumpled into a ball and whined.

"Hmm. I didn't expect that to do much. The way you preen, I figured I wouldn't hit anything vital there."

He gulped air, his face florid.

Tris stood and eyed the standard Enclave pistol. "Have you ever even fired this thing? Don't worry, Nathan. I don't think I'm going to shoot you." She stuck the gun in the armor's built-in holster.

"Hah. You think the Council is going to listen to you?" He forced himself up to his knees, an arm braced through his crotch. "You're fooling yourself. You really believe that nonsense, don't you?"

"I think you're mostly bluffing." She sauntered closer. "The Council already warned you once... and their time of power is coming to an end. Your entire military from the smallest drone to the biggest Guardian hovercraft is about as potent as your little twig of a dick." She tapped her head. "They've all been disabled, and only I've got the codes to turn them back on. It's six thousand against four. What side are you on?"

Nathan growled and pulled a ten-inch blade from his hip. Her combat boosts slowed his motion to a near crawl. She caught his arm, twisted it over, and flipped him onto his back while ripping the knife away from his grip.

"A knife! Why thank you! It's perfect!" She made a show of studying it like a gift.

"What..." Nathan moaned.

"Oh, I guess they didn't tell you." Tris grabbed a fistful of his tunic and hauled him off the ground one-handed. "Apparently, my father's ghost has been rattling around the network. He gave me the full combat package."

She threw him over the chair into the wall. He bounced off, leaving a bloody mark where his mouth made contact, and collapsed in a heap.

"The way you had them strap me down before you had the balls to show up, I figured you knew that... I guess you really are just a sad, sad little man. If you were afraid of a girl my size *without* boosts, you're about to have a really bad day."

Nathan struggled to his feet, clawing at the wall to pull himself up. He pushed away, flying at her with a wobbly roundhouse kick.

Tris caught his ankle in her left hand, smirked, and threw his leg aside.

His eyes flared wide. Growling, he waved his arms about in some manner of martial arts threat display. She tilted her head.

"Is that supposed to be kung fu, tai chi, or did a wasp fly past your face?"

"Stupid bitch." Nathan circled to her left. "You think a little VR is going to matter? I've been training for years. In the *real* world."

"Right." She rubbed her temple over her right eye. "Here, and I thought you were a useless pampered administrator."

Nathan lunged. Her enhancements dragged the world into slow motion again, making his left hand feint obvious. Tris spun under his incoming punch, grabbing his wrist as her back pressed into his chest. A quick thrust of her hips sent him up and over, and she yanked down on his arm to swing him into the floor. Before he could start shouting from the dislocated shoulder, she whirled around and braced her knee against the back of his arm, pulling on his wrist until the arm broke backward at the elbow. She hopped away and eased off the boost.

Time resumed.

Nathan shrieked.

"Guess they ran the wrong software."

As soon as he started to push himself upright, she took a step and kicked him in the stomach, flipping him over on his back. He gurgled, cradling his gut, staring at her with googly eyes bulging from a red face. Whatever he tried to call her came out in a series of harsh barking noises and groans.

Tris glared at him, hands clenched to fists. She never imagined it possible to hate someone as much as she hated Nathan. Every time Abby cried, she wanted to twist his head off. Every time the girl woke up screaming in the middle of the night, haunted by her dreams of what happened in Amarillo, Tris wanted to kill him. The thought of how terrified the girl had to be worrying about them out here boiled over. Snarling, she went in for a field-goal kick to his head. He rolled to the side and scrambled to his feet, catching her foot.

Before he could do anything with her trapped leg, Tris flung herself into a midair corkscrew and cracked him across the chin with her left foot. Nathan torqued around and sailed into the wall face first while she landed on all fours. Tris shoved herself upright and got her arms up to block a series of punches that dragged down to a crawl as soon as her boosters kicked on again. One after the next, she swatted his strikes aside. After six, she caught his wrist.

"Didn't I already break this once?" Narrowing her eyes, she twisted his arm to the side and hammered the handle of the knife down on his forearm, earning a satisfying *crunch*.

Nathan gasped, fell to his knees, and made a noise like a lovesick basset hound. Bloody mucous ran from his lower lip. He fumbled with his rubbery limb, trying to pull it into place for his nanites to mend.

"I really don't like what you bring out in me, Nathan." She eyed the knife. "You killed all those people in Amarillo."

He grunted and hauled himself upright. "They're damaged on a genetic level. Hu"—he wheezed for breath—"Humanity can't afford them."

Tris faked a slash to his face and stomp-kicked him in the sternum when he moved to defend. The hit launched him against the wall, a coconut like *knock* came from his head. Dazed, he started to wobble toward her. She grabbed him, flung him around, and plowed an elbow into his upper back, crushing him against the clean white surface. He struggled, whimpering, but couldn't budge her. Tris tossed the knife up and caught it by the handle.

After admiring the way the light reflected from the edge for a second, she rammed it into his back hard enough to stick it in the wall.

"That's for Emilio."

Nathan let off a long, agonized wail.

Tris leaned up on tiptoe, putting her mouth at his ear. "This is for Abby."

She twisted the knife back and forth, grinding it deeper.

Nathan howled, and shit his pants.

"Don't worry. You've got nanites, right? It'll take them a while to exhaust themselves to the point they start reconfiguring tissues." She tapped the knife handle, making him squeak each time her finger made contact. "You should last fourteen hours before they eat you from the inside out."

She pounded her palm on the knife handle, seating it into the wall. Nathan gasped.

"You are not permitted entry," said the Persephone.

"The bitch is loose," yelled one of the men who broke her finger. He tried to barge past the android, but she palmed his chest and flung him into the wall outside.

The delicate sound of concrete chips falling to the floor followed a loud crash.

"I see you paged your helpers." Tris looked at the door. "Are there five of them out there?"

"That is correct," said the Persephone.

"Those five don't need to remain among the living." Tris let go of the knife, leaving Nathan hanging like a frog tacked to a dissection board. She walked to a terminal a short distance away behind the chair.

"Ngh," wheezed Nathan. He tried to reach around and grab the knife, but screamed at the pain of moving and hung limp. "What... what are you doing?" Fingers splayed against the featureless white wall, he attempted to push himself off the knife, but also gave up with a gasp.

Tris dove through the Enclave file system using the root access Not-Dad gave her, and raided Nathan's personal files. She found a certain list of files he'd put in her head, selected one, and smiled at him.

"What are you doing?" wheezed Nathan, sounding desperate. "You don't honestly expect to simply walk out of here do you?"

A disgusting crunch came from the doorway. Two men and a woman screamed, then rapid footsteps grew quiet and distant. Tris snapped her gaze over to the door at the sound of gunfire. The Persephone leaned out into the hall, her breasts bouncing with the recoil of the assault rifle she fired. Seconds later, she lowered the weapon and took two steps back into the room, standing guard.

Tris glanced at Nathan's twitching figure. Trails of crimson traced pin-straight lines down the wall to the floor, joining a growing pool of blood seeping out under Nathan's shoes. "Goodbye, Nathan."

Her fingernail clicked on the enter key.

The Cure's *Burn* blared out of the speakers.

Head held high, she walked past him slow—without even looking at his feeble struggling. As the drums kicked in, he recognized the song, and shrieked in rage. Satisfaction spread a broad smile across her face.

"Don't you dare leave me here, you fucking bitch!" He screamed, slapping his left hand at the wall; his right arm appeared to have gone numb. "Tris! God dammit, you worthless genetic disaster!" Nathan trailed off into incoherent random obscenities. "You think you've won, but you haven't. You're wrong. You're dead fucking wrong! This isn't over! I'm not done with you!"

She closed her eyes, savoring the music accented by his cries of pain and impotent rage.

At the door, she paused. *The knife was for Abby. This is for me.*

Tris whirled, raised the gun, and put twenty-seven rounds into his back.

Nathan gurgled, sagging over backward. She adjusted her aim, and fired a single shot into his temple, bursting the opposite side of his head open.

The ammo display on the end of the pistol showed 00.

After six seconds of dead weight hanging on the knife, it popped out of the wall and he fell, landing atop an expanding patch of blood. A ruin of plaster and cinderblocks disintegrated from where the bullets had pierced him and gone into the wall beyond.

She stood motionless, staring at him until the song ended.

"Command?" asked the Persephone.

Tris lowered her arm and gazed at the pistol, wanting to kill Nathan another four or five times, but that would have to wait until she could dream again. She turned, finding herself eye-to-chin with her somewhat older, more athletic doppelganger.

"Lead me to the Council of Four."

33

THE COUNCIL OF FOUR

Kevin skidded to a halt on his heels and stared for a half-second at five men in ISF armor. They twisted to face him, looking as startled as he felt.

"Oh, shit."

He flailed his arms and darted back into the corridor, heading for the nearest door to put something more solid than air between him and bullets. Of all things to think about at that moment, the way the Enclave shoes squeaked on the polished floor made him long for his boots... sitting in a locker he might never see again.

The ISF rushed into the hallway behind him.

Shit. Shit. Shit.

"Stop," said a man.

Kevin barged through a door into a conference room with no other exit. Three walls of dry-erase board contained indecipherable mathy stuff, as well as stick figure doggy-style porn with the 'receiver' labeled Whitford and the 'giver' labeled Gerhardt.

A long table and twenty-two comfortable-looking black chairs wouldn't do much for him. He whirled to face the door, raising the Enclave pistol as he backed up.

Head shots. I need head shots.

Shadow spread over the gleaming white floor from the ISF men collecting outside.

Come on. First one in wins a prize.

He fought the urge to tense up on the trigger. *This is like one of those goddamn mouse thing buttons.*

"You're that Wildlander, right?" asked the same man. "We've been looking for you."

No shit. He stared over the gunsights, waiting. The chaos outside had grown so loud it felt like the wall behind him would collapse under the weight of the unrest. Metallic slams suggested cars smashing into things, the occasional *pop* of a gunshot went off, but most of the cacophony consisted of shouting.

"Doctor Jameson has asked us to get you out of here in one piece."

Kevin blinked. "What?"

"We're on your side. I'm gonna look in, don't blow my head off." A man in his early twenties with short white hair and green eyes peeked around. Only his head and one shoulder came past the doorjamb, no sign of a weapon. "I'm Alex. We saw the whole thing... the stasis pods, the Virus..." He looked down. "We had no idea there were so many people out there. They've always told us they were... diseased. Mutated and rotting..."

"That's Infected." Kevin shifted his jaw side to side.

"We know that now," said Alex.

Another man walked into view out in the hallway; he had a rifle, but kept it lowered. Longer black hair wavered at the sides of his head, down to his earlobes. "Yeah. That's completely fucked up and wrong to drop bio weapons on civilians."

Kevin went from staring over the gunsights to staring at the gun. "Umm."

Alex raised an empty hand. "I understand you're hesitant, but if we were trying to kill you we would've fiber-opped the door and shot you without exposing ourselves."

Either way I'm fucked. He lowered his arm. "Where's Tris?"

"What do you mean?" Alex stepped in. He had a hand on a rifle hanging from a strap, but his body language didn't appear aggressive.

"Some of your pals dragged her outta here in cuffs."

The black-haired man shook his head. "That didn't go over official channels. Most of the ISF agrees with her. There's a penis-waving contest going on between us and the military right now, and the civilians are caught in the middle."

A third man, also white-haired but a little older, entered. "Doctor

Jameson advised us to exfil you asap. There's apparently a network of tunnels beneath the city that we can use."

"Whoa." Kevin raised his hands in a 'hold on a moment' gesture. "One, I'm not leaving without Tris. Two, 'exfil' sounds kind of private and painful."

The ISF men chuckled.

Alex recovered first. "It's short for exfiltrate... as in leave."

"There's still the first problem." Kevin relaxed enough to approach them. "Where's Tris?"

"Jameson said she's got things under control." The thirtyish white-haired man waved him to follow. "He said to tell you she's found the cure... whatever that means."

Kevin's expression blanked. "I have no damn idea." He blinked. "Music? Did she escape and go after Nathan?"

"If I knew, I'd tell you," said Alex. "Come on."

He followed the five men into the hallway. "Look. If this goes shitty, I need you guys to help me find her."

A bald man with a face ugly enough to stop a clock gave him a severe look. He exuded the scent of recent shaving, but still appeared to have a deep beard shadow. Large trapezius muscles flowed into equally thick arms, calling into question whether or not he possessed a neck. The dude would've been scary even without the augmentation he no doubt had. "We got your back."

The men walked mostly at his right side with one out front and one trailing behind, ushering him farther down the corridor than the Virus lab, which still rumbled from the distant incinerator. Kevin argued with himself about following Jameson's idea of this 'exfiltration' thing. *No way. As soon as we reach the outside, I'm going after her.*

"Almost there," said the bald man, who had the lead. He jogged around a left corner, barged through a metal door and fast-stepped it down a small stairwell to a landing. "This way." A second set of switchback steps led to a door. He headed for a keypad on the left and punched in a code. "Guess we find out if the old man was right."

A beep emanated from the panel and the door opened.

"Looks that way," said Alex.

Small LED lights at even intervals along the upper left corner of a plain concrete hallway came on in sequence. A trail of light raced off into the distance. About sixty yards away, the corridor angled to the right.

The youngest ISF man, who looked eighteen, whistled. "Wow. Did you guys know this was down here?"

"Nah. Jameson said only First Tier and the Council had access." The bald man strode in, looking around at the walls and ceiling. "Some kind of emergency evacuation route."

"Maybe they used it for all that shady crap," said the young one. "Stuff they didn't want anyone knowing about."

Kevin couldn't think about anything but Tris; the angry screams coming out of her as the other men dragged her away played on continuous loop between his ears. "Yeah. Probably. Look… I know you guys mean well and all, but… I'm not leaving without her."

"We're not even sure what team took her." Alex spoke in a low tone that didn't echo too much in the bare tunnel. "It had to be military dressed up like ISF. Probably on direct orders from the Council."

Kevin narrowed his eyes. "Or Nathan."

They hurried past the bend in the passageway, about a forty-five degree angle. From there, the corridor stretched off to a tiny point. Agonizing minutes passed as they jogged forward. A few offshoots led from both sides along the way. Other than the scuff of shoes, the occasional drip also broke the heavy silence.

The bald one ignored the first branch to the left, hesitated at the second hallway, which led to the right, and kept going.

Is this guy lost?

"None of you know where she is?" asked Kevin.

Alex shook his head. "Jameson said she's not in danger. He didn't give us any more detail than that."

The bald one slowed and hovered at the fourth corridor leading left.

"Hey Tarl, you lost?" said Alex.

"Nah… I'm not seeing those numbers the old ghost said to look for." His already harsh countenance hardened further. Kevin half expected to see the wall crack wherever the man looked.

"Maybe we haven't gone far enough yet?" asked the youngest.

Great. These guys are lost. Kevin bit back the urge to make a wisecrack.

The big man jogged ahead, picking up speed while examining the walls in search of whatever markings he'd been told to find. The tunnel ahead seemed to go on for miles. Traces of tire marks on the floor near another ignored offshoot increased Kevin's worry. If the tunnels went long enough to require a vehicle… anything could happen to Tris before he found a way out.

"This way." Tarl pointed and cut right.

The group jogged another few minutes before the man skidded to a halt and backtracked six feet to a left turn he almost skipped. Alex gave Kevin a 'sorry, we're guessing' kind of face as the group flowed after their point man.

Kevin glanced over, where a tiny black '42' occupied a one-inch square tile by the corner.

"Which one are we looking for?" asked Kevin.

"Four-four." Tarl turned right at the next hallway. "Here."

Twenty yards or so farther, the floor angled downward into a shallow ramp. Urgency to find Tris got Kevin up to a faster jog, which the ISF men inherited. Minutes later, the tunnel leveled off and ended at a room with a single elevator and three, small, four-wheeled carts. Tarl typed a code in a panel by the elevator and it lit up.

"Wow." Two bushy caterpillar eyebrows climbed his bald head. "Code worked."

"Where does this lead?" asked Kevin.

Tarl's brutal face didn't do subtle shades of emotion well. His apparent attempt to project confidence felt more like 'I want to break you in several places.' "Surface. Probably near the HC port."

"Again, that sounds painful." Kevin closed his eyes and tried to radiate some kind of mind powers that could keep Tris alive.

"Hovercraft port," said Alex. "There's a canal leading out from about the middle of the Quar to the Bay. Not as heavily guarded as the primary gate."

The elevator arrived, and opened, revealing a smallish room with walls mirrored from the waist down and polished wood grain inlaid with decorative gold accents around the upper half.

Kevin walked in shaking his head. "I'm not going to leave the Quarantine Section without Tris." He clenched his fists and stared into nowhere. "Even if I'm carrying her body."

Come on, Tris. You got them nanites. Don't fuckin' die.

Heavy glances passed among the ISF team.

Tarl patted him hard on the shoulder. "You got it, man."

Alex entered the elevator last, and spent a few seconds staring at the controls... only two buttons. He pushed the top one, earning a soft electronic *ping* from the wall. "Well, that makes the choice easy."

Kevin glanced to his right, at his reflection in the high-polished woodgrain panels, and past it at two tiny doors. Curiosity got the better of him, and he opened one. A rack held about twenty tiny bottles of various alcohols. *What the hell?* He shrugged and shoved the door closed with contempt. *These people are ridiculous... drinks in an emergency escape elevator?*

The ISF guys discussed where they expected to emerge on the surface. They couldn't reach a consensus. Tarl kept insisting Doctor Jameson told them to take the hallway marked '44.' Kevin bounced with anxiety, squeezing and releasing the grip on the Enclave pistol. The squishy rubberized handle didn't feel right. His beloved .45 sat heavy in his pocket. Even if it couldn't dent this armor, its presence comforted him. He stared at the digital clock on the elevator panel, watching cyan numbers tick up from 04:33:16.

One minute and twenty-two seconds after Alex hit the button, the doors slid open.

A grey floor spread out in front of them, ending at a black curtain about fifteen feet away. Strong overhead lights forward of the curtain made the space outside glow. Several men and two women's shouts echoed as if in an auditorium.

"What do you mean the override is not working?" yelled a man with a hint of a Japanese in his English.

"Not working. The absence of working. Not functioning as intended," snapped a woman with an accent that reminded him of the couple who'd said *'namaste'* at him.

The first man let out an exasperated sigh. "How is it that not *one* of the systems is responding to our commands? Who is this person in our network?"

"The old man or the girl?" asked a calm-sounding voice reminiscent of a stern grandmother. "We're not getting anywhere like this. What are the repair teams reporting?"

"They're reporting that they've been surrounded and captured," yelled the Japanese man. "This is an absolute disaster."

"Do it," bellowed an older-sounding man. "You have permission to use whatever force necessary to contain the situation. Citizens are to return to their homes." He paused a few seconds before yelling, "Please," and dropping back to a hushed speaking tone. "Will you give me a damn moment? I can't record an announcement with you four bickering like children in the background."

Kevin crept across the open space to the curtain. A few seconds of feeling around located a seam, which he pulled aside enough to peer out. About fifteen feet in front of him, four people sat at a wide shared desk with their backs to him. Rows of black seats spread out into the distance, positioned behind thinner tables lined with small silver nameplates he couldn't make out. Larger signs overhead read 'First Tier Administration' near the front, 'Second Tier Administration' near the middle, and 'Third Tier Administration' closest to the exit doors.

Left of the giant desk, a tall man with neat grey hair, somewhere between sixty and seventy, stood at a podium loaded with computer displays. His thick grey eyebrows, dour, square-jawed face, and impeccable appearance made him look too perfect to be real.

If shady military government was a person, he'd be it.

A black-haired man with Japanese features and paper-white skin sat closest to the podium. He looked over sixty, and stared daggers past a somewhat younger, brown-haired Caucasian man between him and a woman with darker skin and black hair. She appeared middle aged, easily in her fifties, and pointed one finger at the Japanese man as if she wanted to ram it through his eyeball.

At the far right end, a pewter-haired woman leaned her elbow on the desk, massaging her temple. She had a hint of a tan, a subtle wrinkling to her face, and looked also in her sixties—with a frustrated scowl as if about ready to throw her arms up and walk away. "So what you're telling me is, there's no way to kill this rogue process that's opening all the pods?"

"I've done everything," said the man at the podium. "Not one of the control routines are responding. The team we sent to the facility encountered resistance."

"Do you mean they encountered Resistance or they encountered resistance," asked the brown-haired man.

The dark-skinned woman slapped the table. "Will you stop babbling?"

"I'm not babbling!" He thrust his hands up. "I mean *the* Resistance or just—"

"Enough!" roared the Japanese man. He closed his eyes as if meditating for a split-second, and continued in a normal speaking tone. "Citizens were resisting reinsertion to the simulation."

"Shit," whispered Alex. "T-that's the Council of Four."

Kevin glanced back at him. "There's five people..."

Alex gestured toward the standing figure. "That's the Speaker." He exhaled. "This is unbelievable. No one but the upper administrators have ever met them face to face."

"No shit?" whispered Kevin. "*These* four old people are what everyone's afraid of?"

"That's Director Gerhardt on the right. She's the Prime Council. Doesn't have *too* much more power than the rest, but she usually gets whatever she wants. Director Khan"—he pointed at the dark-skinned woman—"she's fairly new to the council, only about four years. Whitford's been on it like forever. Same with Kuroyama."

"All we ever see of them is still images and sometimes a recording," said the youngest ISF man. "The Speaker's everywhere. Floating head always talking. All the information the Council needs to pass to the people goes through him."

"Yeah…" He sighed. "Tris said that. I don't think she likes him much."

"What are you doing down there?" roared the Speaker at his podium. He pounded his fist on the top twice. "Find a way to stop it and start getting our people back into their pods."

A faint warble of a voice emanated from the podium.

Kuroyama screamed at a middle-aged man with spiky black hair and military armor on a monitor in front of him. "You're telling me that *all* of the equipment has failed at once? Do you honestly expect me to believe that?"

"Stalemate?" yelled the Speaker, at whoever he had on video chat. "What do you mean the soldiers are refusing to fire? They're traitors, not citizens!"

Whitford, the not-quite-fifty looking man with brown hair, cleared his throat while pointing at something on his section of the giant desk. "A combined force of ISF and military are approaching the council chambers."

"There are still some loyal men out there." Gerhardt stopped rubbing her forehead and sat straighter. "Vogel, put something together to counteract that media kit. Make them understand we are acting in their best interest."

The Speaker's face reddened. "Do you not think I haven't been trying? I've sent four speeches to the distribution cluster, and each time it begins playing, that same young woman appears telling them the truth. These people can't be trusted with the truth. They don't understand the danger."

Shouting from outside became apparent beyond the far wall.

"Perhaps it is time for us to consider relocating to somewhere less conspicuous," said Director Khan.

"And go where?" Gerhardt glared at her. "The entire Enclave is currently engulfed in the throes of chaos. Are you so eager to head off into the wasteland?"

Khan gasped and fanned herself. "You cannot be serious. It's not fit for human habitation."

Oh, fuck this.

Kevin swept the curtain aside and stepped out. "Am I late for bingo?"

The Council of Four froze as if time had stopped—except for Khan who screamed and clutched her chest.

Tarl and the others crept out behind him. Alex gave him a 'huh' face.

"Bingo… it's a game old people play." Kevin chuckled. "I have no idea how it works, but I know old people play it. Sometimes they jump up and yell bingo." He pumped his fists overhead. "Sometimes they pee themselves… you know, old people."

Director Whitford coughed and looked insulted.

"Okay, people." Kevin clapped. "Oh, I'm forgetting something." He pulled the Enclave pistol and almost pointed it at them. "There. Now that I have your attention… I think it's time for you to take a good look at the situation."

"Who do you think you are?" asked the Speaker, invoking a deep bass voice that might've frightened a boy… or someone who gave a shit.

"Me? I'm just some asshole from the Wildlands who's sick and fucking tired of dodging goddamned zombies." He raised his left hand as if about to swear an oath. "I know, I know… They're not technically dead. You think that matters to a little girl watchin' her whole city turn against itself?"

"*You* are from the Wildlands?" asked Gerhardt. Her severe presence eased a bit with genuine surprise before she recovered herself and glowered at him as if her words could kill. "How did you get in here?"

"Same way you were about to go out. Handy little elevator. The wet bar was a nice touch." He smiled. "So, here's the truth… and I know the five of you ain't really on speaking terms with the truth, but I'm gonna try anyway. Your virus… all gone. Burned that shit myself. Five thousand degree incinerator. No more exterminating the innocent. Your people? Yeah, we kinda let 'em out. Doesn't seem to me like they're too happy being stuck in the freezer like leftovers."

"Why are you officers standing there doing nothing?" bellowed the Speaker. "Remove that man."

"Well, for one thing"—Tarl took a step forward, his rifle held sideways across his chest—"the law doesn't explicitly give the Council the legal authority to murder at will. Two, *you* don't actually have any authority or political power. You're a mouthpiece; you don't give anyone orders. Three, we saw the drone footage of those settlements. Agent-94's been wiping out innocent settlers for years. That ain't what any of us signed on for."

Fear showed in the faces of the council, except Gerhardt, who held herself calm, though her slightly narrowed eyes suggested she schemed, or perhaps considered.

"A friend of mine went and got herself lost around town. Tryin' to find her, and we kinda made a wrong turn and wound up here. But..." Kevin grinned. "Since I'm here, I might as well at least say hello to the people who cooked up the idea to spray that shit around. Thanks for the nightmares and stuff by the way. Haven't had a good night's sleep since I was small. Now I gotta kid to take care of who watched her whole damn city implode on itself with paranoia. They shot her father right in front of her. I gotta look into those wide brown eyes every damn night and come up with something to say that makes sense when she asks me why people would do such a thing..."

"Traitors, all of you!" shouted the Speaker at the ISF men. He jabbed a button on the podium. "Get in here now, we've—"

Kevin shot the podium, causing an eruption of sparks that made the older man jump back. "I'm still searching for the reason why I haven't just fucking ended all of you..." He touched two fingers to his forehead for a second and flicked his hand at them. "Damn, you know sometimes that 'humanity' thing gets in the way."

"What do you want?" asked Gerhardt, sounding calm.

"Mostly, I want to find my girl and go the hell home and live in a world without having to watch the friggin' sky all the time for zombie juice... or worry about what kind of marauders are running around hopped up on synthetic narcotics and slingin' around weapons you people are throwing out there." He pointed the gun at the grey-haired woman. "Tell me one thing. Do you really believe the world is disease-ridden and unfit to live in, or do you like killing people for the fuck of it?"

"Uhh, he's pointing a gun at Director Gerhardt," whispered the teenaged ISF officer. "Should we stop him?"

"There are reports indicating that several new strains of pathogen have developed as a result of unexpected interactions with gamma and beta radiation." Gerhardt stared at him, hands on her knees, her tone as even as if she spoke to an old friend who didn't have a gun trained on her face. "Our people have lived in isolation for so long it seemed only logical to eliminate dangerous tribes of nomadic scavengers."

"You're actually talking to this caveman?" yelled the Speaker.

Kuroyama grumbled to himself before shaking his head. "We have other things to worry about now than making the world clean."

"Clean?" Kevin switched to aim at him. "You call a biological weapon attack that has claimed hundreds of thousands... probably more, lives... *cleaning?*"

"The information we had suggested less than two thousand." Gerhardt looked down at her lap. "We thought them all... what is the word you use? Raiders? Slavers? Killers? Savages... People whom the world would be better off without."

Kevin clenched his jaw. "There's a couple of those kinda people right here."

The Speaker scoffed. "Indeed."

Gerhardt shot the old man a warning look. "By the time the reconnaissance drone program had developed to the point where more accurate intelligence became available to us, the agent was already loose. I ordered the program stopped once I learned the true... scope."

"It's still going on." Kevin glared. "They hit Amarillo only months ago. Who knows how many others?"

"What?" Gerhardt looked up, shocked. "Months ago? I never authorized a launch of live agent."

"That was probably our ol' friend Nathan." Kevin scowled. "Still going after Tris."

Gerhardt's jaw shifted and her glare hardened. "I gave that man a direct order."

"What does it matter?" asked the Speaker. "Fewer tribals to remove later on. This fiasco has cost us decades. Our population won't be able to thrive out there at current levels. We need at least another ten thousand."

Tribals? He squeezed the pistol grip, making his hand shake. "We did a number on your computer thingee. There's no going back. As Tris would say, it's time to open the doors and join the world."

"Absolutely not!" roared the Speaker. "Again, I say, why are we still talking with this cretin? We cannot allow the taint of the outside world in."

"Agreed," said Kuroyama.

"It's too dangerous." Khan nodded.

Whitford glanced at Kevin with a contemplative look, but kept quiet.

Gerhardt pursed her lips as if in thought.

"Right now, our priorities need to be getting our citizens back where they are safe"—the Speaker gesticulated at the smoking podium—"and repairing the damage these savages have unleashed."

Director Gerhardt stared down her nose at the Speaker, a hint of a smile showing. "If they're such savages, how have they managed to turn our entire computer system against us?"

The Speaker's face reddened further. "We have spent the past thirty years working to ensure that humanity continues into the future. I will not sit back and tolerate talk of abandoning all we've worked for. There is no discussion. There is no negotiation."

Kevin glanced at the gun. Tris' voice in the back of his mind pleaded with him not to kill a helpless old man. "You've been working for bullshit. Opening the gate is your only option now... unless you're willing to kill more than half your people." He gestured at Gerhardt. "And this one almost had a damn stroke over Nathan getting a handful of soldiers killed."

"Enough!" roared the Speaker. "You are in the Enclave. We are the future of Earth. You do not even deserve to be breathing the same air—"

Bang!

The Speaker's head exploded in a shower of gore.

Kevin raised an arm to shield from the spatter while ducking and hopping to the side. "Fucking hell..." He glanced at the front end of the room.

Above the rows of empty seats, in the middle of a pair of wobbling double doors, stood Tris.

Holding a smoking rifle.

"I've wanted to shut that guy up since I was nine..." She lowered the rifle and marched down the aisle, followed by a naked woman who could've been her somewhat older sister. "He *never* stops talking, and he's frickin' *everywhere.*"

Tris! Kevin rushed to the right, ducking around Gerhardt's chair and heading down a short stairway to meet her at the base of the auditorium.

In the shadow of the Council's tall desk, he wrapped his arms around her and held on; she kept her rifle trained on the four elders. The angle lined his gaze up with a pair of bare breasts on the woman behind her.

He blinked. "Is that a Persephone? Oh, and don't mind those ISF guys… they're with us."

"Yep," said Tris. "Nathan thought it would be ironic for me to kill myself."

34

THE FUTURE OF HUMANITY

T ris held back the need to cling to Kevin and forget the world existed. She glared at the Council, finding them far less intimidating than they'd been when she thought they lived in the center of the Core City surrounded by thousands of soldiers. In person, they seemed so fragile.

"Okay. Now we can talk." Tris stared at Gerhardt. "I'm a little emotional right now, so if I accidentally shoot someone else in the face, don't take it personally."

Kuroyama pointed at the Persephone. "Android, by order of the Council, kill these invaders."

"I'm sorry, Director Kuroyama." The Persephone stood statue still. "A command has been processed at a higher security level that is in direct contradiction. I am unable to comply."

"What?" He blinked. "What is going on here?"

"My father was Doctor Ian Jameson... you know, the crazy old man who invented them. Apparently, he didn't want his inventions being used against him. Or his family. Persephone, if any of them try to give you a command again, please tear off a random arm and beat them to death with it."

"Command accepted," said the android. "Please clarify if you prefer true random or pseudorandom limb selection."

The Council all shifted in their seats.

"How did you get in here?" blurted Director Khan.

Tris grinned. "Watching a Persephone throw a man through a concrete wall convinced the soldiers they might be on the wrong team... now where was I?"

Kevin leaned close and whispered, "Why is this one talking like Bee, but the one I ran into with the Redeemed acted like a person?"

She smiled. "I haven't told her to load a personality matrix yet. She's more intimidating that way. Later. I want to go the hell home."

"Right." He took a step away for some room and kept his pistol ready.

"Gerhardt... I'm sure you know that the Enclave is not equipped to support its true population as you've got things set up. Nice fake out on the Core City by the way... I really believed it." She exhaled a somber sigh. "We're all kinda circling the drain right now. There's a good chance that maybe humans were meant to die off. When we pushed the proverbial button and burned down the sky, we pretty well screwed ourselves. Maybe forty years from now, there won't be anyone left no matter what we do. And if the Enclave is working *against* the rest of humanity, it's not a question—we will die out."

The ISF officers moved closer, standing as if holding the Council under guard.

Tris glanced at them. "As it was before today, the Enclave only hurried this along. People out there, they didn't want to give up. They tried. They established settlements, created trade routes, farms... an attempt at civilization. We had no right to destroy them simply for not being privileged enough to have been born inside these walls.

"Are there bandits, raiders, slavers, and people who deserve to die out there? Sure. It's not like those hist... I mean movies made it look like. There's maybe one slaver for every three hundred settlers, and that's probably overestimating. It seems worse because they band together."

"And you fuckers help them," said Kevin. "Sending them weapons, drugs like Void Salt, vehicles... trying to kick us into the ground all that much faster."

Gerhardt tapped her finger on the desk, glancing away and down. Kuroyama continued to stare at the Persephone as if he expected it to shoot him any second. Khan trembled in her chair.

Whitford leaned back, hands flat on the desk. "What are you proposing we do?"

The noise of rioting outside grew louder.

"Like I said, there's a chance nothing will matter. Maybe the war, the virus, and greed have already killed us all. But… if the Enclave *helps* rebuild, it could be different. If you use the technology we've preserved and improved on in the fifty-one years since the war… we might actually survive. I've been out there. There's no mutant diseases. We're not going to choke to death on the air or drop dead as soon as we eat something not grown in a hydroponic tank. It's *all* bullshit. Question is, did you make up the bullshit or do you believe it too?"

"Dust hoppers are kinda a mutant," whispered Kevin. "I don't think they had seventy pound rabbits before the war."

An uneasy noise leaked from Director Khan's stomach.

"The people within these walls can help humanity get on its feet." Tris looked back and forth among them.

"What if we disagree?" asked Gerhardt.

"Either the Council disbands. Or"—she aimed at Gerhardt—"you all atone for the people the Enclave has murdered."

"And," said Dad-AI from ceiling-mounted speakers. "I will permanently disable the reactor, which will force you to move into the world and find a new source of power. I doubt quite sincerely that even Amarillo has enough solar panels to meet your current energy demands."

Gerhardt chuckled, shaking her head. "I'm surprised you're not demanding to take over."

Tris walked left, up three steps to the dais, and stopped at Gerhardt's side. "That's never what I wanted. I don't know what Nathan told you about me, or what you assumed about me based on what you feared my father had planned, but I'm not after power. Nothing I did was ever motivated by a desire to be in charge. I wanted a life of my own, not be told who I can or can't love, not be shut in a giant human hamster cage. The Enclave… or whatever it will become in the next few weeks, is humanity's best chance to continue and maybe even get back some quality of life."

Khan mumbled to herself. Her expression said she wanted to object, but the woman either lacked a compelling argument or the nerve to voice it. Kuroyama glared at Tris with barely contained hostility. If not for the rifles hovering around him—and a Persephone waiting to rip someone's arm off—he'd likely have attacked her, or at least slapped her by now.

"The Council's power is over," said Tris. "The Enclave needs to change… and the war against innocent people must stop."

CLEANSING

Tris glanced down the length of the rifle at Gerhardt's chest. After a little over a minute of silent staring, she shifted so the weapon pointed in a neutral direction. "Well?"

"We still don't have enough information about the dangers of the outside," said Gerhardt, her voice weak, defeated.

"It's exaggerated," said Tris. "Your predecessor wanted a 'perfect society' ruled by an iron fist."

"You've been deceived, child." Gerhardt looked up at her, weary steel-grey eyes struggling to project sympathy. "Your father is the one who invented the virus you so passionately despise. He was the founder of the Enclave. Everything that's happened here has been his plan all along."

"Helena," said Dad-AI. "If you're going to feed my daughter bullshit, at least have the decency to serve *good* bullshit."

An explosion of light welled up in a banner over the Council's desk, dozens of holographic panels streamed with text data, pictures, charts, and video. A few screens enlarged, bearing emails among members of a 'planning council' discussing the need to modify Jameson's bio agent into a weapon that could 'purge the filth' from the world so 'we can take it back.' Images flicked to later emails and a video message showing a fiftyish man with a strong familial resemblance to Gerhardt detailing the need to eliminate Jameson as he 'cannot see the necessity in the plan.' One called him 'too idealistic.' Another screen enlarged with a chain of emails to select 'replacement parents' for Tris, who they would have simply killed if not for their worry that Jameson somehow buried things in the system that would require her later on down the line. They expressed quite clearly the selection process for 'extremely loyal' individuals to serve as surrogate parents.

"I have all of it, Helena. Your father was nothing if not thorough in his record keeping."

Gerhardt gasped and stared at Kuroyama. "Is this true? The files I was given on Jameson when I took office… They were falsified."

"Women are prone to being too idealistic and emotional." Kuroyama scowled at Tris. "We expected you to hesitate on certain matters. The Enclave couldn't afford to have a Primus who let emotion get the better of them. You were presented with the information you needed to function in the best interests of the people."

"Which people?" snapped Tris. "The three of you or the half a million dead because a handful of assholes in lab coats couldn't read a damn chart and thought the world toxic?"

"It was you." Gerhardt pointed at Kuroyama. "No wonder Nathan got away with half the things he did. You were helping him… and continuing to send Agent-94 out into the world after I ordered that program shut down. It was… too indiscriminate."

"You never should've seen those recon feeds." Kuroyama folded his arms. "Video of a handful of farmers with children doesn't prove the world is survivable. They'll probably grow third legs or blow up with tumors by the time they hit puberty."

Gerhardt bowed her head. "I've been… lied to." She lifted her head with the apparent effort of moving a boulder, and made eye contact with Tris. "I'm sorry. For what it's worth, I'm sorry. You're right. We cannot keep on going like this. We're breeding ourselves into extinction."

"You're being foolish, woman," said Kuroyama. "We are the Enclave."

"Now you're sounding like the jackass with the exploded head." Kevin pointed his pistol at the Japanese man. "One more remark about women out of you, and it's going to be the Council of Three."

Alex chuckled.

A window popped open on the desk in front of Director Khan. A man in a military helmet, bulky, ponderous, and bedecked with hoses connected to his nonfunctional Hoplite appeared.

"Directors… We are unable to hold the perimeter as ordered. Half of my personnel are defecting. There are thousands of people coming out of stasis. They're not listening to orders."

"Probably a bit pissed off at being lied to and kept frozen against their will." Tris smiled as the roar of rioting crowd at the top of the auditorium grew even louder. "It probably no longer matters what the Council wants. Your power is gone." She lowered her rifle and took Kevin's hand. "Come on. Let's go home."

Kevin cocked an eyebrow. "You don't want to kill them?"

Tris sighed. "They deserve it for what they did, but no... I think being exiled into the Wildlands is going to be far worse for them than the instantaneous justice of a bullet. More poetic too." She looked at Gerhardt. "Your dread of the outside world is all in your head. You might even like it out there."

Kuroyama eyed the ISF men. "You traitors plan to simply stand there doing nothing?"

"Sorry, sir," said Alex. "I've been debating placing you all under arrest for war crimes, but I'm not entirely sure it's worth the paperwork."

Tris slung the rifle over her shoulder and pulled Kevin into a long, deep kiss. The fear that had taken her while strapped to the chair came back, and she clung to him tight to chase away the dread she'd felt at the idea of never seeing him again. Basking in his presence calmed her. Her body wanted sleep, craved a few hours of ignoring the world, and went limp. She let him hold her up, moving only enough to keep kissing him. Soon, tears of joy ran down her cheeks, and she clung to keep from collapsing to the floor.

"Is this real? Am I in VR? I can't believe we really did it."

His arms squeezed tight around her. "*You* did it... I only twisted a few valves and gave some crazy, idealistic woman a ride to Harrisburg."

36

REUNION

A sudden clamor of activity by the chamber's main entrance stole the laugh from Tris' throat. She peered over Kevin's shoulder up the aisle. An army swarmed in; more than half of them wore only the dried residue of stasis tank slime streaked with blood from wounds that nanites had already healed. All had armed themselves. Most appeared to be around eighteen, likely frozen as soon as they 'went off to University.' Here and there, those without white hair stood out as if someone had thrown colored paint at random into the crowd.

"Uh oh," muttered Kevin. "Nothing good ever happens when a huge crowd of armed, bloody, angry, naked people storm a room." He chuckled. "Didn't this used to be a college? Probably not the first time a mob like this has run around."

"What?" asked Tris.

"Uhh, movie I saw." He overacted an innocent face. "I may have been too little to be allowed to watch that particular movie."

Tris pulled away from Kevin, raising a hand to the crowd in a gesture she hoped they'd take as greeting. In seconds, the auditorium had filled with citizens. The mass of people swelled wide at the bottom, surrounding Tris and Kevin before spilling up onto the dais. Tris resumed breathing as the ones nearest her aimed their weapons at the Council.

"It's her," said a young woman near the middle. The shape of her small body vanished amid a black jumpsuit much too large for her. "Tris?"

The ISF men by the curtain exchanged a few tense words with the nearest citizens, but soon tensions between the two groups faded. None of the crowd pointed weapons at the ISF, who remained hesitant to aim theirs at the Council.

"Yeah." Tris nodded at the girl. She looked at a nude man within arm's reach. "Guess you're in a hurry?"

"Most of us haven't been out of pods for a full ten minutes yet," said a man a little deeper in the crowd.

"Kill them!" shouted a female voice near the middle of the room.

"No!" yelled Tris.

A hush swept over the citizens.

Dammit. I hate being stared at by two *people much less two hundred.* Grumbling, Tris pulled herself up on the dais, and faced the room with her arms raised.

"You've grown up being fed lies about the supposed barbarians of the Wildlands. Don't turn into them. Before the war, humanity had a system of law and government that we should attempt to preserve."

"Yay, politics," whispered Kevin.

"We can't arrest them," said the same girl in the oversized jumpsuit. "There's no jail here... you showed us Detention was really VR. And you burned out that system."

Tris nodded. "It had to be done, or they might've put you all back in prison. That's what it was." She lowered her hands. "I'm not going to tell you what to do. I have no interest in remaining here. I have a home I want to get back to. You'll need to decide for yourselves where to go from here, though I sincerely hope that you listen to my father's ghost and open the Enclave to the world."

"If we're not going to kill them or freeze them, what do we do with the Council?" shouted a man.

"Either build a prison or... exile them. I think that would punish them more." She paused to breathe. "And I don't mean the Council's definition of exile as a euphemism for murder... I mean real exile."

Director Kuroyama leapt from his chair, hurling himself at Tris from behind. He got a hand on the rifle slung across her back as he came down on his chest and slid forward over the desk. She stumbled to the right, knocking a flat panel monitor into Gerhardt's lap and two others to the floor. Kuroyama's momentum sent him spilling past her. She twisted to the right, tearing her rifle from his grip.

About thirty people shot him the instant he hit the floor.

Kuroyama's body convulsed under a hail of bullets; he gurgled and went still, lying atop an expanding seep darkening the pale grey carpet.

Director Khan screamed.

"Idiot," said Kevin.

Tris sighed. "No… He knew what would happen; he committed suicide." She glanced at the remaining three elders. For some reason, she almost felt bad for Gerhardt. Almost.

"Exile," said a muscular woman on the dais.

"Exile," repeated a man next to her.

The word swept over the crowd like rain, two or three, ten, then a deafening chorus.

Gerhardt bowed her head, calm and reserved, though dread showed clear in her eyes.

Director Khan burst into sobs. "Please don't. At my age… You can't send us out there." She calmed, blinking as sudden inspiration took her. "The old legal system had an appeal process. I wish to appeal."

"I'm sure the half-million or so who died to the Virus would've liked an appeal too," said Tris. "If I were you, the first thing I'd do is get rid of that fancy Enclave suit and never tell anyone out there who you are. I don't think it's possible for you to meet a single person who wouldn't jump at the chance to kill the ones responsible for setting that horror loose on the world."

"How's this gonna work, then?" asked Tarl.

Tris looked from him to Alex to the front row in the crowd. "I don't know why everyone keeps asking me questions. I don't have the answers. The only thing that differentiates me from you is that I saw through the bullshit first. Don't trust anyone from the administration."

"And she's got a combat package," muttered Kevin. "And a great ass, awesome legs, perfect boobs…"

She blushed.

"Good advice," said Not-Dad from the speakers. "I believe I can provide some assistance in that regard."

Most of the citizens looked up with expressions of awe.

"It's not God. It's an AI," said Kevin.

"Wait," asked the girl in the too-large suit. "You're just going to leave?"

"Yep." Tris jumped down to the floor and walked up to Kevin. "We can stay a bit longer to talk about the outside world. I'll help as much as I can, but this isn't my home." *It never was.*

"Tris?" yelled a familiar sounding woman.

"It *is* her," said a familiar sounding man.

Oh, crap. Tris closed her eyes. *If there is a God up there, please let Mom2 and Dad2 have clothes.*

She opened her eyes as a hand grabbed her forearm.

Mom2, Yana according to the AI copy of her real father, stared at her as if looking at a dead person back from the grave. Mercifully, she had appropriated a jumpsuit, blood soaked from the waist up. A few spots of chalky skin showed from bullet holes in the torso, and the five or six inches of her snow-white hair that hung past the shoulders had soaked it up, turning pink. Despite having to be fortyish, the woman didn't appear much older than Tris.

"Tris..." She let go of her arm to cover her mouth.

"Hey kiddo," said Dad2. He had no blood on him, though his clothing consisted of a pale blue bath towel held around his waist by a closed fist. As soon as she looked up at him, he threw his free arm around her back and squeezed.

The AI had called him Marcus, but she'd sooner call him Dad2 to his face. After she gave up insisting that she'd been adopted, every time she'd called him 'Dad' had made her feel guilty, like she'd kicked Doctor Jameson deeper into his grave.

"We're sorry." Yana looked down. "For not believing you."

Tears brimmed across Marcus' eyelids. "We... thought you were ours."

Ugh. "It's not your fault. I'm not angry with you anymore. The AI showed me how they set you up to believe I was really your daughter. I don't know why they ran it in real time without compression... normally sixteen weeks of VR pass in one real week."

"Nine years is too long for a single session to be time compressed. The brain can't handle the rapid influx of data. It would've felt false and might've caused brain damage." Marcus slid his hand from her shoulder up to cradle her cheek. "I realize what happened, but I can't help but think of you as mine."

Tris slung the rifle from her shoulder and handed it to Kevin before embracing her foster parents. "You basically *were* my parents for nine years. I used to think you were part of the conspiracy, but you really did believe I was crazy." She sniffled. "I don't mind continuing to think of you as my parents, but you should know..."

Yana smiled and cried. "We wondered what had happened to you.

You'd been so sweet up until nine... and then every time you smiled at us it felt like you were hiding something. Like one day you all of a sudden couldn't stand us and... were afraid."

Tris looked down. "That's the day we left VR. The daughter you thought you had was a computer program."

The ISF, and a handful of armed citizens, herded the remaining three members of the Council out through the crowd at gunpoint. Kevin shook hands with Alex and the youngest as they passed close enough.

"They tried to give me a memory overlay that would've made me believe I'd grown up with you my whole life. The AI blocked it... as far as I knew, you were adoptive parents they put me with less than a day after they told me my dad died in an accident at his lab." She sighed. "I took in a kid, and... even if you weren't conditioned to believe you'd given birth to me, it doesn't matter. You're my parents."

Marcus smiled and wiped a tear or two.

"Tris..." Yana clamped onto her and sniffled.

"She does kinda resemble you," said Kevin. "Almost the same shade of blue eyes."

"Umm... Mom... Dad... this is Kevin." Tris put a hand on his shoulder and pulled him closer. "He... uhh... we..."

Kevin's face showed a little red.

Her parents exchanged glances.

Say it. I can say it. "We're... well... married."

Yana gasped. "No..."

Tris' eyebrows furrowed. "Yes. We are."

"I mean..." Yana looked at Kevin. "You haven't had any kind of ceremony have you? We weren't there. I don't know what you did. Where were you? They said Detention and the next thing we know you're out and everything is going crazy. Where did he come from?"

Kevin laughed.

Oh... maybe it was better being an orphan. She flashed a cheesy smile. "It's a long story. I've spent about nine months out in the Wildlands. I've got a daughter"—she held up a calming hand—"adopted. Who I feel ten shades of awful for leaving behind to come here. I'm going home soon."

"Home?" asked Marcus. "I suppose we could make room."

"No, Dad." She leaned on Kevin. "We're going to Nederland. This place is... a little too crazy."

"But what about the pairing? Dovarin seemed like such a charming man." Yana blinked, looking confused as to why she wouldn't want him.

"That program was only needed because the Enclave is so isolated." She scowled. "And if Dovarin comes within five feet of me, he's going to wind up missing something rather critical to his anatomy." Tris stared at her hand for a second before making a fist. "As a matter of fact, I'm not quite the same weak little flower I used to be. Maybe I'll pay him back for that mark he left on my face."

"What?" asked Yana. "Mark? What happened?"

"Okay, Mom. I guess if I'm going to accept you as my parents, I should open up with you. I had trust issues after that whole 'she's crazy' situation." Tris looked down. "I thought I'd say something wrong and you'd ship me off to a padded cell or something."

"We had no idea," said Marcus.

"I know that *now*." She held a breath for a second, exhaled, and made eye contact with Mom2. "Dovarin... that son of a bitch hit me within a half hour of being alone with him. He didn't want a wife, he wanted a toy."

Yana gasped. Marcus glowered at the crowd. "I thought I saw him outside somewhere... It was a complete mess. ISF shooting at soldiers. Soldiers shooting at soldiers..."

"The First Tier Administration and the Council had about two hundred military personnel who somehow decided to remain loyal even in the face of the truth," said Not-Dad from above. "The fighting is ebbing at this point. A handful of holdouts have fled into the Wildlands. I counted twenty-eight of fifty members of the first through third tiers gunned down by a vengeful mob. People are starting to calm."

"What about asshole?" asked Kevin.

"I'm sorry. There are no residents of the enclave with that name," said Not-Dad.

Kevin gave Tris the side-eye. "And you say *I'm* a literal bastard."

"Dovarin? He is not dead." The AI paused for a second. "He was wounded, but he's filtered in among the crowd, acting like one of those freed from the pods."

"They'll recognize him eventually." Tris frowned. "He's not worth the effort... though I would like to give him a good shot across the jaw."

Yana gasped. Marcus blinked with a surprised grin.

"I told you, I'm not the same little timid thing I used to be." Tris hugged Marcus and lifted him off his feet for a second.

"She's had some work," said Kevin.

Tris smirked at him.

Marcus patted her on the back and laughed. "I'm glad to see you smiling. I... we've always wondered what we did that you turned into this gloomy, sorrowful little wraith."

"Sorry." Tris bowed her head. "I thought you were part of the lie. Well, I mean you were, but not for wanting to be. And... I think some part of me remembered before the war. I was so little, but the Enclave never truly felt 'real' to me. More like I'd been trapped in some strange, future-techno dream that I couldn't wake up from. I didn't feel like I belonged here. I still don't. I'm going back to Nederland. You two can come with us if you want, but I can't stay here."

Marcus hummed with an exhale, and sent an uneasy glance toward the door. "Out there? Are you sure that's what you want? I mean... they exile people as the greatest punishment."

"Dad..." *It's going to take a while to get used to calling him that.* "They conditioned everyone to think of it as horrible. It's not... I mean, okay it's got its shitty bits, but for the most part it's fine. The technology is lacking, but as this place pulls its collective crap together and starts contributing to the world instead of trying to destroy it..." She choked up. "I haven't felt hope in a long time."

"Well, they did kind of misplace our house." Marcus chuckled. "I couldn't even find it. A lot changed out here in nine years. Wow. Core City never existed. I'm still trying to process that."

"Your house doesn't exist either. Simulation, remember." Tris sighed. "You don't have a home to go back to."

Yana gave Tris a look equal parts happy and terrified. "I suppose we could try your Nederland for a little while. If it doesn't work out, we can come back."

Tris spun into Kevin's arms and kissed him. "I don't know about you, but I am *done* with this place."

"Me too." He nodded at the door. "Any idea how to get back to Amaranth?"

She shrugged. "Well I could always go back the way we came."

He paled.

"No. I said *I*. You are staying right here away from possible Infected in the subway."

He pulled her tight against him. "You know I'm going to go crazy with worry if we split up."

"You won't worry; you'll be unconscious." She winked. "Did I mention my dad is a doctor?"

"So?"

"Hey, Dad." Tris knocked on Kevin's sternum. "Can you fix my man up here with 'some of them Nanites?'"

Kevin laughed.

37

WISHES

After two days of long driving, 'the parents' still sat ramrod straight in the back seat of the Challenger, stuffed into a pile of children's clothes. They stared out the windows with the kind of faces Kevin expected he'd make if someone had taken him on a safari tour through a city full of Infected. They seemed afraid to touch anything.

'The Parents' had more or less kept silent following Tris' retelling of what had happened in Amarillo. They couldn't believe that their Enclave would use such a horrible weapon at all, much less on innocent people. She'd gotten a little short with them, perhaps a taste of what the last year or two of her 'home life' had been like before Detention. He had to keep a hand over his mouth. She'd sounded so much like a teenager while shouting at them he started to feel like a dirty old man.

At least it made for a quiet ride.

Ugh. Kevin shifted in his seat and rubbed the middle of his chest. A slight pressure in his chest felt like a tiny rock balanced atop his heart. According to Marcus, random tingles and pins would continue for a few more days as his new nanites acclimated to his 'DNA profile,' whatever that meant, and repaired old scars. To him it had felt like only a minute or two had gone by, but Tris had been sitting next to him, already returned from the Resistance hideout with his stuff, Amaranth, the Challenger, and the rest of the crew in tow.

She'd spent the ride in the Persephone's lap, rather 'Nikki's.' Since the artificial woman had apparently helped her deal with Nathan, she invited her to Nederland, and the android accepted. At some point between a four-hour meeting with what remained of the leadership structure of the ISF and their leaving, she'd found the time to issue some command or whatever to the android. She didn't act like Bee anymore, or even like Snow, the one he'd met at Pinos Altos. 'Nikki' wasn't scary or intimidating at all despite what that body could do. In some ways, the personality had come out like Tris. Not *quite* as...

He smiled to himself.

Not quite as 'adorable.' Nikki had a soft spot for people who needed a little help, but perhaps that part of her still controlled by tactical analysis algorithms kept her from being like Tris—no regard for personal danger when she *had* to help someone. Seeing the artificial woman giggle and tell jokes like some ordinary twenty-five-ish person unnerved him more than the emotionless android throwing people through walls.

He shivered, picturing the hole in the front of the Council building he'd seen on the way out. The soldier who'd raised a weapon at Tris had more or less liquefied inside his armor when the android hurled him through the wall.

With each mile closer to Nederland, his anxiety grew. Tris told him a drone had been within spitting distance, loaded with Virus. As far as the AI-dad-thing knew, it had turned the drone back before it released any of its payload. Bullet holes in things carrying liquid doom seemed like a horrible idea... who knew what might've leaked.

Kevin rubbed his thumb back and forth across the little plastic button that would unload the M60s on the hood while picturing everyone in Ned lost to the infection. In his mind, Emma perked up from the gate as she so often did to wave when he pulled up, but this time she'd be staring at him with 'nobody home' eyes and bleeding sores on her face.

His knuckles creaked on the wheel.

Tris and Nikki looked at him.

"Can't wait to get back." He kept his gaze forward. *That android really does look like her older sister.*

Before too long, he followed the road west away from Boulder.

"Are those... trucks?" asked Yana.

He snapped out of his fog, startled by the appearance of Nederland's gate. He hadn't even noticed it in his morose thousand-yard stare. Much to his relief, a smiling (and quite normal-looking) Emma jumped up and down on the left side truck. After a few seconds, the thirteen-year-old guard trained a pair of binoculars on them.

Kevin waved and smiled.

Old Socrates emerged next, still wearing the same battered duster coat and hat.

Emma yelled something that reached the Challenger only as a high-pitched warble, and jumped down. The dump truck bin on the left shuddered open. Emma darted across the road to the other side. Kevin rolled to a halt for less than four seconds before the other truck bed scraped over the paving to open.

"Yes, I do believe those are trucks," said Marcus.

"You're back!" Emma ran up to Tris' door and grabbed on. "What happened?"

Tris put her hand on top of Emma's. "It's over. We destroyed the Virus, and all the drones. I'll tell you the whole thing sometime. Right now, I need to get home."

"Yeah." Emma nodded. "Abby's been kind of a mess. She's hanging on, but she'll be thrilled to have you back."

"Thanks." Tris looked down as they pulled away from the gate.

Kevin felt the same guilt, but let it out on a sigh. "She'll understand."

"I hope so," whispered Tris.

He drove through the town, drawing a small group of curious followers, and pulled off the road onto the grass to the right of their house.

"Well, place is still standing." Kevin shut down the car's six switches. "Oh, damn do I need to stretch my legs."

He opened the door and got out before pulling the seat forward to give Marcus room to leave the car with his case of Enclave-tech medical supplies. They'd last a few months here, but a trip to get more once the dust settled would likely occur.

Abby's scream carried from down the road back by Bill's place. Her long brown hair trailed behind her and she made it about halfway before her haste sent her moccasins flying. Kevin left Marcus to fend for himself and rushed around the back end of the car. Tris sprinted to Abby, catching her in a kneeling hug a short distance away from the house.

Everything Abby tried to say came out as sobbing. She reached toward Kevin as he jogged over. Tris stood, lifting Abby off her feet. Kevin embraced the pair of them; such relief and joy washed over him he couldn't find words.

"Kevin!" squealed Zoe. She hit him in the side like a blonde missile, grabbing on and cheering.

Abby clung to them both, bawling uncontrollably. A few times, she came close to forming words like 'you're alive,' or a slurred mumble ending in 'scared.'

Kevin cradled the back of her head in one hand. "We're sorry for scaring you."

"You're back." Abby sniffled, cried for a few seconds more, and gasped for air. "I was scared you weren't gonna make it."

Me too. "Well… we did, and you're stuck with us for a while now."

"We shot down drones," chirped Zoe.

"You did?" Tris gasped. "Or do you mean 'we' as in the town?"

Zoe puffed up her chest, fists on her hips. "I shot one down. Abby spotted it. Militia got another one 'couple days after… and me an' Abby shot at another one, but we scared it away."

Tris burst into tears.

Abby went still; all the color faded from her face. "That was the one, wasn't it? That one had the stuff in it…"

Kevin nodded.

"Uhh." Abby looked ready to throw up.

"It's all gone." Kevin patted her on the back.

Tris clung to them both, fighting back trembles. "All of it. There's no more Virus left in the world."

"Hey." Kevin reached into his armored jacket. "I brought you something."

Abby bit her lip and canted her eyebrows up in the middle.

He pulled out the silver cylinder. "This is a vaccine injector. It's like the one they gave Tris when she was a little kid. Younger than you are now. After this, even if an Infected bites you, you can't get sick. It won't be too long before the Infected are gone for good."

Tris kept rubbing Abby's back. "Some friends gave us that before we went to the Enclave. We had to get through a whole tunnel full of Infected. Kevin didn't take it. He wanted you to have it."

Abby hugged him before breaking down and crying into his shirt.

Kevin hadn't thought much about it, but Tris insisted Marcus inoculate him too. At least the extra half hour in the infirmary let them confirm the cylinder Amaranth gave them checked out. Since they had the means to verify, he couldn't think of giving it to Abby without being absolutely sure what it contained.

"You could've died," wailed Abby.

"Nah." Kevin ruffled her hair. "I'm too sneaky. And I had Tris to watch over me. I was only gonna run past Infected for a couple minutes. You needed to run through your dreams for a bunch of years still."

Abby looked up at him with a guilty smile. "I don't wanna ever catch it." She held out her arm. "Please?"

"Maybe it's a ass needle?" asked Zoe.

"Uhh." Abby glanced at her friend. "Is it?"

"Shoulder's fine," said Marcus, walking over. "Do you know how to work it or would you rather I administer it?"

"Who's that?" Abby shrank behind Kevin.

Tris smiled. "These are my parents. Mom, Dad, this is Abby."

Yana snapped out of a fog at staring around at the countryside. She smiled. "Hello."

How the heck did he do this? Kevin fiddled with the injector, twisting a ring at the back end that caused it to chirp. "Aha!"

"Push that little button there, and hold it against her arm for ten seconds," said Marcus.

Kevin grasped Abby's bicep in his left hand, and pressed the injector down until it made a hiss. She went up on tiptoe and grimaced, emitting a long 'eeeeee' sound a little louder than a whisper.

Bill, Zara, and a handful of militia came jogging up the road. Handshakes and hugs made the rounds.

"Well, it must've gone somewhat okay if you're back." Bill clapped Kevin on the shoulder.

"Yeah, it went okay." Kevin picked Abby up and perched her on his hip.

Zoe gave him a look.

He picked her up and perched her on the other hip. "Ugh... Two of you is too much." He feigned staggering under their weight, making them laugh.

Tris looked up at Abby and took her hand. "The people who were responsible for Amarillo have answered for what they did. The former Council of Four—sorry three—were given the choice of exile or death, and they all opted for exile."

Zara gawked. "Seriously?"

"Well, Kuroyama chose death." Kevin shook his head.

Abby sniffled and wiped her nose on her arm.

"We'll give you all a full rundown of what happened tomorrow. I'm exhausted and starving," said Tris. "Oh, Bill... These are my parents."

When his arms reached critical mass, Kevin eased the girls back to their feet. "Oookay. Enough. Sixteen hours of driving." He leaned forward a step to shake Bill's hand. "Thanks so much for watching her. Hope she wasn't too much trouble."

"She's got panic tacks and bad dreams, but I pa'tected her," said Zoe.

Blush crept over Abby's face as she looked down.

"Hmm," said Kevin, rubbing his chin. "I don't know anyone else with those."

Abby perked up with a grin and jumped into a hug. "You're really back... I'm not dreaming?"

"We're here." Kevin squeezed her. "Oh, hey Bill?"

"Yo?" Bill turned away from a mumbled conversation with the militia and approached.

"One, the drones are gone. Two, we found a store in the middle of Infected central. Got a ton of kid clothes." He pointed at the Challenger. "After Abby and Zoe grab their share, what do you wanna do with the rest? Oh yeah, got a machinegun and a couple thousand rounds of ammo for the militia as well."

Bill laughed. "Well, keep an eye on them so they don't take all of it... We'll send the rest down to Clare and Mitch. They'll get it distributed by size to whoever needs it the most. That'll take some of the load off the people sewin' up new stuff."

"Kevin! Tris!" said Bee. She ambled over and waved. "It is positive to register you on my optical sensors once more."

"You're doing that on purpose." He laughed and pulled Bee into a hug.

Bee hugged him back. "You find it humorous when I talk like that. I like to make you smile."

Nikki smiled and waved at everyone.

"Oh, yeah," said Kevin, pulling Bill close. "Nikki over there is a Persephone. Probably get her on the militia. Might want to let some of the guys know not to play grabass with her."

"What's a Persephone?" asked Bill.

"Long story, but for now..." He nodded at Bee. "Advanced cousin."

"Oh." Bill blinked. "One of *those*?"

"Yep. And she's on our side. Now..." Kevin picked Abby up again. "I need to make dinner. Hungry wife is angry wife."

Tris thumped him on the shoulder.

"There still needs to be a proper wedding," said Yana. "I insist."

"Yeah, yeah," muttered Kevin. "Let me recover from one near death experience first."

He carried Abby inside their *home*, Tris right behind him. The parents followed, as did Zoe, who insisted on having dinner there that night as well as a sleepover. Bee brought up the rear after having retrieved Abby's moccasins from the road.

Abby stayed in the chair he put her down in for all of four seconds before she came up behind him and held on. Kevin gave her hands a quick pat where she clasped them around him, and got to work on food.

"Everyone okay with dust hopper?" asked Kevin.

Yana gagged.

"What is a dust hopper?" asked Marcus.

"I'm ready to eat the plate." Tris rummaged the fridge. "I'll help so we can eat faster."

"It's good," said Abby. "You'll like it."

Kevin grinned to himself and fired up the stove. Abby held on the entire time he cooked.

TRIS KILLED NATHAN AGAIN IN HER DREAMS. THE SEVENTH TIME SHE stabbed him in the back, his body morphed into a giant block of 'beef spread,' a staple Enclave lunch product often smeared onto pitas.

The utter oddity of it woke her up.

She squinted at a sliver of sunlight that leaked in from the window. Her stomach churned, demanding beef paste and pears. The idea of combining those two particular flavors made her grab her gut and gag.

Kevin, at her side, snored with his mouth wide open.

Wow... we both slept late. She peered at the hollow between them where Abby had spent the night. Not like either of them had the energy to do much anyway. *She didn't wake up in the middle of the night... that's something.*

The room swirled around. Tris sat up fast, expecting to throw up, but only a cough came out. She held her head for a few seconds waiting for the dizzy to go away. *Great. I get a cold. All the technology of the Enclave, and nanites still can't kill colds.* She sat on the edge of the bed clutching the mattress on either side of her legs, head bowed. Deep breaths, in and out. The beginnings of a headache faded. *Okay, maybe this one won't be so bad. Maybe that meat spoiled.*

Abby padded in, still wearing her dust hopper hide dress despite her windfall of six or seven pieces from the clothing haul. "Mom?"

Tris looked up smiling. A tear ran down her cheek. "Yeah?"

"Is it okay if I go to the lake to swim? Zoe and a couple of other kids are going." She crept over, looking angelic, as if she *really* wanted to go and expected Tris to say no.

The last three times kids had asked her to go play before they left, she'd hid in her room. "You want to go?"

Abby nodded and raked her toes at the carpet. "Yeah. Can I?"

Sounds of impatient kids outside reached Tris' weary ears. "Will there be an adult there watching?"

"Yes." Abby clasped her hands in front. "Ann is gonna be there… and Cassie too."

A stabbing pain lanced her gut from an imaginary ten-inch long needle. She tensed, but kept it hidden. "All right. Stay careful, and come home for lunch."

"Thanks, Mom." Abby hugged her, headed to the door, and peered back. "Why don't you come swimming too?"

"Let me finish waking up first and I'll see how I feel."

"Okay." Abby grinned and darted off.

The soft *thump-thump-thump* of her running down carpeted stairs faded. Children's voices got loud for a second as the front door opened, and cut off when it closed.

Tris sighed and rubbed her stomach. "Ow."

Maybe someday she'd tell Abby about killing Nathan. Her arm clenched with the memory of the knife twist. *That was for Abby.* It seemed inappropriate to tell an eleven-year-old about such a grisly scene, so she'd left it at saying she'd personally killed the man who sent the Virus to Amarillo.

The need to pee swelled.

Tris stared at her crotch. "Go to hell."

"What did I do?" asked Kevin, behind her.

"Not you." She tried to shift her weight in a way that lessened the need to go.

He groaned and crawled out of bed. "Shit, we overslept pretty hard."

"Yeah."

Kevin headed for the door, scratching his stomach. "Gonna slap something together for breakfast… Where's Abby?"

"Swimming. Ann and Cassie are watching them."

He nodded while yawning. "I'll be downstairs."

How can he just get out of bed and not go straight to the bathroom? In another minute or three of sitting there staring at the wall, the discomfort advanced to pain.

"Fine... fine." She stood and swooned with vertigo. Nausea came back hard enough to nudge her stiff legs into a run.

Seconds later, her ass perched on the bowl and her face hovered over a small wastebasket. Tris hugged the plastic, waiting for vomit, but only a little trail of saliva dangled off her bottom lip. She sat for a while listening to Kevin rattle around the kitchen, savoring the absence of pain in her bladder. Again, she lurched and dry heaved, but nothing came out.

"What the hell is wrong with me?"

A mild pins-and-needles effect washed over her abdomen and a faint *beep* came from nowhere.

Great. What are the nanites fixing? I guess that dust hopper really did go to hell.

The little blue clock that always floated in the lower left corner of her vision, something that she'd gotten so used to she didn't even notice it there unless she looked for it, flashed a few times and went off. *Crap. Are my implants going?*

Text scrolled along the space where the time had been in bright blue letters. Digital information fed into her optic nerve on platinum wires thinner than a human hair.

Self-diagnostic running.

"Oh, that's new." She swallowed a mouthful of spit and sat up straight, feeling a little better already.

Diagnostic Pass. No problems detected.

"So what is—"

Status:

She blinked.

Pregnant.

The wastebasket slipped out of her hands and hit the floor with a hollow, plastic *thoomp.*

"What!"

Dual zygotes detected. Double egg release. Progress: normal.

Tris' scream of shock turned to a jubilant cheer halfway before her lungs ran out of air.

38

NOWHERE ELSE

Eggs made for a welcome respite from dust hopper. The damnable enormous rabbit-like critters continued to raid the farm, so they piled up in the larders of everyone in Nederland. Meat was meat, but another week of rabbit twice a day and he'd drive to Hagerman just to eat the piss-coated scorpions off the ground behind Wayne's.

He poked a wooden spatula around the little frying pan, hoping the electric heating element stayed on. Bill would probably want them to take a ride to Amarillo on the sooner side of later to grab more panels, but maybe he could talk them into working out some kind of thing with whatever would replace the Enclave. Having them make new ones beat taking a long ride again. He didn't want to leave Abby behind and he didn't want to bring her back to that place. Yeah sure, the pair of them had been inoculated, but having her return to the birthplace of her nightmares would not end well. Bill had filled him in on her panic attacks, so he'd do everything possible to make sure she felt completely safe.

Of course, being inoculated also made him the best person to go. Him, Tris, Zara, Nikki… the four of them could handle it.

Fuck. I'm gonna need a good goddamned excuse to ask them to have someone else do that. No way am I gonna make Abby watch us shoot people she used to know. He grumbled to himself at the sudden wonder if witnessing Amarillo purged of Infected might help her cope instead of traumatizing her more. *Nah. She doesn't need to see that.*

White caught his eye, and he glanced left at Tris creeping into the kitchen. He started to smile, but froze stone-faced at the red around her eyes.

"What's wrong?"

Tris walked up to him; her sky-blue T-shirt didn't hide much of her shape, and stopped only an inch or two below her crotch. If not for her making a face like someone had shot her dog, he'd have made a move. "Umm?"

"Abby?"

"No." She shook her head. "Abby's fine. It's not about her."

"Did your parents say something bad?" He tended the eggs one-handed while grasping her arm. "What's wrong?"

"I'm..." She shrank in on herself and whispered, "pregnant."

He dropped the spatula.

Tris' lip quivered.

Holy shit. "That's fucking awesome." He grabbed her in a bear hug. "Ack." He relaxed.

"You're not going to snap me in half now." She laughed, sniffling a bit.

He waved his hand around in a small circular motion. "What's with the tears? This is what you've wanted, isn't it?"

"Two." She flashed a cheesy smile laced with guilt as if she'd run off and spent all their money without telling him. "Fraternal twins..."

He blinked. "They joined a fraternity already?"

Her eyebrows formed a single, flat line across her head. "Really?"

"What?"

She leapt into him and bawled on his shoulder.

He leaned to the right to pull the eggs up from the stove and flicked the switch to off. After putting the pan on a cold element, he hugged her. "I'm still not sure what about this warrants crying."

"I figured it out... it must've happened that night at the roadhouse, when we were on the way to the Enclave." She shuddered. "I almost got myself killed while pregnant. No *wonder* I've been feeling like mothering the crap out of everyone. I guess they didn't take my ovaries out... only some eggs."

"So..." He put on his rogue's grin. "When do your boobs get bigger?"

She punched him in the shoulder and cracked up laughing. "I'm serious... what if that failsafe didn't exist... Or..."

He kissed her to stop her from talking. Minutes later, he leaned back and smiled. "No what-ifs. Forget it. Calm down. It's over. You saved the world…"

She blushed and bowed her head against his chest.

"At least from the Virus." He kissed the top of her head. "We're safe here."

"Yeah."

Gunfire popped and rippled in the distance.

She snapped her head up and glared at the wall.

Kevin listened to the tempo of the shots for ten seconds, and relaxed. "Militia practicing. The shots are too paced and regular to be combat… and no one's shouting."

Tris moved to a chair by the table and sat. "That smells amazing." She absentmindedly rubbed her stomach, watching him slide eggs and toast onto two plates. "We're not perfectly safe here."

"Nowhere is *perfectly* safe." He moved up behind her and reached around to set breakfast in front of her.

She turned in the chair to face the table and attacked her food.

"But…" He rested his hands on her shoulders with a gentle squeeze. "Right now, there's nowhere else I'd rather be."

Tris looked back and up at him with wide, urgent eyes, a bit of egg on her lip. "You…"

"Missed a bit." He plucked the egg from her lip on his fingertip and held it up before poking it into her mouth.

She sputtered and giggled.

"You're eating for three now. Don't waste any." He bent down to kiss her.

Tris leaned back after a moment, and grinned. "You should eat yours before it gets cold."

He grabbed his plate from the counter and sat as close as he could get a chair to her.

"I guess. Nederland's pretty nice." Tris leaned against him. "I can't really think of anywhere else I'd rather be either."

Kevin draped an arm around her shoulders. She reached up and held his hand over her heart. "I didn't mean Ned. There's nowhere else I'd rather be than with you."

She blushed. "Even Dallas?"

"Even Dallas." He leaned to his right and kissed her again.

Tris nibbled on his lip.

"Ow, hey." He chuckled.

"You taste like eggs."

He scraped more food onto his fork. "I better eat this before you take it all."

She half-closed her eyes. "Even on a bus in the middle of a street packed with Infected?"

"Hey now. Let's not get crazy." He winked.

Tris laughed and snuggled into him. "I'm pregnant..."

"If you say so." He smiled. "You think you're ready for this?"

"After the Enclave? I'm ready for anything." She patted her stomach. "Well, maybe if one of them's a boy, he'll turn out like you."

"And?"

"Then we're both in trouble."

Kevin laughed. "I can't argue that."

She tilted her head back to look up at him. "Kevin?"

He peered down at her. "Tris?"

"I love you." Tears welled in her eyes, but she wore the biggest smile he'd ever seen on that snow-white face.

Kevin brushed at her hair for a little while, taking in how beautiful she looked. "I love you more than I've ever loved anything or anyone in my life."

"More than your own roadhouse?"

"Roadhouse?" He furrowed his brows with a rogue's grin. "What the heck's a roadhouse?"

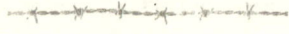

fin

ACKNOWLEDGMENTS

Thank you for reading the Roadhouse Chronicles series!

Additional thanks to:

Mark Woodring, for his insightful editing and polishing—even if he did utterly despise the Cure pun.

Will Stanton for making the suggestion that turned a single short story into a three-novel series.

ABOUT THE AUTHOR

Originally from South Amboy NJ, Matthew has been creating science fiction and fantasy worlds for most of his reasoning life. Since 1996, he has developed the "Divergent Fates" world, in which *Division Zero, Virtual Immortality, The Awakened Series, The Harmony Paradox, and the Daughter of Mars series* take place. Along with being an editor at Curiosity Quills press, he has worked in IT and technical support.

Matthew is an avid gamer, a recovered WoW addict, Gamemaster for two custom RPG systems, and a fan of anime, British humour, and intellectual science fiction that questions the nature of reality, life, and what happens after it.

He is also fond of cats.

Visit me online at:
    Facebook: https://www.facebook.com/MatthewSCoxAuthor
    Amazon: https://www.amazon.com/author/mscox
    Pinterest: https://www.pinterest.com/matthewcox10420/
    Goodreads: https://www.goodreads.com/author/show/7712730.Matthew_S_Cox
    Email: mcox2112@gmail.com

OTHER BOOKS BY MATTHEW S. COX

Divergent Fates Universe Novels

Division Zero series

- Division Zero
- Lex De Mortuis
- Thrall
- Guardian

The Awakened series

- Prophet of the Badlands
- Archon's Queen
- Grey Ronin
- Daughter of Ash
- Zero Rogue
- Angel Descended

Daughter of Mars series

- The Hand of Raziel
- Araphel
- Ghost Black

Virtual Immortality series

- Virtual Immortality
- The Harmony Paradox

Divergent Fates Anthology

(Fiction Novels - Adult)

The Roadhouse Chronicles Series

- One More Run
- The Redeemed
- Dead Man's Number

- Heir Ascendant
- Ascendant Unrest
- Ascendant Revolution

Temporal Armistice Series

- Nascent Shadow
- The Shadow Collector

Vampire Innocent series

- A Nighttime of Forever
- A Beginner's Guide to Fangs
- The Artist of Ruin
- The Last Family Road Trip

Standalones

- Wayfarer: AV494
- Axillon99
- Chiaroscuro: The Mouse and the Candle
- The Far Side of Promise anthology
- Operation: Chimera (with Tony Healey)
- The Dysfunctional Conspiracy (with Christopher Veltmann)

Winter Solstice series (with J.R. Rain)

- Convergence
- Containment

Alexis Silver series (with J.R. Rain)

- Silver Light
- Deep Silver

Samantha Moon Origins series (with J.R. Rain)

- New Moon Rising
- Moon Mourning

Maddy Wimsey series (with J.R. Rain)

- The Devil's Eye
- The Drifting Gloom

Samantha Moon Case Files series (with J.R. Rain)

- Blood Moon
- Dead Moon

Young Adult Novels

- Caller 107
- The Summer the World Ended
- Nine Candles of Deepest Black
- The Eldritch Heart
- The Forest Beyond the Earth
- Out of Sight

Middle Grade Novels

Tales of Widowswood series

- Emma and the Banderwigh
- Emma and the Silk Thieves
- Emma and the Silverbell Faeries
- Emma and the Elixir of Madness
- Emma and the Weeping Spirit

Standalones

- Citadel: The Concordant Sequence
- The Cursed Codex
- The Menagerie of Jenkins Bailey
- Sophie's Light

www.ingramcontent.com/pod-product-compliance
Lightning Source LLC
Chambersburg PA
CBHW051937240626
47153CB00005B/1522